PR[...]H
HIS ROYAL TWINS

BY
LOUISA HEATON

CANCELLED

MILLS &
BOON

All rights reserved including the right of reproduction in whole or in part in any form. This edition is published by arrangement with Harlequin Books S.A.

This is a work of fiction. Names, characters, places, locations and incidents are purely fictional and bear no relationship to any real life individuals, living or dead, or to any actual places, business establishments, locations, events or incidents. Any resemblance is entirely coincidental.

This book is sold subject to the condition that it shall not, by way of trade or otherwise, be lent, resold, hired out or otherwise circulated without the prior consent of the publisher in any form of binding or cover other than that in which it is published and without a similar condition including this condition being imposed on the subsequent purchaser.

® and TM are trademarks owned and used by the trademark owner and/or its licensee. Trademarks marked with ® are registered with the United Kingdom Patent Office and/or the Office for Harmonisation in the Internal Market and in other countries.

Published in Great Britain 2017
By Mills & Boon, an imprint of HarperCollins*Publishers*
1 London Bridge Street, London, SE1 9GF

© 2017 Louisa Heaton

ISBN: 978-0-263-93329-1

Our policy is to use papers that are natural, renewable and recyclable products and made from wood grown in sustainable forests. The logging and manufacturing processes conform to the legal environmental regulations of the country of origin.

Printed and bound in Spain
by CPI, Barcelona

Dear Reader,

Many years ago I suffered from panic attacks and anxiety—so much so that I was housebound for a long, long time. No one seemed to understand the fear I had in my heart about such a scary world, and going outside terrified me…

I've always wanted to write about a heroine who suffers from anxiety—who hides from the world, getting by as best as she can in such a limited way. But of course my heroine would find freedom from her fear and achieve the happy-ever-after that everyone with anxiety or panic attacks hopes for.

Strength comes from within—but it also helps if you have someone who is prepared to stand by your side and love you, no matter what. So I gave Freya the lovely Jamie.

I do hope you enjoy their story!

Louisa xxx

This book is for anyone who suffers from anxiety.

Who has to find the courage from deep within
just to leave the house.

It's an endless battle, but this book is for you.
xxx

Books by Louisa Heaton

Mills & Boon Medical Romance

The Baby That Changed Her Life
His Perfect Bride?
A Father This Christmas?
One Life-Changing Night
Seven Nights with Her Ex
Christmas with the Single Dad
Reunited by Their Pregnancy Surprise
Their Double Baby Gift

Visit the Author Profile page
at millsandboon.co.uk for more titles.

CHAPTER ONE

FREYA SURREPTITIOUSLY SLIPPED the packet from her locker and into her uniform pocket, hiding it under her notepad. The lack of her period and the increasing nausea she was experiencing each morning seemed obvious signs enough, but Freya wanted proof. Scientific proof.

Night shift it might be, but to her this was morning, and walking into the staff room and smelling the strong coffee that had been put on to brew had almost made her share with everyone the ginger biscuits she had forced down for breakfast. It had taken a gargantuan effort to control her stomach, and a sheen of sweat had prickled her brow and top lip as she'd fumbled with her locker. Her fingers had almost tripped over themselves in her haste.

Heading to the ladies' loo, she told Mona she'd just be five minutes and that she'd catch up to her at the staff briefing in a moment.

'Okay, hun, see you in five.' Mona smiled and headed off, her hand clutched around a mug of that nausea-inducing coffee.

The toilets were right next door to the hub, so Freya slipped in and locked the door behind her, leaning back against it, letting out a long, slow breath of relief. She took a moment to stand there and see if her stomach settled.

There didn't seem any doubt about what was happening

to her, but she needed to do this just the same. She pulled the pregnancy test from her pocket and stared hard at it, not quite believing that she was actually going to.

She'd always *hoped* that one day she would become a mother. But the actual chances of that ever happening to her had—she believed—become very slim the day she had been scarred for life. Because who would want her now?

'Come on, Freya…you're better than this,' she whispered to herself, trying to drum up the courage to get herself through the next few minutes.

Freya loved the nightshift, working on Maternity here at Queen's Hospital. There was something extra-special about working nights. The quiet. The solitude. The intimate joy of bringing a new life into the world and being with that family as they watched their first sunrise together. A new day. A new family. Life changing. Getting *better*. New hopes. New dreams. There weren't the distractions of daytime—telephones constantly ringing, visiting families all over the place. It was secluded. Fewer busybodies.

It was the perfect hiding place for her, the hospital at night time, and those nights afforded Freya the anonymity that she craved. Lights were kept low. There were shadows to stay in, no harsh fluorescent lighting to reveal to her patients the true extent of her scarring.

It was better now than it had been. She had some smooth skin now, over her cheeks and forehead, where just two years before she'd had angry red pits and lines, her face constantly set and immovable, like a horrific Halloween mask.

Not now. Not now she'd had her many, *many* reconstructive surgeries. Thirty-three times under the skilled scalpel of her plastic surgeon.

And yet she was still hiding—even more so—in a bathroom. Her hands sweating and fidgety as she kept glancing down at the testing kit.

'Only one thing to do, really,' she told herself aloud, shaking her head at the absolute silliness of giving herself a pep talk.

She peed on the stick and laid it on the back of the sink as she washed her hands and then took a step back. She stared at her reflection in the mirror, refusing to look down and see the result. She saw the fear in her eyes, but she also recognised something she hadn't seen for years—*hope.*

'This is what you've always wanted,' she whispered.

But wanting something and actually *achieving* it, when you believed it to be impossible, was another thing altogether. If it *were* possible then she'd finally get her childhood dream. To hold her own child in her arms and not just other people's. To have her own baby and be a mum. Even if that meant she'd have to revert back to living in sunlight. With all those other people.

Even if they didn't stare at her, or do that second glance thing, she still felt that they were looking. It was human nature to look at someone different and pretend that you weren't. And your face was the hardest thing to hide.

Still…this wasn't exactly how she'd imagined it happening. As a little girl she'd dreamt of marrying a handsome man, having his babies and being in a settled relationship.

She had no one. Even 'the guy' had been a mad, terrific impulse, when her body had been thrumming with joy about the fact that she was out amongst people, having fun, enjoying a party behind the veil of her fancy dress costume.

It had been so long since she'd last been to a social event. Too long. Years since she'd stood in a room full of people, chatting, laughing at poor jokes, being *normal.*

Mike had taken that away from her. That joy and freedom. His jealous actions had imprisoned her in a world of night and pain, surgeries and hiding. Feeling unable to show her face to the world without fearing people's reactions. A

frightened child turning away as if to clutch her mother's skirts when a stranger did a double-take and tried not to look appalled or disgusted or worse.

The veil she'd worn that night had hidden everything. The high-necked Victorian steam punk outfit had hidden the scars on her neck that had not yet been tackled, and the veil had added a note of mystery.

That night people had looked at her with intrigue and with delight. They'd smiled...they'd complimented her on how *wonderful* she looked. Their words had made her giddy with happiness. She'd been normal there. Like them.

And then *he'd* been there. The guy. The pirate. He'd seemed uncomfortable. Had appeared to be waiting for enough time to pass so he could make his escape.

She knew how that felt. She'd felt a kind of companionship with him, despite their not having exchanged a word.

It had helped, of course, that he had seductively dark eyes and a wickedly tempting mouth, and she'd almost stopped herself. She'd taken a moment to register the fact that she was *attracted* to a man when the very idea of that had been anathema to her for so many years.

But not that night. The costume, the veil, had given her a sense of bravery she hadn't felt for a long time.

'I'm Freya. Pleased to meet you.'

'Jamie.'

'I saw you eyeing up the exit. Getting ready to make a break for it?'

'I've been thinking about it.'

'Please don't. Stay for a little while longer. Let me get you a drink.'

It had been crazy how emboldened she'd felt. Her entire body had been thrumming with adrenaline and serotonin, her heart pounding like a revved-up engine. She'd felt alive,

happy, normal again—having a conversation with an attractive man, feeling the thrill of first attraction.

Silly. Childish, maybe, when she really ought to have known better, but it had just felt so good!

He had made her feel that way. The way he'd looked at her, his eyes sparkling with inky delight, his full lips curved in a wicked smile. He'd laughed with joy at her anecdotes, had genuinely seemed happy to stay.

She'd felt warm and wanted again. Desire had filled her the second he'd let go of the stem of his glass and let his fingers trail delicately over the back of her hand. She'd focused on that movement, watched his fingertips on her skin—her very sensitive skin. She'd looked up and met his eyes, and the most extraordinary question had left her lips.

'Are you married?'

'No.'

'With someone?'

'No.'

'Do you want to be?'

She'd startled herself with the sheer audacity of her question. That wasn't *her*! Freya MacFadden did not proposition strange men!

She'd pulled her hand away then, retreating into the shell she was so accustomed to being inside. But then he'd reached for her hand again. Not to stop her from running away. Not to try and possess her or control her. But just to get her to make eye contact with him.

'I'm guessing you didn't mean to say that?'

'No.'

'Then we can both forget it. Don't worry.'

'I'm sorry.'

'Don't ever be.'

He'd been so kind. So understanding. So she hadn't bolted and neither had he.

They'd continued to sit with each other and talk about what the other guests were wearing and why the charity they were there to support was so important. They'd laughed and had a good time, enjoying each other's company.

He'd offered to walk her out at the end, and she'd let him, intending to say goodbye at the door. To fetch her coat and leave. For ever to remain an enigmatic stranger at a party that he would remember with fondness. Like Cinderella leaving the ball at midnight, only without the glass slipper.

Freya let out a deep breath. She couldn't stay here in the bathroom for too long. There was a hand-over from the day shift.

Freya loved her daytime colleagues, and they her, but she was happy when they went home. Because then she could begin to craft the intimacy that the night shift brought. Lowering the lights. Softening the voices.

It was time.

She couldn't wait any longer.

It was now or never.

She looked down.

And sucked in a breath.

'I'm pregnant.'

She looked back at her reflection, disbelieving.

'I'm *pregnant*?'

She didn't know whether to laugh hysterically or to cry, to gasp or anything else!

She was pregnant.

There was no question as to *how* it had happened. She remembered that night all too well. The father of her child was quite clear in her mind. How could he *not* be? Even if she didn't actually know *who* he was. Or where he came from.

Their meeting that night had been quite by chance—as

sudden and exciting and as passionate as she'd imagined it could be. Scary and exhilarating, and one of the best nights of her life. She'd thrown caution to the wind and felt fully alive again for just a moment. For one desperate moment she had been someone else.

She had gone to the ball knowing she would be able to hide behind her veil and costume all night. It had been very gothic-looking, high-necked, with lots of black and dark purple, layers and petticoats. And there had been a top hat, embellished with a large swathe of plum ribbon, copper cogs and whatnots, and a veil of amethyst silk covering her nose and mouth like a Bedouin bride, leaving only her eyes visible.

Her best feature. The only part of her face not scarred or damaged by the acid. She'd been lucky in that respect. Most acid attack victims were blinded.

Her dashing admirer had tried to remove her veil when he'd leant in to kiss her, but she'd stopped him.

'Don't, please. It's better this way.'

He'd smiled and used his mouth in other ways...

Now everyone at the hand-over would be waiting for her, and they'd all look at her when she went back through. The longer she left it, the worse it would be.

She put the cap on the test stick and slipped it into her pocket, then unlocked the bathroom door. Shoulders back, trying to feel relaxed, she headed off to the briefing.

Okay. I can do this. I'm an expert at pretending everything is fine.

The staff were all gathered around the hub of the unit. Whenever a new patient was admitted, or whenever family came to visit, they would walk down this one corridor that led to the hub. From there they would be directed down different corridors—to the right for postnatal and discharges, straight ahead for medical assessment and long-

stay patients, to the left for labour and delivery, and beyond that, Theatre.

From the hub, they could see who was trying to buzz through the main doors to gain access to the ward, with the help of a security camera. They could also see the admissions boards, listing who was in which bed and what stage they were at.

There were usually thank-you cards there, perched on the desk, or stuck to the wall behind them, along with a tin or a box of chocolates kindly donated by a grateful family, and on the walls were some very beautiful black and white photographs of babies, taken by their very skilled photographer Addison.

Senior midwife Jules was leaning up against the hub, and she smiled when she saw Freya coming. 'Here she is! Last but not least.'

Freya sidled in amongst the group, keeping her eyes down and trying desperately to blend in. She could feel all eyes upon her and folded herself down into a chair to make herself smaller. She had kept people waiting when they just wanted to go home.

She gratefully accepted a copy of the admissions sheet that Mona passed over to her.

'It's been a busy day today, and it looks like you girls aren't going to have it easy tonight either. In the labour suite, we've got two labouring mums. In Bed One is Andrea Simpson—she's a gravida one, para zero at term plus two days, currently at three centimetres dilated and comfortable, but she had a spontaneous rupture of membranes at home. She's currently on the trace machine and will need to come off in about ten minutes. In Bed Two we have Lisa Chambers, she's a gravida three, para four. Two lots of twins and currently about to deliver her first singleton

baby. She's had two previous elective Caesareans and is trying for a VBAC on this one.'

Freya nodded, scribbling notes. A VBAC was a vaginal birth after Caesarean—a 'trial of scar', as some people put it, to see if the mother could deliver vaginally.

'She's labouring fast. At six-thirty she was at six centimetres and she's currently making do on gas and air.'

Freya sat and listened to the rest of Jules's assessment. They had in total twenty-one patients: two on the labour ward, seven on Antenatal and twelve on Postnatal, five of whom were post-surgery.

And the phones would continue to ring. There would also be unexpected walk-ins, and no doubt A&E would send up one or two.

But she didn't mind. Her job was her life. Her passion. The only thing that brought her real joy. It was all she'd ever wanted to be, growing up. A midwife and a mum. And, as of ten startling minutes ago, it looked as if she was going to achieve being both of those.

Freya was excellent at her job, and she truly believed she was only so good at it because it was something she adored doing. Every new baby born was a minor miracle. Every witnessed birth a joy and a privilege. Every moment she sat and held a mother's hand through a contraction was another courageous moment.

It was a weird place, Maternity. A place where staff and patients met often for the first time, total strangers, and then just hours later Freya would know so much about a person—about their family, their hopes and dreams, their sense of humour, what their favourite foods were, what they craved, what they wanted to be, what they wanted to name their children...

She saw them at their worst, but more often at their best and bravest, and when her patients left Freya knew she

would always be remembered as being a part of that family's life. Someone who had shared in their most special and cherished moments. Never to be forgotten.

It was an immense responsibility.

Jules put down her papers. 'Now, ladies, I want you to calm yourselves, but we have in our midst a new midwife! His name's Jamie and he's hiding at the back. Give us all a wave, Jamie!'

Jamie? No. Relax. It's a common name.

Freya didn't want to turn and look. She knew how that would make the poor guy feel, having all those women turning and staring at him, eyeing him up. But she knew that it would look odd if hers was the only head that didn't turn. It would single her out. So she gave him a quick glance.

Lovely. No...wait a minute...

She whipped her head back round, her mind whirling, and pretended to scribble some more notes about what Jules had just reported on her sheet. But her pen remained still above the paper.

It's him. It's him! Oh, God, oh, God, oh...

Her trembling fingers touched her lips and her nausea returned in a torrent so powerful she thought she might be sick with nerves right there and then—all over Mona's shoes. She wanted to get up and bolt. Run as fast as she could. But it was impossible.

She frantically eyed the spaces between the rows of staff and wondered how quickly she could make a break for it at the end of the briefing.

It couldn't be possible. How *could* it be him? Her one-night stand.

'Jamie is with us for a couple of months, filling in for Sandra who's away on maternity leave, so I'd like to say welcome to the team, Jamie, it's good to have you here. For the rest of you—Jamie has been working all over the

country in various midwifery posts, so he's got a lot of experience, and I hope you'll all take the time to welcome him here, to Queen's.'

Jules smiled.

'Right, then. We're all off. Have a good shift, ladies. And Jamie!'

She smiled, waved, and the majority of staff disappeared off to the locker room, to grab their things and go.

Freya, frozen to the spot, wished she could do the same.

Okay, so the simplest thing to do is to stay out of his way.

So far she'd done a sterling job of that.

Mona was showing him around, pointing out where everything was, getting him acquainted with the temperamental computer and how to admit people to the ward—that kind of thing. Freya, on the other hand, had just been given the task to introduce herself to the two labouring mothers and work on the labour ward—which she was very happy about because that gave her the opportunity to stay in her patients' rooms and not see or have to engage with *him*.

The irony of the situation was not lost on her. The first time they had met she had been brimming with temporary confidence, an urge to experience life again as a normal woman meeting a handsome guy at a party. But now she was back to reality. Hiding and skulking around corners, trying her best to avoid him. The man she'd propositioned.

And what the hell were the odds of him turning up on the very same day that she took a pregnancy test? It had to be millions to one, didn't it? Or at the very least a few hundred thousand to one?

Jules had said he'd been working in various posts around the country. Why hadn't he got a job at one of those? Why did he keep moving?

What's wrong with him?

The weight of the pregnancy test in her left pocket seemed to increase, its weight like a millstone.

She entered Andrea Simpson's room quietly.

'Hello, it's Andrea, isn't it? I'm Freya and I'm going to be your midwife tonight.'

She smiled at her new charge and then glanced over at her partner, who was putting his phone in his back pocket and standing up to say hello.

He reached over to shake her hand and she saw him do that thing with his eyes that everyone did when they noticed her face—noticed that she'd been burned, somehow, despite her corrective surgery and skin grafts. Noticed that she'd had *work done*.

His gaze flittered across her features and then there was *that* pause.

'Hi, I'm George,' he introduced himself. 'I'm just here to do what I'm told.'

Freya smiled. 'Mum's the boss in this room.'

She glanced over at the belt placement on Andrea's abdomen and checked the trace on the machine. The trace looked good. No decelerations and the occasional contraction, currently seven or eight minutes apart. Still a way to go for Andrea.

'I want you to stay on this for ten more minutes, then I'll take it off—is that all right?'

Andrea nodded, reaching for a bottle of water and taking a short drink.

'Do you have a birth plan?'

'Just to have as much pain relief as I can get.'

'Okay. And what sort of pain relief are you thinking of?'

'I want to start with gas and air, see how I go with that, and then maybe get pethidine. But I'm open to whatever you suggest at the time.'

Freya smiled. 'So am I. This is *your* birth, *your* body. I'll be guided by you as long as it's safe. Okay?'

'Yes...'

Freya could see that Andrea had questions. 'Nervous?'

Andrea giggled. 'A bit. This is all so *new*!'

Tell me about it.

Freya had seen hundreds of babies come into the world. She never tired of it. Each birth was different and special, and now she knew that if all went well and she didn't miscarry she'd be doing this herself in a few months. Lying on a bed...labouring. It was actually going to happen.

'You'll do fine.'

She laid a reassuring hand on her patient's and wondered who'd be there to hold *her* hand during labour? Her mum?

Her mind treacherously placed Jamie beside her bed and she felt goosebumps shiver down her skin.

No. It can't be him.

It can't be.

But isn't that what you always wanted? A cosy, happy family unit?

It had been. Once.

It was *her*. He'd have known those blue eyes anywhere. The eyes that had been haunting his dreams for weeks now.

He'd been invited to that charity ball after he'd attended a small event in Brighton that was meant to have been low-key. But word must have reached the ears of the hospital that the heir to the throne of Majidar, Prince Jameel Al Bakhari, was around and an invitation had got through to his people.

It had been for such a good cause he hadn't been able to refuse it. A children's burns unit. He'd seen the damage burns could cause, from a simple firework accident right through to injuries sustained in a war zone, and it was

shocking for anyone. A painful, arduous road to recovery. But for it to happen to a child was doubly devastating.

So he'd attended, dressed as a pirate, complete with a large hoop earring and a curved plastic scimitar that had hung from his waist by a sash.

He'd not intended to stay for very long. He'd made them keep his presence there quiet, as he didn't enjoy people bowing and scraping around him. He hated that whole sycophantic thing that happened around members of his royal family. It was part of why he'd left Majidar. To be a normal person.

It was why he tried to live his life following his passion. And his passion was to deliver babies. Something that was not considered 'suitable' for a prince back in his own country.

But what could you do when it was your calling? Delivering babies was what he had always yearned to do, and he'd never been destined for the throne. His elder brother had been the heir and was now ruler. So surely, he'd reasoned, it was better to spend his life doing something worthwhile and selfless instead of parading around crowds of people, smiling and waving, a spare heir that no one needed?

He'd faced some considerable opposition. Mostly from his father, who'd been appalled that his second son wanted to do what he viewed as 'women's work'. His father had forbidden him ever to speak of it again and, respecting his father, he had kept that promise. Until his father had passed away. Then his brother Ilias had taken the throne, and Jamie had approached his new King and told him of his vocation.

Ilias had proudly granted his younger brother the freedom to pursue it.

So he'd gone to the ball, telling the organisers that he didn't want to draw attention to himself, and asking that

they did not make any special announcement that he was there, just let him join in as any other person would.

Jamie had mingled, smiled, shaken people's hands—and found himself losing the will to live and wondering when would be a polite time to leave… And then he'd spotted *her* in a corner of the room.

Almost as tall as he, she'd been dressed from top to toe in black, accented in dark purple, with some weird cogs and a strange pair of pilot goggles attached to her hat. Her face had been covered by a Bedouin-style gauze veil that had reminded him of home.

Her honey-blonde hair had tumbled down her back, almost to her waist, and above that veil had sparkled the most gorgeous blue eyes he had ever seen. Blue like the ocean and the sky, and just as wild and free.

'I'm Freya. Pleased to meet you.'

'Jamie.'

'I saw you eyeing up the exit. Getting ready to make a break for it?'

He had been. But not any more.

So he'd stayed. And they'd talked. And laughed.

Freya had been delightful, charming and intelligent, and so easy to be with. She'd told him a story about the last time she'd attempted to flee a party. She'd been eleven years old and it had been the first time her parents hadn't stayed with her. She'd been frightened by all the noise and all the people and had scurried away when no one was looking and run home to hide in her dad's garden shed.

She'd grimaced as she'd recalled how she'd stayed there, terrified out of her wits not only about being found out, but also because there had been a massive spider in the corner, watching her. He'd laughed when she'd told him she'd almost peed her pants because her bladder had been killing her from drinking too much pop. But she hadn't been able

to go home too early, or her parents would have known
that she'd run away.

'No spiders here,' he'd said.

'No.'

'Nothing to be afraid of. I'll protect you.'

*'Now, why would you do that? You hardly know me. I
might be dangerous.'*

'I think I can handle you.'

His pulse had thrummed against his skin, his tempera-
ture rising, his whole body aware. Of *her*. She hadn't re-
moved the veil, but she'd kept on peering at him over it with
devilment in her gaze, and he'd felt drawn to her excitement
and bravado. She hadn't been drunk on alcohol. Her eyes
had been clear, pupils not pinpointed, so no drugs. But she'd
definitely been intoxicated by *something*, and he'd begun
to suspect that he was feeling the same way, too.

There'd been something about her. So different from ev-
eryone else at the party. But what had it been? What had
made her unique? Had it been the veil? The air of mystery?
Or just those eyes? Eyes that had looked so young, but had
also spoken of a wisdom beyond her years. As if she knew
something that no one else did. As if she'd experienced life
and the gamut of emotions that came with it. And yet that
night she'd been drawn to him, and he to her. She a purple
and black veiled moth and he the flame.

'Do you trust me?'

She'd smiled. *'Can any woman trust a pirate?'*

'I'm not just a pirate.'

The corners of her mouth had twitched and she'd glanced
at his mouth, then back to his eyes, and he'd been hit with
such a blow of lust he hadn't been able to help himself. He'd
tried to look away, to take a deep breath, to regain control
over his senses.

'I need to go,' she'd said.

'Let me walk you home.'

'No need. I have transport.'

'Then let me walk you to it.'

He'd offered her his arm and she'd taken it, smiling through the gauze and looking up at him, her eyes gleaming.

He'd been overcome by a bolt of desire.

But what to do about it? He considered himself a gentleman. He had principles…he'd only just met her…but there was *something*…

They'd stood there staring at each other, each of them trying to force the words to say goodbye, but neither of them ready to leave just yet. Her eyes had glinted at him in the darkness, with a look that said she wanted more than this…

The first door they'd tried had been unlocked, and they'd found themselves inside a supply closet, filled with clean linen and pressed staff uniforms.

He'd stood in front of her, just looking at her, noticing the small flecks of green and gold in her eyes. They'd shone like jewels, and her pupils had been large and black as she'd reached for his shirt and pulled him close.

He'd lost himself in her. Completely forgotten who he was, where he was. All that had mattered had been the feel of her, the taste of her, as he'd hitched up her skirts, her million and one petticoats, slid his hands up those long, slim legs…

Freya…

Like two lost souls that had found each other, they had clutched and grasped, gasped and groaned. He'd reached to remove the veil, so that he could kiss her, so that he could seek out her lips and claim her for his very own, but she'd stopped him, stilled his hand.

'Leave it. Please.'

'But, Freya...'

'No kissing...please.'

He'd respected her wishes. That veil had made her seem like forbidden fruit. An enigma. Her hat had fallen to the floor and her long blonde locks had tumbled around her shoulders like golden waves. And the dark stockings on her ever so creamy thighs had aroused a feeling in him that he'd never quite experienced before.

They'd given each other everything.

And when they were spent they had slumped against each other and just stood there, wrapped in each other. Just breathing. Just existing. It was all that they'd needed.

A sound by the door had made them break apart and rearrange their clothing.

She'd glanced at him, guiltily. 'I must go.'

He'd stared at her, not knowing what to say. He'd felt as if there was so much he *wanted* to say to her, but it had all got stuck in his throat and he'd remained silent. He'd wanted to tell her to stay. To come back to the hotel with him. He'd wanted to ask her if he could see her again and that had both shocked and scared him—because he *never* made commitments.

But she'd slipped from the closet, and by the time he'd adjusted his clothes and made himself presentable again she'd been gone.

He'd scanned the ballroom, looking for her fall of blonde hair, looking for those all-seeing eyes, but she'd gone.

Jamie had signalled his security people and told them to look out for her, to check the car park, but like an enigmatic spy she had simply disappeared. Disappointed, he had got into his own car and been driven home.

But now she was here.

She'd turned to look at him after Jules had asked everyone to welcome him. She was *here*. Of all the places in

the world he could have looked. In this hospital. On this ward. With him. Those eyes of hers had pierced his soul once again, reawakening his dormant desire and making every cell of his body cry out for her.

But there'd been something else. Something that had rocked him. Something he hadn't noticed before. And now he understood about the veil.

Freya was scarred. Something had happened to her. To her face. She'd had work done. Skin grafts, no doubt. Painful surgeries and recovery. How many? What had happened to her? A house fire? Was that why she'd been at the charity event for the burns unit?

And he'd sensed her fear. Her shock. Had seen the horror in her eyes as she'd realised who he was. Then he'd seen her shame, because she'd noticed how he'd reacted when he saw her properly.

Angry with himself, he'd wanted to reach out, touch her, tell her that she should not be ashamed—but she'd bolted.

Jamie sensed a soul like his own. Someone who preferred the everyday to the limelight. Someone who avoided crowds and adulation. Someone who preferred to hide behind a mask.

He felt her magnetism. Her draw.

And helplessly he allowed himself to be pulled in.

'It is you, isn't it?'

Freya had quickly run to the kitchenette to make her patient's husband a cup of tea. She'd slid into the small room, breathing a sigh of relief, wondering just how the hell she was going to get through work for the next few weeks if *he* was going to be here, covering for Sandra.

She'd just been kneeling down to put the milk back in the fridge when she'd heard the door open behind her and then his voice.

Freya closed her eyes and looked down, hoping the loose tendrils of her hair would cover her face. She didn't want this. Didn't *need* this. Tonight had already been overwhelming—finding out she was pregnant—but to have him here too? To have to have *this* conversation? Now? At work?

'I'm sorry, I need to take this drink to my patient.'

She held the mug of tea in her hand, not turning to face him, but so very aware of his presence behind her in this small, suddenly claustrophobic room.

This man had made her body sing. Nerve-endings that she'd thought were dead had come alive that night and she had felt every single part of her body as he'd played her like a delicate harp. Knowing what to touch and how to touch, how to make her gasp, sigh and groan. She'd experienced things with this man that she had never felt before. He'd made her reveal a side to herself that she'd never known.

But he'd been with a woman who didn't exist in reality, and she didn't need to see his disappointment when he realised.

Just being this close to him now was doing crazy things to her insides and turning her legs to jelly. And was it hot? Her armpits were tingling with sweat.

They'd had an amazing night. And it would stay that way as long as he didn't ruin the illusion by seeing her for who she really was. He'd probably thought that she was some rare beauty, but if he saw her properly he would soon be surprised. No doubt about that.

She didn't want to have to watch it happen right in front of her. That *look*. She'd already noticed his shock when they were at the hub, and work was meant to be her happy place. He was ruining everything.

Holding the mug of tea before her, she kept her head down to pass him so she could get to the door.

He stepped back, keeping a respectful distance, which

she appreciated, but as she reached for the handle he spoke again.

'It *is* you.'

Keeping her eyes downcast, she stared at the floor, not wanting to see him take in her scars, her wounds. To see that she was damaged goods. This man had *wanted* her! Wanted her so badly! And it had been wondrous—a memory she'd cherished since that night. A moment of freedom from the poor existence with which Mike had left her. And she had revelled in that.

Did she want to see him realise that the woman he had given himself to was not the one of his dreams? No. Just for once she wanted to be a good memory for someone. For them to believe her beautiful.

'I'm sorry, I have to go.'

'Look at me.'

'Jamie, please…' She glanced upwards for just a moment and painfully met his gaze, her eyes blurry with unshed tears, waiting to see him realise his mistake…

Only it didn't happen. He simply looked directly at her. Showed no shock this time. No horror.

'If only you knew how much I've wanted to see you again.'

Confused, she stared back. Felt the tears finally escape her eyes and trickle down her cheeks.

'What…?'

What was he saying? What did he mean? Why wasn't he reacting to her face like everyone else did?

'You're unforgettable—do you know that?'

She swallowed hard, looking away, down at the steaming mug. 'For all the wrong reasons.'

She got out of the kitchenette as quickly as she could. What *was* it with them and small rooms? Kitchenettes. Supply cupboards. Was Jamie set to startle her in anything

less than six by six? Should she stay away from bathroom cubicles, too?

As she hurried back to her patient's room she madly wiped her eyes and sniffed a few times, to try and look presentable for Andrea and her husband.

What had just happened? How had he managed to turn her understanding of the world completely on its head?

She slipped her hand into her pocket, to reassure herself that the pregnancy test was still there. Only it wasn't. Her pocket was empty except for her notebook and pen.

She looked back to the kitchenette and saw Jamie come out, his face a mass of confused emotions as his eyes met hers.

Over the small white stick in his hand.

CHAPTER TWO

IT MUST HAVE fallen from her pocket. But when? And how?

And then she remembered crouching down to get the milk from the fridge. Something similar had happened before, due to the design of the pocket on her uniform. It was below the waist, low down. She'd lost her mobile phone once that way, hearing it clatter onto the floor. She'd not heard the test stick fall. Probably because she'd heard his voice instead. Felt his presence.

'It is you. Isn't it?'

His words had cut through everything.

Her mind had been on other things. Other concerns. She'd closed that fridge fast. Stood up quickly and made that tea, trying not to look at him, trying to get away as quickly as she could.

She was saved from going over to him and taking the test from his hands. The call light above Bed Two flashed and she went in to see how Lisa Chambers, her labouring mother there, was doing.

Lisa was pacing the room, her abdomen swollen before her, her hands pressed into her back.

'I felt the need to push with that last one, Freya.'

She handed the mug of tea over to Lisa's husband and then guided Lisa back to the bed. 'I'll need to check you before you can push.'

She didn't need Lisa pushing too early. It might cause a swelling of the cervix and make delivery more difficult.

Regaining control of her own body, she checked her patient's. 'You're right, Lisa. You're ten centimetres. You can push with the next contraction.'

Lisa got up off the bed. 'I can't lie down, though.'

'That's fine. Let your body lead you and I'll help. Just tell me when you're ready.'

Lisa beckoned to her husband to stand on the other side of the bed and take her hands. Then she squatted on the other side.

'When the contraction comes, take a big, deep breath, Lisa—chin to your chest and *push*, right into your bottom.'

Lisa nodded, waiting, then closed her eyes and sucked in that breath.

Freya quickly washed her hands, dried them and gloved up. Lisa might be five times a mother, but this was her first vaginal delivery. It might take some time and, with the best will in the world and not wanting to prolong her patient's suffering, she hoped that it would.

Because she herself needed some time before she could leave this room. Needed to think of what she would say. What she would do. How she could escape this situation she'd found herself in.

Lisa was an excellent patient, though, and obviously keen to see her fifth child. Because within forty-five minutes of her first needing to push, her son slithered into Freya's waiting hands.

She passed the baby to his sobbing mother, clamped and cut the cord, then helped Lisa into bed and wrapped a towel around her son to help keep him warm.

The baby cried—bursts of pure sound, a completely new person announcing his arrival. Freya smiled at the newly created family of seven and quietly gave Lisa the injection

of syntocinon that would hasten delivery of the placenta, as per her patient's request.

It seemed to take no time at all to deliver it, check it, assess the baby's APGAR score, then Lisa's, and realise that Lisa hadn't torn at all. Her five-pound, twelve-ounce son had arrived perfectly.

There was no reason for Freya to stay at all. She prided herself on leaving her families to have some private time as soon as she could after the birth. So they could welcome and get to know their new baby on their own. But tonight she hesitated by the door.

'Congratulations, you two.'

'Thanks, Freya. I couldn't have done it without you.'

'Nonsense. You were a model patient.' She smiled, trying to pluck up the courage to go out there and face him. *That* conversation.

She could only hope and pray that he was busy with a patient of his own.

But she had no such luck.

Jamie was just walking back to the hub desk, sliding his pen into his top pocket. His dark eyes instantly met hers. Challenged her. Demanded an explanation.

She almost faltered. But she had Lisa's notes to finish writing up, and when that was done she needed to check on Andrea. She'd taken her off the trace a while ago and she'd been steadily contracting every five minutes the last time she'd seen her.

Jamie stood still as she walked past him, and she hoped he wouldn't see that her nerves were making her hands tremble and shake as she sat down at the desk.

'It's not what you think.' She glanced up at him, then away again. *Dammit*. He was just as handsome as she remembered. Even more so, this close. He was hauntingly beautiful.

Jamie sat down in the chair next to her. 'What *do* I think?'

She paused, her pen over Lisa's notes. 'It belongs to a patient.'

'A patient?'

'Yes. I must have put it in my pocket without realising and—'

'We don't do pregnancy testing here. Mona was quite clear when she showed me around that the fertility clinic is in a whole other ward next to this one.'

She tried her hardest not to look at him. Not to meet the searing gaze that she knew would instantly divine the truth. If her cheeks could have flamed red, then they would.

She looked at him, guilt filling her eyes.

He gazed at her for a moment, his face deadly serious. 'Tell me the truth. It's yours?'

Her eyes closed, almost as if the admission would cause her pain. 'Yes…' A whisper.

'Am I…?'

The words choked in his throat and she opened her eyes again in anguish. She hardly knew this man. He was a temp. A locum. A drifter. How could she tell this stranger that the baby in her womb was most definitely his? Because she didn't sleep around. She never met anyone—never gave herself the chance to.

She didn't need to get that kind of close to any man, to develop feelings for any man, because look at what had happened to her when she did. She'd suffered more than she'd ever believed it was possible for one body to suffer after getting involved with Mike. The pain she'd gone through, both emotionally and physically, had almost destroyed her.

She never wanted that again. Never wanted to risk it. Having that one night with Jamie—a stranger—had been a moment in which she'd thrown caution to the wind, feeling herself so physically attracted to the pirate she'd met at the

ball that she'd decided she would risk it. Keeping her anonymity, she would never have to deal with him afterwards.

Because why *shouldn't* she have slept with him? It was allowed, and it had felt *so good* to let all that other stuff go.

But they'd both been stupid. Believing that one night wouldn't have consequences. Believing that they could walk away.

They should have known the risks.

They'd been wrong! And no one could be angrier with her than she was with herself.

She'd once sat on a hospital bed, with a plastic compression mask over her burnt features, and promised her mother that she would never get involved with another man ever again. Would never cause her family anguish ever again. Because what Mike had done—throwing that acid at her face—hadn't just affected her. The tragedy had affected her family and even Mike's family, who were distraught that their son was in prison.

And all because she'd got involved with him.

And now she was pregnant. With Jamie's baby.

'Yes. You're the father.'

She saw him look down at the ground. Could almost hear the cogs going around in his skull, almost sense his thoughts as he tried to distance himself from her. Maybe even planned to leave this place. Get a temporary post somewhere else less complicated.

'Right.' A pause. 'It's very early on. Four…maybe five weeks?'

She nodded.

'You need to start taking folic acid.'

'I know.'

'You need to look after yourself.'

She knew he was just trying to say the sensible thing, trying to help and maybe trying to make sense of it in his

own head. This had to be a huge shock to him too. But to Freya it sounded as if he was telling her what to do, and no man would ever tell her what to do again.

Her control was slipping. 'You don't need to tell me how to do anything. You don't own me.'

'I'm not. I'm just trying—'

'You're just trying to take over! So back off, Jamie, I don't need this in my life!'

She tried her hardest not to shout, but it was difficult. All she wanted to do was run away, but it was as if the walls were closing in and she would soon be trapped with him. A man. A stranger. Tied to him for eternity when she knew nothing about him. He could be anybody.

He sat forward in his chair. 'You're pregnant with *my child*. I don't think you realise what this means.'

She leaned forward too, anger and rage fuelling her bravado, matching his stance. 'I'm a midwife. Of course I know what it means.'

She stood, grabbing her notes and pen, deciding she would check on Andrea. She would finish her notes in there—give Jamie a chance to think about what she'd said.

He was *not* going to tell what to do.

He was going to be a father.

Of course if nothing went wrong they would have to marry. If the people of Majidar ever found out that he'd got a woman pregnant and then abandoned her to have the child alone they'd be appalled. And so would he. He wasn't just a prince, he was a man, and as such he had a responsibility to do the right thing. No child of his would grow up to be illegitimate—he just wouldn't accept it. The baby was his and he would be its father.

Honour in this country was different from honour in his. He saw it on the television every day—men getting

women pregnant and then leaving them to raise the child alone. There were single parents everywhere, and that was fine for them—but not for him. Not at all. He could never knowingly sire a child and then abandon it to God only knew what kind of future.

This was *his* child. And, whether Freya liked it or not, he had a duty to it.

And to her.

But what had happened to her? What was making her so frightened and on edge? Why couldn't she look him directly in the eye? Was it her scars? Her face? Did her shame stem from that? Or was it the unexpected pregnancy?

Clearly she was in shock. All he'd tried to do was make this easier for her. Try and shoulder some of the responsibility.

Because it was his and his alone. And because of who he was it was imperative that he do the right thing.

He would need to speak to his advisor.

At just after six in the morning Andrea delivered a healthy baby girl.

Freya was reluctant to leave her patient's room and go back out there and face Jamie again, but she knew that she had to.

She could only hope that as there was less than one hour until the end of her shift he might be busy elsewhere and she would be able to get through it without having to see him.

She'd had her fill of pushy men. To be fair, she'd only been with one, but that one—Mike—had been enough for two lifetimes.

It had started innocently enough. Mike had asked her not to go out with her friends from college one evening.

'Why not?'

'I just can't bear to imagine you out on the town like

that. I've seen gaggles of girls dressed to impress and off their heads on tequila shots. I know what guys think of girls like that, and I don't want them looking at you like you're a piece of meat.'

She'd thought he was being sweet! That he cared so much about her.

He'd begged her not to go, and to make him feel better she'd cancelled. The next week, when the girls had wanted to go out again, rather than just accept the invitation straight away she'd said she needed to check with Mike first.

Slowly she had stopped having any contact with her friends. Then he'd started making comments about how her family looked down their noses at him and how family meet-ups made him uncomfortable—could they stay home?

Bit by bit he had isolated her, until her entire life had been his to control and manipulate. She'd felt as if she couldn't breathe and she'd tried to break away. He'd found her, begged her to stay, promised he would change.

Only he hadn't. If anything he had got worse—his insecurities, his paranoia.

She'd bolted one day when he was at work and run home to live with her mum again. She'd thought she was free, that her life was hers again, until that terrible day on the high street...

Freya was grateful to see that the hub looked clear and she headed over, her back aching slightly, and slumped into a chair to complete Andrea's notes. The open tin of chocolates called her name and she unwrapped one and popped a caramel barrel into her mouth.

Mmm...just what I need.

The chocolate began to soften in her mouth, and as she chewed she realised just how hungry she was. She'd not really taken a proper break whilst Andrea laboured, and

suddenly she was starving—craving a full English break-fast, washed down with a mug of strong tea.

A banana was placed right in front of her. She frowned and looked up to see who had given it to her.

'Jamie…'

'Eat this. You haven't had anything all night.'

She moved the banana away from her. 'Thank you, but I have other plans.'

'So you say—but you're not the only one who gets to make decisions about yourself any more. This is my baby too and you need to eat. *Healthily*, preferably.'

He grabbed hold of the tin of sweets and moved it away from her.

Angrily, Freya grabbed the tin back. 'Keep your voice down. I don't need the whole ward hearing about it.'

'Are you going to eat the banana?'

She glanced at the fruit, lying harmlessly on the desk, and felt repulsed by it. The idea of taking a bite of it turned her stomach. She craved hot food. Preferably dripping in grease.

'Not right now.' She felt a little hypocritical. She'd often lectured pregnant women about eating well for a healthy pregnancy and here she was craving fat. And maybe another chocolate from that tin.

'So when are you going to eat?'

'When I get out of here. At home, where I can cook myself something.'

She didn't want to tell him that she didn't like to go out during the day. Didn't like to sit by herself in cafés filled with staring people.

'Where do you live?'

She looked at him incredulously. 'Why would I tell you that?'

'Because, like it or not, we're involved now and I want to look after you.'

'I don't know you!'

'You knew me enough to make a child with me.'

He stared hard at her, his eyes dark and dangerous, as if daring her to try and wriggle out of that one.

'Well, I didn't know I was doing that at the time.'

It was enough to make her remember their assignation—her back against the wall as he hoisted her legs around his waist and thrust into her, her hands frantically grasping at him. Both of them made courageous by darkness and anonymity.

No. She would not tell him her address. He might be anyone and her home was her safe space. Her haven. A place where she could relax and just *be*. It was her bolt-hole, and there was no way she was going to give him that information.

'You're not going to do this, you know.'

'Do what?'

'Go all alpha on me. Order me about.' She could hear her own voice quaking as she stood up for herself.

'I care about you.'

'No, you don't. You got me pregnant and now you think that you've got to be seen to be doing the right thing. Well, I'm giving you an out. You're off the hook—you can walk away.'

It would be easier, wouldn't it? To do it alone? Without a man? Because men were frightening. They didn't know what it felt like to be a woman. To know that half the population was bigger and physically stronger than you. That they could overpower you if they cared to try. Not to be able to walk down a street without fearing the footsteps you could hear behind you. Always having to be aware of your

surroundings. Of who might be looking at you strangely.
Were they just curious, or were they about to pounce?

He leaned forward and stared at her. 'I don't know what
experiences previous men have given you, but let me tell
you something. *I am not that kind of man.* When I do some-
thing I take full responsibility for it. And that means tak-
ing care of you and taking care of that baby.'

'But you don't have to. I can do it alone.'

'I do have to. It's my child. It has to be honourable.'

'Why does it have to be *honourable*?'

Even as she said the words she realised how childish she
sounded. Why wouldn't she want her baby to be honour-
able? Was she cheapening it already? By saying it didn't
matter if it was 'honourable'?

But this was *her* baby! She had dreamt of this for years!

He recoiled as if she'd slapped him, as if he was appalled
that she could think anything else.

'Because it has to be. I won't have it any other way.'

She moved the banana. She could smell it and it was be-
ginning to turn her stomach.

'If everything you do is "honourable", then how come
you had a quickie with a stranger in a closet? Surely being
honourable would make you at least a hotel-room-with-
satin-sheets kind of man?'

'Maybe I am?' he challenged, pushing the banana back
towards her. 'There is plenty that you don't know about
me, Freya MacFadden.'

The use of her name made her narrow her eyes as she
looked at him. God, he was beautiful. Almond-shaped eyes,
dark as ink, cheekbones a model would die for, and his
lips...

Oh, goodness, I remember those...

Freya cleared her throat and tried to sound as if she was

in control of this conversation. 'Well, perhaps you'd care to enlighten me?'

Jamie checked around them, as if keen to make sure they were alone and no one was listening in.

'I can't tell you right now. You wouldn't believe me. Perhaps if you agreed to meet me here?'

He pulled a card from his uniform pocket and slid it across to her. It was a glossy black card with the name of a hotel in silver.

Why did he want to meet her in a hotel? What kind of movie did Jamie think he was living in? He was deluded. This was normal life. People didn't do that. There was no way she was going to meet a total stranger in a *hotel*!

'Can't you just tell me?'

'You wouldn't believe it. Please meet me there.'

It would be a public place. Safe. But it would be in daylight. When there were other people about. Not in his room. Nowhere they could be alone. But she would have to face other people's stares.

'When?'

'Tomorrow? Before your shift? We do need to talk about this and we can't do it here.'

She could maybe put on some sunglasses and wrap a thick scarf around her neck, then no one would stare at her. She could get there before everyone else was up and milling around for breakfast. She could listen to what he had to say, give him his five minutes, then slink out quietly.

'Fine. About six? That gives us an hour before work.'

'Thank you.'

She nodded, then picked up the banana, gave it back to him and said, 'Now, take that away, please, before I throw up all over this desk.'

His mouth curled slightly at the corners. 'Tomorrow I'll bring you grapes.'

* * *

The Franklin Hotel sat atop a hill, so that as Freya drove towards it she had a sense of awe and magnificence as she approached the beautiful Georgian manor. Looking at it from a distance, she wondered how Jamie could afford to stay in such an opulent place.

I don't have to go in. I don't have to hear what he has to say.

But she knew she would. Because, no matter how terrified she felt, she knew that she owed her baby the chance to know something about its father. So she could look her child in the eye and tell him, or her, that she'd tried everything.

It looked welcoming and warm, with yellow lights gleaming out in the darkness of the early morning, the sky above a blue which was fading from inky navy to palest azure.

Parking her little hatchback next to rows of expensive cars with chauffeurs sitting in them made her feel a little uneasy. Why had Jamie asked her to meet him here? What was it that she was about to learn from him?

He was a midwife. A damned sexy one, if she was honest, with an accent to die for and eyes that looked right into her soul and grasped her by the heart. She'd never met anyone like him. The mystery was what could he tell her here that she would never have believed if he'd just told her at work?

Whether she liked it or not, whilst this baby nestled in her womb they would be tied to one another—and Jamie seemed determined to be in her life.

Adjusting her scarf and lowering her sunglasses, she strolled across the gravel driveway, her nerves jittery, her legs weak. In the hotel, gentle music playing from a piano met her ears. To her right was a reception desk, where ex-

quisite and perfectly presented staff waited to attend to every guest's needs.

'May I help you, madam?' asked a young man in a navy suit with enough gel in his hair to sink a ship.

No, it's fine. I'm just leaving.

'I'm supposed to be meeting a Mr Jamie Baker?'

'Miss MacFadden? We've been expecting you.' He smiled, revealing perfectly white teeth. 'Please take the lift to my right and go up to the third floor.'

Take the lift? Go to the third floor? That wasn't meeting in a public space. That meant going to his room. Where there was a bed.

'Oh…um… What room number?'

'Mr Baker has the entire third floor.'

Freya blinked. What? Who went to a hotel and took up an entire floor? That was the sort of thing celebrities did with their entourages, or royalty, or…

'You wouldn't believe me if I told you.'

What was going on? It was all so confusing. He was just a guy, right? A normal guy.

Was he rich?

The night they'd met at the gala she'd known there was a member of royalty there. She'd heard the rumour but she'd never been introduced to anyone. There'd been no announcement. Everyone had hidden behind their masks and it had been exciting. You could talk to *anyone* and not know it!

Including royalty.

Have sex in a closet with them, if you so chose…

Freya swallowed hard, trying to control her rapidly weakening legs as she hesitantly went over to the lifts and pressed the button.

I could still go. I could run. Just get the hell out of here!

She stood there, fidgeting with the tassels on her scarf, as she waited for the lift to come down to the ground floor.

I owe it to our baby.

Was Jamie a member of some royal family? How could that be?

She thought about turning tail and running—changing her mind and hiding somewhere. Her parents' beach house on Hayling Island, perhaps. It was the place she went when she needed to hide and think. She'd gone there when she'd first been released from hospital, months after the acid attack, and she'd had to wear that damned orthotic burns mask every day, marking her out as different.

She'd felt like a leper. As if there was a bright neon arrow over her head screaming that here was someone *not normal*.

The house on Hayling Island would soon be filling up with summer rentals, but hopefully no one was there right now. Jamie wouldn't know where to find her. It would be good for her to take a break while the morning sickness was in full swing.

The lift pinged, signalling its arrival, and the doors slid open. On the back wall of the lift was an ornate mirror and she gazed at her reflection, wondering what the woman in the mirror should do. Run like hell? It was like staring into a prison.

All ye who enter here...

But Freya had seen more than enough women arrive on her ward to give birth alone, without a father involved, and she had felt sorry for all those children who would grow up without an interested father.

Jamie *wanted* to be involved. He'd said he would not shirk his responsibility. All she'd ever wanted was to be loved and to have a baby—something she'd thought would never happen after her acid attack—and here she was, pregnant and with a guy who said he wanted to be involved.

She owed him a chance, the opportunity to show her what he could provide for their child.

With hesitation Freya stepped into the lift and pressed the button for the third floor, eyeing the reception area with longing as the lift doors closed her in.

As the lift ascended she gripped the strap of her bag as if it was a lifeline. An anchor to real life. The sensation that her world was about to change for ever was drowning her in anticipation, and she wished she'd eaten more of those ginger biscuits before coming, because her stomach felt as if it was about to explode.

The lift stopped rising. *Ping!* The doors slid open to reveal two men in dark suits.

Her stomach flipped and she looked from one to the other.

Guards? Why does Jamie need guards?

They were wearing those earpieces that secret service men had on television. They asked her to put her bag through a scanner, and then she had to walk through a metal detector shaped like a doorway before they escorted her down the corridor towards a pair of ornate doors.

What on earth have I got myself into?

Silently she followed, feeling like a little girl between giants. Were they wearing guns beneath their jackets? Her mouth went dry at the thought of it and she gripped her bag tighter, as if that small item would somehow protect her from what was to come.

At ornate double doors the men stopped and grabbed a handle each, stepping back to open the doors wide.

Freya sucked in a steadying breath as her eyes hungrily took in the details of the room. A four-poster bed set with golden drapes in an opulent room adorned with fine art and floor-to-ceiling windows. Gilt-edged tables, fresh flowers in vases that were almost as tall as she was. And stand-

ing in the middle, in a long white tunic and trousers, was Jamie. As if he'd been waiting for her.

She stared at him, not sure what to do. Or say.

Now she could understand why he hadn't just told her all this.

'You're right,' she said, clearing her throat and looking straight at him. 'I would never have believed you.'

Jamie poured her some tea, adding two cubes of sugar to the drink. He frowned slightly when he saw how her hands were shaking when she went to take it from him, then set it down on the table instead and took her hands in his to calm them.

'It's all right, Freya.'

'Is it?' She looked at him askance. 'Who *are* you, Jamie?'

'My name is Jameel Al Bakhari and I am heir to the throne of Majidar. My older brother Ilias is King, ruling with his wife Queen Jasmeen, but they have been unable to sire any children so I am next in line. I also have a younger sister, Zahra, who has just married.'

It all sounded as if it was from a film. 'Heir to the throne...?'

'Yes.'

'Royalty?'

'Yes.'

It was a struggle to process. 'But...but you work as a midwife.'

'Yes.'

'Why? Why do that, when you're a...a prince?'

He smiled. 'I did not ask to be born a prince. Ruling a kingdom and waving at crowds from a distance is not what I felt I was meant to do. I want to *know* people. Help them personally. When my father sat upon the throne he took us with him to a hospital, where he was opening a new neo-

natal unit. I was very young—maybe eight or nine. We toured the labour ward, saw the new state-of-the-art theatre and the incubators that held tiny newborns. I was fascinated by the babies, and when we returned to the palace an idea took hold. The more I thought about it, the more I realised I wanted to deliver babies. To hold the miracle of life in my own two hands and experience the joy of bringing a new life into the world.'

Freya nodded. 'But why be a midwife? You could have been a doctor. An obstetrician. A surgeon!'

'I could. But those paths didn't interest me. I wanted to deliver the babies. An obstetrician gets called in only if there's a problem. A surgeon just takes care of Caesareans. I wanted to be there through the whole labour—to monitor progress, develop that close relationship a midwife creates with each patient. My mother spoke fondly of all her midwives. I would beg her to tell me, over and over again, the stories of our births—mine, my brother's and my sister's. Even after all those years she could remember every detail, and it was the midwives of whom she spoke the most highly. I wanted to be that person. To have that impact on people's lives. To be remembered in such a way. Selfish, perhaps, but true.'

'I don't think it's selfish.'

He inclined his head in thanks. 'I asked my father if I could study towards midwifery. Focus on the sciences so that midwifery could be my calling. But he would not allow it. He said it was not appropriate for a prince of my standing to attend to such work usually reserved for women.'

Freya couldn't imagine what she might have felt if her mother had forbidden her from becoming a midwife. 'What happened?'

'I had to put my wishes to one side until my father died and my brother Ilias took the throne. I assumed then, like

they did, that they would soon overwhelm the palace with little babies and that I would no longer be next in line to sit upon the throne and rule. So I begged Ilias to let me come to England to follow my education and have the life that I wanted. Ilias is much more modern in his thinking and he agreed that I should have the life of my own choosing.'

'You said your brother doesn't have any children?'

'No. Ilias and Jasmeen have never been blessed. Therefore I am still next in line to sit on the throne—something I have no desire to do, but must endure when the time comes. And it *will* come. Eventually. My brother, as considerate as he is, has begun asking me when I will return. He tells me that I must be seen to be upholding some of my royal duties, so that when my time comes the people will know me better and accept my succession.'

'So you have to go back?'

'Not immediately. Ilias is still young—just a few years older than me—but his health is not the best.'

Freya looked down at her tea. The nausea and shock had subsided somewhat now, and she felt more comfortable about taking a sip. 'So what you're trying to say, in a round-about way, is that I'm carrying the heir to your throne?'

Jamie inhaled a deep breath as he looked at her. She seemed tiny suddenly. He hadn't wanted to scare her, or overwhelm her, but he'd known if he'd tried to explain this on the hospital ward she would never have believed it. She needed to see it. Experience this.

'Yes.'

His acknowledgement was too much. Too overwhelming. She suddenly felt as if she was being suffocated as her mind whirled with all the possibilities that would entail. She got up and began to pace. Walking back and forth, back and forth as she thought hard about how she could get out of this situation.

A royal baby? Heir to a throne? It would mean her life changing. Never to be hers again. All her choices taken from her. All her control gone and given over to someone else.

'Tradition dictates that if everything remains well we should marry before the child is born.'

What? Marriage? No, no, no, no…

She shook her head frantically. 'I'm sorry, but no. I can't. I can't do that, Jamie. I *won't*!'

He stood up too, and reached for her arm, but she swiped his hand away.

'Marrying you would make me…what? A princess? A *queen*? I can't be that! Stared at… With people judging me on a global scale… Why do you think I do night shifts? I love my little world. I'm happy there. I'm accepted. Do you think I want *any* of what you're offering?'

'But, Freya, we need to—'

It was all spiralling away. Her control—everything. Disappearing into a black hole that was vast and powerful. It couldn't happen. She wouldn't let it! She had the right to say no!

She didn't know this man. Even though she'd been intimate with him, conceived a child with him, worked with him. She didn't know him.

Didn't know how he would react if she backed away…

Would he be like Mike? Refuse to let her go?

I need to get away.

Her hand reached into her bag and grasped her mobile phone. She pulled it out and activated the phone keypad, pressed the numbers nine-nine-nine and hesitated. Ready to press 'Call' if anything went wrong.

'No, Jamie. *We* don't need to do anything. *You* don't need to do anything. You can forget about me—you can walk away and pretend that I never existed. You can go

back to your kingdom, when the time arrives, and marry a proper princess—someone beautiful, someone the people will expect.'

'You *are* beautiful.'

She laughed at his response. 'You're just saying that. Do you really think you would have asked a girl like me to marry you if I wasn't pregnant? With *this* face? I don't think so.'

He stood in front of her. 'Your face doesn't matter. You are a strong, beautiful woman.'

'Of course it matters. It's what people see! It's what they judge you on. I know this better than anyone. I appreciate that you're trying to say and do the right thing, but it's not the right thing for Majidar. It's not the right thing for *me*. Your people don't need me by the side of their King. A one-night stand who got pregnant? A commoner from another country? *No.* I absolve you of all responsibility. Send me money each month, if that will make you feel better about it, but please, Jamie, I beg of you, walk away. It will be better for you if you just let me go.'

She was trying to sound reasonable. Trying to sound calm and steady so that he would remain so, too. Her thumb hovered over the 'Call' button. He hadn't seen the number she had keyed in and she appreciated that he was keeping his distance physically. But she would press it if she had to.

'I cannot. I *will* not.'

Freya sighed, her eyes filling with sorrow. 'I can't be who you need me to be. I can't live that sort of life. That's not who I am.'

'Neither am I. But it is my destiny. And now, because of the child, it is also yours.'

Freya closed her eyes as if she were in pain, and then she opened them again, looking at him with tears in her eyes,

as if she were sorry to be causing such distress. Sorry to have to deny him.

She was afraid to say the next words, but knew she had to, so that he was clear on where she stood. 'No, Jamie. Never.'

And then she backed away. She yanked open the large doors to his suite and hurried down the corridor, expecting at any moment that the guards would drag her back, her finger still hovering over the button on her phone.

But the guards simply followed her at a respectful distance.

The lift was waiting for her and she got in and punched the button for the ground floor. Only when the doors slid closed and she was safe inside did she clear the numbers and slip her phone back into her bag.

It had taken every ounce of her strength to refuse him. To say no and walk away, not knowing how he might react. The likelihood of him being like Mike was slim, but then she'd thought Mike was okay, too. And look at what had happened there.

As she ran across Reception and out into the cool morning air she hoped this meant it was all over. That he would not bother her again.

She had given him her answer.

He would do much better if he were to accept it.

CHAPTER THREE

SHE TRIED TO stay away from Jamie at work. She sensed
he was giving her space, and she appreciated that, but she
could tell by the way he looked at her from across the room
that as far as *he* was concerned this was far from over.

There was no way she could accept his terms. *Marry*
him? Become a princess, or whatever she would be? Have
her child schooled to become a king or queen themselves?
Living a life of privilege, no doubt, but one that would be
like a prison. Never to pop to the shops when she wanted,
go for a walk when she liked, without fearing that some-
one might get too close to the royal person…

It was ridiculous.

Her child wouldn't live like that. She wanted a normal
life for her baby—a normal education, real friends, a real
life and choices. She wanted to sit on the South Downs and
have a picnic with her child. Fly a kite and take a dog for a
walk. She wanted to walk barefoot on the beach and jump
waves with him or her, laugh out loud and eat ice cream
and fish and chips.

Normality.

It was the only thing she craved for her child. For her-
self. To live a normal life. Not the life that she had had
since the attack, hiding from people and crowds. Not the
childhood that Jamie had had, raised behind the walls of

a palace. Something else. The childhood she'd had when she'd been growing up. When her face had been unspoilt by sulphuric acid—when her future had looked bright and the whole world had been a possibility.

Mike had limited her. Told her what she should wear, what she should eat, who she could talk to. And when he hadn't been able to control her, hadn't been able to keep her, he had tried to make sure that no one else would want her.

Saying no to Jamie had taken every ounce of bravery she had. But she wouldn't allow another man to control her, and Jamie's request demanded something of her that she couldn't give. Basically, it seemed to her that he wanted her whole life—her dedication, her child—to be given to him and his country. A country she had never even heard of just one week ago.

Jamie had a duty to his throne, but she didn't. Nor did their child. And she refused to tie either of them down to it.

A person's skin is made up of proteins. Protein makes up the structure of cells and the enzymes within them. Acid, when it comes into contact with protein, changes its innate structure and causes it to break down immediately upon contact. It's excruciating, the pain—difficult to relieve. The strongest medications often have no effect...

Freya sat in the hospital staffroom, waiting for her shift to start. Her mind was torturing her with the memory of that day so long ago, when her world had been turned upside down.

She'd tried to hold up her hands to protect her face, but it had been too late, and then suddenly—instantly—the terrifying scorching of her skin had begun.

She'd thought those screams were from other people, but they'd been her own. Freya had collapsed onto the pave-

ment, her eyes squeezed tightly shut, afraid to open them in case she couldn't see, screaming at people to help her.

Some guy had tried pouring water over her face to dilute the acid, but it had simply run down her neck and begun burning her there, too.

It had seemed an age before the paramedics had arrived. Before the morphine had hit her veins, before they'd tried to irrigate her skin and whisked her to hospital.

Despite the burning she'd begun to feel cold. Shock, they said. Apparently, burns could cause hypothermia. Who knew?

It was a day she would never forget. And all because a man had refused to let her go.

She'd told Jamie no. She'd turned down his marriage proposal, refused to let him take her and the baby back to his country. How would he react now?

As if her worries had summoned him, Jamie entered the staffroom. His gaze met hers, briefly, and then he looked away.

What did that mean? Was he upset? Angry? Was he the type to seek revenge?

So far he seemed reasonable. Normal. A little sad, maybe, but nothing like Mike. But for how long? What about when he got called back to his country and the time came for him to leave? Would he put pressure on her then? Would he try to blackmail her? Threaten her?

She didn't want to tar him with the same brush as Mike, but her history with men so far had not been good. She couldn't read him yet. Didn't understand him. Perhaps if she remained polite and respectful he would remain that way too? Perhaps if she got to know him a little more she might understand him better?

But she was afraid to do that.

Getting to know him meant spending time with him…

* * *

Caroline Müller was well into her labour—contracting every two minutes, alternating between taking amusing selfies with her husband Stefan when she was between contractions, and breathing and retreating into herself when she was having pain, going all Zen, peaceful and in control.

It was a marvel to behold.

Freya was happy she could distract herself at work—the place where she could absorb herself in her patient's labour and just for a few hours forget about her own life.

'How are you doing, Caroline? Still coping?'

Caroline had requested no pain relief. She wanted to try and give birth naturally to her first child. Freya wanted to support her in that, but also to let her know that she could change her mind whenever she needed to.

'I'm good, I think.' Her patient nodded, as if she were reassuring herself that she could do this. 'Do you think I'm doing okay?'

Freya smiled. 'You're coping wonderfully. Eight centimetres dilated and still no pain relief! You're a marvel.'

Freya was very keen on honouring a woman's choice. Of all the things in the world a woman could do, going through labour and childbirth was an extremely personal thing. No one else could do it for her. She was on her own. Pulling on the resources and reserves that only she had within her own body.

It was an eye-opening and eye-watering experience. No one could know how they would cope with those levels of pain. And if a mother wanted to give birth without pain relief or with every medication going then Freya would support her either way. Childbirth wasn't a competition, and the mother alone was the one who must decide her course of treatment. It was important to empower a woman with the knowledge that any choice over her body was her own.

Caroline blew out a breath and nodded. 'Thanks. Did you know Stefan's mother wanted to be here at the birth?'

Freya looked at Stefan. 'I didn't.'

'I told her she wasn't welcome—which didn't go down very well. I didn't want my own mother here, so there was no way I was having my in-laws loitering around my nether regions.'

Freya and Stefan smiled at each other.

'My mother can be quite controlling,' he said. 'This is her first grandchild and we've had to be quite firm with her about not booking things in advance.'

'What sort of things?'

'Enrolling him or her in a private nursery, hiring a nanny, booking her personal swimming instructor to give our newborn swimming lessons, *and* pre-book a German teacher so that our child will grow up to be bilingual. German is my mother's natural tongue,' he explained, smiling with amusement.

'Wow!' Freya mused. 'She sounds wonderfully keen to provide your little one with the very best.'

'She has to be reined in or she doesn't know when to stop!' Caroline said, and grimaced as another contraction began to build.

She closed her eyes, relaxed her brow and began to breathe steadily in through her nose and then slowly and smoothly out through her mouth. She stood to one side of the bed, leaning on the mattress, swaying her hips from side to side as the contraction intensified.

'That's it, Caroline, you're doing really well. Keep breathing.'

Freya rubbed the small of her patient's back, wondering how royal families raised their babies.

Weren't they all surrounded by nannies? Whisked off

to nurseries and only brought to their parents to hold when they were clean and fed and presentable?

Actually, she had no idea how royals looked after a new baby. Nor did she have any idea about a desert kingdom's culture.

But what she *did* know was that she didn't want her child to be taken away from her. This was *her* baby and she wanted to raise it. With Jamie's help, if he wanted, but she would have the final say in everything.

There would be no taking the baby away to a nursery at night time. She wanted to deal with midnight feeds and nappy explosions. She wanted to soothe her baby when it started to teethe. She wanted to be the one who took her child to the doctor for vaccinations and check-ups, to comfort it when it cried because some stranger had poked at it with a needle or a stethoscope.

Was it too much to ask? This might be Jamie's baby too, and he might come from a royal line of kings, but it was also *her* baby and she *wasn't* royal. She was normal—girl-next-door. And she wanted her child to have a normal life.

Caroline began to groan out loud—thick guttural noises coming from deep within her. 'Oh, I think I want to push!'

'Try not to. Not just yet. I need to check you again… make sure you're fully dilated.'

She was. With a wide smile she informed Caroline that with the next contraction she could start pushing, and that hopefully, within the next hour, they would have their longed-for baby.

'Will I really?' Caroline began to cry. Happy tears springing from her eyes as she reached for her husband's hand, clutching it tightly.

He squeezed back. 'We will.'

Caroline wanted to remain standing between contractions, and then lowered herself into a crouch beside by the

bed each time she pushed. She pushed long and hard, her face reddening, sweat pouring down with her efforts, until after about forty minutes she began to crown.

'You're nearly there now!' Freya watched intently and quietly as Caroline gave birth to the baby's head. It had thick black hair and Caroline reached down to touch.

'My baby!' she cried.

'One final push, Caroline! You can do this!'

Freya supported the baby with her gloved hands as it was delivered, and then passed the crying baby over to its mother, who lifted her up from between her legs to cradle her against her chest.

'Oh, my God! It's a girl! We have a little girl, Stefan!'

Freya clamped the cord and Stefan cut it, and then she helped guide the new mum onto the bed, so she could rest whilst Freya took care of all the little things that needed doing. The syntocinon. Checking to see if mum needed stitches. For any sign of haemorrhage.

She draped a couple of towels around the baby to help keep it warm as Caroline placed her daughter against her skin beneath her hospital gown. Then Freya checked the placenta to make sure it was complete and healthy.

After she'd written the pertinent times and details into her patient's file, she took the baby to weigh it and check its APGAR score—the scale against which all newborn babies were measured to ensure they were coping with life outside of the womb.

Handing the baby back for more skin-to-skin, she asked if Caroline and Stefan had chosen a name yet?

'Hannah Rose.'

'That's beautiful,' she said.

'Thank you. Thank you for everything, Freya—we really mean it. We couldn't have done it without you.'

She smiled her thanks. 'I couldn't have done it, without

you! I'll leave you on your own for a little while. Press the buzzer if you need me, but I'll be back to take you down to the postnatal ward.'

She left the new parents to it—Stefan already taking pictures with his phone—and quietly closed the door behind her. Then, carrying her patient's notes, she headed over to the desk and sat down.

Freya was hungry…thirsty. She hadn't had anything for hours, having stayed with her patient for most of the night, popping out only once to use the toilet because her bladder had threatened to explode if she didn't.

Mona came out of the small kitchenette, carrying a tray filled with mugs of tea. 'Ah! Perfect timing. Want one?'

'Ooh, yes, please!' Freya grabbed a hot mug and gratefully took a sip. 'My patient just delivered a baby girl— Hannah Rose. Isn't that a beautiful name?'

'Gorgeous! How did she get through it?'

'Not a single scrap of pain medication!' Freya stated proudly.

'Good for her! I have no pain threshold whatsoever. I practically needed an epidural for a tiny blister I got on my heel. What about you?' Then Mona's face darkened as she realised what she'd said. 'Sorry…'

But Freya wasn't offended. Mona was her closest friend here, and she knew she hadn't meant anything nasty by it.

Freya thought back to her days spent in hospital after the acid attack. The pain she'd been in. The pain she'd had to live through for months as her face recovered. The nightmares. The flashbacks. The searing, agonising torture of debridement. She'd had enough pain for one lifetime.

She smiled. 'I want everything they can give me.'

Jamie had been watching her carefully over the last few weeks. As much as he could, anyway. Clearly she was try-

ing to avoid being with him. He kept catching her noticing him arrive in the staffroom or at the reception desk and suddenly getting that *I'm busy* look before she got up to go and do something.

He was finding it terribly frustrating when all he wanted to do was talk to her. Find out how she was. Whether she was feeling okay. She had to be due for the first scan of the baby any day now, but she'd made no mention of it to him and he didn't want to miss it. Nor did he like this distance she was creating between them, as if she didn't want him involved, because that was not how he planned to have his first child. Being cast aside as if he was just a sperm donor.

Having a baby was one of the most wonderful things a woman could do. To become a parent one of the most rewarding privileges. He really hoped that Freya would thaw towards him, but he could understand why she hadn't yet.

Mona had told him what had happened to her years ago. Some possessive ex had thrown acid in her face. The very idea of that made him feel sick. It caused a rage to build in him towards a man he knew was already in prison.

Mona hadn't said much else, clearly reluctant to gossip about her friend, but he'd had to ask. He'd spent so many nights wondering why she was keeping him at such a distance. Why she seemed so edgy and uncomfortable. Why she kept looking at him as if he was some firework that might go off at any minute. It had made him wonder what had happened to her. And now he knew.

Freya MacFadden was having a strange effect on him. She was so petite, so dainty, and he loved seeing her walk in with her long blonde hair hanging loose down her back, watching her scoop it up, twist it and pin it into place each shift. It was an action so casually done, without looking in a mirror, and she always managed a tousled look which, with those big blue eyes of hers, was a winning combination.

The scars didn't bother him at all. Not like that. What bothered him about them was that someone had done that to her. Intentionally. That she had suffered, and that her life had been changed for evermore. He'd visited clinics that cared for women attacked like this, and he'd never seen such suffering before or since. It was a memory that haunted him, but he'd learnt something from those women—that they had tremendous courage. That they bore a bravery within them that he could never hope to emulate.

Freya was the same.

He was worried that she didn't seem to be letting him in, but he understood why and knew that he would have to bide his time if she were to trust him.

He leaned against her locker, straightening when he heard her coming down the corridor, chatting to Mona. He hoped to end this stalemate between them—to get them talking again. Ask her how she was…if she needed anything.

He saw her notice him. Watched as she debated whether to avoid using her locker after all. But then she seemed to overcome that hesitation and came over to him.

'Excuse me, I need to get inside.'

He stepped back, giving her space. 'Could we talk for a moment?'

She looked up at him hesitantly. 'About what?'

'About us.'

'There is no "us".' She glanced over at their colleagues, afraid of being overheard. But no one appeared to be listening.

She shoved her bag into her locker and hung up her coat. Then she did the hair thing that he loved and clipped her ID badge to her uniform.

'Can you tell me if you're feeling okay? If there's anything I can do?'

'I'm feeling fine. A bit sick, but eating often seems to help.'

He could see in her face that she was still closed off from him. Unwilling to share. He understood that, and he was willing to wait.

'Well, if there's anything I can do for you then please let me know.'

She nodded and bit her lip.

'Can I get you a tea? A coffee?'

She glanced over at their friends by the kettle and the sink. 'No, but thank you.'

'Have you told anyone?'

Her eyes darkened. 'No. Not yet. Have you?'

He shook his head. 'No.'

'Right. What will happen when you do?'

He imagined the reaction of his family. They would be insistent upon marriage. They would be insistent about him coming home and building his life as a father and future King of Majidar.

'They'll be delighted.'

Her eyes narrowed, as if she were trying to assess him for the truth. *'Right.'*

'Oh, I brought you these.' From behind his back he drew out a brown paper bag filled with grapes. 'As promised.'

A small smile *almost* broke out across her face, but she checked it and instead frowned. 'I'm not sick.'

'No, I know.'

'You don't have to do this…' she whispered.

He nodded and whispered back, 'I do. So if you need anything—*anything*—I hope you will ask me.'

And he left her at her locker to go and grab himself a drink.

Little inroads…small kindnesses. That was what she needed. He needed to build her trust. He needed to show

her that he could be relied upon to look out for her and keep
her safe. She needed to see that he was everything that the
man who'd attacked her was not. That he believed in kind-
ness and respect and love. That he believed in honour and
duty and that he would shirk neither.

Baby steps.

The next shift they had together Freya nodded her head
towards him, as if to say *good morning*. The one after that
she actually said hello.

Jamie gave her more space and time.

One night shift she came in and straight away headed
for the staff toilet, emerging fifteen minutes later looking
a little green. He presented her with ginger tea—some-
thing that his mother had sworn by. Another time when
she looked queasy and was meant to check on a patient in
Postnatal, he offered to answer the call bell instead.

Where he could, he took the time to try and lighten her
load. To make it easier for her whilst she was going through
this difficult time.

Their colleagues had begun to suspect that something
was up, and Mona had been the one to ask Freya during
a night shift.

'Are you *pregnant*?'

Clearly Freya had realised it was pointless to try and
deny it. Not when the signs were so obvious and she was
surrounded by people who specialised in pregnancy and
babies.

The team had been delighted! Hugging her and con-
gratulating her.

'Who's the father?'

Freya had baulked at answering, but she had looked at
him, as if to give him permission to answer.

He'd stepped forward. 'I am.'

Well, that had sent the gossip mill into high speed!

He had seen that Freya wasn't overly happy about being the centre of attention, but she'd seemed to cope with it—probably because these were her friends and people she trusted.

After that everyone had tried their best to help Freya out whilst the morning sickness was so devastating. She really was suffering, poor thing.

'Are you guys, like, together?' Mona had asked him.

Jamie had longed to say *Not yet*, but had felt that would be pushing too far, before Freya was ready. This was not a world in which two people could be forced into marriage. It was not something that had been arranged since they were children. It was not a unification of two countries solidifying a pact by marrying off a prince and princess.

This was real life. Freya was a commoner. A woman from the west. She had different expectations from life and a whole lot of baggage that she needed to sift through before she realised he was a good guy.

'Your first scan should be soon,' he said as he brought her another cup of ginger tea one day.

'It is.'

'I was wondering…only if you feel right about it…if I might come with you?'

She looked at him carefully, almost as if she were appraising him. She'd been giving him this look a lot just lately.

'Okay.'

His heart almost burst with joy. *'Okay?'*

'Sure. It's your baby too.'

'Thank you, Freya!'

He almost imploded with excitement, but managed to contain himself. Strong emotions, sudden reactions, were not the kind of thing that would make Freya feel safe. She

needed to see that he was stable, even if his insides were fizzing with glee and he wanted to jump about and yell for all the world to hear.

They sat together, waiting for the ultrasound technician to call Freya's name.

She felt uncomfortable. Not just because she'd had to drink a huge amount of water beforehand, and hold it in, but also because she was back in what she considered the 'normal' world. Daylight hours. Where there were too many people about. People who, she noticed, kept glancing at her, trying to work out what was different about her. Noticing her face…

Part of her wanted to stare back at them. Challenge them with a single raised eyebrow as if to ask, *What are you looking at?* But she wasn't brave enough or rude enough.

Freya had been raised to show respect to people. To be polite and to treat others the way she wished to be treated herself. She couldn't do that to strangers. They didn't deserve it. They were just being curious. It was human nature to take a second look at something that didn't quite fit.

She wondered how many of them were wondering how on earth she could be sitting there with this gorgeous man next to her.

Jamie clearly had no idea of his allure. Ink-dark hair, midnight eyes that penetrated the soul, and a bearing that screamed royalty—due, no doubt, to a childhood that had consisted of years of being told to sit up straight, shoulders back. Not to slouch. To meet people's eyes. Assess the situation. Listen. Look commanding.

She felt tiny next to him. Inconsequential. He was so tall, proud and strong, and she was small, scarred and nauseous.

How much of her feeling sick was due to the pregnancy, though? Her stress levels were high. She dreaded to think

what her blood pressure was. But she had to admit she wouldn't have got through these last few weeks of her first trimester without Jamie's help.

He had been instrumental in getting her through it, and she'd quickly come to realise that she had begun to rely on him being close. Always there with a hot, steaming mug of ginger tea, or some peppermints, or one of the strawberry milkshakes which she had begun craving. Whatever she'd needed—a rest, a moment to herself, someone to take care of her patients whilst she clutched the toilet bowl—he'd provided it. Her friends, too, yes. But Jamie had been the most considerate and for that she was grateful.

And scared.

He was getting under her skin. She was beginning to like him. Once she'd come on shift and, when she'd realised that he wasn't rostered on with her, a huge sense of disappointment and loss had hit her like a brick.

How had that happened?

She never wanted to rely on a man again.

And yet here she was. Not only was she tied to this man but he was also a prince, he had a duty, and she was refusing to accept that. She knew she must somehow be tearing him in two. He had a duty to his country. To his people.

I'm hurting him and yet he doesn't complain.

They didn't look right together—no wonder people were staring. She was just a girl. A scarred, damaged girl. And he… Well, Jamie was something else entirely, and he deserved a beautiful princess to stand by his side and make pretty babies with him.

'Freya MacFadden?'

She straightened, rising to her feet. Behind her, she felt Jamie stand and follow her into the darkened room.

They went through the preliminaries with the techni-

cian. Date of last period, how many weeks pregnant she was, whether she felt well.

Frightened, she lay down, not sure what was scaring her more—the prospect of seeing her baby on screen, at last, or the fact that she wanted Jamie at her side. She'd anticipated doing this alone. Not telling him. Sneaking in to the appointment after everyone on the night shift had gone and having this moment all to herself. Knowing she would cry. Knowing she would get emotional because finally, *finally* this day had come. The day she would see irrefutable proof that she was pregnant. With a baby she'd thought she would never have.

The technician squirted the gel and applied the probe to Freya's abdomen.

Freya bit her lip. She might have got this all wrong. Perhaps she wasn't even pregnant at all? A false positive? A molar pregnancy? Then everyone could go back to their normal lives. Jamie could leave and go on to another post, or back to his country, and she could remain unchanged on the night shift, revelling in the joy of other people's babies and just imagining what it might feel like to hold her own baby...

The technician was smiling. 'Everything looks wonderful here.'

Freya let out a breath she hadn't realised she'd been holding. 'Really?'

'Any history of multiples in either family?'

What?

The technician turned the screen so that Freya and Jamie could see. There, in black and white, was her womb. Filled with not one but *two* babies, separated by a very fine line which meant...

'Twins? Non-identical twins?' Jamie stared at the screen, laughing with shock and delight.

Freya had to remind herself to breathe. She couldn't

quite believe it! Twins? Her grandmother had been one of a pair of twins, but she'd never imagined that this would happen to her. 'Oh, my God…'

'Freya, can you believe it?' Jamie scooped up her hand in his and kissed it, his dark eyes sparkling with unshed tears in the shadows of the room.

She stared at him, seeing his joy, his beaming face, his eyes twinkling in the semi-darkness of the room.

She felt her body flooding with adrenaline. *Twins.* Non-identical twins.

This was crazy. Unbelievable! It was…

She stared at the screen once again. Counted again. Two babies. Growing inside her.

Two.

'I don't believe it.'

The technician continued to make her checks. Measuring the babies, the length of their femurs, checking the Nuchal fold at the backs of their necks.

'Your babies look beautiful. Perfectly healthy and a good size. It probably accounts for all that morning sickness you've been having. You'll get more scans and check-ups due to this being a twin pregnancy, so if you have any problems don't hesitate to shout.' She smiled at them both. 'You ought to go and celebrate.'

Perhaps. But Freya didn't foresee having a party. She liked the idea of keeping it quiet. Just telling family and the people at work. They were the only people she knew anyway.

Jamie probably had loads of people he needed to tell. His family. His staff. His advisors. What would they all tell him to do? He couldn't walk away now, could he? She was carrying *two* royal children.

If she hadn't felt trapped before, she most definitely felt it now.

She began to hyperventilate and felt Jamie's fingers wrap around her own.

'It's okay, Freya. Just breathe slowly. In and out. That's it, slow your breathing.'

She focused on his face. On his voice. On him, her only connection to this world. She felt spaced out, as if she was adrift in a vast universe and he was the umbilical cord connecting her to reality.

He had intensely dark eyes. Eyes she could lose herself in. She had once before and now she needed to again.

Was she about to get swept up into a load of royal political intrigue? Be married and whisked away to live in a desert? Something like that?

How could she continue to live the private life that she loved? Was she about to lose all control over her every decision? Because she wasn't sure she could do that.

This life, her *babies'* lives, were too important. Jamie's demands were not more important than her own.

She'd lost all control once. Had all decisions taken from her. She had lived a life trapped in a hospital, in pain and afraid, with staff all around her, checking on her every hour of the day, waiting on her hand and foot. It had been unbearable. Living a half-life, staring out of windows, watching the world go by and wishing she could be in it. Wishing that the pain would go away, so she could escape…

I won't have that happen again.

Slowly her breathing came back under her control. Jamie was smiling at her, with relief on his face that she was calming down. Sitting up, she pulled her hand from his. She had relied on him enough.

'I'm okay. I'm all right.'

The sonographer passed her a couple of scan pictures. 'Twins can be a bit of a shock. It might take some time to get used to.'

Jamie was watching her, assessing her. He offered her his hand, so she could get up off the bed, but she did it without his help.

She couldn't keep relying on him. He had other commitments. Other duties. No matter what he said their lives were incompatible, and no matter how much she might want something else she couldn't have him and he couldn't have her.

I just need to keep telling myself that.

The rush hour traffic was building around the hospital. The car park was filling with vehicles. Staff were arriving, visitors...

Freya pulled up the collar of her jacket and adjusted her scarf. Aware of too many pairs of eyes all around her.

Jamie stood beside her, gazing down at the scan pictures the technician had given them.

'This doesn't change anything,' she said, hoisting her bag strap firmly into place on her shoulder.

'No?'

'No.'

He stared back at her, frowning, a small divot forming between his dark brows. 'There must be something I can do. To make this easier for you.'

Why did he have to have such a beautiful voice? Deep, slightly accented, smooth and delightful. He was already handsome and charming. Helpful and kind. Did he have to be sexy, too? Couldn't the man have one single fault?

He does. He's royal.

She was struggling not to cry again. Her hormones washed through her with renewed force now that she knew she was carrying twins.

'You could leave. Get a contract someplace else.'

'That's never going to happen. You think I'm going to walk away from you? All three of you?'

With eyes blurred from unshed tears, she glanced up at him and then away as she headed for her car to go home.

'You're under no obligation to be with me, Jamie. I told you that. Why can't you just go? Pretend this never happened? I'll never ask anything of you.'

She heard his footsteps as he hurried to catch up with her. Felt his hand upon her arm, turning her.

'I'm *never* walking away from you. You need to stop asking me to do that.'

She wasn't sure she could do this. How had she got herself into another situation where a man was refusing to let her go? Demanding to stay in her life? It was scary. She didn't want it. *Any* of it! She just wanted to be left in peace. To deal with this alone. Why couldn't she be living her happy dream? The one where she was married and was about to have a family with the man she loved and who loved her and where everything was normal and light and easy? And not terrifying.

'Jamie, I can't be who you need me to be.'

'Who do you think I need?'

'A princess. A queen. A *wife*. Someone who can stand by your side proudly. Someone who can wave to cheering crowds. Someone who can be loved by your people.'

'They'd love any woman I chose to have by my side.'

'Because of their duty?'

'Yes.'

'I don't want love out of *duty*, Jamie. And I could never stand beside you like that. I could never live away from my family. My job. My life. My life and my babies' lives will be *here*. Not in Majidar. You need to accept that.'

She pointed her key fob at her car to unlock it and opened the door.

'You *will* be called at some point to take your brother's throne and be King, so leave me now, leave *us* now and then no one will have to get hurt.' She got in, closed the car door shut after her and gave him one last look.

Did he not understand how much this was hurting *her*? She'd dreamed of this day! She'd never imagined she would ever be blessed by one baby, never mind two, but in that dream of having babies she'd hoped to have a wonderful man by her side too. In her imagination he'd always been a tall, dark and handsome figure, his face blurred. She'd never been sure who he might be. She'd dreamt of a family. Her children, her husband.

Mike had taken that dream away from her the second he'd thrown that acid, but now it was within her grasp again. And it was all wrong.

She wished she could develop something with Jamie, but he had another calling, apart from midwifery.

He was going to be King.

And she could not leave everything and everyone she knew to live her life beside him. A life of publicity, of always having her photograph taken, with her every choice of clothing or hairstyle criticised and appraised. Her face discussed and talked about in newspapers and on television channels, her relationship with Mike dredged up from history, where she'd consigned it. They'd no doubt track him down in prison, interview him, get the inside scoop on their relationship and publish that too.

A life with Jamie would mean a lifetime of judgement.

All she'd ever wanted was to be loved.

And love did not come from duty.

Jamie pressed his hands against her window and begged her to lower it so he could speak.

She dropped the window slightly and the coolness of the outside air filtered into the car's interior.

Jamie stared at her. 'People are already hurting, Freya. You are. I am. We need to work together to sort this—not just for us, but for our children.'

Her hands went to her belly, protectively wrapping around them. 'They're who I'm thinking of.'

His eyes had narrowed slightly and frustration crept into his voice. '*Are* you, Freya? Or are you just thinking of the man who did that to you? Letting his actions dictate how you think your life must be?'

She bit her lip. Because he was right. Mike—his actions years ago, his attack, her fear—was being allowed to run every decision she made.

But who was Jamie to think he could tell her this? Say it? Confront her with it? As if he had the right?

'I'm their father, Freya. Let me be with my children!'

CHAPTER FOUR

WALK AWAY AND no one would get hurt? Did she think he was made of stone? He already had feelings about this. About the babies. About *her*.

Freya didn't seem to understand that.

He was *already* involved. Already in too deep and he always would be—until the day he took his last breath. These were his *children*!

And she…she was *scared*.

He understood that. What she'd been through… He couldn't even begin to imagine *half* the pain she must have experienced. She must have thought her life was over. Her face ruined. Her life destroyed by what had happened. Had she believed she didn't have a future?

All he wanted to do was help her feel safe. Make sure she was all right. But she seemed determined to keep pushing him away. It was very frustrating and he was trying his hardest not to make demands.

She truly was remarkable. He had nothing but admiration for her. Her spirit, her bravery made her shine from within. She didn't understand that. She didn't realise just how much people cared for her because of who she was. She believed they judged her purely on what she looked like.

She was still beautiful. Imperfections on her face meant nothing. It was who someone was that made them attractive.

Clearly Freya was still bothered by her face and he understood that. Women today were bombarded with messages about what constituted beauty, and it was all focused on outward appearances—being model-thin, having long, luscious hair, drop-dead gorgeous features. Beauty was never seen in acts of charity, or kindness, or caring. No one was ever told that having a good, loving heart was beautiful.

So he would protect her. Care for her as much as she would let him. And hopefully she would begin to let down her walls. To trust him.

He tried to make sure she always had a drink or a snack, as she kept staying in her patients' rooms and not coming out for a break, and he couldn't allow that. She needed to keep her strength up. But when he did these things for her she would give him a look that was almost like fear. As if she was worried about what he might do next. A look that said *You really don't have to do this.*

But he did. Whether she liked it or not they were joined now. For evermore. With or without rings on their fingers.

He brought her mugs of tea. He'd even offered to massage her aching feet once, when she'd complained about them, but all she'd done in response was look at him as if he was mad and then she'd got up to go and do something else. When she should have been resting!

She wouldn't let him in. Wouldn't let him get close.

His security people had told him that after she left the hospital and went home she stayed in. Never went anywhere. Didn't seem to have a life. There had been one visit, where she'd gone to someone's house, but a quick background check had discovered that it was her mother's home. He'd debated about calling in, hoping to meet her mother, but had refrained, not knowing how she'd react to that. If she thought his making her a cup of tea at work was

bad, he felt sure she wouldn't want him pushing into her life before he was invited.

The security detail he'd assigned to her reported in every day. It broke his heart that she lived such an isolated life. Was there some way in which he could help her to open up her world? Or perhaps she was happy? Perhaps she was an introvert who enjoyed her own company? He wasn't in any position to judge.

'Would you like to meet me for coffee one day?' he asked her during a break on the ward.

She looked at him askance. 'Why? I see you every day at work.'

He smiled. 'It's different at work. We don't really get a chance to talk. We should be getting to know one another a bit more. We could meet in the open somewhere. In a public place, if that will make you feel better.'

He thought he was suggesting a *good* thing. Neutrality. Safety and security in numbers.

'I was attacked in a public place, Jamie. Surrounded by people. Numbers don't always make you safer.'

No. Of course not. He should have considered that. Freya liked privacy and quietness. She liked being alone.

'Chichester Cathedral.'

She frowned. 'What?'

'Let's meet at Chichester Cathedral. It's quiet, not too many people. There's a place to get coffee. Some grounds to wander in where we could find a private nook.'

'Because you want to talk?'

'Because we *need* to talk. Please, Freya, I beg of you.'

She seemed to consider his proposal. A divot formed in her brow. 'It's still too public for me.'

'Then where? Name it and I will arrange it.'

She thought of her bolthole on Hayling Island. The place she'd gone to after the attack. Her sanctuary.

'There's a path called the Billy Trail on Hayling Island. It starts just after the bridge to the mainland, on your right. We could meet there. I'll bring Rebel.'

Now it was his turn to frown. 'Who's Rebel?'

'My mother's dog.'

He wasn't the biggest fan of dogs, but he could get past that if she could get past her fears. 'Okay. When?'

It was Sunday afternoon, and the sun was burning down through a pure blue sky. He'd had to have the air-conditioning put on full when he'd got into the car because it was so hot. But he was glad the weather was good. He thought that if it had been raining, or bad weather in some way, Freya would have cancelled and they *needed* this. This time together. They needed to know more about one another. More beyond work and pregnancy and past horrors.

He and Freya were from vastly different backgrounds. It was no wonder they were clashing. But they both had the same desire and that was to do the best thing for their babies.

His driver located the small car park just past the bridge. He'd never been this way before, and he'd been positively delighted at the beautiful harbours the bridge had driven them through. The soft stillness of the calm water, the white boats sitting on the surface, the stretch of coastline and beyond, across the water, the views to Portsmouth and the spire of the Spinnaker Tower.

He stood waiting for her to arrive and pretty soon saw her small car turn into the car park. He gave her a smile and a wave. He had butterflies in his stomach! He so wanted this meeting to go well between them. It was imperative that it did so.

His nerves grew worse when he saw her let a large German Shepherd dog out of the boot of her car. For some

reason he'd expected something smaller, but Rebel was massive! He was dark with intense eyes, his ears up and alert, ready to protect his mistress.

His mouth dry, he began to walk towards them.

'Hi.'

He stopped, looking down at the dog. Rebel was panting from the heat, but all Jamie could see were rows of sharp white teeth.

Freya had him on a short leash. 'Rebel, sit.'

Instantly the dog sat and looked up to her, waiting for the next order.

He was impressed, but also trying to control the feeling that he needed to bolt. He desperately wanted to run away from this dog, but he had no doubt that it would run after him and pull him to the ground with a well-placed jaw around his arm or leg. Or somewhere worse!

'Are you okay?' she asked.

'Bit nervous of dogs, to be honest.'

She smiled, amused. 'Rebel's all right. You can trust him.'

'Does he know he can trust *me*?'

Her smile broadened. 'We're both still trying to work that out. So, shall we get going?' She slung a backpack over her shoulder and locked her car.

'Sure. How…um…how close should I get to you?'

'Beside me is fine. Don't worry, he won't rip your throat out unless I tell him to.'

'Oh, good. That makes me feel a lot better.'

She laughed. 'Come on!'

Clearly Freya felt at ease with the dog at her side, and he had to admit he really rather liked this relaxed Freya. The dog? Not so much.

Freya looked relaxed in her white tee shirt and blue shorts, sunglasses over her eyes and her hair swept back

in a ponytail. She looked fresh and happy, and already he could see a slight swelling to her abdomen. Only three months pregnant, maybe, but this was twins so she was slightly bigger than normal.

Three or four people on mountain bikes went cycling past as they headed onto the path.

'You found the place all right, then?' she asked.

'My driver did.'

'Of course. You have servants. I forget that when I see you at work.'

'Just a driver. Some security. A valet at the hotel. Not much.'

'Not much, huh? You have the entire third floor. I think you have plenty.'

'Just a security issue, that's all.'

'Where are your guards today? Are they lurking behind bushes on the trail? Are they going to walk behind us at twenty paces?' She looked behind them, as if to check.

'Nothing like that.'

He didn't tell her that his security team had already swept the entire five-mile length of the trail. That he had one or two undercover men posing as walkers and another pretending to be a wildlife photographer. The trail passed a nature reserve, so it was the perfect place to hide men in plain sight.

'It must be hard to live a life that's watched over like that.'

'You tell *me*.'

She frowned. 'What do you mean?'

'Don't you think that everyone is constantly looking at *you*? Watching your every move?'

She looked away. 'That's different. That's a perception. Your life is a reality. One you can't escape from.'

'Is that why you don't want to be a part of it? Because people are always watching? Observing? Making judgements?'

'Partly.'

At least she was being honest.

'You don't notice it after a while,' he said.

'I would. I notice everything. Every little glance. Every raise of an eyebrow. Every frown. Every reaction—shock, fear, disgust. That last one I get more than you'd realise. Have you ever thought what that might feel like? To observe someone looking at your face and see that they're disgusted? Of course you haven't. Not looking the way you do. The world is open to those who are good-looking. It's a proven scientific fact. Beautiful and handsome people get better jobs, better pay, more opportunities. Disabled and disfigured people always seem to be at the bottom of the pile.'

'Life must have been hard for you.'

'Must have been? It still is.'

He didn't know how to answer that. He would never know exactly what she had been through. What she still went through, looking in the mirror and seeing a different face.

'But a new phase of our lives is opening up to both of us now.'

She nodded, stopping as Rebel bent his head to sniff at a small post in the ground. 'We have two separate, completely incompatible lives, Jamie. How are we going to manage this?'

The truth? He didn't know. He wanted to be a father to these babies, and to be in their lives, but he would be called upon to rule Majidar at some point and would have to leave this country. He didn't want to leave them behind and she refused to go with him.

He *loved* Majidar. Even though he had left it to come to

England and make his life there. It was still his home. It was still the place where his family was. Where his heart was. His people were gracious and kind and understanding, but would they understand when they learned that he had left his children behind? Because he wouldn't. He couldn't get his head around it.

He loved these babies. Already. He'd seen their little hearts beating, had seen them in her womb, two gorgeous little beans that were *his*. He felt he would die for them. Lay down his life for them. Already he dreamed of holding them in his arms, teaching them, playing with them, laughing at their chuckles and watching them grow.

Be a king. Or be a father.

It seemed to be one or the other, and it was an impossible decision to make.

'We *must* manage it. We must find a way.'

'But how?'

He smiled at her. 'Today is a good step forward. We can't afford to shut each other out; we don't have that luxury. I know it's hard for you—hard for you to trust me and let me in.' He paused over his next words, but knew he had to let her know that he *knew*. 'I know what happened to you.'

Freya stopped walking. So did Rebel, who turned back to look at her. 'Who told you?'

'No one was gossiping. I asked. I brought it up. I needed to know why you were shutting me out.'

She started walking again, Rebel loping by her side. 'I see.'

'I don't want you to be frightened of me, Freya. I'm not that kind of man.'

'I can't tell any more. My perspective on men is skewed.'

'Hence the big dog?' He smiled.

She glanced at him. 'Tell me why you're afraid of dogs.'

He thought about why he was afraid, glancing at Rebel's

teeth. 'My brother and I were once playing out on the sand dunes. We'd gone out with our father, who was hunting with his falcons and his dogs. We had these big boards—like surfboards—and if we threw them right down the sloping side of a dune we could jump on and surf to the bottom. We were doing that…laughing and joking…having a brilliant time. I'd jumped onto my board and was sitting on it, surfing down the dune, when one of the dogs must have had his hunting instincts activated by our movement and high-pitched cries. This dog—this hound that was almost as tall as I was—raced over to me, and when the board stopped moving it grabbed onto my head, sinking its teeth into my scalp.'

Freya looked fascinated. Interested.

'My father got the dog to stop. It let go and I was rushed to the hospital with four puncture wounds to my skull. After that I couldn't go near any dogs. They made me too nervous.'

She nodded. 'So you know how it feels.'

He looked at her. 'I do. I know you don't know me well enough to be sure I'm not going to pounce, not going to sink my teeth in, but all I can say is I'm not like the man that did this to you. Just like Rebel, there, is probably nothing like the dog that attacked me.'

'You have to trust that.'

'As do you.'

He touched her on the arm, making her stop. Then he sucked in a breath as he contemplated what he had to do. Show her that if he was willing to work past his fear, then so should she. With some hesitation he held his hand out towards Rebel, hoping the dog wouldn't sense his fear. Hoping he wasn't about to lose a chunk of his hand. His heart racing, he watching in horrid fascination as Rebel licked his fingers, then began sniffing the cuff of his shirt.

Jamie knelt down in front of the dog and reached out to stroke it. His arms were trembling, but he was determined to do this. Rebel's fur was soft and thick and, most surprisingly, the dog didn't seem to mind him at all. Slowly he stood up and breathed a sigh of relief, a smile breaking across his face.

'Well, that went better than I'd imagined.'

A small smile broke across her face. 'That must have taken a lot of courage. Were you really that scared?'

'Terrified. But I trusted that I'd be okay. I hope you can do the same with me. Because only then can we get through this. As equals.'

They began walking again, side by side, enjoying the views over the harbour and its old oyster beds, where masses of birds were nesting.

'I'll try. That's all I can do.'

Jamie nodded. 'It's all I ask.'

Freya looked about her, then sucked in a breath and began talking. 'I guess I ought to tell you about him. About Mike—the guy that did this.'

'Only if you want to.'

'I do.'

Freya stooped to undo the clip on Rebel's lead and set him free.

Jamie felt a surge of anxiety, but decided he had to stay calm. She still had control of the dog. And the way the dog kept looking at her, waiting for instruction, showed that she did.

'Mike made me think we were equals. At the beginning. He seemed to adore me. Wanted to be with me all the time. I thought that was just so wonderful, you know? But over time it became insidious, the way he manipulated that. He made me feel bad about going out to see other people. He questioned my clothing. He wanted to know why I needed

to wear make-up. Was it for someone else? Was I flirting? I tried to prove him wrong by not wearing make-up, but then he wanted me to cut my hair short. Said it made me look flirty, being so long, that men looked at women with long hair in the wrong way.'

She paused.

'It sounds crazy now, but at the time I was just so afraid of upsetting him. His moods were terrible. We were so good together when he was happy, and I wanted to do what I could to keep him that way. But I refused to cut my hair, so he told me to wear it up, so that it looked a bit less feminine. Less pretty. He began questioning me if I was ever late coming home from work. Who had I been talking to? Was it a man? Didn't I know how scared it made him feel when I didn't come home on time? It was just a part time job at a bar, to help with college fees, but he figured the place was filled with nothing but lecherous guys.'

She paused again.

'I began to realise I had no life outside of college and work. I hadn't seen my family in ages. My friends no longer asked me out. All I did was spend time in the flat with Mike. I was just eighteen. It seemed like no life at all, and I didn't want it to stay that way. It had seemed like a compliment at first, the way he seemed to need me. But I began to see that my life had become a prison. A prison I needed to escape.'

'And he let you go?'

'I waited until he went to work, then packed what few possessions I had and took a bus home to Mum. He went crazy when he came home and found out I wasn't there. Called me on my phone. When I told him we were over there was the longest silence, and then he called me all these vile names, said my life wouldn't be worth living without

him, and that if I didn't come back to him by the morning
I would regret it.'

'Freya…'

'I thought it was just him letting off steam. I thought he
was saying stuff like that because his pride had been hurt.
But he really was that crazy. I was shopping when it hap-
pened. Out on the high street and suddenly he was there,
throwing acid into my face.'

'My God! I'm so sorry.'

'I should have seen it coming. I knew he couldn't let
go—knew he was a little unstable. I should have expected
it.'

'You can't blame yourself.'

'I do, though. For getting involved with a man like that
in the first place.'

'You were just *eighteen*, Freya.'

'I know, but…but I feel I should have had more sense.'

Rebel had been up ahead, but now he came loping back,
his large paws pounding the ground. He came running up
to Jamie, sniffing around his jacket.

Jamie tried not to freeze. Tried to keep walking. To act
normal.

'Rebel, heel!'

The dog left him instantly and went back to its mistress.
Jamie breathed a sigh of relief. He understood how hard it
was for Freya. She couldn't know. Even if she suspected
the worst, she couldn't know if or when it would happen.
It was impossible. His own hesitation and fear around dogs
was similar, but Freya's fear had to be tenfold. He would do
whatever he could to make things easier for her.

'You did what you thought was right at the time, with
the knowledge you had. You couldn't have asked any more
of yourself back then. Or now, come to think of it.'

'What are we going to do, Jamie? I can't marry you. I

can't be your wife and leave everything to go and be Queen in some foreign country. That's not me. That's not what I want from my life. And I can't have my children raised behind walls with security guards for protection. I want them to be free.'

'I know. I understand. I *do*. But I can't leave you behind. A king has to be, above all, a good role model for his citizens. I can't leave my children here and go back to rule as an absent father. But I can't let my people down, either. They'll need me. At some point they'll need me on that throne.'

'We have a stalemate, then.' She pulled a small treat from her pocket and fed it to the dog.

'In the future, yes, but right now we can try and work something out.'

'How do you mean?'

'I might not have to be King for many years. In the meantime let me be with you—and them. Let me be who I need to be. I *have* to be in their lives.'

Could she hear the desperation in his voice?

She looked up at him, considering him, judging him. He knew she was still scared. There was no way that was just going to disappear. But he could see that she was thinking about acquiescing to his request.

'I want my children to know their father,' she said.

'That's good.'

'But I don't want their father running out on them. I won't have their hearts broken, Jamie. I won't.'

'I would never want to hurt them in any way.'

'But it will happen. Eventually. Wouldn't it be easier if—?'

'No.'

He knew what she was going to say. *Wouldn't it be easier for them if they just didn't know about you at all?*

'I can't forget about them. They're here. They're a part of me. They are my sons or my daughters. I can't walk away from that. Could you?'

She let out a heavy sigh. 'No, I couldn't.'

They walked on a little more. An older couple were walking towards them, holding hands, chatting. They looked so comfortable with each other. So safe in their little bubble.

He envied them. Envied them their easy lives.

'I have a responsibility to do the right thing. A father stands by his children *and* the mother of those children. As a man, I have to show them that's what I should do. Take responsibility for my actions. As King, I need to think about my people and how they need a good, strong leader they can respect. But most of all I have to respect myself, and that means doing the best by all of you. That doesn't mean, and nor would it ever mean, walking away.'

Freya nodded. 'Okay. We'll work something out.'

He nodded too, sure they would find a way.

'We will.'

'I've brought you something.' Back at work, Freya stood awkwardly in front of Jamie, holding two mugs of tea.

Jamie put down the magazine he'd been reading and looked up at her in surprise.

'It's tea.' She thrust the mug towards him.

He took it. 'Thank you. That's very kind.'

'It's just tea.'

But they both knew it was more than that. It was an olive branch. A step forward. A slight lowering of the barricades. The walls were still there. Freya didn't know if she would ever be able to trust another man. But she was willing to give him a chance to show her that she was wrong after

the way he had approached Rebel. Willing to trust. Being scared, but doing it anyway.

'May I sit with you for a moment?'

'Please do.' He sat up, straightening, and watched her as she lowered herself into the chair opposite him.

'We…er…ought to get to know one another a bit more.'

He smiled, pleased. 'That's a very good idea.'

'Thank you.'

'How do you suppose we do that?'

She wasn't sure. She hadn't thought that far ahead. To be honest, she hadn't thought she'd get past offering him the tea before chickening out and walking away again, but she had done it. And now here she was.

'We should meet outside of work. What sort of things do you like to do?' he asked. 'That don't involve big dogs?'

She smiled. 'I like to read.' Then she realised that they were hardly going to sit and *read* together, were they? 'I don't really have any other hobbies.'

'What did you do when you were little? There must have been something.'

She thought for a moment. 'I loved to swim. But I haven't done that for years.'

'Swimming's very good for pregnant women. We should do that.'

'Oh, I couldn't possibly—'

'I'll arrange for us to have the pool area at my hotel all to ourselves. What day do you fancy?'

Oh. She hadn't thought he would be able to do that. But what did she know? He was a prince—he could probably do anything he wanted. He was right. There was so much they didn't know about each other. But swimming? Wearing just a swimsuit? Was it too late to back out?

'Saturday evening?' she said.

'Perfect. Thank you, Freya.'

'For what?'

'The olive branch.' He sipped at his tea and smiled. 'It tastes lovely.'

She'd had to get herself a new swimsuit, and had bought one online. She'd had to go for one especially for pregnant women, that allowed for a burgeoning belly, and had found a nice dark navy one with a crimson and cream pleat around her boobs.

Trying it on at home, she stood in front of the mirror to see what Jamie would see. She needed to shave her legs, that was for sure. Maybe paint her toenails?

The swimsuit covered her nicely, though, and even coped with her growing breasts without making her look as if she was hanging out of it. So all in all she was quite pleased with her purchase.

It revealed the scars on her neck, though.

She reached to touch the roughened skin where a graft had failed to take and was reminded of the first time she had looked in a mirror after the attack. The doctors had given her a small hand mirror and then left her to look by herself. Even her mum had left the room, giving her privacy for such a moment.

She'd almost not looked. Why had they all left like that? she'd wondered. Was it because the damage was so bad that they didn't want to see her distress?

Lifting up the mirror, turning to see, had been the most heartbreaking moment of her life. Her face had been ravaged by the acid, her nose almost gone. Angry, red, livid skin...

She'd wanted to die. Right at that moment she had thought that life was no longer worth living. That she would never look better than she did there and then. That her life was over at eighteen years of age and that she would now

be one of those relatives kept hidden away in a house, never to be seen again.

But time was a great healer. And the body had an amazing ability to repair itself. It had been a long, hard, painful road, but after each surgery, after each debriding, after each skin graft, she had looked into the mirror and seen progress. Incremental progress. The skin had become less angry. Smoother. Flatter. Her nose had been rebuilt, new eyebrows tattooed into place.

Slowly but surely, normality had seemed to be within reach. She knew she would never be perfect again. Never have the face she used to have. But she would no longer look like some kind of monster.

She'd grown used to the scars, but to everyone she met they were brand-new and she still feared their judgement.

Swimming, though... She hadn't done it in years, because she'd been too afraid to go to a public pool. All those people? Not likely. But she had missed it. So much so, she actually felt a small frisson of excitement at the idea of having a pool to herself and just being allowed to float in the water, quiet and serene, without the worry of people watching her.

She knew she shouldn't be so sensitive to that, but she couldn't help it. A person's face was what they presented to the world, and *her* face was different. Not different in that she had too big a nose, or a massive spot on her chin. Her face just had *that look* after all the skin grafts. The hint of something that was awful underneath in the way her top lip was slightly pulled to one side, her nostrils not quite normal.

The thought of returning to the Franklin Hotel caused butterflies in her stomach. The last time she'd been there it had been made clear to her just exactly who Jamie was. This time she already knew. But he would find out who

she was. And she wasn't used to people probing around inside her life like that.

Suck it up. You're doing this for your babies.

She parked the car and crunched across the stones on the driveway into the entrance hall. Jamie was already there, waiting to meet her, and he surprised her by kissing her on both cheeks.

'I'm glad you came.'

She nodded, trying to make sense—quickly—of how it had felt when his lips had pressed against her face. She'd stopped breathing. Felt hot. Uncertain.

It's nothing. Just get on with it.

But she hadn't been ready for him to touch her face like that. And with his lips. His perfect lips…

'Shall we go through to the pool? I can show you where the changing rooms are.'

Freya nodded hurriedly, glad that she didn't blush any more the way she'd used to. Following him through the reception area, down a small corridor, through a set of double doors, she was suddenly hit by the smell of chlorine.

It was like going back through time. She'd both forgotten that smell and remembered it intently at the same time. It was so strong! And there was that slight echo in the room, the reflection of the blue water, bouncing off the walls…

'The ladies' changing rooms are off to the right.'

'Thank you.'

Freya headed off to get changed, letting out a strained breath as she got to the changing area.

What was she doing—coming here? Doing this? Was she really about to strip down to a swimming costume in front of Jamie? It was practically like being naked. Naked meant vulnerable, and she didn't like feeling that way.

She sat down on a wooden bench for a moment, to breathe and gather herself.

I'm not doing this for me. I'm doing this for my children, so that when they're grown up I can tell them that I tried my best.

Suitably emboldened, she got up and began to undress. She put on her swimsuit and wrapped herself in a large towel before heading out to the pool.

Jamie was waiting for her. Wearing just a pair of trunks that emphasised his physique. She tried not to stare as she took in his beautiful body. His slightly hairy chest, his toned muscles, his flat stomach and long, strong, powerful thighs...

He was a thing of beauty, with his dark toned skin, whereas *she* hadn't been out in the sun for ages and was milky white, pale, swollen and...

She almost chickened out. Almost turned around to go back inside the changing room saying *I'm not doing this*, but then he smiled at her, padding towards her to take her hand.

'Are you all right?'

She nodded, not trusting herself to speak, fighting the urge to flee, but also wanting to get into that water so very much! She'd missed it. Swimming. Relaxing. Floating in the water with the weight of the world off her body.

'Let's get you in, then.'

He walked ahead of her down the steps, her hand in his, allowing her to slip off the towel and get chest-deep in the water before he turned back to look at her.

She appreciated him being a gentleman like that.

'How does the water feel?' he asked.

It felt wonderful. She felt instantly lighter—her bump supported, the strain off her back—and the temperature was perfect.

'Amazing!' She smiled, treading water and moving her arms.

'How many years has it been?'

'Erm… About twenty years. Maybe more.'

He swam alongside her, dipping his head to get his hair wet.

She glanced at him when he came up for air, and then looked away again. God, the man was sexy, all wet like that! Flustered, she allowed the weight of her legs to drop to the bottom of the pool and stood up. She was feeling strange things happening in her body. Tingling anticipation.

'When did *you* last swim?' she asked, to try and think of anything else but her body's primal reaction to this man beside her.

'Yesterday.' He smiled. 'I always do a few lengths after a shift.'

'*After?* How do you have the energy?'

'I just do. But, then again, I'm not growing babies inside me. How are you feeling?'

'Better now the morning sickness has disappeared. It wasn't too bad. I was never actually sick. But I'm feeling much better, thank you.'

'I'm glad.'

She stared at him for a moment. They were facing each other, about a metre apart, treading water. He looked so relaxed, and she wondered how he could be that way with so many worries upon his broad shoulders.

'How do you do it?'

He frowned. 'Do what?'

'Have those men following you around all the time? Your security? I've noticed I've got some of my own now. They're discreet, but they're there. It scared the hell out of me when I realised I was being followed.'

'I should have mentioned them to you. I'm sorry, I should have thought.'

'You should.'

'You get used to it. After a while you hardly notice.'

'Really?'

'Really.'

'I wonder what they think of all this? Having to follow *me* around?'

'I don't know. They do it because I order them to.'

'To protect me?'

He nodded.

'I don't need protection.'

'Maybe not, but those babies of mine do.' *Duty.* Would it always come back to that? He had a duty to his children, not to her. He *had* to do it, not because he wanted to.

She felt some similarity in her own life. She'd survived because she'd had to. She was trying to let him in because she had to. She owed it to her babies. But was it what she wanted? Yes—in a way. Her desire to be a mother was incredibly strong, and the need for her children to know their father was equally so. Even if she did suspect that at some point he would have to leave them behind.

She thought of women who were married to soldiers. Didn't they do the same thing? Knowing that at some point they might lose their husbands? That one day they just wouldn't come home?

But Jamie wouldn't be dying, would he? He would be choosing his duty, his country, over them.

She turned and began to swim breaststroke across the pool. Jamie swam alongside her. And now that the olive branch had been accepted, now that she wasn't having that knee-jerk reaction to keeping him at arm's length, she was curious about the man whose babies she was carrying. His life. His past.

'Tell me about your childhood. What was it like, growing up as a prince?'

He gave a wry smile. 'It was privileged life—no surprise there. But it was also very difficult.'

'In what way?'

'I was a young boy who wanted to run off and explore. Beyond the palace was a thriving town, and beyond that an oasis. I wanted to go there all on my own, but that was never allowed. I felt my freedom was restricted, and along with my schooling I was given many hours of instruction on politics and court etiquette and council procedures, which was all very dry and uninteresting to a boy who only wanted to be able to go to the falconry or the stables or have friends round after school.'

She tried to imagine him. Tried to imagine her own children having such a life. It didn't sound the best.

'Sounds lonely.'

'I was never lonely—which was half the trouble. There was always someone there, standing in the background, waiting, watching. Once my father had forbidden me to learn midwifery I was very angry for a while, and I would often try my best to evade my guards so I could sneak out of the palace grounds and be free for a little while.'

'Did you manage to do that often?'

He smiled. 'I did—much to their disappointment and anger. But I really felt like I didn't belong there.'

Neither did she belong there. Or her babies. It was part of their heritage, but did they deserve to spend their lives like that? Yearning for freedom and escape? She knew how that felt. She'd been there. Wanting to escape from four walls and having family and doctors constantly watching over her. It had been stifling.

'But you have a wonderful brother?'

'I do. He's only a few years older than me, so hopefully he'll be on the throne for a long time. Who knows? Maybe our children will be fully grown and living lives of their own before I have to return to Majidar.'

She stopped swimming as she came to the edge of the

pool and leaned back against it. Wouldn't it be wonderful if it happened that way?

'I hope so, Jamie. I do.'

He smiled, before sinking under the surface and swimming towards her, rising from the depths like a merman, his face right in front of hers. It was unnerving, having him this close. She could see him looking at her, taking in every feature of her face.

'Tell me about *your* childhood, Freya.'

His dark eyes were looking into her own with such concentration. Nervous, she began to talk.

'I've lived my whole life here in Chichester. I was very much a girly girl, playing with dolls and babies. I would line them all up like they were in a hospital nursery, covered with little blankets I'd made myself on my mother's sewing machine.'

'You can sew?'

She shrugged. 'Moderately. Simple things—cushions, blankets, curtains.'

'Go on.'

'I loved to play mum. I wanted a brother or sister desperately, but I never got one.'

It had been lonely, growing up without siblings. At least her twins would have each other. Didn't twins usually have a strong bond?

'I loved to swim. I wanted to have horse-riding lessons, but Mum could never afford it.'

'I have horses.'

She lifted her eyebrows in surprise, smiling. 'You do?'

'In Majidar, yes.'

'Oh.'

'Beautiful stallions. Racehorses.'

'Do you miss them?'

'I'm kept up to date on their progress.'

'But only from afar. It must be hard to be kept from something you love?'

Jamie stared at her. 'It can be.'

She could see him having a proper look now. Seeing the edges of her scars around her hairline. Tracking the damage that must have been done and had been repaired. Realising how many operations she must have gone through to look as she did today.

The intense scrutiny made her uncomfortable.

'Love does strange things to people. Makes them act out of character. Makes them crazy. Makes them not think straight.'

Jamie's hand reached up out of the water and she sucked in a breath as his fingers traced the edges of her face, down her cheek, along her jaw. Such a tender touch—respectful and gentle.

'You're beautiful, you know?'

What?

She hadn't expected him to say that. Never in a million years had she expected to hear *anyone* say that to her. Not the way he had. As if he meant it. He'd not been patronising her. His voice had spoken the truth as he saw it.

Moved to strong emotion, Freya blinked back tears at his words.

'Have I upset you?'

'No.' She wiped her eyes hurriedly and tried to smile bravely, to show him that she was okay. Her mum would tell her she was beautiful, but she'd always dismissed that— mums were duty-bound to say that.

'You're crying.' He reached out and pulled her gently towards him.

At first she resisted. Just slightly. But then she gave in, allowing herself that moment. She rested her head against his shoulder, put her arms around his back, completely in

shock that this was even happening. This, she had *not* expected. To be held like this...

'I'm okay,' she said, her face against his wet shoulder.

His hand smoothed down her hair. 'No, you're not. But I'll hold you until you are.'

And he did. They both stood there, in the warmth of the pool, in each other's arms, until the tears dried in her eyes, she stopped sniffing and the water was still, like a pond.

When everything was calm again, and her breathing had settled into a steady in and out motion, she felt him release her.

'We should have a change of scene. Let's go to dinner,' he said. 'Before you get cold.'

And she suddenly couldn't think of anything she wanted more than to sit with him. Talk. This man had been nothing but gentlemanly and kind to her. He'd never shown her pity. Never reacted the way everyone else had.

'I'd love to have dinner with you.' She meant it. Smiled her thanks. And, though she tried her hardest not to look down at his mouth, at those lips that had once brushed her skin in the most intimate way, she couldn't help herself.

She wondered what it would be like to let down her guard completely and kiss him all over again?

The hotel's restaurant was dimly lit, and they were seated in a small alcove near the back, away from prying eyes, where they could pretend it was just the two of them.

From the reception area she could hear the piano being played—gentle, soothing music.

She'd got out of the pool and gone back to the changing room to get dressed on very shaky legs, unsure as to what was happening between the two of them. She wanted to let him in—but just a little bit. To let him know that they could

talk about things, discuss the future. But something else seemed to have happened. An anticipation of so much more.

Hope.

Never in her wildest dreams had she ever thought she would be in this position—pregnant, about to become a mother, but also having a man tell her that she was *beautiful*.

It was a word she'd never thought would be used to describe her again. *Brave* got used an awful lot. *Courageous*. *Stubborn*, maybe.

But beautiful?

She'd stared at the mirror as she blow-dried her hair, focusing intently on her own face, gazing at the façade that it had taken her years to get used to. Inside, she still felt that she looked the way she had before the accident, so every time she looked in the mirror it was a stark reminder that she was different.

She'd tried to embrace that and look forward. Never allowing the melancholy and disappointment to overwhelm her. Never letting what Mike had done beat her down, because then he would have done what he'd set out to do. Never allowing the depression to set in, as it had with so many others affected in a similar way.

She was living the best way that she could. Under *her* rules. *Her* control. And now she was handing some of that control over to him.

She was different now. Not just in looks, but in character. She cared more for the underdogs in society; she listened, empathised, and she worked damned hard to make sure her patients felt empowered and brave and strong. She was their cheerleader. Their support. She knew she could coach women through the scariest moments of their lives, even as they felt they were being split in two, and she knew they *all* had the strength within them to get through it. She

gave them everything they needed and asked for nothing in return.

But now Jamie was here and he wanted to pay her attention. He wasn't family, but he was trying to give her everything she needed and a whole lot more besides. He was able, it seemed, to see past the prickly exterior that she had first presented to him. He had pushed it to one side, had powered through, because he was invested in *her* well-being. *Her* thoughts and feelings. *Her* health. *Her* happiness.

And that felt odd. Disconcerting.

Good, but strange.

It had happened at university, too. During her training. Her teachers and lecturers had seen past her face and made sure she qualified, made sure she became the midwife she'd always wanted to be.

Perhaps she needed to give more people the benefit of the doubt?

'I'll have the Caesar salad to start, please, and I think I'll have the pan-seared chicken for my main, thank you,' she said to the waiter from behind her menu card.

'Smoked salmon and the pheasant for me, thanks.'

The waiter disappeared, having removed the menu cards with him.

Freya took a sip of her water. 'You must be used to English food now. Is there anything you miss from back home that you can't get here?'

'You don't serve as much goat as there was back home.' He smiled. 'Or *luqmat al-qadi.*'

She frowned, having never heard of that before. 'What is that?'

'They're like your pastries. A leavened dough that has been deep-fried, then soaked in a very sweet syrup.'

'Like a doughnut?'

'Not quite. My mother made them. Sometimes she would

add cinnamon or sweet spices to them. They were out of this world.'

'Your mother cooked?'

'Occasionally. Not as often as she would have liked.'

'My mum likes to cook. She likes to feed people. There's always something on at her house.'

'It was the same at mine.'

She smiled. 'But, to be fair, your house was a palace, so…'

He laughed, good-naturedly. 'True.'

She took another sip of water. 'Is your mother still alive?'

His eyes darkened. 'No. She passed away a few months after my father did. It was a huge shock to lose them both so quickly like that. But I believe she died of a broken heart, after losing my father so suddenly.'

'She must have loved him very much.'

He nodded. 'Al Bakharis love deeply.'

Her breath caught in her throat as she imagined that sort of passion. The depth of love that one person could have for another. It was the type of love she had once imagined for herself. The type of love she had thought she had found with Mike, in the way he had so quickly and deeply fallen for her.

That kind of love was scary. Terrifying. It could totally condemn you to a future filled with pain, misery and grief. Case in point: Jamie's mother dying of a broken heart. Perhaps love was more dangerous than people realised and they were fools to seek it out? It was best to keep things light. Casual. Even if it did leave you wanting…

'Have you ever felt that way about someone?' she asked.

'Not yet. That kind of love is the kind that stays for eternity. You will always be together, until the end of your days. If I had already found that, then you and I would not be in the situation we now find ourselves in.'

It was a stark reminder of exactly what this was between them.

A *situation*.

That was all. There was no point in reading anything else into it—even if he *had* told her she was beautiful. Even though he had cradled her in his arms until she'd stopped crying. Even if they had shared that one magical night together.

They'd been caught out by Mother Nature and now they were having to deal with the consequences.

That was all this was. Nothing more, nothing less.

So, despite the fact that they were sitting together in a restaurant, having only just a few minutes before shared a most intimate connection as she was wrapped in his embrace, Freya had to remind herself not to get carried away with *hope*. With *possibility*.

But she'd always been a dreamer and it was hard to switch that part of her brain off.

If the accident hadn't happened she would never have been at that charity ball. She would never have had that night with Jamie. She wouldn't be pregnant with twins. But they still would have met at work, and she would still have been attracted to him. The way she was now.

It was hard to tell herself that he probably didn't feel the same way. No matter what he'd said.

Reality hurt when she thought about that. She might have defied the odds and got pregnant, but Jamie was *not* going to be her knight in shining armour and she would do well to remember that.

'Please excuse me a moment.'

She stood, needing to escape to the bathroom for a minute alone—because she could feel tears threatening to fall down her face, and if she cried again he would comfort her again. He would touch her. Hold her. Try to make her

feel better. And, despite her best instincts, she realised she *wanted* that.

Even though she shouldn't.

And she couldn't have that.

She stared at her tear-stained reflection in the bathroom mirror.

Why was life testing her so harshly?

CHAPTER FIVE

Jamie was very pleased with the way their relationship was progressing. Freya's walls were starting to come down, and now she was letting him sit and talk to her at work. They socialised together sometimes, getting to know one another, and when they went to her check-ups and other appointments with her consultant they asked questions as if they were a real couple.

He'd sat by her side when she'd had her twenty-one-week scan, gripping her hand tightly in his, and they'd both been over the moon when the scan had confirmed that they were going to have non-identical twin boys.

Sons!

That was a big deal for Jamie. He'd always dreamed of having sons and raising them to be good, strong men. Sons to be proud of…sons he would support in their desire to do anything. He would not restrict their lives the way his had been, and if they wanted to become pilots or nurses, whatever their dreams could possibly be, he vowed to himself that he would help them achieve them in any way that he could.

His sons would be his heirs. Heirs to the throne. It was their destiny, but what would they know of it? What would they know of Majidar? With its rolling dunes, its intense heat and its beautiful people. He himself had yearned to

leave and live a life he couldn't get there. Should he be the one to tell them that they must follow that path when he didn't want it for himself? Who was he to decide what they should do? He was their father, so shouldn't he want them to be happy more than anything else?

He'd sent news of the babies to his brother Ilias and younger sister Zahra. Both had responded with joy and delight, but both had asked him when he was coming home. With Freya at his side.

It was an awkward question to which he had no answer.

Zahra was already gushing about their wedding and all the things they'd need to organise. How could he tell her that it was probably never going to happen?

So he'd kept silent, swearing them to secrecy in his last email, until he knew what the next few months would bring. He'd used work as his main excuse. Said he was still under contract for another six months, with the possibility of a permanent post, and that he would not let people down when they were depending upon him.

Zahra had emailed back.

Six months? But the babies will be born by then!

It was all so difficult. So confusing. If he'd had his way then he and Freya would already be married. No need for a big ceremony in Majidar…no need to be driven down the streets in an open-topped car, waving to adoring crowds. He would present his marriage as a *fait accompli*. Everyone would just have to accept it.

If only Freya would accept it!

That would be easier, wouldn't it?

He hadn't mentioned it to her for a while, not wanting to raise such a difficult subject again when things between them seemed to be going so well.

When he'd first mentioned marriage he'd done it out of duty. Done it because of the moral code that told him it was the right thing to do. Not for him, or for her, but for their children. Whether Freya liked it or not, her babies carried royal blood and he would not have them being illegitimate. He hadn't thought too much about whether a marriage between them would work out or not. It just had to be. Details, emotions, feelings—all those could be worked out later, as time allowed them to know each other more.

But now...?

Life was even more complicated.

He liked Freya a lot. He cared for her. And the more he got to know her, the more he realised that if they were to get married then he would have a happy life with her, a happy marriage. He felt it in his bones. She was strong and loving and kind, the bravest woman he had ever known, and he felt proud that a woman like that was carrying his children. What a role model she would be! How much she would love them!

His feelings for her were deepening every day. Each time she laughed or smiled his heart expanded a little bit more. Each time she trusted him with a hint of intimacy— a confession, a secret, a story from her past—his feelings for her grew.

It was confusing. The line between emotion and duty was blending, merging. How could he get her to understand how he felt if he didn't even understand it, himself?

It was the end of November, and at seven months pregnant Freya felt huge. It had been many weeks since she had last been able to reach her own feet, and she thanked the Lord that Jamie, at least, seemed quite happy to lift her feet up onto his lap and massage them for her when they had a break at work.

Her body was protesting. She was knocking back strawberry milkshakes as if they were going out of fashion, and she dreaded to think about how much extra weight she was putting on. But it was all for a good cause, so she was trying to be relaxed about it.

There wasn't long left, and this probably wouldn't happen again, so she was trying to enjoy her pregnancy for as long as she could.

The babies were good movers, kicking and stretching at all hours of the day and night, and she would often sit at work with one hand on her swollen baby, feeling their movements. It was very reassuring.

They were good sizes, too. She and Jamie had attended many scans which had not only marked the growth of the babies, but also the growth of their ever-changing relationship.

She'd started to get the nursery ready at home. Jamie had even come over one evening to help paint the walls and put up some stencils. He'd even climbed a ladder to hang up the new curtains she'd made.

It was almost as if they were a real couple getting ready for their future.

Only without the living together and the sex.

And sex had been high on her mind lately, despite her burgeoning size. It had to be the hormones! She was blaming them entirely as her mind filled with X-rated images of her and Jamie doing really naughty things together.

It didn't help that he was so easy on the eye. Or that he was kind and thoughtful and gentlemanly. Seeing him smile delighted her, and she often found herself reaching out to touch him—a hand on his arm, his shoulder. Touching the small of his back as she passed behind him at work. Just a small contact. But enough to make her desires surge and make her brain remind her of what that one night had

been like and how wonderful it would feel to experience that again. To touch him in other places. To have him touch her...

Enough, Freya!

It would never be like that between them again.

Would it?

She blinked, trying to dismiss the thrilling images she'd created, and instead focused on the patient notes she was filling out. Her patient, Rosie Clay, had been progressing through labour quite well until suddenly the baby had started showing decelerations. The infant had gone into distress and Rosie had been rushed to theatre for an emergency Caesarean section. Rosie was now fine, but her baby girl was in the NICU, having aspirated meconium, which meant she had passed her first stool whilst still in the womb.

She dropped the pen to stretch out her shoulders, thrusting them back and trying to roll them. She suddenly felt hands slide down over them.

'Tense?' Jamie asked.

You betcha.

'Yeah, a little. It got a bit frantic in Theatre just now.'

'I heard. The baby's in NICU?'

'A little girl.'

'Little girls are strong.'

She thought of her own babies. Of the struggles they might have in the future together. Alone, without a father.

'So are little boys.'

Jamie's hands felt great, massaging away the tenseness of her muscles, releasing the knots and strain that she'd been carrying all night. She could groan because he was making her feel so good!

'You can stop now.'

She pulled away, not wanting to embarrass herself. Jamie was just doing it out of duty, anyway. She'd accepted that

ages ago, and reminded herself daily not to get too carried away with what was happening between them. It was the babies he was interested in. And she was dreaming again. Allowing herself to get carried away with fantasy.

It was her ability to dream and fantasise that had got her through the long, painful days after her attack; it had been the only way she could escape the pain and the four walls that had bound her so tightly.

He settled into a seat beside her. 'Do you need anything to drink? Eat?'

'No, I'm fine, thank you,' she answered, and heard a harshness coming out in her voice that she hadn't intended. But this was so frustrating! Having something so close she could almost touch it. Wanting something—*someone*—so badly, but knowing it could never happen.

'You're sure?'

She nodded, fighting the urge to yell at him, to tell him to leave her alone because that was what he was going to do anyway. At some point. And the idea of it was breaking her heart.

She'd grown to love his friendship, his kindness, his support—even his attentiveness. But sometimes she got angry—mostly with herself—knowing it wouldn't be for ever.

Freya had tried to keep herself distanced from it, but lately it had become nigh on impossible and her hormones were probably to blame for that too! It was as if her body had become conditioned to let him in. To allow him to care for her as the natural father of her children. But she had other feelings developing too, and they were dangerous and stupid!

Beside them, the buzzer rang. Someone required admission.

In the evening, the doors were locked for security, so

anyone turning up in the middle of the night, in labour or otherwise, had to buzz to be let in. There was a security camera so the staff could see who was there.

Freya looked at the monitor and its grainy black and white image. A man stood there, desperately looking up at the camera, wrapped in a coat and scarf.

She picked up the phone to speak through the inter-com. 'Hello?'

'My wife! My wife's having the baby!'

'Okay, sir, I'm going to buzz you through.' She went to press the button.

'No, you don't understand! She's having it *now*. In the car! I can see the head!'

Freya glanced at Jamie, who got up at a run and raced down the corridor, grabbing a mobile pack from the supply room as he did so.

'Someone will be with you in a moment. Hang on!'

She knew she wouldn't be able to run like Jamie, but he would need back-up. It was freezing out. And there was a frost.

She got to her feet and moved down the corridor as fast as she could, her feet protesting, the babies kicking at the sudden rush of adrenaline in her system. She grabbed extra blankets and slapped the button release to open the doors, then took the stairs.

It would be quicker than waiting for the lift. It was just two flights.

She held her belly with one hand as she hurried down the stairs, her other hand on the rail, and by the time she got to the bottom she was out of breath and the twins were kicking madly. She burst through another set of double doors, hur-ried across the lobby and pressed the buzzer for the outer doors, feeling a wall of cold air hit her as she raced outside.

There was a car parked in the dropping-off bay, its doors

open on one side—the guy from the monitor was in the
front and Jamie was crouching by the back. She could see
there was already a little bit of ice forming on the path. She
hoped the gritters would be along soon…

'That's it, Catherine, push as hard as you can!' she heard
Jamie say.

'What have we got?' She pulled her penlight torch from
her top pocket and shone it into the interior of the car.

A woman was lying in the back, her dress up around her
waist and her baby's head already born. There was no point
in trying to get this patient into a wheelchair and whizzed
upstairs now. She was going to have this baby in the car.

'Catherine—thirty-nine, forty weeks' gestation.'

'Okay, anything we need to be worried about?'

'Just the cold.'

'I've brought extra blankets.'

Jamie turned to grab them and laid them over the head-
rest, so they'd be ready when he needed them. He already
had his gloves on, had the kit open, and was ready to clip
off the cord.

'Catherine, one more push with the next contraction. I
want you to push as hard as you can, okay? Let's get this
baby out and safe into your arms.'

Catherine nodded furiously, sucked in a huge breath
and began to push.

At first nothing happened, and for a brief second Freya
worried about there being a possible shoulder dystocia, but
then slowly the baby began to emerge. Catherine sucked in
another breath and began to push again, and this time the
baby slithered out, crying immediately in protest.

'Well done, Catherine!' Jamie had caught the baby and
immediately put it into its mother's arms, grabbing the
blankets to drape over them both before he clipped and
cut the cord.

'Oh, my God!' Catherine cried, looking down at her baby with love and joy.

'You did it! You gave birth in the car!' cried the new dad. 'The upholstery's probably ruined, but I don't care!'

Behind her, Freya heard the doors open and Mona appeared, pushing a wheelchair. They needed to get the new mum and baby inside so they could do the proper checks and get the placenta delivered.

Jamie took the baby and passed it to Freya, so that he could help get Catherine out of the car, lowering her gently into the wheelchair. She was shivering and shaking, so he wrapped the last blanket around her shoulders.

'Let's get her inside.'

They all hurried into the lobby, and Freya pressed the button for the lift before passing the baby back to its mother.

Catherine gazed into the loving eyes of her husband. 'We have a *son*!'

The man laid his forehead against his wife's and kissed her. 'We do. Well done! I'm so proud of you.'

He turned to look at Freya and Jamie.

'I'm Martin—pleased to meet you.' He shook their hands. 'This little one is so precious to us. He's an IVF baby.'

'Congratulations.'

'We thought we'd left it too late, but now we have him. A son. Thank you all so much!'

'Catherine did all the hard work,' said Freya, and smiled.

The lift doors pinged open and they wheeled Catherine through to an empty room and helped her onto the bed. They injected the syntocinon and the placenta was delivered almost without Catherine noticing as she cradled her little boy.

'Have you thought of a name yet?' asked Freya, who'd donned gloves and was beginning to check it.

Catherine smiled wanly, looking tired. 'Jackson.'

'That's a beautiful name.'

But something was wrong. The placenta was not as it should be. Freya felt the hairs go up on the back of her neck and instinctively knew. Catherine had gone incredibly pale, and now she rested her head back against the pillow.

She caught the baby before Catherine could drop him. 'Martin, take the baby!'

'What's going on?'

Jamie lifted up the sheet and grimaced. 'Haemorrhage.'

He smacked the red button behind Catherine's head and an alarm sounded. Before they knew it the room was filling with people and Catherine was being whisked out on her bed, headed for Theatre. Jamie went with them.

Freya was left with Martin and the baby, in a room with blood all over the floor.

'What just happened?' asked Martin.

'It looks like Catherine is losing too much blood.' She examined the placenta more and realised there was a piece missing. 'Retained placenta. That's why she began to bleed so heavily.' She laid a hand upon his arm. 'They'll look after her.'

'I *can't* lose her. I can't lose my wife!'

'Come and take a seat, Martin.'

She guided him safely to a chair and helped him sit. She needed to examine the baby, but she was very conscious of the fact that Martin would probably be reluctant to hand his son over right now.

'Emergencies can be frightening, but she was in the right place when it happened. If she'd given birth earlier and you hadn't made it here... You did, though. She's in good hands.'

'She'll be okay?'

'Everyone will do their best.'

She couldn't promise him anything. She couldn't tell him everything would be all right because she didn't know. Haemorrhages happened, and sometimes they went badly. The medical team would do everything they could for her.

'I need to check Jackson. I'll just take him over to this cot—is that okay? You can come with me. Watch what I'm doing.'

He nodded and handed her the baby.

Freya took him gently and with the utmost respect. This man had just watched his wife collapse and be taken from him. He felt lost and bereft, and the only thing he had to cling on to with any certainty was his son.

She decided to talk him through it, so he would understand all that she was doing. If he understood what she was doing perhaps he would feel he had a bit of control over *something*.

'First I'll check his breathing.' She looked to Martin to make sure he was listening.

He nodded.

'He cried immediately after birth, and his respiratory rate is good, so he scores two points on the APGAR scale. The scale is out of ten points overall, and the higher the score, the better.'

'Okay...'

'Now I'm going to use my stethoscope to check his heart rate, and this is the most important.'

She put the earbuds in her ears and laid the stethoscope on Jackson's chest. Over a hundred beats per minute.

'He scores two for this as well. His heart rate is *good*, Martin.'

'Good.'

'Next I need to check his muscle tone, and I can see here that he has good active motion, so again he scores two.'

She talked Martin through checking for a grimace re-

sponse or reflex irritability, and because Jackson began to cry she again scored him two.

'And now skin colour. His entire body is nicely pink, except his hands and feet, but that's normal. His circulation is good, so that's another point. A score of nine. You have a healthy little baby boy, Martin.' She wrapped Jackson up again and handed him back to his father. 'Do you have clothes and a nappy for him?'

Martin thought for a moment. 'Oh, it's all in the car.'

It was important to get Jackson dressed and wrapped up warmly. 'I can go and fetch them for you, if you want?'

'Would you mind?'

'Of course not.'

He reached into his back pocket and pulled out some keys. 'It's all in the boot. The lock release is on the key fob.'

'Okay. I'll do that, and then I'll get you a cup of tea. I think you've earned it.'

'You too, I would imagine.' He looked at her belly. 'How far along are you?'

'Seven months. With twins.'

'Life's about to get crazy for us all, then?'

She nodded. He had no idea how crazy her life already was.

'I'll be back in a few minutes. Any problems, just hit the orange call button on the side of the bed. Someone will come and check on you.'

She closed the door behind her and began to waddle down the corridor once again.

Boy, were her ankles killing her! And what a night shift this was turning out to be! The last time she'd helped deliver a baby in a car parked outside it had been in the middle of summer, when the nights were a lot warmer and they didn't have to worry about tiny babies freezing in the night air.

And this had been her first delivery working with Jamie.

Usually they got to work alone, sometimes with another midwife, but she'd not yet had the chance to watch him in action like that. She'd been with him in Theatre before, but that had been different—their patient had been unconscious under a general anaesthetic, because it had been an emergency delivery.

Tonight she'd seen how good he was with a patient. How calm and encouraging. How he'd coached his patient to breathe and push. She could see why he loved midwifery so much, because he'd simply been alive with all that had been going on around him, and even though it had been an unusual delivery, out of the hospital, he had remained cool and in control. Even when the haemorrhage had begun he had worked quickly and calmly.

The lift doors pinged open. She didn't feel like taking the stairs again so soon. She waddled her way across the lobby and opened the double doors to go outside. The cold air hit her again and she glanced down at the keys in her hand to see which side of the fob she needed to open the boot of the car.

She walked straight out, without thinking, onto the pathway, and it happened almost instantly.

Her feet began to slide on the black ice, she lost her footing and slipped and, not having any control over her centre of gravity, she went up into the air backwards, her arms flailing, and landed heavily on the ground, the back of her head smacking hard onto the concrete.

Pain shot through her skull and her back and her belly. She reached up to rub at her head, but felt the world begin to fade and grow dark.

The last thing she saw was the clear dark sky, inky black with shining stars twinkling way beyond her, and then there was the sight of two men in dark suits appearing over her,

one reaching into his jacket for a walkie-talkie and saying something in a language she didn't understand.

She closed her eyes and drifted away.

Jamie was relieved. They'd managed to save their patient. Catherine's haemorrhage had been contained, the retained piece of placenta removed and checked. The bleeding had slowed and Catherine's womb had contracted fully. Her pressure was slowly coming back up and her heart rate was getting better.

The surgeons had done it.

He let out a huge sigh of relief and removed his mask and gown, disposing of them in the trash and going to wash his hands, whilst a porter took his patient to a side room for recovery and to be monitored.

It had been touch and go there for a while, he thought as he stood washing his hands. But they had prevailed. *All* of them. Working together to save their patient and give her a chance at life. There was nothing like this feeling in the whole wide world. This miracle they called life. He watched new life coming into the world every day, and it was a privilege to be amongst those who helped women achieve it.

Days like today reiterated for him the rightness of his choice. It had been *right* to leave Majidar, and it had been *right* to pursue this dream of his. Look at what he had done this night. Earlier he'd delivered one baby, safely in a hospital bed, and now he'd safely delivered not only a baby in a car, but a mother too. Everyone in the team had done that.

Outside, he could hear a bit of a commotion. Loud voices. Men. His guards, by the sound of it. What on earth was going on?

He dried his hands on paper towels and disposed of them in the bin. He wanted to see whatever this noise was about,

sort it out, and then go check on the new baby. He'd delivered the little boy—it was up to him to write up the notes.

When he pushed through the doors he froze as he saw his security men were on the ward, arguing with Jules. Whatever were they doing in here? Why did they seem so upset? They had strict instructions not to come onto the ward unless there was a just cause.

The only thing he could think of was Freya, but she'd been safe in that delivery room when he'd left with his patient for Theatre, so that left something to do with his brother the King.

Ilias? No, it can't be. He's sick, sometimes, but it can't be now!

Jules threw her hands into the air as the two guards barged past her towards Jamie.

'Jamie, these men—'

'Sadiq? Mujab? What's going on?'

But before they could say anything Jules barged through them and laid a hand upon his arm. 'It's Freya. She's had an accident.'

CHAPTER SIX

IT WAS THE pain she felt first, as she began to become aware of the world once more. Everything felt sore, but the worst thing was her headache. It was as if she had a crown of intense burning fire around her skull. Her mouth felt dry too, and she tried to lick her lips.

'Freya? Open your eyes.'

Jamie.

Jamie was here. Why was he in her bedroom? What had happened?

As she struggled to implement his instruction to open her eyes she began to remember some weird, hazy things.

A woman in a car.

A baby wrapped in blankets in her arms.

The cold.

A set of car keys.

The twinkling stars above.

Two stern-looking men crouching over her, babbling in a language she didn't understand.

And then she remembered.

The black ice.

Slipping on the pavement and falling.

She opened her eyes, struggling to focus, but she could only just make out a face. A man's face. Dark hair and midnight eyes.

'Jamie…'

She saw a relieved smile break across his face and she tried to reach up to touch him, to make sure he was real, but it was as if she was uncoordinated, or didn't have the strength.

'You've had a nasty fall. Knocked yourself out. The babies are okay. You've had a little bleeding, but they're okay. We're keeping you in for monitoring and bed rest.'

Freya blinked as she processed this huge amount of information. 'What? Keeping me in? No.'

She panicked, tried to get up, tried to get out of bed, but dizziness assailed her and she felt his firm hands holding her arms, pressing her down.

'You need to stay in bed.'

'No, I'm—'

'Freya, for once you are going to have to do as you are told!'

And then she heard it in his voice. *Fear.*

He *cared.*

She blinked again and tried to focus on his face, but she just felt so tired. Slowly, inexorably, her eyes closed once again and she drifted off to sleep.

'Concussion?' She stared at Jamie.

'Yes. You're also still bleeding and you have high blood pressure, so you're staying in on bed rest.'

Staying in. In hospital.

Adrenaline was pulsing through her, making her legs twitch. She wanted to run. Wanted to get out of there.

'But the babies are fine, you said.'

'I did.'

'But I need to stay on bed rest? Are you kidding me?'

'What would *you* say to a patient seven months pregnant with twins, who's had a nasty fall, hit her head, has

high BP and is bleeding? Would you tell her to carry on, or would you tell her to stay in bed?'

She bit her bottom lip, eyeing the door. He was right, but she didn't want to admit it. She *would* tell a patient in that situation that she needed to stay in. But this was different.

She'd been trapped in a hospital bed before. Lying there, gripping onto the bedrails, whilst a doctor and a nurse debrided the dead tissue from her face. It had felt as if the acid was being splashed onto her all over again. The pain interminable.

Being back in a hospital bed, being told she had to stay there, was making her feel trapped. Claustrophobic. As if she couldn't breathe.

She turned away, upset but not wanting to let him see her cry, her gaze falling on the fruit baskets and the balloons filling her room and all the cards on the windowsill that sent best wishes from her work colleagues and her family.

It was all terribly familiar. She was unable to move, feeling terrified and afraid. Her own life was out of her control. In the hands of doctors.

How had she forgotten what that felt like?

'I'm not sure I can do this,' she whispered.

'You have to.'

'You can't make me. I can discharge myself.'

'You'd have to get past the guards I'll put on your door first.' He raised an eyebrow. Daring her to challenge his authority.

She stared at him. He'd never ordered her about like this before. Never challenged her.

She baulked at his attempt. 'You wouldn't…?'

He leaned forward over the end of the bed. 'Try me. I've let you do this your way ever since day one. I have acquiesced to your wishes and tried my best not to upset you. But, damn you, Freya, if you get out of that bed and en-

danger yourself and those babies then, so help me, I will not be held responsible for my actions!'

He meant it. Every word.

She crossed her arms and looked away.

Again her life was being taken out of her control by other people. She had vowed never to let that happen to her again. This was *her* life and she wanted to be the one in charge, making all the decisions.

However, she had no doubt that he would post guards on her door, and then everyone would know who Jamie was. And as soon as that little nugget got out her life would most definitely not be her own. There would be reporters and gossip and her happy, quiet little life, hidden away on the night shift, would be destroyed.

'Fine.'

It wasn't fine. Far from it. But this wasn't just about her any more. She wasn't in this bed alone. She had two babies to think of.

He stared hard at her, his hands on his hips. 'Fine?'

'I'll stay in bed.'

'Good.'

'But on one condition.'

There was that eyebrow again. Wary. 'Yes?'

'Someone brings me a goddamned strawberry milk-shake!'

There was the ghost of a smile and then he bowed, almost to the floor. 'Yes, Your Majesty.'

Freya was a cranky patient. Short on temper, irritable, bad of mood. Nervous.

But didn't they say that medics made the worst patients?

'I know it's difficult, but you need to try and relax,' he'd told her.

She'd glared at him. 'How can I? When being here reminds me of what it was like before?'

He'd placed his hand on hers. 'I know. But this is different. No one is going to hurt you now. I won't let them.'

She'd had another scan, and the babies looked fine. The consultant believed the bleeding was coming from a small lesion on her cervix, but it was nothing sinister. They'd tested it and believed the lesion had occurred as a result of her fall. The pressure of two babies on her cervix as well as the severity of the impact of her hitting the concrete had caused a small tear.

He'd given her books to read, had brought delicious yet healthy treats, and he would often sit with her, slowly massaging her feet or her shoulders as she tried to relax.

His favourite moments were spent watching her as she read. The small divot that formed between her brows, the cute way she sometimes bit her bottom lip, the way she would hurriedly turn the page, as if she just couldn't wait to find out what would happen next. Those were the moments when she forgot where she was.

She looked up at him and caught him staring. 'What are you doing?'

He smiled. 'Looking at you.'

Freya frowned and smiled at the same time. 'Well, don't.'

'Why not?'

'It's weird. I don't like people looking at me.'

'No, and you don't like people making assumptions about what happened to you. You don't like people showing sympathy. Was I doing *any* of those things?'

She looked as if she was thinking about that. 'I guess not.'

'Well, then, I'll continue to look at you.'

'But why?'

'Because I like doing it.'

It was true. He did. She was such a complicated person, prickly when scared, but fascinating. And she really was beautiful. Outwardly and inside. Her scars—shocking because of how she'd got them—were totally a part of her character. Who she was.

'But why?' She really sounded confused.

He sighed. 'Does it ever occur to you that you might be worth looking at?'

Her eyes clouded over. 'No.'

'Well, then, you're wrong.'

'Are you sure *you* didn't get the bump on the head? Perhaps you should be lying here instead of me?'

'Perhaps I should be lying *next* to you? Beside you?'

That stopped her from speaking. She immediately looked down at her book, tried to read on, but he could see that she wasn't taking anything in.

Eventually she looked up at him, exasperated, and said, 'You can't say things like that, Jamie. It's not fair.'

'Even if it's true?'

'Even if it's true. Even if you did want to be lying here next to me you shouldn't say it—because then I start to get the feelings, and I don't want to get the feelings, because some day you're going to leave. You'll leave us, Jamie, you *will*. You can't deny that.'

No. He couldn't. She was right. One day he would get called back and then what? If he tried to start a relationship with this woman it would always be there, hanging over them like a swinging blade, ready to fall down and sever them in two. Was that fair? On either of them? On the babies?

'I'll go and make us some tea.'

He got up and slipped from the room, his mind dark with thoughts of ascension to the throne and responsibil-

ity and living a life behind walls. Never to enjoy himself again. Never to deliver another baby.

Away from Freya and his sons.

He fought the urge to punch a wall. It was all just so maddening! He'd fought to get access into her life, which she had finally given, and they were becoming used to one another, liked one another—but for what?

Either way, he was going to lose someone or something.

Majidar, or Freya and the babies.

Or maybe he'd just lose himself?

'Mona, please stop fussing.' Freya laid a hand on her friend's as she continued to fiddle about with Freya's sheets.

If she was going to visit, she'd prefer it if her friend just kept her up to date with what was happening on the ward, had a cup of tea with her and chatted. Not fussed about like an old mother hen.

'I can't help it.'

Freya smiled. 'Sit. Eat one of these.' She passed over a box of chocolates that her mum had brought on her last visit. 'They're truffles.'

'Oh! Okay.' Mona took the box.

'The praline one is nice.'

Mona checked to see which one that was, and then popped it into her mouth and began to make appreciative sounds.

'Told you.'

Freya lay back against the pillows and turned away from the bright light pouring in through the window. It made a pleasant change from the dark, grey wintry days they had been having recently. Life was passing her by and she was still stuck here.

'I got the Christmas decorations out just now. I'm going to pop them up later.'

Freya frowned. 'It's still November.'

'It's never too early.'

'I beg to differ.'

'Well, *you* would. You've always been a Grumpus around Christmas.'

Mona was wrong. Freya loved Christmas. But these last few years she'd begun to resent it. Everyone she knew was married or in a relationship, or had kids, or both, so they had a reason to enjoy Christmas. They were with their loved ones. They were making memories. For Freya every Christmas was spent with her mum, and though she loved her mum it wasn't what Freya wanted.

She had big dreams of what Christmas should be. Of a Christmas morning on which she could sit and watch her children open their presents with squeals of delight. Of a festive season during which she could go out and build snowmen and have snowball fights, visit Santa in his grotto, go to see a pantomime.

Her mum was great company, but she didn't want to do any of those things. She liked a quiet, understated Christmas, where her only concern was whether the turkey would be cooked and whether they'd finish eating in time to watch the Queen's Speech. Then she'd fall asleep in her chair, until Freya woke her later in the evening to see if she wanted a mince pie.

'Wait 'til next Christmas. You'll have twins!' exclaimed Mona.

Freya nodded. But would she be alone with them? Or would Jamie be there? How was she going to cope with raising two babies? She would have to brave *everything*. Living during the day time. Seeing all those people. Changing her shifts at work because the hospital nursery only took children during daylight hours.

Her whole life was going to change.

It wasn't meant to have happened like this! She was meant to have been *happy*! Thrilled that she was having children. She *was* thrilled, but it wasn't turning out to be the fairy tale she'd imagined it would be.

'Are you and Jamie spending Christmas together?'

'I think he's working.'

'But he'll have *some* time at home. Are you going to do anything special?'

'I don't think so. I'll be at Mum's, as usual, I guess.'

'You aren't spending *any* time together?'

This line of questioning was making her feel very uncomfortable. 'He hasn't said anything.'

Mona handed her back the box of chocolates, looking sceptical. 'Is there something you're not telling me, Freya?'

'Like what?'

'About Jamie? Who were those men in suits? They looked like bodyguards.'

She hurried to try and put Mona off the scent. 'Oh, I don't know. Just some guys who were passing, I think.'

'Well, for guys who were *just passing* they hang around a lot. And they talk to Jamie a lot.'

'He's probably just thanking them.'

'He's not some secret undercover boss, or anything?' Mona grinned. 'Because if he's secretly the CEO of the NHS then I think we need to enlighten him about a few things.'

Freya laughed. 'Jamie? No!'

'I just think it's strange, that's all. They even wear those earpiece things…like Secret Service guys.'

Thank goodness she didn't blush as she'd used to. 'Really? That's weird. But, no, Jamie is just a midwife. Honestly.'

Mona nodded, watching her. 'Okay.' She got up and went to the door, put her hand on the handle. 'You know,

I still don't understand why you two aren't together. You obviously slept together, and you seem to get on. So what's keeping you apart?'

Freya shrugged. 'He's a temp. He'll be leaving soon—there's no point.'

'But Sarah from HR told me that they've offered him a permanent post, which he's accepted.'

That was news to Freya. Why hadn't Jamie told her? That he was planning on sticking around for her and the babies?

'I didn't know.'

'It's clear he has feelings for you.'

Her smile was tinged with sadness. 'For the babies, not me.'

'You really think that? I've seen the way his eyes shine when he talks about you. The way his face lights up.'

'He talks about me?'

Mona nodded. 'Frequently. He *cares* about you. You must see it.'

She cared about him, too. Probably more than she should. But she'd been holding back. Afraid of showing any of it. Alone in the day, she dreamed about what it would be like to be with him, and at night her dreams were filled with his smiling face and his steaming hot kisses.

No wonder she woke up cranky. She couldn't have what she wanted the most. Was afraid to let herself have him in case she lost him.

'It's complicated.'

Mona laughed. 'When isn't it? Look, I've got to go, but he'll be in later. Do me a favour and be nice to him. He's doing his best, but you're a bloody expert at keeping people at a distance. Let him care for you, Freya. He's not Mike.'

No. She knew that.

'It's difficult.'

'"*'Tis better to have loved and lost, than never to have loved at all.*" Who was it who said that? Was it Shakespeare?'

'I never was any good at English.'

'Me neither.' Mona opened the door. 'But we're very good at chemistry!'

And she gave Freya a tiny wave before she headed off to do her shift.

Freya lay there on the bed, thinking over all the things her friend had said. Jamie was staying on permanently. He had feelings for her. She had feelings for him. The babies would be here soon.

We could be a family.

If she were only brave enough to let it happen.

Was it better to love someone and then lose them than not to love at all?

It sounded to her like devastation. And Jamie's mother had died of it.

Could she let her babies grow to love their father in the knowledge that he would desert them at some point? And would her babies one day leave her too?

But the temptation to give in, to try it, to accept the love and care that Jamie clearly wanted to give her, was extremely potent. The proximity of all that imagined happiness was intoxicating.

If she gave herself the chance to explore that happiness, to cast all her concerns to one side and just live in the moment with him, what would that be like?

Her heart soared at the idea. At the hope. At the possibility of such happiness.

Didn't she deserve it?

No matter how short-lived?

Jamie opened the door to Freya's room and stopped, frozen in place, when he saw how she looked.

Out of bed. Getting dressed.

Smiling. No. *Beaming.*

'What's happened?'

'I've been told I can go home and start my maternity leave. As long as I rest.'

He frowned and went to the end of her bed, picked up her chart and began to read it. 'The bleeding's stopped?'

'For almost a day now.'

'And your blood pressure is down?'

'Almost to normal levels. I can get out of here. You've no idea how much I've longed to hear that.'

'Well, I know how much you've been bugging your consultant about it, so I have a fair idea.'

He smiled. These last few days had been hard for her.

'All this bed rest… I could have done it at home in the first place. There was no need for me to have taken up a bed.'

'There was *every* need. Here, I've brought you a milkshake.' He passed her the drink he'd bought from the café downstairs. 'Why don't you sit down? I'll do your packing for you.'

She held up her hand. 'No, thank you! I don't need you seeing all my knickers and things.'

He smiled, picking up a pair of unflattering maternity pants. 'Why ever not? I've seen—no, *tasted*—what's underneath.'

And then he grinned, because he saw how flustered that comment made her.

She snatched them from him. 'I haven't been allowed to do anything for myself for days now. At least let me do this.'

'Okay.' He sank onto her bed and watched her busily pack her holdall, the excitement in her eyes at finally being able to leave the hospital almost palpable. 'I hope when you get home you do actually rest.'

'I'm fine. I've been discharged. There are things I have to get done. The nursery isn't ready and—'

'Then I'll help you. Tell me what needs doing and I'll get it sorted.'

She stopped to look at him. 'How will you have the time? Now that you're a *permanent* member of staff? Yes, I know about that. Why didn't you tell me?'

'I was waiting until I'd actually signed the contract. Which I did about twenty minutes ago. So here I am. Telling you. Don't change the subject.'

'I'm not.'

'You did. Now, what do you need help with in the nursery?'

'I've ordered two cribs, which are going to be delivered, and some furniture—all of which will need building.'

He nodded. 'I'll do it.'

'I can do it. I'm not helpless.'

'I know you're not, Freya, but you are still meant to be resting.'

'Don't I get *any* say in this?'

He thought for a moment, then smiled. 'No.'

She smiled back. 'You're infuriating, you know?'

Jamie nodded, happy to be so if it meant she was taking it easy. He had no doubt that if he let her go home without supervision she'd be up ladders and cleaning and painting and building wardrobes and putting herself straight back into a hospital bed. He couldn't allow that to happen.

'How are you getting home?'

'Mum's coming over on the bus, then we're using my car to drive back. It's been in the staff car park ever since my fall on the ice.'

'Okay.' He knew her mum would take good care of her. 'I'm on shift now until seven, but I'll pop round straight after—see what needs doing and formulate a plan.'

'You don't need to babysit me.'

'I know.' He stood up and dropped a kiss onto her cheek. She looked a little startled. 'I'm a grown woman.'

He smiled again, as his mind handily provided him with flashbacks to that steamy night many moons ago. 'I *know*.'

'Stop it.'

'What?'

'Remembering what we did.'

'I'm not allowed to remember?'

'Not that, no.'

'Why?'

'Because of the way it makes you smile. The way you look like you hope it will happen again.'

He stood up and stepped between her and the holdall. 'Would that be a bad thing?'

She was breathing heavily, and licked her lips. She tried her hardest not to look at his lips, but failed.

'Yes.'

'We wouldn't know unless we tried.'

She licked her lips again, bit the lower one and then looked away. Then back again.

'I'm on bed rest.'

'We could be in bed.' He smiled.

She swallowed. 'Please don't, Jamie.'

'Why?'

'Because we *can't*!'

'Who says?'

'The consultant. He said no sex.'

Well, wasn't *that* interesting? Freya herself wasn't saying no. She wasn't turning him down because *she* didn't want to, but because it was a strict order from her consultant.

He smiled, feeling a swell of joy not only in his heart, but elsewhere too.

'I can wait.' He paused to stare at her, then laid his hand

on her arm, stilling her, drawing her close. 'Won't you give us a chance to be together?' he whispered.

Her eyes looked up at him, full of conflict, yearning and desire.

Until he bent his head and kissed her.

CHAPTER SEVEN

HIS LIPS WERE SOFT, gentle. It was the most tender kiss. As his lips met hers it was as if the world slowed. Everything around her faded into nothingness, and all that mattered, all she could feel, was his lips pressed against her own. She forgot her scars, forgot her fears.

Tenderness. Heat. Her heart racing inside her chest... pounding away within the cage that contained it.

He's kissing me!

She'd thought about what it would be like to kiss him again, without hiding behind masks and anonymity.

She knew him now. Knew who Jamie was. *What* he was. He'd become her friend as well as her colleague, and somehow, without her realising how, he had wormed his way into her affections. She cared for him. Worried about him. Feared for their future.

And she had wondered what it might be like for them both if their lives were different. If he weren't heir to the throne of some faraway kingdom, and if she weren't the woman who hid behind the scars on her face.

And now he's kissing me.

She felt herself sink further into his embrace. Felt her body press up against his. God, she needed this! Needed *him*.

Freya had never imagined losing herself to something so wonderful as this.

But it felt so right. It felt so *good*.

She was almost dizzy with all the sensations running rampant through her system, with all the emotions she was experiencing. What was it doing to her blood pressure?

I need to breathe.

She pulled back, looked at him, her eyes dazed with confusion.

'You kissed me.'

'Yes.' His eyes shone darkly, with a heat in them she had never noticed before.

'Why?' It was a whisper.

'Because I needed to.'

'Needed?'

A smile. 'Wanted.'

'Me?'

Another smile. Broader this time. 'Of *course* you. When will you start to believe that?'

Her words caught in her throat for a moment, a painful lump of disbelief that she had to swallow down, blinking rapidly to stop the tears from falling.

'I see you, Freya. Who you are. I see the woman who stands before me today and she's the bravest, strongest, most wonderful woman I know.'

'I don't…'

'You keep comparing yourself to who you used to be. I don't know who you used to be, or what you looked like before, and I don't need to know. That was the past. What matters is the present, the *now*, and the woman before me is beautiful. She is caring and loving, fragile yet strong and courageous. As beautiful on the inside as she is on the outside. That's who I see.'

He tucked a strand of her hair behind her ear.

'But…'

'No buts. No whys or maybes. Just accept it. Can you

accept the fact that I have feelings for you and that I'd like us to be more than just friends?'

It was everything she could possibly want to hear. Everything she's thought she'd never hear. And here he was. This man. This drop-dead gorgeous, handsome *prince* was saying it to her!

And suddenly she felt afraid. Afraid of what it all meant. If she accepted it—if she let him in—then wouldn't she be making herself vulnerable all over again?

But she was teetering on the edge of a giant abyss and she wanted to fall for him. Wanted to believe so much!

Her heartbeat pounded in her ears. She felt hot and dizzy with it all. But she wasn't ill. Just lovesick. And she wanted that happiness, even if it was just for a short while. She'd accept it and have him for as long as she could have him.

'I can.'

Hesitantly she smiled at him, watching as his face lit up.

He let out a heavy breath and beamed at her, before pulling her back into his embrace. 'Then let's get you safely home and we'll take it from there.'

It was strange to be back home. Her mum put on a pot of decaffeinated coffee to brew. Freya sat on the couch, her feet up, cradling her mug.

'I think Jamie and I are going to give things a go.'

It felt odd to say it. *Jamie and I.*

Her mum smiled at her over her own mug. 'Really? Oh, I'm so pleased to hear that. I really am.'

'We don't know what's going to happen, but we're going to take it a day at a time. It's all we *can* do, really.'

'Stop downplaying it, Freya. You're already making it sound like it's doomed before it starts.'

'I'm just being realistic.'

'No, you're trying to protect yourself before you get hurt

and it won't work that way. If you are going to give it a try with Jamie then you've got to be in it wholeheartedly. One hundred per cent. Not with one foot already out of the door.'

'You think that's what I'm doing?'

Her mum put her mug down and came over to sit beside her. Took her hand in her own. 'I know that's what you're doing. But Jamie's different. He's honourable and kind and I think he cares deeply about you. You can't play with his feelings because you're scared. Be in it totally, give everything of your heart, one hundred per cent, or don't give anything at all.'

Tears began to sting her eyes. 'I want to be with him.'

'Then do it.'

'But what if—?'

'No what ifs, Freya. No fear. You are having two babies with this man, and whether it works or not he will be in your life until your last day on this earth. So make it work. Give him your whole heart, not half of it.'

The tears began to fall. 'I think I might love him.'

Her mum was tearing up too.

'Then you both have my blessing.'

She leaned forward and kissed Freya on the cheek, then pulled her into a hug.

Casey Benson looked calm. She was sitting in her hospital bed, serenely tapping a message into her mobile phone. But then again, Jamie mused, Casey had been through this three times before. She was an experienced mother.

'Hi, Casey. I'm Jamie, and I'm going to be your midwife today.'

She turned and smiled, her smile freezing slightly when she saw him. 'I get *you*?'

He nodded. 'You do.'

'For when I give birth?'

'That's the plan!'

'Oh.'

She looked a little perturbed, and he wondered if she was feeling uncomfortable at having a man deliver her child.

'Is that all right?'

'Yes! Course it is, it's just…'

'Yes?'

She blushed. 'You're very attractive.'

Well, that was very flattering, but he didn't understand why that should be a problem.

'An attractive man down at my—' She stopped and blushed again. Her face going very red.

He tried to change the subject, feeling amused. 'Are you here alone today?'

'I always do this alone.'

He saw on her file that she was married. 'Is your husband at work?'

'You could say that. He's in the Antarctic.'

'Oh, really? Doing what?'

'He's part of a research team studying the biodiversity of a special organism, or some such thing. He hopes to be back when this one is about two months old.'

'No other family who can be with you?'

'There is, but I'm happy to do this myself. It never takes long—they usually pop out after an hour or two. I'll be home in a few hours.'

'Who's babysitting the others?'

'Mum is. She's not very good with blood and gore, but she's an absolute whizz with spilt milk and baby dribble, so she's keeping an eye on the troops.'

'Glad to hear it. So it's just you and me, then. Unless you'd like a chaperone?'

She smiled at him over her mobile. 'Just you and me is fine.'

* * *

Casey had been right. She did labour easily. Though her contractions were showing up good and strong on the trace she remained calm, breathing easily through each of them as she leaned over the back of her bed, her knees on the mattress.

'You're doing brilliantly, Casey.'

Casey beckoned him over. 'Come and join me for a selfie. Otherwise no one is going to believe I had *you* deliver my baby.'

He capitulated, and put his head close to hers for a photo, smiling as the camera on her phone clicked the two of them together.

'You still all right with just the gas and air?'

'Absolutely!' She settled back on her haunches whilst she waited for the next contraction. 'Still all systems go here. Though, if I'm honest with you, I can't believe I'm back here, doing this again. I swore the last time that Benji was going to be my last baby, yet here I am.'

'Does your husband get to come home often?'

'Every six months. He gets home for about four weeks and then he goes off again. And obviously, because we haven't seen each other in all that time, we're very keen to see each other as much as we can, if you get my drift, and that usually results in me peeing on another of those ruddy sticks. Mind you, I love being a mum. I love all my kids—we have such a great time.'

'Do they miss their dad? What with him not being around?'

'Of course they do! They play up every now and again, but don't all children? They know their dad loves them, and that he's off doing some very special scientific work, and it's good for them to see that their dad is dedicated

and works hard for a cause he believes in. It's good moral grounding for them.'

'It must be hard for him, too. Being away from his children?'

She nodded. 'It is. But he absolutely adores what he does, and I don't think he could be away from them unless he did. Why would he lose all that time he could have with them if he was stuck somewhere hating what he did? No, it's good he has that passion. Do you have kids?'

He smiled. 'I have two on the way.'

'Twins, huh? Wow. But I imagine you'll be the same. You must love what you do? Because when they're born... when they're finally here and you hold them in your own arms...you can't imagine spending any time away from them. Missing any of it. Not unless you love what you do.'

He nodded. She was right. He wanted to spend as much time as he possibly could with his babies when they came. And if at some point he got called away to be King of Majidar that would be his crisis point.

Because he could *never* imagine himself wanting to do that. Could not imagine himself being stuck inside a glittering palace, getting bogged down in politics and laws, stuff he didn't care for, when instead he could be with his children. Doing a job he adored.

Majidar was never meant to be his. Ilias should have had his own heirs. He was a midwife. It had always been his calling. His vocation. He'd never wanted to rule, but it was the family he had been born into. And he felt a responsibility there, too.

The people of Majidar expected him to be their next King. And he knew, because it had been reported to him, that his people were *proud* of him for following his passion, for working far away from them in another country,

bringing life into the world. But they knew he would come back. They *expected* him to come back.

But he wanted to be with his children. And Freya.

Unexpectedly, he had built a life here. Was putting down roots for the first time ever. And it was exciting and thrilling and the most terrifying thing he had ever done.

But it also felt like the *right* thing.

Knowing he would have to leave at some point, knowing he would have to walk away from them, was killing him inside.

Casey pulled herself back up over the bed railing and began to breathe heavily. 'Okay, let's do this.'

'I'm ready when you are.'

Casey gave birth to a healthy seven-pound, four-ounce baby girl that she called Francesca.

Jamie escorted her through to Postnatal for a little while and, as she'd predicted, waved her on her way home a few hours after that.

She'd given him a lot to think about, and he wondered if she'd made light of her situation at home. It had to be hard for her, living as a single parent, with her husband away for long periods of time.

Would that be Freya's life too? Stuck here in England alone? Knowing that he was away, and knowing that he'd put his *duty* to his country before his duty to his own children?

Casey was able to do it because she knew her husband was passionate about what he did, and she valued the life lessons she could show her children—that their dad was working hard at something he believed in. That he was doing it for *them*.

Would Freya be able to say the same to their two boys? Jamie *did* believe in the honour and privilege that it would

be to sit on his country's throne, but would he be able to like himself for doing something he didn't actually want to do? Forcing himself out of duty?

He arrived at Freya's flat bright and early, knocking on her door and waiting for her to answer.

She opened it and he held up his box. 'I've brought tools.'

She smiled at him. 'Milkshakes or chocolates are my preferred gifts.'

'Maybe, but milkshakes and chocolates can't build bedroom furniture, can they?' He stepped past her, then stopped, turned, smiled and lowered his head to kiss her. 'Almost forgot this part,' he whispered, his lips closing over hers.

He'd missed her. Even more so since spending time with Casey. He felt the need to be with her. Her and the babies. Whilst he could. Her lips were full, soft and warm. She was comforting to him. It made him feel good just to be with her, and already he could feel his cares and worries being soothed away.

He wanted more. Could feel his body awakening to her touch, her presence. But more was forbidden. Which made the idea of it all the more desirable, and he had to pull back, bite his lip and just look at her with adoration and maddening frustration.

'Has everything arrived?'

'It's all in the nursery, awaiting your attention.'

'Good.'

She stared back at him, licked her lips, and he tracked every motion. The way her tongue swept over her lips, wetting them, leaving them glistening, before slipping back into her mouth.

'Can I make you a drink?'

He let out a sigh, imagining what that tongue could do to his body. 'Tea, please.'

He watched her head off to the kitchen and forcibly pushed aside his very sinful thoughts of all the things he wanted to do to her. That would have to wait. They had time. Time, at least, was on their side.

'I thought it might snow.' He followed her and watched her make the tea. 'They've forecast it in the paper.'

Freya laughed cynically. 'Let me tell you something about England, Jamie. They *always* forecast snow. They give us dire warnings every year, but we never get it. We can barely manage a frost down here, near the coast. It's very disappointing, actually.'

He smiled. 'This time last year I was working in Edinburgh, and we had snow. First time I'd ever experienced a heavy snowfall and it was wonderful.'

'Well, you'd better keep a hold of that memory, because you probably won't get it again.' She handed him his tea, smiling. 'Shall we get to it?'

'I'd love to. But apparently there's furniture that needs building.' He smiled.

She smiled back. 'That's what I meant.'

'You can supervise. And pass me things.' He pointed at her. 'No heavy lifting.'

Freya saluted him. 'Yes, sir.'

'Orders from your consultant.'

'I get it—don't worry. Are you sure you don't want something to eat before we start?'

He turned to look at her, devilment in his eyes. 'Freya, what I want to eat is, unfortunately, not on the menu at this moment in time.'

The instructions for the two cots seemed to be written in gibberish, and the pictures showing where to place the locking nuts didn't seem all that clear either. It took over an hour to do the first cot, through a process of elimination,

but by the time he'd started the second he actually felt he knew what he was doing.

Freya sat beside him in a rocking chair, reading a book about what to expect in the first year of their child's life. She looked so cute, rocking away, one hand resting on her ample stomach, intensely concentrating on the words. He sat and watched her for a moment, quite unable to believe that this was his family now.

'Good book?'

She closed it and wiggled her eyebrows. 'Scary book. There seems so much to watch out for and worry about.'

'Like what?'

'Like colic, whooping cough, vaccinations and sterilising everything to within an inch of its life! What if they choke on something? What if I wean them too early and it does them more harm than good?' She let out a sigh. 'Being a mum seemed so much easier when it was just hypothetical.'

He could see that she was feeling nervous and needed reassurance. 'We'll be absolutely fine. We can do this. Thousands do.'

'And thousands of parents end up in A&E with their babies—we both know that. They get gastroenteritis and need rehydration drips and monitoring, or they swallow some coin or a marble or a little toy gun—I don't know, *something*—and they need an operation.'

He went to kneel beside her and took her hands in his. 'We can't protect them from everything.'

'But we're their parents. We're meant to protect them from things that will cause them harm!'

'You can't protect them from illness. Germs will get in no matter what you do. And, yes, they might swallow something they shouldn't. I believe I swallowed a small plastic camel when I was two years old, but here I am, absolutely

fine and without trauma to my system. It's okay to worry, Freya. It's part of being a parent.'

'But I never thought I'd get the chance at this and now I am! And it's getting closer now, and I'm just worried that I'll get it all wrong!'

'Every mother worries. This is natural. Let's focus our energies on things we can control—like baby names, for instance. Have you had any thoughts on what you might want to call them?'

She let out a sigh and he saw a small smile begin to emerge as she focused on happier things. 'I quite like the name Samuel.'

He mused on it. 'Samuel MacFadden. That sounds like a good strong name.'

She smiled. 'Samuel Al Bakhari. I'm going to give them your surname.'

He sat back on his heels, pleasantly surprised. And honoured. 'You are?'

'And I figured if you let me pick their first names, then you could pick their middle names. Something Arabic? So they get a name from both our cultures?'

'Wow... I don't quite know what to say.' The gesture meant a lot to him.

'Just suggest some good names!'

He smiled back at her, stroking her beautiful face and staring into her eyes.

They decided upon Samuel Dawoud and James Kadin. 'Good, strong names.'

'For good, strong boys.' She rubbed her tummy. 'They'll be here soon.'

He squeezed her hands. 'And we'll be ready for them.'

Once the cots were up, and Jamie had powered through constructing a wardrobe, a baby-changing station and a set of drawers, Freya cooked them both something to eat.

It was wonderful to have Jamie there with her, now that she was determined to step forward into the future with him at her side, instead of fighting him every inch of the way. Watching him work on the bedroom furniture, seeing how careful he was, how focused, making sure everything was put together correctly and securely, made her feel warm inside.

'I can't wait to see them in those cots.'

She smiled. 'Me too.'

'Can't wait to see their little faces. Hold them. Love them.'

She knew exactly what he meant. She felt it too.

Passing him a bowl of pasta, she sat down on the couch opposite. 'Thanks for today, Jamie. It feels good to see the nursery taking shape. Makes me feel like I'm a bit more prepared.'

'I'm glad. I'd do anything to make this easier for you.'

'It must be difficult for you too. Not knowing what's ahead?'

He nodded. 'I don't want to screw this up. Us… The twins… Majidar…'

'I never wanted to come between you and your country, Jamie. You have to know that.'

'Of course I do.'

'I just feel like…'

'Like what?'

'Like I'm making you choose. And I know I won't win.'

He put the pasta down. Sat beside her. Kissed her on the forehead. 'This isn't your fault. You're not making me do anything I don't want to.'

'But you have a responsibility to your people. A million of them. I'm just one. Soon to be three. I can't compete with that. I don't want to think of the day when you'll have to make that decision.'

His eyes darkened as he felt her pain. 'I don't want to leave you. You know that?'

She nodded.

Jamie let out a heavy sigh. 'We can't worry about that yet. It could be decades away. Let's consider brighter, better things.' He thought for a moment. 'What do you want to do over Christmas?'

Christmas? She hadn't really thought about it. She'd figured she'd be spending it in the normal way. 'I'll be at my mum's house.'

'I'm scheduled to work over Christmas. The afternoon shift from two p.m. But I wondered…well, I *hoped* that maybe we could spend the morning together?'

'Oh… Okay… Well, why don't you come to Mum's? It'll give you both an opportunity to get to know each other a bit more and we'll get to share the day together. We eat at midday, so you'll get lunch.'

He smiled and nodded. 'Sounds good. I'd love that—thank you.'

'I'll let Mum know there'll be an extra mouth to feed!'

Freya felt good about that. This would be her last Christmas without children. Maybe next year she and Jamie would be living together? Inviting her mum over to their place? Cooking for her instead? And there would be the joy of watching the babies rip open their presents. Would they be toddling by then? Crawling? Making mischief between the pair of them? Babbling away in their own little twins' language?

The idea of it made her smile. Made her feel warm and happy. Her future with Jamie might be uncertain, but whilst he was here they would make good memories together. Memories they would both cherish. Every moment would be precious.

Life was changing—and for the better. She couldn't

quite believe she'd resisted this so much! Look at how well she and Jamie got along! All she'd needed to do was give him a chance. Give *them* a chance. And, even though she still felt apprehensive about the future, everything was looking much brighter now.

Maybe they *could* do this?

Together.

'We're going out.'

Freya frowned at Jamie. She'd just opened the door to him, expecting to invite him in for them to spend the evening together the way they usually did—watching a movie, eating popcorn, that kind of thing. She hadn't been expecting to go out, and she was wearing jogging bottoms and a maternity tee shirt that was having difficulty stretching over her twins-filled abdomen.

'What?'

'I've arranged something special. Just for you. So get dressed—we're heading into town.'

'Into town? Oh, no, I really don't think that I could—'

He pressed a finger to her lips, silencing her with a smile. 'Trust me.'

Freya stared back at him. Going into town was not her favourite thing. She'd done it a few times after the attack. It had been part of her therapy—heading out with her counsellor to show that she was okay being around crowds of people.

She'd been in a crowd of people when Mike had thrown the acid at her. It had happened in town. On the main street. He'd been lucky it hadn't hit anyone else and scarred them too. For a long time she'd been afraid to go out. Had almost become agoraphobic. Her counsellor had worked on exposing her gradually, getting her back out into the world.

It had been a long, difficult road, but one she had accom-

plished with much pride, even standing in the very spot on which the attack had happened, her eyes closed, breathing everything in—the familiar sounds of people all around her, the faint music from a clothing store playing far away, a busker a little further along, the aroma of freshly brewed coffee, the ringing of the church bells, the hustle and bustle of life all around her.

She'd done it. It had been fine. Until she'd opened her eyes.

Then she'd seen it. The stares of people passing her by. Had watched them notice her scarred face, seen the looks of repulsion, the pity, the sympathy, the recognition of who she was—that girl from the news who was attacked.

Her counsellor had told her not to worry about other people's reactions, but that had been easy for her to say— she hadn't been the one with a ruined face. It had been horrible to be looked at so differently.

Freya had always been pretty. Had always been aware that people looked at her with appreciation. That they'd wanted to know her, be her friend. She'd never had to try too hard with her looks, hadn't needed loads of make-up or anything like that. A natural beauty—wasn't that what everyone had said?

It had been torture to see that change. To look in the mirror and see what everyone else saw. Her face told her story. Her past relationship, her pain, her journey to recovery. Every operation, every painful skin graft—all there on her face for the world to judge. She would always be 'the acid girl'.

It was easier not to expose herself to people like that. To work nights, to order online, to keep to her small group of family and friends and the patients she saw on shift.

She had to admit that her patients had all been fine with her. No one had reacted with shock or pity. One or two had

asked her what had happened, but the majority had decided it wasn't any of their business and hadn't asked at all.

Perhaps she needed to let the rest of the world have that chance?

'What have you got planned?' she asked nervously.

'It's a surprise.'

'I don't like surprises. Besides, I'm meant to be resting,' she added, trying to use her pregnancy as one last grip on the door.

'I've taken all that into consideration.' He stepped into her flat and closed the door behind him. 'Now, go and get dressed.'

'Jamie, the town…for me, it's—'

He pulled her towards him and held her tightly. 'I know. I *do*. But we won't be going anywhere near that part of it and I'll be with you every step of the way.'

What had he got planned? She didn't like surprises. Surprises were bad news.

Reluctantly she rummaged in her wardrobe for anything that might fit her and found a pair of maternity jeans and a pink hoodie that said *I'm Doing Nine Months Inside*.

Then she brushed her hair, put it up into a ponytail, added a bit of mascara to her lashes and some lip gloss, a quick spritz of perfume and stood in front of the mirror. Psyching herself up for this 'surprise'.

When she was ready she headed out, grabbing her handbag. 'Will I do?'

His face lit up in a smile. 'You look perfect.'

'Where are you taking me?'

'I told you—it's a surprise.' He got her coat and helped her put it on, slipping her arms into the sleeves, and then grabbed her long, woolly scarf and wrapped it gently around her neck, before dropping a soft kiss on her nose.

She followed him down to his car and he opened the door for her, closing it again once she was safely inside.

Butterflies gathered in her belly as he drove her towards town. They could be going *anywhere*. To do *anything*! She was meant to be resting—which was why Jamie had been spending every spare moment with her when he wasn't on shift. How he got any sleep and managed to function, she had no idea, but he must be power-napping or something, because he always seemed wide awake when he was with her.

And she liked it that he was spending this time with her. It was good for them. Snuggling on the sofa, holding hands, each kiss he gave her heartfelt and meaningful, warming her, making her feel safe and secure and loved.

Oh, there'd been times when she'd wanted a whole lot more! But they were both on strict instructions. No sex until the babies were born! And, as they were determined to keep the twins inside her for as long as they could, they were both being extremely diligent about that rule.

Jamie drove them through the streets towards town, and Freya had to admit it looked really pretty at night. The Christmas lights were up, adorning most of the streets in the city centre, Christmas music was being played, and everyone seemed to be in a happy, relaxed mood. Perhaps everyone was feeling goodwill to all men?

Jamie parked in a small service road to the rear of one of the big shopping centres.

Where on earth were they?

Jamie got out, walked around the outside of the car and then opened her door. 'Madam?'

She smiled nervously. 'Where are we? What are we doing?'

'I need my guys to watch the car, so I've parked here;

it means my security looks a little less conspicuous. And I think you'll find that we'll be met in just a moment.'

He pressed a buzzer beside a set of double doors and instantly they were opened by a woman wearing a pretty blue dress and a name tag that read *'Michelle'*.

'Mr Bakhari? Miss MacFadden? Good evening and welcome to The Nesting Site.'

The Nesting Site? She'd read about that store in the local paper when it had opened up a few years ago. It was a stylish baby store, selling everything from plain muslin squares right through to the most hi-tech buggy anyone could possibly hope to purchase. It was exclusive—and a bit pricey, too. She'd heard some of her patients, when they'd come in to give birth, talking about browsing there, just to look at the beautiful things.

'I have a lift on hold, waiting for us.'

Michelle stood back to let them in and Freya breathed in the woman's perfume as she passed her by, feeling completely underdressed in her jeans and hoodie. She leant in towards Jamie for security and comfort, and felt better when he took her hand in his and give it a squeeze.

Michelle was looking at her with a polite smile. 'How many months are you?'

'Seven and a half, but it's twins, so...'

Michelle nodded, as if she understood perfectly. 'I had twins. One of each. Do you know what flavours you're expecting?'

'Two boys.'

Michelle smiled. 'Two princes. How wonderful!'

Freya looked at Jamie in shock. Did this woman know *who* and *what* Jamie was? She'd thought he didn't tell anyone that. But Jamie just smiled enigmatically at her and said nothing.

The lift doors pinged open and Michelle invited them in to the amazing store.

Freya sucked in a breath at all the beautiful things she could see—cribs with white lace curtains, the most beautiful rocking chairs, baby clothes in all manner of colours and designs, from plain white with gold embroidery through to brightly patterned Babygros in pinks and blues and the palest of palettes.

Michelle indicated a large reclining chair, stuffed with cushions, for Freya to sit down upon—which she did, wondering just what was about to happen here.

'I've arranged for us to have the store to ourselves, and for personal shoppers to bring us anything we wish to see. We don't have any clothes yet for the little ones, and I'd like us to get a few things.' Jamie smiled and squeezed her hand once more.

'Jamie, you didn't have to do this. I could have ordered online, like I always do.'

'I thought it would be better to see the items in person, before we buy. And I know you don't like crowds, so we have the place to ourselves. Now, what sort of thing should we look at first?'

'How about their going-home outfits?' Michelle suggested, snapping her fingers at some staff who must be were hidden away beyond Freya's eyeline. 'Would you like some tea? I can have a tray brought in.'

She almost felt dizzy with the possibility of it all.

Was this what it felt like to be a princess?

A princess in a hoodie and jeans…

CHAPTER EIGHT

'JAMIE, THIS FEELS WEIRD.' She leant over to whisper to him.

He smiled at her. 'Why?'

'All these people running around after me. Fetching and carrying. It's not right.'

'It's what *you* do when you're at work. Don't you look after your pregnant mothers? Fetching them cups of tea? Getting them epidurals or pethidine or gas and air? Don't you rub their backs and mop their heads with cool flannels when they need it? Hold their hands?'

She could understand his point. But that was different, surely? That was her *job*. Her patients needed her to do that because that was what she was trained to do. It was what she was there for.

'It's what they're here for, Freya,' Jamie said, echoing her thought process. 'It's what they're paid to do.'

'It just doesn't feel right to be on the receiving end of it, that's all.'

'Enjoy it whilst you can. When Samuel and James get here you'll look back on this moment and wonder why you didn't take full advantage of getting to put your feet up for a short while.'

She smiled as she imagined her babies in her arms. Who would they look like? Would they be dark-haired, like Jamie? Or blonde, like her? Would they have his in-

tense midnight-dark eyes or her blue ones? Would they be happy, giggly babies? Or cry all the time with colic?

It was getting so close now, and she couldn't wait to hold them in her arms. To feel their little bodies snuggled up close to hers. She was looking forward to breastfeeding, if she could, although she worried about producing enough milk for both of them. She knew her body was designed to produce as much milk as the babies needed, but she couldn't stop worrying. Fretting about this and that. All the *what ifs* and all the horrors that might befall them.

She knew it was a normal part of being a new parent. She and Jamie were about to take on a huge responsibility and that they, more than anyone else, had uncertain futures.

I can't think about that now. I told myself I wouldn't.

The personal shoppers arrived, pushing a small clothes rail from which hung a plethora of baby clothes on tiny hangers. She went through them one by one, holding them, touching them. Laughing and smiling with Jamie as they imagined their sons dressed in each item and cooing over the small size of each piece.

She picked out baby vests and Babygros, tee shirts and tiny pairs of trousers. There were the most gorgeous pairs of baby shoes and trainers, pure white scratch mitts and the cutest knitted hats that looked like raccoons and foxes. She chose them both a winter snow suit, and picked out towels with white stripes that were adorned with tiny white sheep, and a gorgeous set of soft cherrywood brushes for their hair.

Michelle suggested a range of handmade bibs that were more like neckerchiefs, and then they moved on to car seats, and a double buggy that they both practised putting up and collapsing down. Freya chose a V-shaped pillow to assist with breastfeeding support, and a cute bedroom thermometer that looked like an owl. Plain and patterned fitted sheets and cellular blankets went onto the purchase

pile. Then there were all the toys—teddy bears and rattles and soothers.

As each item was scanned Freya began to feel a little queasy. She saw the total totting up but, glancing at Jamie, she saw he was totally unfazed and realised that cost was not a concern for him. How nice it must be, she thought, not to have to worry about the pennies.

'And where shall we deliver this?' Michelle asked.

Jamie gave them her address and arranged a time for delivery tomorrow, promising Freya that the men would bring everything up to her flat and pack it away for her, so that she didn't have to do a thing.

'Oh, no—I'd like to do it, if that's okay.' She very much wanted to go through everything by herself. Sorting out where to put the clothes and how to organise everything in the wardrobes that Jamie had put up the other day.

'Just the clothes,' Jamie agreed. 'You're meant to be resting.'

Michelle escorted them back through the store, down into the lift and back to their car, waving at them as they drove off, with a big smile on her face.

'Well, if she works on commission I think we've just bought enough to give her the rest of the year off,' Freya joked.

Jamie laid his hand on hers. 'Did you enjoy it?'

She smiled. 'I did. You were right—it was lovely to actually see the items in person, rather than online. Some of those clothes were just so *dinky*!'

He laughed. 'They were, weren't they?'

Freya out a long sigh. 'So, are we going back home now?'

'I thought we could go and get something to eat, if that's okay?'

She thought of the crowds, and her mood dipped slightly. 'What did you have in mind?'

'How about pizza?'

Oh, yes! 'You read my mind.'

Jamie parked the car by the marina and left the engine on, keeping them warm as they ate their pizza. The boats were lit with security lights and bobbed about on the gently rocking waves as the wind whipped across the bay, biting at any exposed flesh on passers-by.

'Thanks for tonight, Jamie. It was amazing—it really was.'

'Once you got over what it felt like to be looked after for a change?'

She laughed. 'I guess.'

He peered out of the window. 'Still no snow.'

'I told you.'

'Yes, you did.' He wiped at his mouth and fingers with a napkin, before closing the lid on his pizza. 'That was delicious.'

'The pizza? Or me being right?'

He smiled at her. 'Both. And I wouldn't have it any other way.'

Wouldn't he? She knew this situation wasn't ideal for either of them. They both wanted the same things for the years ahead. They wanted to stay here in England. But he knew he would have to leave at some point. To be King. It was a dark thought that cast a long shadow over both of them.

'I'm sorry, Jamie.'

He turned to her and frowned. 'For what?'

'For not being able to leave here. For not agreeing to be your wife. I know it's me that's making this difficult for

you and that if I just changed my mind then everything would be okay.'

Jamie shook his head. 'I would never force you to do anything. *Never.* I love the fact that you have been honest with me.' He took one of her hands in his and kissed the back of it. 'You were true to yourself. You told me the truth and I appreciate that. It makes what we have all the more special.'

She squeezed his fingers. 'What *do* we have, Jamie? Sometimes I'm not sure of anything.'

'We have a promise to be there for our children together, as much as we can be. To love them, and each other, until we can no longer do so.'

And each other? What did he mean by that? That he loved her? Or that the babies would love each other? That they would have a loving family? What he'd said was ambiguous. It could mean anything. And, although she was desperate to know whether he loved her, she felt at that moment that she couldn't ask him. The words were stuck in her throat.

She nodded. 'I don't want them to miss out on anything.'

'They won't.'

'I don't mean we should spoil them. I mean…' She looked away, out across the bay, past the boats and out to sea, where God only knew what was waiting. 'I mean that they should know just how much they are loved, by *both* of us. Even if one of us isn't there.'

'They will.' Jamie's voice was deep and full of emotion.

She loved it that he cared about this as much as she did. That his love for their babies ran as deeply as hers. Desperately she wanted to grab his hands and beg him never to go. Never to leave them. But she knew she couldn't ask him that. He had a duty. Over a million people would need him one day.

She couldn't make him choose between Majidar and her! He would always resent her for making him do it. So she knew that one day he would have to leave, and the idea of that, as her babies' birth grew closer, was beginning to break her heart.

Her feelings for Jamie had changed and grown. Especially over these last few weeks. Why did they have to be in this situation? Why did he have to be born to such a duty? Why couldn't he just be a midwife? Some random guy whom she'd met one day?

Why did he have to be a prince? Heir to a throne?

Why would she have to break her own heart one day and let go of him?

It wasn't fair.

Christmas morning arrived in the middle of a downpour.

Freya would not let the rain sully her day. It didn't matter. What mattered was that today was a day for family, and that for the first time in for ever she wouldn't be spending it alone with her mum. Jamie would be with them, arriving mid-morning, having lunch with them, before he had to leave for his shift at the hospital.

She hoped he'd like the present she'd got him. It had taken her ages to find something she thought he might like. What did you buy a *prince*—a man who could buy anything?

In the end she'd been rather sneaky, asking the security guys who followed her to get her a picture of Jamie's most successful racehorse so that she could have a painting done. One of her patients was an artist, and she'd commissioned her to do it.

Freya had to admit the painting looked amazing. Jamie's horse, Pride of Jameel, was a magnificent-looking animal,

and Susie had painted the stallion standing tall and proud on a sand dune, his black coat gleaming.

As a little something extra—something silly—she'd got him a pair of teddy bears that played a recording of their twins' heartbeats when their bellies were squeezed.

'Merry Christmas, Mum!'

'Merry Christmas, Freya!' Her mum turned and blew her a kiss before turning her attention back to the frying pan. 'Full English for you?'

'Erm...just bacon and eggs, please.'

'What time are we expecting your young man?'

'Around ten, I think.'

'You've told him we don't open our gifts until after lunch?'

Freya nodded.

'And he's okay with turkey?'

'Yes, Mum.'

'What about the sausages? They're pork.'

'If there's anything he doesn't want he'll just leave it.'

'I don't want to offend him.'

'You won't, Mum. Honestly.'

'It's such an important day. I wouldn't want to ruin it.'

She helped her mum prepare all the vegetables, peel the potatoes and baste the turkey, which was already in the oven. The kitchen was filled with succulent aromas as they made the bread sauce, the cranberry sauce, and her mum's special stuffing. In the background Christmas carols played from the radio, and Freya realised as she sliced and chopped that she had never felt happier. It was Christmas, she was going to be a mother, and she had a man in her life whom she loved.

She'd fought it. Oh, how she'd tried to fight it! But she had to be honest with herself and admit the truth. She loved Jamie. He'd made it impossible for her not to.

Part of her still couldn't quite believe she had made herself that vulnerable again, but the other part—her love for Jamie—kept telling her it didn't matter, because she felt sure he loved her too and that he would never try to hurt her the way that Mike had, that by opening her heart and allowing him in she was not going to get burned this time.

There was only one way Jamie could hurt her, and that was by leaving, but she was being optimistic and trusting in what Jamie had said. They might have *years* together yet. Samuel and James might be grown men before he got called back to Majidar, so why waste all that time being lonely and miserable when they could be together, happy and loved?

The doorbell rang, breaking her thoughts, and instantly a smile lit her face. Wiping her hands on a tea towel, she went to answer the door.

Jamie stood on the doorstep beneath the shadow of a large black umbrella, holding a small sack of Christmas presents in his other hand.

'Merry Christmas!'

He smiled and stepped forward, planting a kiss upon her lips that made her hungry for more. She could have stood there all day, kissing him in the doorway, if it hadn't been for her mum coming to the door.

'Well, let the poor man in, Freya—it's bucketing down out there!'

'Something smells good.'

'It's your lunch. I hope you're hungry?'

He met her gaze. 'Starving.'

Freya could have melted there and then. The heat between them had been growing uncontrollably, and it was a terrible struggle not to let things advance between them physically when it was what they both wanted.

'Come on through. I'll make you a cup of tea.'

'Nope.' He took the bag of presents back from her. 'I'll make the tea. You put your feet up. Just show me where to put these and I'll get right on it.'

Freya showed him where to put the presents and then allowed him to settle her down on the couch, lifting her feet onto a foot rest.

He leaned over her, his hands either side of her, his face close to her own. 'I've missed you.'

'You saw me just yesterday.' She smiled, glancing down at his soft, sultry lips.

'And I missed you the second I left. I'm so happy to be here with you today. You have no idea.'

How was everything going so right for her? How was she so lucky? To have this—Jamie, the babies, Christmas, the *future*. Just a year or so ago her future had seemed quite lonely, but now…now she had everything she could possibly want. Perhaps it *was* her turn to be happy. She'd had what felt like a lifetime of pain, disappointment and grief. Her luck was turning at last.

Jamie slid onto the couch next to her and she rested her head against his strong, broad shoulder. She sat there feeling content. *Happy*.

CHAPTER NINE

'You've not got long now. Just a few more weeks before those babies arrive. What are you planning on doing once they get here?'

Freya frowned at her mum. 'How do you mean?'

'Well I know you're getting the flat ready, and the nursery is all decked out, but do you have any plans to move in together?'

Freya looked at Jamie, unsure. They hadn't talked about this.

'I'd be lying if I said I hadn't thought about the future, but I don't want to push Freya unless she's ready,' Jamie answered diplomatically.

It was scary. Terrifying. But she said it anyway. 'I might be ready.'

He raised an eyebrow, smiling. 'Really?'

'I'll need all the help I can get when the twins are born, and it would make sense, wouldn't it?'

Freya's mum was looking between them. 'What a romantic you are, Freya! You could sound a little more enthusiastic if you're asking him to move in!'

If she'd been able to blush properly she would have. Instead she looked at Jamie uncertainly. 'I'd love you to move in. If *you're* ready?'

Did he know how much it was taking for her to say this?

Jamie put down his knife and fork, dabbed at his mouth with a napkin and then got to his feet, walking around the table to kneel by her side. He took her hand in his and kissed it. 'I'd love to move in.'

Freya's mum clapped her hands together in excitement. 'Oh, yes! What a merry Christmas it is, indeed!'

Jamie embraced Freya in a quick hug, kissed her on the lips and then went back to his seat. 'Let's have a toast.' He raised his glass of juice and waited for Freya and her mum to do the same. 'To moving in and to bright futures.'

'To moving in and to bright futures!'

Their glasses clinked.

Freya had got her mum a scarf, hat and mittens set, along with a couple of books she wanted and some Belgian chocolates to satisfy her sweet tooth.

In return she'd received a gift voucher, some perfume, a new pair of pyjamas and a book in which to record all the twins' milestones as they grew.

'Thanks, Mum.'

'You're welcome, love.'

'Your turn, Jamie.'

Her mum had bought him a bottle of aftershave and a jumper, which he immediately tried on and declared that it fitted perfectly.

'Thank you, Mrs MacFadden.'

He handed Freya's mum an envelope, and when she opened it she realised, to her immense delight, that she'd been given a pass for a spa day at the Franklin Hotel.

'Jamie, that's brilliant—thank you!'

'After all your hard work in the kitchen today, you deserve it.'

'Open this next.'

Freya passed Jamie her present. The painting of his fa-

vourite horse, wrapped in bubble wrap and Christmas paper and tied with a huge, sparkly silver bow.

Curious, he began to unwrap it, struggling a little with all the tape Freya had used, until eventually he turned it around to see what it was.

'Freya, that's just *gorgeous*! It looks like Pride of Jameel.'

'It *is*!'

She laughed at the pure delight and amazement on his face, pleased that she could make him so happy—the same way he made *her* feel. This was what it was all about. Moments like these. When you could make the person you loved feel joy.

'How did you manage it?'

'Well, seeing as you've insisted I have bodyguards follow me around, I put them to actual work and told them to get me a photo of your most beloved horse.'

'It's amazing!' He kept admiring it, turning it this way and that to catch the light and admire new aspects of the painting. Then he put it down and kissed her. 'Thank you.'

'There's this, too.' She handed him the wrapped teddy bears.

He opened the gift, smiling when he saw it was two honey-coloured bears.

'Squeeze their tummies.'

He did, and his face broke into a huge smile when he heard the babies' heartbeats, which she'd had recorded at one of her antenatal visits.

'Samuel and James. I'll treasure them. Always.'

Freya felt she could burst with happiness! She hadn't been sure how he'd feel about the gifts, but she was thrilled with how much he liked the painting of his horse. It meant so much to her that he did.

'There's only two gifts left. Both for you, Freya.' Her mum smiled, passing over the gifts.

They were both small boxes. Jewellery-sized boxes. The type that rings came in...

Feeling nervous, Freya accepted the first one and began to unwrap it.

She'd been right. It was a small, red velvet box, shaped like a heart.

What if he was going to ask her to marry him again? Here and now? What would she say?

Sucking in a deep breath, she pushed open the lid.

There, nestled on a cushion of dark blue silk, was a pair of beautiful earrings. Silver, each encircling a beautiful jewel.

'They're platinum, and the jewels are black diamonds. The largest I could find.'

'They're beautiful!'

'Put them in, Freya,' urged her mum.

Part of her felt relief that his gift wasn't a ring. But there was still that second box. There could be a ring in there. It wasn't over yet.

She smiled nervously and put in the earrings, which both her mum and Jamie admired.

'They look beautiful on you, love.'

'Diamonds for my diamond.' Jamie smiled.

She leant over as much as she was able to and kissed him, meeting his gaze and holding it, trying to tell him without words just how much he meant to her and how frightened she was by his next gift.

It had to be the ring in that box, didn't it? And she wanted to say yes, but how could she? When the worst happened and Jamie got called back to Majidar she would have to go with him if she were his wife. It would be expected. But if she said no then she'd be ruining this beau-

tiful day and breaking both their hearts, when right now they were both so happy.

Why had he done this? *Why?*

She felt a small surge of anger inside, irritation flooding her that it was all about to go wrong. She was about to feign a headache, or something, when the front doorbell rang.

Her mum frowned. 'Who on earth could that be? It's Christmas!'

'I'll go,' Jamie said, getting to his feet.

But Freya, feeling the need to escape the anticipation of what was in that tiny box, laid her hand upon his arm, stopping him. 'No. I'll go. You two have been looking after me all day—I need to stretch my legs for a moment.'

It was an excuse, but a welcome one, whoever it was. She just needed time to try and think. To try and decide what to do.

More than anything she would love to be Jamie's wife. To stand by his side with their babies as part of a loving family. But she knew she couldn't put herself under that much scrutiny. The world's press would have a field-day.

'Just coming!' She waddled down the hallway, exhaling loudly as she approached the door. She had no idea who it could be.

Standing before her was a man wearing a long white robe and a traditional *keffiyeh* on his head. He looked sombre, and bowed slightly at her appearance. 'Madam Mac-Fadden. My name is Faiz and I am the personal emissary of His Majesty King Ilias Al Bakhari. It is imperative that I speak with his brother, Prince Jameel.'

Freya froze for a moment as she took in his appearance and his message. Personal emissary? Why would Jamie's brother send a message on Christmas Day? It could hardly be a festive greeting. She was sure that they didn't celebrate Christmas over there in Majidar.

'An emissary?'

Faiz bowed again. 'Time is of the essence. If I may be allowed entry to speak with My Prince?'

Freya blinked rapidly as her brain raced through a thousand and one possibilities. Numb, she moved back and said nothing as Faiz stepped inside and past her.

'Who is it, Freya?' she heard her mum call from the room where moments ago everything had been perfect.

A chill crept over her as she began to suspect the reason for Faiz's visit. No. It *couldn't* be that. Could it?

Fighting back tears, she followed Faiz to the living room, where he stood just inside the doorway.

Jamie had got to his feet, his face stoic and ashen. 'Faiz?'

'My Prince. I must speak with you privately.'

Jamie glanced at her. The briefest eye contact. He must have seen the horror on her face before he looked away again.

'Anything you have to say, Faiz, can be said in front of everyone here.'

Faiz gave her a considered look, then nodded. 'Your brother has been taken ill. He is in hospital and it is imperative that you return to the kingdom.'

'Ill?'

'It is believed that His Majesty has suffered a stroke.'

Jamie stared at the floor, his body tense, his fists clenched at his side. 'Is Jasmeen with him?'

'The Queen has not left his side.'

'So you need me to return?'

His voice was thick with emotion, and more than anything Freya wanted to go to him and put her arms around him and comfort him, but her own grief kept her glued to the spot.

Jamie was leaving.

Now.

She wasn't ready. She wasn't ready to let him go! They'd only just started to be happy. They'd only just decided to be together. This wasn't fair! What about the babies? It was so close to her due date…he'd miss seeing them born!

'Jamie?' Her voice croaked in a painful whisper of grief.

He couldn't look at her. He just kept staring at the floor.

'Faiz? Are you absolutely sure that I must return?'

'I am not to return without you.'

Her mum hurried over to her and draped an arm around her shoulders. She turned into her mum's body and began to cry.

Behind them, she heard Jamie dismiss Faiz. 'Give me a moment.'

'Yes, My Prince.'

'Freya?'

She couldn't look at him. It hurt too much. She just clutched her mother harder.

'Freya? Please…'

Her mother released her and stepped away. 'I'll be in the kitchen.'

Freya folded her arms around herself and stared at Jamie through her tears. 'You can't go!'

'I must.'

He stepped forward and reached for her, intending to hold her, but she couldn't bear the idea of him touching her. If she let him hold her then she would never let him go.

She stepped back. 'Don't.'

'I never expected this. We were meant to have years…'

'But we both knew that it would happen one day,' she threw back.

'I'm so sorry. I never wanted this.'

She couldn't say anything. Words were not enough to express how she felt right now.

He looked remorseful. 'I could be back in time for the birth. Ilias may recover.'

'He might. But I can't compete with a million people who need you. And that's how it should be. The needs of a million people outweigh my own. You have to go. I understand.'

'I want to stay.'

'But you *can't*!' Her voice broke. 'We knew this day would come. We were fools to think we could cheat it.'

'There must be a way?'

She nodded. 'There is. Accept your fate. It's always been there for you. Coming to England, meeting me…it could never stop that wheel from turning.'

He looked hurt. 'You know that I would stay if I could?'

She nodded, fresh tears running down her cheeks.

'You'll keep me informed?'

She frowned. 'How?'

'I'll leave my men. They can get messages to me.'

'No, Jamie. Take them all with you. Leave nothing behind.'

'I'm leaving *you* behind.'

She stared directly at him, through her tears and her pain. 'Exactly.'

He shook his head. 'I can't believe this is happening. Do we have to end this? Now?'

'We do. Because I can't live a half-life, Jamie. I've already done that for far too long…hiding from the world, living in the shadows. I've got to live for me now. For my children. And I deserve—*we* deserve—a happy, full life.'

'I can't walk away from my children.'

She winced. So he *could* walk away from her?

'But you will, Jamie. You've already made your choice. You've been called and you're going and you *should* go. Your brother is sick—has had a stroke. You need to see him,

just in case his condition does not improve. You will be called upon to rule the country in his stead, and if he does not recover you will rule permanently. By going now you're choosing Majidar over us—as it should be. It's your duty.'

'You truly are the bravest woman I have ever known.'

She swallowed down her pain. 'You need to go now. Just *go*, Jamie.'

He looked away, his gaze taking in the twinkling Christmas tree, the wrapping paper discarded on the floor, the presents, the painting of his horse. And the small gift that she still had to open.

Jamie picked it up and held it in his hands. Staring at it for a moment, twisting it this way and that. Then he put it in his pocket, bent to pick up the teddy bears and gave her one last look.

'I love you, Freya MacFadden.'

She stared back, her heart breaking at this one last message, more tears falling freely down her face. 'And I love you, Jameel.'

And he went.

He turned his back and disappeared through the doorway.

Grief and pain tore sobs from her as she sank to her knees on the floor.

And on the television was the Queen, in her annual speech, talking to the nation. She focused on the Queen's face. A monarch addressing her people. Her whole life committed to her country.

How had she ever believed she could come between a man and such a love?

The house on Hayling Island had been closed up for a while.

Freya went through it, opening windows, letting in the aroma of the sea air despite the winter cold.

She turned up the thermostat on the central heating, made herself a mug of tea, and then stood outside on the small balcony and looked out to sea.

It was very still, calm, as if it was waiting for something. Grey-green, dully reflecting the grey sky above.

Down by the water she could see a dog walker, wrapped up in a thick jacket, throwing a tennis ball for three small dogs that chased after it happily.

This was what she needed—calm. The relaxed, unhurried way of life here, where no demands could be made of her and where she wouldn't have to find a brave face when inside she could feel herself crumbling.

She and Jamie had had their time cut short. Much too short. Both of them had believed—hoped—that they would have years…decades, perhaps. She'd begun to believe that her two sons would have a father. A great father. One who would adore them, teach them, raise them to be good boys. Good men.

Only now she would have that task alone.

What would she tell them about him? And when? As they got older they would begin to understand what a prince was, what a king was. Would they want to go to him?

She toyed with the idea of going with them one day. But she could only foresee agony in doing so. Meeting Jamie after many years… What if he had moved on? Married, as a king would be expected to do? What if he had a new family? Would she be welcomed in Majidar? Or spurned? Would Samuel and James always be known in Majidar as the King's illegitimate children?

And if they did visit there would always have to be another goodbye, and it wouldn't just be Freya who would be distraught afterwards it would be the boys, too, and *she* would be the one who would have to deal with the fallout.

She would be the one to pick up the pieces of her children and slowly put them back together again.

Perhaps it might be best not to tell the boys who their father was? But the idea of lying to them, of manipulating the truth, made her feel sick.

What to do?

This was why she had come here to Hayling Island. To get some space. To think clearly. Not to see the nursery every day and be reminded of the ticking of the clock. She had mere weeks left of her pregnancy, and as if in reminder of that she felt her first Braxton Hicks contraction. A tightening of her belly. Her body preparing itself for the battle to come.

She rubbed her hand underneath her bump and breathed through it. There wasn't any pain, just a tightness, her belly going hard and rigid before slowly softening and relaxing again.

'I'll always be here for you,' she said to them, before going to close all the windows she'd opened. so she'd feel the benefit of the central heating.

She wanted to go down to the water, to walk along the beach and feel that sea air invigorate her lungs.

She grabbed her coat, hat and scarf and wrapped up well, then opened the door and stepped out, locking up behind her.

As she turned to begin her walk she felt something touch her cheek. Then her nose.

She looked up and saw that snow was finally beginning to fall, and it pained her to know that he was missing it.

'Oh, Jamie…'

Security guards lined the floor of the private hospital in which his brother the King lay. Escorted by Faiz and his

own personal assistant, Rafiq, Jamie strode down the corridor towards his brother's room.

He had been kept informed throughout his seven-hour flight back home on the Bakhari private jet. And the briefcase of documents awaiting his attention on the plane had reminded him of the life he had left behind when he'd first come to England.

He was trying his hardest to remain stoic, but his mind was a mess. He'd left her behind.

I left her behind!

Freya and his two babies. His sons. His heirs.

My heart.

But duty had called him and he felt helpless to try and fight it. He would never be the same again now that he'd been ripped in two.

Part of him hoped that when he walked into that hospital room and saw his brother lying in a hospital bed Ilias would open his mouth to speak and smile, maybe hold his brother in greeting, give him a hug, pat him on the back and say, *Welcome home, brother.*

That would be the best solution for them all.

His duty, his future, hung over him like a guillotine. He hated to refer to his noble duty in such a way, but it was how it had always felt to him. He'd never asked to be royal, never asked to be born into such a family, and being King had *never* interested him. Not once.

Leaving his country, his family, and flying thousands of miles away as a young man had taken a lot of courage, but he had followed his heart and done what he'd thought was right.

He came to his brother's room and placed his hand upon the door. The doctors had informed him that Ilias appeared to have a blood disorder. They weren't sure of it yet, but they were running tests.

He hoped they would learn what it was soon. So his brother could be treated and recover as quickly as possible. He opened the door.

CHAPTER TEN

THERE WERE MONITORS sounding out the beats of his brother's heart.

He is alive.

But then he saw him—pale and wan against the hospital pillows, with his wife Jasmeen dutifully by his bedside, clutching his hand.

The shock of seeing him looking so ill stopped Jamie in his tracks.

'Jameel? You're here!' Jasmeen let go of her husband's hand and came over to embrace her brother-in-law.

'How is he?'

'The doctors say he is stable…but I have never seen him like this before.'

'Nor I.'

Jamie took a seat by his brother's bed and took hold of Ilias's hand.

'Ilias? It's Jameel. I'm here. I've come home.'

'He sleeps deeply since the stroke. It's like he has a tiredness that cannot be quenched.'

'Can he speak yet?'

'Sounds, but not words. It distresses him greatly. He tries to write, but he is right-handed, so it takes a while to read his words.'

Jamie squeezed his brother's fingers and felt tears sting

the backs of his eyes. But he refused to cry here. Crying would be an admission of just how out of control he was, when he was desperately clinging to the one bit of hope that he still had.

'Ilias?'

His brother moaned and then began to blink, looking about him to find the source of his brother's voice.

'Nurgh…'

Tears appeared in Ilias's eyes when he saw his brother, and Jamie leant forward to kiss his brother's cheeks.

'I am here, brother. I am here.' He held his brother's face in his hands, touching his forehead to Ilias's.

His brother signalled for his writing pad and Jasmeen presented it to him.

I'm sorry you had to come home.

Jamie read the tight scrawl and smiled. 'Don't be sorry. You couldn't have known this was going to happen.'

You're about to become a father.

He nodded, thinking of Freya and her huge belly, of his hand resting on her abdomen, feeling the boys kick and stretch inside. He'd left them. Left them behind. Maybe never to see them again.

The ache in his chest was palpable. 'Yes.'

I did not want to do this to you.

'It's not your fault, brother. None of this is. I am just so grateful that you are still alive. You must fight hard, Ilias. Fight hard to get better.'

He turned to look at Jasmeen.

'Has he seen any physiotherapists yet?'

'They come three times a day.'

Ilias began to scribble again.

I don't think I can remain King like this.

Jamie's stomach dropped like a stone. 'You don't know what the future holds.'

Jasmeen gave a weak smile. 'The doctors hoped that his speech would be back by now, and though the weakness on his right side has yet to improve they hope with time that it will get a little better. But they are unsure of a full recovery.'

Jamie thought about what that meant for a moment. 'I see.'

'I have been talking to Ilias, Jameel. We have talked long and hard and taken everything into consideration. Ilias loves Majidar and its people so much—he believes it needs a strong leader. Right now he does not feel that that is him.'

Jamie shook his head and tried to implore his brother. 'It *is* you.'

'He wants to abdicate.'

Jasmeen's words dropped into the room like a grenade.

Abdicate? *Abdicate?* But if Ilias abdicated that would mean that he...

Jamie stood up and began to pace the room, coming to a stop by the window to stare out, far and wide over the desert in the distance, on the outskirts of the city. Freya was so far away.

'*Nurgh...*'

Jamie's eyes closed at the sound of his brother's voice. He felt awful. Pathetic. Thinking only of himself when his brother was in such distress and pain! What sort of man did that make him?

He turned to see that Ilias was holding up his writing pad. He read the words.

It doesn't have to be you.

It was New Year's Eve and the snow had been falling for a few days now. Thick, heavy flakes, tumbling silently, covering the world in a white blanket of softness.

It made everything look beautiful, but it had certainly put paid to Freya's ideas of getting some walks in. All the heavy rain there had been before the snow meant that there was a thick layer of ice beneath it, so the pavements and roads were treacherous.

The weather forecasters predicted more heavy snow and informed people that they should not travel unless they had to. Gritters were out, trying to line the roads, but they were fighting an endless battle.

Freya stayed in the small house, drinking lots of tea and eating plenty of warm, buttery toast in front of the log fire, flicking from channel to channel on the television to try and find something interesting to watch.

Today she'd found a few films and had settled in to watch those, aware that her Braxton Hicks contractions had been coming a lot more frequently just recently. This morning they had begun to start hurting, and every now and then she'd find herself having to stop and breathe, clutching onto the back of the sofa or a kitchen unit.

She dutifully called her mum and told her she was fine.

'I'm so worried about you, stuck out there with all this snow. What if you go into labour?'

'Then I'll call an ambulance, Mum. Stop worrying, I'm fine. I've got a few weeks left.'

'Two weeks left, Freya. *Two weeks.* Those babies could come any time.'

'Well, I *am* a midwife, Mum, so I'll know what to do.'

She managed to get her mum off the phone eventually, sighing heavily, and decided to run herself a bath.

A soak in warm water helped soothe her troubled nerves, and she was soon settled back on the couch with a nice cup of tea.

A sudden pain, low in her belly, had her gasping, and she had to reach under her bump to rub at her abdomen. Slowly the pain eased and she lay back again, wondering if she'd sat down awkwardly and maybe pulled a muscle?

But the pain was gone now, and she felt confident that she'd know if she was really in labour.

On the screen, a newsflash came up on the local news to say that most roads in the area were becoming inaccessible and it was recommended that people did not drive anywhere unless it was absolutely necessary.

She glanced out of the window. The snow was still falling and there were drifts right up to the ledge.

She'd never known it to snow like this before. Not down here. Not by the coast, where you'd imagine there'd be enough salt around to prevent it. But there it all was. A thick white blanket. Would it snow like this next year? Would she be able to let the twins out in it? See the wonder on their faces?

The thought made her smile—a smile that soon faded when she got another pain.

Oh, God. Is this it? Is this labour?

All her bravery, all her bravado because she was a midwife, went out of the window. She suddenly realised just how *alone* she was here, how isolated. And if she needed to call an ambulance would it be able to get here?

There was only a single road on and off the island, connected to the mainland by a bridge. What if that was blocked? Impassable?

She hauled herself up and began to breathe through the panic, pacing back and forth.

Okay...okay. This could just be early labour, and I'm a first-time mother so my labour could be hours yet. Plus, it could still die down. There's nothing to say that these pains will continue.

But they did. Every eight minutes she got a pain, and as the hours passed they increased to every five minutes.

She picked up the phone, but the line was dead. She scrabbled in her handbag for her mobile and dialled 999.

'Ambulance, please.'

She was put through to Control and gave her address and situation. The guy on the phone told her that someone would be with her as quickly as they could, but because of the snowfall their ambulances were busy elsewhere. She was to try and find someone to be with her, so they could call again later if she needed to deliver at home.

Panicking, she put down her phone and began to think. Who could she get to help her? These properties were mostly summer holiday lets, and it was New Year's Eve!

A knock at the door had her struggling to walk over to it. Whoever it was, she would tell them what was happening. See if they could help her or if they knew someone else who could help. There were first responders on the island, surely? Perhaps they could get to her? She knew they didn't usually attend labouring women, but when needs must...

She grabbed hold of the door handle, turned the key and yanked the door open.

And there—shivering, wet, and very, very cold-looking—was Jamie. His face was red and glistening, his hair flattened by snowflakes.

Hesitantly, he smiled. 'I told you it would snow.'

'Jamie?'

'The one and only. Can I come in? Only I've been trudging through snow for the last couple of hours.'

'How did you know where to find me?'

But before he could answer another contraction ripped through her, and she gasped and let go of the door to bend over and put both hands on her knees to breathe through it.

'Freya? Are you in *labour*?'

She couldn't answer him for a moment. The contraction had completely obliterated her ability to talk whilst it was going on. The most she could do—the *only* thing she could do—was remain upright and breathe.

When it receded, and when normal thought and the real world returned, she stood straight again and looked at him with tears in her eyes. Her heart felt overwhelmed with relief and love for this man before her.

'For about four hours now.'

'*Four hours?* Why didn't you call for an ambulance? Stranded out here like this!'

'I did. They don't know when they can get to me. Apparently they're busy.'

He rummaged in his pocket for his mobile. 'I'll get someone here.'

He tapped at the screen and then held the phone to his ear, shouting instructions in Arabic before snapping it shut again.

'I've got a paramedic being choppered in.'

'A helicopter? In this? How did you know where to find me?'

'There's a GPS tracker on your phone.'

'What?'

'They all have them. Don't worry—I didn't place some secret bug in it, or anything. I'm not that kind of guy.'

Another contraction began to build. 'Oh, God!'

She turned to lean against the stairs and felt Jamie's

hands hold her steady and rub the small of her back. When it was done, he guided her back to the lounge so she could sit down.

'That last contraction was about a minute and they're coming fast.'

'You don't need to tell *me* that. I'm the one having them.'

'We need to prepare. Where are your towels? I'll put on some hot water, and we'll need scissors I can sterilise for cutting the cord—just in case.'

'Wait a minute. You can't come sweeping in here like a white knight. You need to tell me what's happening. How's your brother? Are you King?'

'Ilias has Von Willebrand's disease. He's being treated for it. The stroke has caused deficits, which hopefully will improve over time, but he has decided to abdicate, feeling that it's in the best interests of our country to have a ruler in full health.'

'He's *abdicated*? Can he do that?'

Her abdomen tightened with another vice-like contraction.

'Ohhhhh...'

She leaned forward and gripped the sofa, her eyes tightly shut as the feelings within her body overwhelmed her. Pain. Intensity. Breathing was the only thing she could manage for sure.

She felt Jamie take her hand and she gripped his fingers tightly, squeezing the blood from his digits. 'Oh, I think I need to push.'

'I'll need to check you first. Can I do that?'

She nodded quickly and removed her pyjama bottoms and underwear, wincing at the dying pain in her belly.

'I'll wash my hands. Do you have any gloves?'

Freya pointed into the kitchen. 'Beneath the kitchen sink are some latex gloves. Mum uses them for when she has to

touch raw meat.' She tried to laugh, recalling her mother's squeamish nature.

'I'll be back in a moment.'

She lay back on the couch and wiped the sweat from her forehead.

Jamie was back. But how? If Ilias had abdicated, didn't that mean that Jamie was now King? *Why* had he returned? Had they allowed him some kind of compassionate leave to be with her for when the babies arrived? So he could see them and *then* leave? She hoped not. Because even if that was good for him, it would be doubly difficult for *her*.

Having him here, holding her hand, mopping her brow, seeing the joy and love on his face as he looked at his sons and then having to wave him goodbye again… *No*. She couldn't allow that. She wouldn't survive it. The birth would be hard enough without being deserted right afterwards.

Jamie came back into the living room wearing a pair of latex gloves. 'Right, let's take a look. Has the contraction gone?'

'Yes. But maybe you should leave, Jamie?'

He looked up at her, confused. 'Leave? I just got here— and I don't think there's anyone more suitably qualified to help than me right now. I don't think I'll be fetching your elderly neighbour from next door, who needs a magnifying glass to read the evening paper.'

Now it was her turn to frown. 'Does he? How do you even *know* that?'

'I have *people*, remember? I'm going to examine you now. Try to relax.'

She lay back, opening her legs. 'Why does every man say that when he has to do an internal? Perhaps if men had a vagina they'd realise exactly how hard it is to *relax*!'

'Good point.' He smiled up at her. 'And good news. You're fully dilated. You can start to push with the next contraction.'

Freya's eyes finally began to leak tears of relief and happiness. 'I can?'

'You can.'

Jamie removed the gloves, pulling them inside out before discarding them in a small wastepaper bin. Then he pulled another pair from his pocket.

'Now—quickly—where are the towels kept?'

I can push. They'll be here soon. Samuel and James.

'Upstairs. Second door to the left is a small airing cupboard.'

'Don't do anything exciting without me.'

He kissed her on the cheek and raced upstairs and she watched him go, shocked by the feel of his kiss still upon her skin.

He seemed okay. He seemed as if he was in control. Was he really? Or was this all a front?

She still didn't know what was happening. Still didn't know whether he was staying. The hope that he might stay was building much too quickly, and she was struggling to fight it down, because she really wanted him to stay with her.

But reality told her that if Ilias had abdicated then Jamie was soon to be King, and he was only here on loan. His country had claimed him. And the knowledge of that was destroying her.

She began to cry.

Why was he doing this to her? Why had he come back and made her think there was hope? Made her think there was a chance for them still? It wasn't fair. Did he not know how hard it had been for her after he'd left the first time? If he did know then he wouldn't have done this.

She heard him come running back down the stairs and he appeared at her side with a huge pile of towels.

'You need to go.'

He frowned. 'Don't be ridiculous. I'm not going anywhere. What kind of man would I be to leave you in this state in the middle of a white-out?'

'A man with principles. I can't have you here, Jamie. Not like this! Not knowing you're going to leave me again!'

Another contraction hit and she heard nothing as his words faded beyond the pain she could feel surround her whole body. She sucked in a breath and, remembering all the advice she gave to labouring mothers, tucked her chin into her chest, curled around her baby and pushed down into her bottom.

It felt *good* to push! Excellent, in fact. There was almost relief there, because now she wasn't a passive observer of her pain, letting it roll over her in waves. Now she could do something about it!

She pushed against it, shoved back, using the pain of the contraction to start moving and birthing her babies.

'That's it, Freya! You're doing really well! Keep pushing right there. That's *it*!'

She let out a breath, then immediately sucked in another and began again. She managed two more huge breaths and two more pushes before the contraction died down and she could breathe properly again.

'Freya…' He took her hand and made her look him in the eyes. 'I'm not going to leave you. Not tonight. Not tomorrow. Not ever.'

Not ever?

'But—'

Another contraction began. *God, they're coming thick and fast now!* But she knew that was good. This was what was *meant* to happen.

'I can see a head, Freya! You're *doing* this! You're really doing this!'

When it was over, she reached down to touch the head of her first son and gasped when she felt it. 'Oh, my God!'

'With the next contraction his head will be born. Okay?'

She nodded, sucked in a breath, and began pushing again as the next contraction built.

'Keep pushing! Keep pushing! That's it—just like that. Now, stop! Pant it out!'

She panted, huffing away like an old-fashioned steam train, and then Jamie was telling her to give one last push.

She felt her son slither from her body and into Jamie's safe, waiting hands. He lifted Samuel up onto her belly. 'Here he is!'

'Oh, Jamie!' She grasped her son, her darling Samuel, ignoring all the stuff he was covered in—the white vernix, the smears of blood—and cried again out loud when her son opened up his lungs for the first time, letting out a long, strangled cry. 'Oh, he's so beautiful!'

He was. He was a good size—between six and seven pounds, she estimated—and with a thick, full head of dark hair like his father.

Jamie draped a couple of towels over his son, so he wouldn't get cold, then tied off the cord with string and cut it with the scissors he'd sterilised in a bowl of steaming hot water.

Then he looked at them. With *such* pride. 'I'm so proud of you.'

Freya beamed at him as she cradled her son. 'I can't believe he's here.'

'Safe and sound.'

'Thanks to you.'

'Thanks to *you*.'

She smiled and reached for him, so that he would lean

forward and place a kiss upon her lips. A soft, gentle, reaffirming kiss. And then he stooped over his son's head and laid a kiss on his son's head, too.

'Oh, my! I can't believe this has happened so quickly!' She looked at him. 'And you're here! And you can *stay*?'

He nodded, smiling. 'I can stay.'

'How?'

'Ilias told me that I didn't have to take the throne. That my sister Zahra wants to do it. She's a good, strong woman. She's always wanted to get more involved with the running of things and she's a good choice. The people will look up to her.'

'But I thought you *had* to do it?'

'So did I. But what kind of King would I be? With my people knowing that I had deserted my own two sons to sit on the throne? Knowing that I had left behind the woman I loved? Above all, my people would want me to be happy—as my brother Ilias wanted me to be happy by letting me come to England in the first place. He knows my life is here now, as do my people. They will understand. And Zahra is much loved. She will make a fine monarch. A brilliant one.'

He could stay? For good? With her and Samuel and James and without any possibility of his desertion hanging over them?

Another contraction began to make itself known. 'It's starting again...'

'Do you want me to take Samuel?'

'Please. I don't want to squash him.'

She passed her firstborn safely over to Jamie and began to breathe through the contraction. Jamie would need to check her first, before she began pushing again. To make sure James was in a good position.

He checked her and smiled. 'He's head down. He's right there, Freya.'

'Okay. I can do this again, right?'

He smiled back at her. 'You can do *anything*!'

She had to believe him. Had to believe that she could give birth again even though she felt exhausted after delivering Samuel.

Hunkering down, she began to push.

It felt a little easier this time. She pushed and pushed, and before she knew what was happening the head was delivered.

'One more push and it will all be over.'

'I hope so!'

She gave a quick glance to Samuel, lying on the floor beside Jamie, wrapped up in towels, resting from the trauma of being pushed through the birth canal.

She'd often wondered if babies cried because of the pain in their skull bones, overlapping to fit through, or whether it was just the shock of all the tiny alveoli in their lungs suddenly inflating for the first time. Maybe it was both?

But Samuel was here and he was safe, and he had a mother *and* a father, and of course she could do it again.

She sucked in a breath.

'That's it, Freya! Push! Harder!'

From somewhere she found a reserve she hadn't known she had. Whether it came from the knowledge that if she just did this one last push, as hard as she could, it would all be over, or whether she really did have that endless supply of energy distinctly found in women giving birth she didn't know. But she found it, and she used it, and she pushed with all of her might.

James was born. Into his father's hands and then up onto her stomach, the same as Samuel had been.

Crying with relief, she held him weakly, glad the pain was over, overjoyed that her babies were finally here, safe and well.

And Jamie…? Jamie was here to stay, it seemed. They could have the future that both of them wanted.

With the cord cut and the placentas delivered, Jamie sat himself next to her. They held a baby each. From above they could hear a helicopter, looking for a suitable place to land.

She smiled at her babies' little faces, gasping with delight at each tiny noise, each little snuffle, each beautiful yawn.

'Look at them, Jamie. They're so beautiful.'

'How could they not be with a mother like you?'

She smiled and leant her forehead against his. 'You're truly here to stay?'

'I'm here to stay. If you'll have me, of course.'

She turned to look at him. Looked deeply into those midnight-black eyes of his. Of course she wanted him! It was what she had always wanted but had been too afraid to admit, because she'd always thought he would have to desert her.

But that threat was gone now.

'Can I ask you something?'

She waited for him to look at her. He was still gazing at his sons with such love.

'Of course you can. You can ask me anything.'

'Will you marry me, Jamie?'

His gaze locked with hers and a delighted smile appeared upon his face. 'Yes. A thousand times, yes!' He leant forward until their lips touched.

Closing her eyes in exhausted delight, she kissed him back, pouring every ounce of her love for him into it. Oh, how she needed this man! She'd never known what was missing from her life. She'd convinced herself that her life was fine, hiding herself away on the night shift, pretending she was doing herself a favour.

That hadn't been any way to live. And Jamie had seen

that. Known that. He'd looked beyond the mask she was wearing and called her on it. Not allowing her to get away with it.

He'd made her into the woman she'd been *before*. The woman she'd thought she would never be again.

'I love you, Jameel.'

He stroked her face. 'And I love *you*.'

EPILOGUE

MAJIDAR WAS MORE beautiful than she could ever have imagined. A vast desert kingdom, filled with a thriving populace that had roared and cheered their delight at Jamie's return for a two-week visit.

She'd been nervous. All those people! And she had taken Jamie from them. She had stopped him from being their king.

But the people were thrilled to have her there. They waved and smiled, and small children brought her bouquet after bouquet, which she passed back to the bodyguards who escorted them on their tour wherever they went. Everyone had treated her with deference, and she did not doubt their love for her as Jamie's wife.

Now, as she stood on the palace balcony, looking out across the oasis beyond, she felt Jamie's arms come around her from behind.

'How do you feel?'

She smiled and laid her head against his shoulder. 'Loved.'

'I told you they would all love you.'

She turned to face him, to look deeply into his eyes. 'But to be loved *this much*... I never would have thought it was possible.'

Jamie smiled back and lowered one of his hands to her slightly rounded abdomen. 'When should we tell them?'

She was pregnant again. This time carrying only one baby. She hoped it might be a girl, but she didn't really mind.

'Let's do it tomorrow. Let's tell the whole world.'

She knew it would be all right.

He smiled and pulled her towards him.

* * * * *

If you enjoyed this story,
check out these other great reads from
Louisa Heaton

THEIR DOUBLE BABY GIFT
REUNITED BY THEIR PREGNANCY SURPRISE
CHRISTMAS WITH THE SINGLE DAD
SEVEN NIGHTS WITH HER EX

All available now!

THE SURGEON
KING'S SECRET BABY

BY

AMY RUTTAN

MILLS
BOON

All rights reserved including the right of reproduction in whole
or in part in any form. This edition is published by arrangement with
Harlequin Books S.A.

This is a work of fiction. Names, characters, places, locations and
incidents are purely fictional and bear no relationship to any real
life individuals, living or dead, or to any actual places, business
establishments, locations, events or incidents. Any resemblance is
entirely coincidental.

This book is sold subject to the condition that it shall not, by way of
trade or otherwise, be lent, resold, hired out or otherwise circulated
without the prior consent of the publisher in any form of binding or
cover other than that in which it is published and without a similar
condition including this condition being imposed on the subsequent
purchaser.

® and TM are trademarks owned and used by the trademark owner
and/or its licensee. Trademarks marked with ® are registered with the
United Kingdom Patent Office and/or the Office for Harmonisation in
the Internal Market and in other countries.

Published in Great Britain 2017
By Mills & Boon, an imprint of HarperCollins*Publishers*
1 London Bridge Street, London, SE1 9GF

© 2017 Amy Ruttan

ISBN: 978-0-263-93329-1

Our policy is to use papers that are natural, renewable and recyclable
products and made from wood grown in sustainable forests. The logging
and manufacturing processes conform to the legal environmental
regulations of the country of origin.

Printed and bound in Spain
by CPI, Barcelona

Dear Reader,

Thank you for picking up a copy of *The Surgeon King's Secret Baby*.

I have to say this book was one of the hardest books I've ever had to write, because of the piece of me that goes into writing *all* my books. It was emotional. Still, this story needed to be told—but I can tell you it was a challenge, writing a book with a hero who had no voice!

Kainan has had a lot put on his shoulders, and his life is changed after the war that broke out in his country—as lives are always changed after war.

Reagan has never really had love, but she finds something special with Kainan and then thinks she's lost it.

Writing about strong heroines is one of my favourite things to do. I was always taught to be strong and independent, and what Reagan endures when she gives birth to her medically fragile son alone is what makes her a superhero in my eyes.

I remember vividly being in Reagan's shoes, but thankfully my son didn't have the severity of illness that Reagan's son did.

I hope you enjoy Kainan and Reagan's second chance at happiness.

I love hearing from readers, so please drop by my website amyruttan.com or give me a shout on Twitter @ruttanamy.

With warmest wishes,

Amy Ruttan

This book is dedicated to all the mothers waiting
next to their child's hospital bed. Waiting for a miracle.

And this book is also dedicated to all those doctors
out there who perform those miracles on tiny humans.

Thank you.

PROLOGUE

Isla Hermosa—war-torn country

"I NEED A unit of packed cells—stat!" Reagan shouted over her shoulder. But no sooner had the words left her mouth than another explosion rocked the mobile hospital unit.

She had a wounded man open on her table, and instinctively she threw her body over her patient's to try and prevent dust and debris from entering into the exposed body cavity.

After working in this war-torn place for over a year, throwing herself over a patient came as second nature. It shouldn't have to, but such was the nature of war.

Isla Hermosa had been a beautiful, peaceful country once. A paradise in the Atlantic for vacation-goers. A country founded by Spanish and Greek settlers over seven hundred years ago, full of pristine beaches and tall palm trees.

Now the beach they were on just held the charred remains of its tall palms, and the blue sky was blackened with plumes of smoke rising from the capital. Dust filled the hot air, making it hard to breathe. There was no relief.

It was not ideal to be operating out in the open like this, but it was stiflingly hot on the beach, and being closed up in a tent in this humidity would not make matters any better. What they needed was a hospital, but that was impos-

sible. Most of Isla Hermosa had been taken over by the rebellion, and Canadian peacekeepers, along with those on Isla Hermosa who remained loyal to the dysfunctional Hermosian King Aleksander, had been pushed out of the city and back to the Atlantic Ocean.

The mortar fire stopped and Reagan went back to work on saving this Hermosian soldier's life. As a trauma surgeon for the Canadian Armed Forces she had seen her share of war-torn countries. As soon as she'd had her medical training she'd joined up for active duty. She wanted to serve her country. To prove to herself.

To whom?

She shook that thought away and continued her work. It wouldn't matter soon. Her agreed-upon tour of duty was ending and she had to return to the attending position that was waiting for her in Toronto.

She didn't know quite what she was going to do with herself back there, besides work. During patients there was down time, card games and a camaraderie. She didn't really have any one in Toronto. The people she served with were like a family. Not like *her* family, though. Not really, because her real family was cold and barely in her life.

The people she served with were her family.

In Toronto she'd be all alone. Again.

Toronto was her home town in the sense that she had been born there, and knew it well. She had a job waiting for her, but it wasn't really home. Her parents weren't there anymore.

Her parents had retired and moved to warmer climes while she'd served. They hadn't even told her that they sold her childhood home until a letter she'd sent them came back marked "Return to Sender."

Only the Canadian Army had ever wanted her, but she had to return to Toronto. She'd served the time she'd signed

up for and her leave of absence from the Toronto hospital was ending.

The friends she'd made here would forget her soon enough. No relationship ever lasted and that was fine. She was used to that. She didn't want to rely on anyone.

Her parents had taught her well. They'd always told her to make a life for herself. Not to rely on them. So she didn't.

I wish I had someone.

She was annoyed that she'd let that little thought sneak in.

Get a grip on yourself, Reagan.

Now was not the time to get maudlin.

"The packed cells you were looking for," a rich, deep voice said, and her body instantly reacted.

Dr. Kainan Laskaris, the foremost trauma surgeon in all of Isla Hermosa, stood beside her. Kainan always unnerved her. He made her feel exposed, vulnerable, as if he knew the pain she was hiding. Knew all her insecurities.

He was the first man in a long time to unnerve her in a *good* way.

"Thanks," she said, barely glancing at him.

When she'd first arrived there she'd tried to keep him at a distance, but it had never worked. He'd wiggled his way in and, though they didn't really talk much about personal stuff, she enjoyed his company. And he was a damn fine surgeon.

He hung the unit of packed cells, calmly drowning out the chaos of the war that was going on in the background.

His presence made her very aware of how very close the quarters were in this tent, but he helped her focus. He distracted her from all that was going on outside.

"How do you keep such a calm demeanor?" she'd asked, the first time they'd worked together on the wounded during mortar fire.

"I drown it out. I ignore it. I think of it as thunder, or something else, and focus on the person in front of me. I try to picture my patient's life and on my duty to return this patient to those who love him or her. Clear your mind and picture the life you're saving."

It had worked. The tactic had worked and helped her focus.

She was going to miss working with him.

"Do you need help, Dr. Cote?" Kainan asked, but he was already pulling on a pair of surgical gloves.

If he had been any other surgeon she would have barked orders to him, as she outranked most in her unit, but there was something about Kainan that commanded respect.

She could never turn him down, and she didn't want to. He knew what she needed in surgery without asking. He was like a second set of hands for her.

"Thank you," she said. "Are there no others?"

"No, the fighting is ending. The rebels are being driven back—that's the last report that I heard."

Kainan went straight to work, helping her repair the damage to the soldier.

He shook his head and *tsked* in disgust. "This situation should never have happened."

"I agree," she responded.

She didn't know much about what had caused the once peaceful island kingdom of Isla Hermosa to erupt into revolution, but she knew it had something to do with King Aleksander, after he'd been crowned after his father's death.

The former King, Mateo, had been instrumental in aligning his kingdom with Canada, and had had a good relationship with the country and good trade agreements.

King Mateo had been a great king for more than fifty years, but his eldest son, Aleksander, was not proving to be so great.

Isla Hermosa had severed its ties with Spain five hundred years ago, so when the revolution had broken out Canada had promised to help. Isla Hermosa had called to Canada and Canada had responded.

Which was why she was there.

"I hope this is over soon," she said as she finished her repair of the spleen. "My orders came in last night and I'm shipping out tomorrow."

"So soon?"

There was a hint of disappointment in Kainan's voice, which made her heart skip a beat.

Don't get hung up. It's probably nothing. You're a good surgeon and he can see that.

The mortar fire had become distant and the unit of soldiers that had been lying in wait to protect the hospital began to move. Tanks were soon going by, kicking up dust.

Reagan cursed under her breath and covered her patient again.

Kainan helped her. She was very aware of his body close to hers as they protected their patient.

"I thought you would stay until the end," he said, after the roar of the tanks had died down.

They went back to work as the dust settled.

"No, a new unit has come in to relieve us. They'll stay until Isla Hermosa is back on its feet."

"That could be some time," Kainan muttered darkly. "I wonder if Isla Hermosa will ever recover from this."

"Hopefully it will. Your country has seen enough bloodshed."

"Yes." There was sadness in his voice.

She wondered if he'd lost loved ones. They worked well together, and he was a brilliant surgeon, but they didn't delve much into personal issues beyond the sphere of this surgical unit.

Which was fine with her.

Even though she knew little about Kainan, there was still camaraderie between them. They'd experienced the war together here, patching up soldiers and civilians. They were friends and she'd miss him.

Even though it would be good to put some distance between them. She didn't want to do something she'd regret.

Live a little.

"I've grown accustomed to working with you," he said, and those dark eyes held her captive.

It thrilled her, unnerved her, this effect he had on her.

Reagan smiled behind her surgical mask. "I like working with you too, but it looks like this is the end."

Kainan nodded. "I guess so."

Reagan finished her repair and began to close up. Her patient would be taken to Spain which was the closest hospital they could get to, where he would be monitored in a military hospital. At least now he would survive the journey.

They didn't say anything as they prepared the soldier for transport, loading him onto the waiting helicopter that would carry him to an American aircraft carrier. A medical plane would take the soldier on to Spain.

When Reagan pulled off her surgical mask and gloves she let out a sigh of exhaustion. She had been working straight for almost twenty-four hours, since the peacekeepers had been pushed back to the beach. It was late afternoon, and though the sun was no longer beating down on them it was still sweltering, and she had the urge to run into the ocean and cool herself off.

Except for the fact that the beach was littered with boats belonging to the allied forces coming ashore.

Kainan was staring back toward the hill where the tall, ancient city gates were. There was smoke rising from the city and he was frowning.

"I'm sorry," she whispered.

She wanted to tell him she knew how he felt, but really she didn't. She didn't know what it was like to lose the country of your birth. To have it mangled and everything destroyed.

She couldn't even imagine what he was going through.

"You okay?" Kainan asked.

Reagan closed her eyes and shook her head. "You don't need to worry about me. I'm just exhausted."

He cocked his head to one side, those dark brown eyes penetrating her to her very core, and she fought back the urge to run her hands through his thick chestnut curls.

"I think there is more. Sadness has come over you."

"I was just thinking of leaving here. I was thinking…" She trailed off, getting choked up.

She didn't want to tell him that she was sad she was leaving the people she considered friends, the people who were like her family, in order to return to a lonely life in Toronto.

It had never bothered her until now.

"I hate leaving a job undone. There is so much work here, but my tour is over."

He sighed and dragged his hand through his hair. "Yes, there will be many pieces to pick up once the dust settles, but Isla Hermosa will rise again. There have been other wars, other strife that has hit our shores, and we have stood the test of time."

Reagan smiled and they walked in silence back to the tent. There were no more critical patients. Just those with minor wounds that were being made ready for transport off the island.

"Captain Cote, you're officially off duty," said Major Smart as she came to the hospital tent. "You've done a wonderful job, but we're getting ready to pull out. The next rotation is here and you need your rest."

"When does my transport leave, Major?" Reagan asked.

"Zero one hundred. I suggest you get some rest—and that's an order."

Reagan saluted Major Smart and stood there for a few moments. She had been relieved of duty and at one in the morning she'd leave Isla Hermosa and head back to Petawawa, before being formally and honorably discharged from the Canadian Armed Forces.

"You hungry?" Kainan asked. "You look like you need food and rest."

"I do—but don't you have to move to the front with the Hermosian Army?"

Kainan shook his head, a strange expression crossing his face. "Not yet. I have time. Why do you think I came here to help with the wounded when our mobile medical unit is further up the line?"

Reagan smiled. "I've just got used to seeing you hanging around these last few months. Usually getting in my way."

Kainan grinned that mischievous grin which always caused her pulse to race. If they weren't here in the middle of a war… But they were, and Kainan was off-limits. She was leaving in a matter of hours and she wasn't even sure that she'd ever see him again.

"You have a beautiful smile, Reagan."

A blush crept up her cheeks. "What?"

"You never smile for me. You're always so serious."

"This is war. I don't feel much like smiling."

Kainan stopped and took her hand, those intense dark eyes focused on her. She wasn't used to that. She wasn't used to the attention.

"You look tired, Reagan. You need sleep and food."

"I'm fine."

"Come."

It wasn't a request, it was an order, and technically he outranked her. Kainan placed his hand on the small of her back and led her toward the mess tent.

She was so exhausted that she let him get food and a Thermos of coffee, but he didn't let her sit down at a table. Instead he led her outside.

"Where are we going?" Reagan asked tiredly. "The beach is full of armed personnel."

"We're not going to the beach. We're going to my tent. It's in a shady spot and we won't be in any danger."

"There was mortar fire not that long ago," she said, falling into step beside him.

Kainan sighed. "The rebels have surrendered and there's a cease-fire. We should be at peace for a while."

Kainan's tent was on the edge of the Hermosian camp that bordered the Canadian forces' camp. And it *was* in a shady spot, with camouflage netting. They took a seat down in the sand under the awning, and felt the breeze blow in off the Atlantic.

Reagan closed her eyes and let the cool air wash over her.

"Here, drink this." Kainan passed her some coffee.

"I'm supposed to be resting."

She took a drink of the dark, sweet Hermosian coffee. She couldn't remember the last time she'd been able to savor a cup of coffee. Usually she downed it quickly, burning her tongue in the process, as she tried to patch together the wounded soldiers and the unfortunate civilians who'd got in the line of fire.

"If you go to bed now you will be even more tired by the time your transport comes because you won't sleep when you're so stressed. Unwind and relax."

"This is nice," she admitted.

"I will miss you," he said out of the blue, and he smiled sadly at her. "You have been a great friend and you're an amazing surgeon. I've enjoyed working with you."

Reagan was shocked, but pleased, and she squeezed his hand. "Ditto."

"Really?" he asked, surprised.

"Of course."

"You could've fooled me. You're so closed-off around me sometimes."

"Then why will you miss me?"

Kainan grinned. "Because you're brave, compassionate…"

"You just called me closed-off," she teased.

"Compassionate with your patients. You have a kind heart."

She blushed again. "Thank you."

"You're also beautiful."

He ran his thumb across her knuckles. His hands were rough from the dry heat and the tough conditions, but they were strong, surgical hands. And the simple touch was both calming and exciting at the same time.

"You're the most beautiful soldier I have ever seen."

His eyes twinkled and he smiled, causing a dimple to pucker in his cheek under his stubble.

Blood heated her cheeks at the compliment. No one ever paid her compliments. She wasn't sure how to take it.

"Why do you need my approval all the time, Reagan? For goodness' sakes, leave me alone. You don't need validation for something that is so ordinary."

Her mother's harsh words rang in her ears.

She began to tremble, thinking about her mother and the lack of parental compassion she'd had growing up.

"You're trembling." Kainan pulled her close and whispered, "Why?"

"Tired. That's all." She was lying, but she didn't want to think of her mother now.

Kainan held her. She buried her head in his chest, drinking in the scent of him, and the human connection she hadn't realized she'd been craving calmed her.

"Where are you going after we pull out?" she asked, still clinging to him.

"To the front lines," he said tersely. "Tonight."

Her heart skipped a beat. The front lines were dangerous. Even if there was a cease-fire, the capital city of Helicia had become a tangled mess of debris, mines and IEDs. The thought of him getting hurt scared her.

"You're shivering again," he whispered as he rubbed her back.

"I'm just worried about you advancing tonight." She looked up at him. "It'll be dangerous."

He grinned at her. "I will be okay. I will worry about you too, you know."

"I'll be on military transport, headed back to Canada."

"Things happen—and Canada is a long way away. A whole ocean divides us."

He reached out and stroked her cheek, wiping the tears from her face, and before she knew what was happening he was kissing her. Tenderly at first, and then possessively, but it felt so good and she kissed him back, gripping the collar of his tattered linen shirt as if his life and hers depended on it.

"I'm sorry," he whispered breathlessly against her mouth. "I don't know what came over me. I've gotten so used to being around you, seeing you every day, just the thought of not seeing you…"

She should put an end to it, the kissing, but she just wanted to *feel*. She wanted to give in to the attraction she felt for him. The white-hot lust.

It would be once.

Just one time.

It had been so long since she'd been with someone, since she had any kind of intimacy.

"No apologies—and don't stop." She kissed him again, running her hands through his hair.

"Reagan, we need to stop."

"Why?"

"I'm advancing and you're leaving. What future do we have?"

"Right now, none. But I'm not asking for a future, Kainan. I just want to *feel* tonight. I just want a connection with you. I've been fighting it since I met you."

He nodded, his gaze holding hers. "Me as well."

"So don't stop," she whispered, pulling him into another kiss which seared her very soul.

He stood to his feet, helping her up. "Come."

Reagan thought that he was going to take her back to her camp, but instead he led her inside his tent, taking her in his arms.

"I want you so much, Reagan. I wanted you the first moment I saw you. But I don't want to make you a promise I may not be able to keep," he whispered against her ear.

"I care for you too. And you don't need to promise me anything. I just want this."

"As you wish," he said, before kissing her again, making her melt into his arms completely.

It was dark outside and she could hear movement. People on the move to the front lines. She rolled over in the narrow cot that she and Kainan were sharing and glanced at her watch. It was midnight. In an hour her transport would be leaving. She had to pack up what little gear she had and get to the rendezvous point.

Kainan was already up and dressed in his uniform, which she'd rarely seen him wear at the mobile hospital. It was a bit surreal, and thinking about him in danger made her stomach knot with unease.

"I was just about to wake you," he said gently.

"Sorry I slept so long here."

"No, it's okay." He leaned over and kissed her. "I have to go with the next transport to the front lines. There is fighting going on in the city. More wounded. I'm needed there."

"I thought there was a cease-fire?" she said, dressing quickly in her wrinkled clothes.

"There was, but some insurgents have been found hiding in the city. It will be taken care of."

He said that with a finality which sent a shiver down her spine.

She finished dressing.

He took her in his arms and held her close.

"Please be safe," she whispered, drinking in the scent of him. She wanted to remember every moment of this time with him, and she sent up a silent prayer that he would be safe.

"You too, Reagan. My beautiful Reagan. I shall never forget you." Kainan kissed her. "Come, we'd better go."

They walked out of his tent and saw the Hermosian camp was a flurry of activity. He walked her as far as he could, to where the Canadian forces were packing up what they could, ready to join the Hermosian Army.

"I'll never forget you," she said, and she wouldn't.

How could she forget him? A man who had seemed to see past her façade. A dangerous and yet gentle man, and one heck of a surgeon.

A man she'd been proud to serve with.

"Ditto."

He kissed her hand one last time and then headed toward a large transporter that was waiting for him. He climbed up into the back of the armored vehicle and waved at her as the truck rumbled away into the darkness toward the front lines.

Please keep him safe.

Reagan headed back to the tent she shared with another surgeon. She packed up her kit bag and then waited for her transport.

It was past 1:00 a.m. when the radio in the mess hall crackled to life.

"Explosion. Hermosian medical transport attacked. All personnel dead."

The words hit her like a rock and her stomach knotted. She closed her eyes and bit her lip as the words hit her.

Maybe it wasn't Kainan's transport?

She wanted to stay and find out if his name was on the list, but her transport came then.

She was airlifted to the waiting Canadian vessel which would take her back home. She was assigned her berth, but as soon as she'd set her bag down she found the nearest commanding officer from her unit.

"General Travis, do you have a list of casualties from that Hermosian medical transport?"

General Travis shook his head. "No, not a full list, but I know who you're asking about and I'm sorry, Captain Cote. I know that you worked with Dr. Laskaris, but his name *is* on the list of those who perished. His dog tags were found and not much else. An IED near the palace went off."

Reagan's stomach twisted and she ran to the side of the boat, losing what little food she'd managed to eat since leaving Kainan and arriving on the transport, over the side of the ship.

General Travis patted her back. "I'm sorry, Captain."

She nodded, and managed to keep the tears at bay.

This was why she kept people at distance, why she never let anyone in. Because in an instant they could be taken from you. They left. They died.

Kainan had wormed his way in past her defenses and now he was gone.

She was alone.

Completely alone.

She should have known better. She was *meant* to be alone.

It was easier that way.

CHAPTER ONE

A year later, Toronto

REAGAN WALKED THROUGH the halls of the hospital in a daze. There wasn't enough coffee in the world to wake her up. It had been a long shift at the hospital and then her infant son had a bad night. The cot in her son's hospital room in the pediatric critical care unit wasn't exactly comfortable, and she could use a break to go home and have a shower.

The problem was there was no one to give her a break.

It was just her and Peter in the world.

A year ago she'd spent an unforgettable night in Kainan's arms. A night that she would cherish forever. Then he'd gone to the front lines and died for his country.

She'd come back to her life in Toronto, empty and alone.

Although it had turned out she was not completely alone, because her one night with Kainan had resulted in pregnancy.

It was the best gift.

A piece of Kainan.

A child.

Someone to love.

And she wasn't going to make Peter feel like a mistake, the way her parents had made *her* feel.

Nothing she'd ever done had pleased them.

Her father had never wanted kids. When her mother had

got pregnant with Reagan he'd stuck around, but he had always been distant. Over time, her mother had come to resent her for causing such distance in her marriage.

There had been times when she'd got shreds of love and affection from her mother, but it they had been few and far between.

She'd thought maybe being grandparents would soften her parents' hearts.

She'd been wrong.

When she'd told her mother about the situation—about the baby and the father dying—her mother's response had been heartless. Painful.

"Get rid of the problem, Reagan. You can't raise a baby on your own."

"I'm not getting rid of the baby, Mother."

"Then what do you want from me, Reagan?"

Honestly, she didn't know. Some part of her had hoped her mother would change, but she should have known better.

Reagan had always been a burden to them. And her getting pregnant overseas on a mission was just another disappointment for her parents. They were even more disappointed that she'd kept the baby.

As soon as Reagan had found out she was pregnant she'd vowed that she'd protect Peter. She'd give him the love she had never had, the compassion she had to learn by herself.

No one would hurt Peter. *Ever.*

Her parents had never cared about her. They'd only taken care of her because they were legally obligated to do so.

"I've never run from my mistakes, Reagan. That's why I took care of you. At the time, abortion wasn't an option."

Reagan was a mistake. It hurt to hear it time and time again.

She focused on the lukewarm coffee she was drinking.

A baby had never been in her plan, but she was responsible for her actions. There were plenty of single parents out there, going it alone. And she would do the same. She would *never* let Peter feel as if he was an obligation or a mistake.

But what should have been one of the most joyous days of her life, when Peter was born, had quickly turned into her worst nightmare.

In all her years as an intern and then a resident in hospital, and then her time in the field with the Canadian military, serving as a trauma surgeon during natural disasters and being tossed into the fray of war zones, she'd seen many sick children. Critically ill children. It had always been a deep-rooted fear of hers that one day, if she ever had a child, something might happen to that child.

She had never been able to handle the thought of it.

And then it had happened.

She'd had Peter.

"Let me see him!" she'd cried, relieved that the birth was over.

Only none of the doctors had answered her. Marisa, her OB/GYN, hadn't looked at her. It was in that moment that Reagan had realized the baby wasn't crying. There wasn't a sound coming from him at all.

"What's wrong?" Reagan had asked.

She'd craned her neck as Marisa had turned back to her, watching the pediatrician on call with her baby in his hands, blue-grey and barely moving.

It had only been a couple of hours later when she'd learned that her baby had cardiomyopathy and would be staying in the hospital indefinitely. The only reminder of her and Kainan's time together was placed on the list for UNOS and would be staying there while he waited for a new heart.

The nursery she had so painstakingly started to prepare

in her small apartment before his birth was still unused, and she hadn't been able to look at it the few fleeting times she'd managed to get home.

Don't think about it—and don't think about Kainan.

Even a year since his death often Kainan crept into her thoughts because Peter looked like him so much. And she couldn't help but wonder what it would have been like had Kainan lived.

Reagan had had a couple of relationships before Kainan, but they'd failed because of *her*—because she couldn't trust. At the back of her mind she was terrified she'd disappoint, that she'd never be good enough and her heart would be broken. Again.

It was better this way.

She was better off alone.

"Reagan, you look like you didn't get a wink of sleep!"

Reagan rubbed her tired, sore eyes and saw the Chief of Surgery leaning over the central desk, where he'd been studying a chart.

Michael McNeil had been so understanding. He'd trained her as a resident, and encouraged her into the Canadian Armed Forces to expand her skills, and since she'd announced her pregnancy and Peter's birth he'd been accommodating, knowing she needed to work. Right now he was looking at her with pity. Like most people. She hated pity.

"We need better cots on the NICU floor," she mumbled, stifling a yawn.

"Are you going to be able to work with this new doctor?" he asked.

Reagan nodded. She needed this job. It was more pay, and not so much time spent doing surgical rounds. Right now she couldn't do a lot of surgery. A call about a heart might come in at any time, and she needed to be near Peter.

Peter was all she had.

She really needed sleep, but right now she needed work more. It kept her sane. And she was looking forward to this new job. It was more flexible.

"Yeah, I'm good." She walked to the other side of the central desk and poured herself another cup of coffee into a plastic cup and capped it.

"Good. I know things have been hard—"

She held up her hand to cut the chief off. "Michael, I'm okay. I need the work. I *love* the work. And Peter is not that far away. Besides, I'm the only staff member available who knows American Sign Language."

"And you worked in Isla Hermosa as well," Michael said, setting down his chart.

Reagan's heart skipped a beat—which was silly. "The new specialist is from Isla Hermosa?"

Michael nodded. "The Canadian government is giving him asylum. His work is important. That's all I know. And he's a brilliant teacher. I think he will be an asset to our medical students."

"I wonder if I worked with him?" Reagan said, taking another sip of the bitter coffee. The caffeine was doing its job. There had been many other Hermosian physicians out in the field whom she'd worked alongside, but none had been like Kainan.

No one will ever be like Kainan.

She couldn't think about him now.

"I don't know, but the Canadian government was very adamant that he should be given asylum here, and after chatting with him over email I'm very excited to have him on board."

"I'm looking forward to meeting him," said Reagan. "To become a surgical consultant when you can't speak— that's impressive."

She couldn't recall any nonverbal surgeons out in the

field on Isla Hermosa. Of course it had been a war zone. Everything was a bit blurry about her experience. Except…

"Well, he could speak before. He was injured at the front and a badly placed endotracheal tube damaged his vocal cords. I'm told he can speak a bit—but not much, and not for long periods of time. He will be getting corrective surgery here before the New Year, but for now you'll help him."

"Of course," she agreed. She would be happy to. "Does he know about my son and my need for flexibility?"

"No," Michael said. "I told him you needed a flexible schedule, but I thought it best if you tell him about Peter if you want to."

She breathed a sigh of relief. "Thanks."

It was exhausting, constantly explaining Peter's condition to people. It drained her. The new surgeon didn't need to know about Peter, he just needed to know she needed flexibility—which Michael had taken care of.

Reagan fell into step beside Michael as they walked toward his office, where she would meet this Hermosian doctor and they could get to work.

"So, my job consists of interpreting American Sign Language to the students so he doesn't overtax his voice?"

Michael nodded. "You can use my office to draw up your plans. The first medical students will be coming at one—after the lunch rotation."

Reagan nodded. "Sounds good, Chief."

Michael smiled, and then said softly, "You know we're all here for you, Reagan. If there's anything more we can do…"

Reagan gave Michael a quick nod. She appreciated it, but she didn't want pity or help. Too many people pitied her, and she was tired of it. She was still a surgeon. She was still Reagan Cote, even if it sometimes didn't feel that way.

"I'm good."

"Are you sure?" Michael asked, and there again was that expression of pity that she loathed, directed toward her.

She couldn't push Michael away like she did so many. He had been her mentor when she was resident. He'd taught her compassion and patient care. Things she hadn't been able to learn from her parents. When she'd started her bedside manner had been atrocious, but Michael had guided her, and he had been the one who welcomed her back with open arms when she'd finished her tour of duty.

"I appreciate it so much, Michael. You know that, but I'm fine. Let me work—it keeps me busy."

Michael gave her a quick kiss on the top of her head and whispered, "He'll pull through."

She nodded, blinking back the tears that always threatened to fall when someone started talking about Peter and his condition. Tears that she had learned to swallow because she had to be strong for Peter.

And for herself.

She had to be tough. There was no time for weeping or sorrow. If she gave in to the grief that she was actually feeling she would collapse and be useless.

This new assignment had come at the perfect time. Even though it would take her off her precious surgical rotation, it would keep her at the hospital.

It would keep her busy and close to Peter.

And that was the most important thing.

"You okay?" Michael asked.

"Perfectly."

Reagan plastered on the fake smile she was used to wearing. The one she'd perfected when she was a small girl, because her father had liked her just a bit better when she'd smiled, and had been nicer to her mother when Reagan had smiled and behaved.

Michael nodded and then opened the door.

Reagan stepped in, seeing the Hermosian doctor had his back to her. Something tugged at the corner of her mind, but she couldn't sift through the fog—or maybe she was having a hard time seeing. Maybe she was so sleep-deprived that this was just a dream.

She began to tremble.

"Dr. Kainan Laskaris—I would like to introduce you to Dr. Reagan Cote, who will be working with you here at the hospital."

The ghost turned around, those dark, expressive eyes of his hollow and wide with shock. The beautifully chiseled face was marred with scars, and on his throat she could see where they had put the botched endotracheal tube. It was almost as if his throat had been slit, the scar was so bad. The dark brown curls were tamed, and streaked with silver. He'd aged. The war had aged him. But he was still devastatingly handsome.

He opened his mouth, as if to say something, but then snapped it shut. And his lips pressed together firmly, as if he was angry.

Her coffee shook in the cup she was gripping so tightly. Her world was spinning and her tight rein on those emotions she'd become so darn good at locking away had gone slack.

She was losing control.

"Never lose control, Reagan. Don't show your weakness to anyone or they'll take advantage of you."

Her mother's voice was screaming in her head.

"Kainan?" her voice finally squeaked out in disbelief.

"You two know each other?" Michael asked.

She waited for that deep, rich voice to answer, *Si.* That affirmation had always made her go a bit weak in the knees.

But of course it couldn't.

His voice had been taken from him.

Instead he just nodded quickly and looked away. As if he was annoyed she was there.

"We worked together on Isla Hermosa during my last tour of duty," Reagan answered, steadying her hand so Michael wouldn't see her tremble. "And we worked well together."

Michael looked visibly relieved. "I'm glad to hear it! Well, I'll leave you two to it. I'm sure you have a lot of catching up to do."

Reagan didn't even see Michael leave. She just heard the door shut, her gaze focused on Kainan. The man she'd thought was dead.

He stared back at her, but he didn't smile at her the way he'd used to. There was no twinkle in his eyes. Just darkness. It was cold. It didn't faze her, didn't hurt her. She was used to people looking at her that way. It did sting a little, and it gave her confirmation that Kainan was like all the other men she'd met. Like her father. Cold and distant.

"You're alive." It wasn't so much a question as it was a statement of fact, because she'd thought he'd died.

Clearly, he signed in American Sign Language, barely looking at her.

"They told me you had died."

His expression softened briefly. *I'm sorry. There was a lot of confusion at first. I was reported dead for days...*

"Your medical transport was attacked and they found your dog tags in the rubble."

Again, there was a lot of confusion.

It was obvious that he wasn't going to give any further information about it.

Reagan sat down on one of the chairs at the table in Michael's office. There was a stack of materials there. New orientation information for Kainan. She needed to keep busy and not think about why he never reached out to her.

"Has anyone explained all this stuff to you?" she asked as she quickly scanned the binder full of information. If she kept busy she could ignore the racing of her pulse, her trembling hands, the urge to hug him and cry because he was alive.

He shook his head and took a seat across from her. Then he cleared his throat. "Best…come…from…you."

His voice was broken, harsh and guttural. And color bloomed in his cheeks. It was either embarrassment or anger, and knowing Kainan it was most likely anger.

She knew how much he liked to be in control of every situation. He'd commanded all those around him during surgery, and those working with him had followed him blindly.

When he lost control he got angry, but that would drive him to work harder to solve the problem and regain control.

He was an amazing surgeon.

And this loss of control…

She could only imagine what he was going through. She liked control in *her* life, but she'd learned a humble lesson when Peter was born. Control was just an illusion.

Reagan had to admit that she was angry too. That he was alive and hadn't let her know. He'd known where she was going. He'd known so much about her. Why hadn't he reached out?

Only she couldn't think about that right now. She'd swallow the anger she had and do her job. Keep moving forward as she had always done. If she stopped for a second everything would fall apart.

"Okay," she said, setting her half-empty coffee cup down and opening up the materials. "We can do this together."

Is there anyone else? he signed.

The words were like a slap. He didn't want her here. She realized his body language was more than just embarrass-

ment or anger over his situation. He was annoyed that she was here, helping him.

Her spine stiffened.

She should have known his attention to her back then had just been seduction. He didn't want to see her again. He'd just been using her.

You wanted it too.

Well, she wasn't going to let him shove her aside. She had a job to do, and anyway she'd got the best part of him. She had Peter, and she didn't regret that for anything.

"No, there is no one else. I am the only doctor here who can interpret American Sign Language and who's free to support you." Now she was really annoyed with him. She wasn't going to let him ruin this job for her.

Fine, he signed. He crossed his arms and leaned back in the chair. His gaze was fixed on her, but instead of anger or annoyance, like before, there was bit of humor. Some smugness.

She wanted to wipe that off his face. "What?" she snapped.

I forgot how prickly you get. How fast your walls go up.

The twinkle she knew so well returned to his eyes. It was meant to lighten the mood, but she wasn't in the mood for that.

"I get prickly when people are acting like jerks."

"Sorry." He spoke, his voice now barely a whisper.

Reagan shut the binder and, though she knew she was going to regret it, she had to ask. "Why don't you want to work with me?"

The question caught him off guard. Of course this whole situation had caught him off guard. He'd known that Reagan was Canadian, but hadn't realized that she worked at *this* hospital, in *this* city. Canada was a large country. He'd

chosen this hospital simply because Dr. Shaw, his otolaryngologist was here.

He hadn't known that Reagan was here. And he hadn't known that she knew American Sign Language or that she would be working in the education part of the hospital. He'd have thought she would be on the surgical floor, wherever she worked, which was where *he* wanted to be, but couldn't be any longer.

How could a man with no voice convey what he needed to his surgical staff during an emergency situation? He couldn't, so his surgical career was over.

Of course that wasn't the only reason his career was over.

His throat tightened at the thought of why it was over. It always tightened when his stress levels rose, and he was certainly stressed now.

Seeing Reagan again was a shock.

And he'd had to hold himself back, because his first reaction when he'd seen her had been to run to her and take her in his arms and kiss her. But this wasn't the time or place.

Nowhere was the time or place.

Still, seeing her again had brought back so many memories. Even though they'd served during a war—a brutal war which had torn his country apart—working alongside her had been some of the happiest moments of his life.

He loved his country, but being called back to serve had been painful. Since his mother had died Isla Hermosa had reminded him only of loneliness and pain.

Reagan had brought back joy into his life.

One of the hardest things he'd had to do in his life was to leave her behind, knowing that she was going back home to her country and that he was going to the front lines. That he might never see her again.

It had nearly broken him, but it had been for the best that she'd left when all was said and done. Now circumstances had changed and they could never be together. He'd never trap her the way his mother had been trapped in her marriage to his father.

Still, he wanted Reagan—even though he shouldn't. Their year apart had done nothing to extinguish the flames of passion that he felt for her.

He still wanted her.

That long, silky brown hair that was so neatly tied back. The long, graceful neck that he'd once run his hands over. And those lips he'd kissed and wanted to taste again.

Only he couldn't now. Not because he'd lost his voice, but because he would never, *ever* put her inside the dangerous situation he now found himself in.

He was a displaced king, of a country that was precarious and about to sink into oblivion, and he couldn't bring her into that situation.

There were people who wanted to assassinate him. And he would gladly take a bullet for his country, because *he* felt responsible for Isla Hermosa's downfall.

He hadn't been able to control his late brother. Kainan had tried, but his brother had ruined the country in six months after their father had ruled gracefully for fifty years.

Now Kainan was King of a broken, bleeding country. And instead of being there he was here in Canada. First in Ottawa, to recuperate from all the injuries that he'd sustained when the palace had been attacked, and now here at this hospital in Toronto, working and waiting for surgery that might or might not return his voice to him. Surgery he might not survive due to the damage in his throat.

Still, he needed a voice to rule. As King, he had a duty

to his country—a tradition to uphold and a service which had so depressed his mother and made her feel trapped.

His father had been a great king, but cold, and protocol had come first. Kainan had watched his mother take second place to Isla Hermosa.

So, no, he couldn't drag Reagan into that. The crown would die out with him. And maybe it was better that way.

What's first? he signed.

"Have you got your hospital identification yet?" she asked, leafing through all the papers from Human Resources that Kainan had just skimmed.

No. I haven't got that yet.

"Okay, we'll fill out this paperwork and—"

Kainan touched her arm and got her attention. *Why aren't you practicing surgery?*

"I told you. I'm the only one fluent in American Sign Language here who has room in her schedule to assist you."

So this is a punishment for you?

"What?"

Surgery was your life.

She frowned, and continued to leaf through the binder. "It still is, but I was asked to do this and—" She was interrupted by a knock at the door. "Yes?"

A nurse stuck her head round the door. "I'm sorry to interrupt, Dr. Cote, but it's Peter."

Reagan's expression changed. She frowned, looking worried as she slammed the binder shut. "I'll be right up."

The nurse nodded and shut the door.

"I'm sorry, Kainan. I'll try to be as fast as I can but…it could take a while."

Is it a patient? he asked.

Reagan sighed sadly. Her expression was tired, broken, and Kainan couldn't help but wonder who Peter was. Was Peter her husband?

That brief, fleeting thought of her with another man enraged him. It made him jealous to think of another man loving her.

Not that he deserved to feel *any* sense of jealousy when it came to Reagan. He'd given up those rights when he'd let her go in Isla Hermosa.

"No, it's not a patient." Then she sighed again and looked almost as if she was going to be sick. "Kainan, I'm… He's my son. Peter is my son."

She stood up to leave, her body tense.

Kainan was shocked, and sat back as reality sank in. He hoarsely asked, "Your son?"

And then it dawned on him—because he knew that she hadn't had a child when she was serving alongside him in Isla Hermosa.

A cold tendril of dread unfurled in his belly. He jumped up and stood in front of her, blocking her escape and he cleared his throat. "How. Old?"

"He's three months now. He's your son, Kainan."

Reagan didn't offer any other explanation.

"Never trust women, Kainan. Never. Your mother tried to hide you from me when she wanted to divorce me, but you were a prince of Isla Hermosa. She had no right to do that. But she did try. Women are fickle. They are not devoted, they only think of themselves. Never trust them. Close your heart to them or you'll be hurt!"

Kainan didn't want to hear his late father's voice in his head. He'd been a fine king, but a terrible husband and father.

Still, Reagan hadn't told him he had a son.

"I have to go and check on him. Kainan, please move."

Numb, he stepped to the side so she could open the door. Of course Kainan was going to let her go, but he needed

more answers. His *son*? It couldn't be. Why was his son at the hospital? Why was a nurse taking care of him?

He dashed after Reagan, cursing himself inwardly because he couldn't call out to her to stop, but he caught up with her quickly and grabbed her arm, holding on to her.

She tried to shrug out of his grip until she saw it was him and relaxed.

My son? he signed.

"Yes."

Why didn't you tell me I had a son? Were you trying to hide him from me? He instantly regretted the words. They were so much like something his father would have said.

Her eyes narrowed. "I thought you were dead. They told me you were dead. I wouldn't hide him from you—you know that."

He wanted to believe that, but his own mother had tried to hide him from his father when she was pregnant.

"I never wanted you locked away in the palace, Kainan. I didn't want you locked away like me. I tried to leave, but I couldn't hide you from him either," his mother had said on her death bed. *"I just wanted us to be happy. To be free. I didn't want you to grow up with him as a father."*

"Why?" He'd felt as if his life was a prison sentence. He was guarded and watched all the time, and though surrounded by people he'd always felt alone. *"Why did you tell him?"*

"I had to. I loved him." His mother had sighed. *"I am sorry I am leaving you. You will never be free. Even as the spare. You will never be your own man. I wanted more for you, Kainan. I'm sorry."*

His mother had died then, and his father had told him woman weren't to be trusted.

"Never trust a woman, Kainan. Never."

Kainan rubbed his temple, where a pounding headache was brewing.

Reagan didn't hide your son from you. She thought you were dead.

That was little consolation to him at this moment.

"I have to go see him," Reagan whispered.

What is wrong with him? he asked as they waited for the elevator.

"Cardiomyopathy." There was a glitter of moisture in her eyes as she cleared her throat. "He was born that way. He was born with a failing heart."

Oh, God.

His heart sank. It was too much. He'd learned he was a father and that his son was dying all in the same day.

He was no fool. He knew the severity of cardiomyopathy in a child.

Run. Turn and leave.

But he couldn't do that either. He was not the cold, unfeeling man his father had been.

The elevator dinged as the doors opened, and they stood to the side as people got off, before getting in.

Kainan didn't say anything as they rode in silence. Everything was still sinking in.

He had a son.

And his son was the Crown Prince of Isla Hermosa.

He felt bad for inflicting that burden on him. And his son was ill. Cardiomyopathy in an infant was horrific, and Kainan could only assume that he was on the UNOS wait list for a new heart, because that was his only chance at life.

Reagan led him to the NICU, giving him a disposable gown and mask. He didn't really hear anything that anyone was saying as he was led into the room.

In the far corner stood an incubator that was covered with a blue blanket.

His heart was hammering.

He had never wanted a child. He didn't want to sentence any child to a life where he couldn't live, where he was under constant scrutiny. He'd never wanted a family. Relationships didn't work. His father and late brother had shown him that. He didn't want to trap a woman the way his mother had been trapped.

Reagan raised the blue blanket and Kainan gasped as he saw a baby with dark hair. A baby who looked like him and Reagan.

A baby hooked up to a machine.

His heart ached to hold him. It was instant love. It surprised him.

This child was the future of his country. But how could a voiceless king and a broken-hearted crown prince rule a country that was already broken and bleeding?

His heart shattered and guilt washed over him. Reagan had done this on her own. He hadn't been there. He'd failed her. He'd failed them both.

All Kainan could do was turn and leave.

His heart was breaking along with his son's.

CHAPTER TWO

THERE WAS SUCH a flurry of activity that Reagan forgot Kainan had followed her in. When Peter was stable again, and she'd spoken to the doctors, she turned to introduce Kainan to Peter's team. But Kainan had slipped out.

Where did he go?

That was her first thought, and then she was disappointed that he'd left. He hadn't even come over to the incubator. She'd lifted the blanket and he'd looked once, before she'd turned her attention to the nurse. Then she'd drowned out everything else. Her main focus had been her son.

With every day that she stepped through those doors, rinsing her hands, a deep, dark part of her told her over and over again that any future with her son became darker and darker.

The other part of her—the part that had sustained her since she'd found out she was carrying Kainan's child— told her not to give up hope.

To keep going.

To be strong.

To drown out everything else and pour all that she had into her son.

And that was what she did. Day after day since he was born.

She had no other choice.

So she hadn't noticed when Kainan had left because he'd never been there before. She was used to being on her own.

Reagan turned back to Sophie, Peter's nurse in the PCCU. "I'm only a text away."

Sophie nodded. "Sorry for dragging you away from your work. I know your first priority is to work with the new Hermosian doctor."

"My first priority is Peter. *Always*."

Reagan smiled and gave Sophie's arm a squeeze. She wanted to tell Sophie that Kainan was Peter's father, but she couldn't really form the words. Like Sophie, everyone in the hospital had been told that Peter's father was dead.

And that was not the case.

Kainan was alive. He'd have rights over Peter. She would no longer be in complete control. Kainan would have a say, and that made her nervous. Kainan might return to Isla Hermosa. What if he wanted to take Peter with him?

Don't think about it now.

She didn't want to make herself sick with worry.

"You okay, Reagan?" Sophie asked.

"Yes. I'm fine. I'll swing by later, Sophie, if I don't hear from you before then."

"Okay, Reagan."

Sophie turned back to the incubator and Reagan sent a mental kiss to her boy, since at the moment she couldn't actually kiss him. She'd only kissed him once, before he was intubated.

Her heart ached at the thought that maybe she'd never be able to really kiss him, see his eyes open and look at her in wonder.

Focus. Find Kainan.

Once she was out of the PCCU she peeled off the disposable gown and mask, tossing them in the nearest receptacle. She was contemplating how she was going to page Kainan

when she saw that he was pacing at the end of a dead-end hall near the PCCU.

All the annoyance and anger she'd briefly had for him walking out on their son melted away. She put herself in Kainan's shoes. He'd just learned he had a son and that same son was gravely ill.

She remembered how she'd felt when she'd found out that Peter was so ill. When they'd whisked him away from her. When she hadn't heard any wail when he was born and she'd been left alone.

Still, he had left.

"You left?" she said gently.

Kainan's dark eyes were a bit wild, and he ran his hand through his thick, dark curls. He nodded and signed, *Sorry.*

"It was a lot to take in. I'm sorry I didn't prepare you better."

Hard to prepare for that. Hard to prepare for learning about a son you never knew you had. He closed his eyes.

"Are you okay?"

I will be fine. The question is, are you? Are you okay?

The question took her aback, because she *wasn't* fine. How *could* she be fine? Her son was ill, Kainan was alive, and she needed sleep. No, she wasn't fine.

"I'm okay." *Liar.* "I should've told you sooner."

You didn't even know I was alive until earlier today.

"True."

They both smiled then, and a bit of the tension melted away.

What's wrong with him? Kainan signed finally. *You said before, but...*

"Cardiomyopathy." The word stuck in her throat. She rarely said it out loud, because if she said it out loud it became real. And she didn't want it to be real.

She was deluding herself. It was *very* real—and scary.

At least she didn't have to explain what cardiomyopathy was to Kainan. He understood the gravity of the situation.

Is he on the transplant list?

"Yes. We're waiting."

How terrible for you. How do you do it?

A spark of anger flared up in her. It was an innocent enough remark, but it had cut her to the quick.

How do you do it?

How could she *not*? There was really no choice in the matter. Just one foot in front of the other.

"There's no choice," she said wearily.

No. I suppose not. Kainan scrubbed a hand over his face. He didn't sign anything else.

Reagan was waiting for him to sign *I'm sorry I wasn't there for you.* Or *Let me help*, but he didn't offer any of these things.

Instead he signed, *Is he stable now? Can we get back to work?*

It was a slap to the face—but then again a lot of stuff had happened to Kainan in a very short span of time. Still, he hadn't even asked their son's name.

Don't take it personally. It's a lot to process.

She'd been disappointed before. Countless times, when her parents had been too busy for her.

"I need help, Mom. Please. I'm tired and Peter is sick..."

"It was your choice to have the baby, Reagan. I told you to get rid of it."

Her mother's callous words still haunted her.

What's wrong? Kainan signed.

"Nothing."

Your expression says otherwise.

"He's stable," she said, answering Kainan and yet ignoring his questioning.

Good.

There was a hint of relief on his face, but only a brief hint. Reagan hoped it was in regard to their son, but again she'd been disappointed before.

"Let's get back to Michael's office and we'll go through everything," she offered.

Kainan nodded and fell into step beside her. There was silence between them, which was good, because right now she was having a hard time to keeping it all together.

Kainan listened to Reagan go over protocols and some other things that he couldn't seem to focus on. All he could think about was taking care of Reagan and Peter. Doing his duty to them.

Even though it would kill him to trap them both in royal protocol.

If his brother had still been alive there wouldn't be this guilt about forcing Reagan into this life Kainan never wanted. He was the "spare," so he's pursued medicine in order to escape Isla Hermosa. He'd gone to medical school in Switzerland and worked there. He'd been happy.

He hadn't ever planned on returning to Isla Hermosa after his brother became King, but then war had broke out and his brother had been killed.

Kainan's freedom had evaporated then. It had been obliterated.

Inside he was screaming and raging, but if he tried to let it all out there would be no sound, and that made him rage all the more at his own stupidity. Yet he still wanted Reagan, and now his son. She'd been alone. She shouldn't have been alone.

I should never have let Reagan go.

If he'd have been with her… He didn't finish that thought, because it wouldn't have changed the outcome at all.

Their son would have been born with cardiomyopathy anyway. That was if he'd survived being born in a war-torn country. The thought made his stomach clench. He tried not to think about it.

"Alek, you have to surrender. It's done. Too many lives have been lost!"

"I will not surrender! Father never would've backed down."

"He would if innocent blood was being spilled. What you're doing is folly!"

"You just want the crown for yourself, Kainan. I know you."

"You don't know me. You're completely absurd. I never wanted this. Never."

"Then why are you here?"

"To save your life. You're my brother, Alek..."

"I'm your half brother."

"Half, then—but still I'm here to save you."

"Why?"

"Because Father loved you. I'm doing this for Father."

Alek had sneered and shaken his head.

"Always trying to please Father. But he's dead and I am King. I will always be King."

Kainan shook those thoughts away. They were treading on dangerous ground. They were threatening his control. He'd tried to save his half brother's life before Alek had been overthrown. He'd been trying to drag Alek out of the palace to safety just before the IED had gone off in the throne room.

Kainan had survived the blast, but had lost his voice for his brother…his King.

In the end his brother hadn't survived after the explosion. So it had all been for naught.

Which now made *him* King and his critically ill son his heir.

His son who was dying.

"Kainan, are you okay?"

He turned and saw Reagan was looking up from the piles of paperwork.

"Overwhelmed?" she asked gently.

He smiled. "Under…" Only he couldn't finish the word because his throat closed up, He felt humiliated by it.

Her expression softened. "Statement? Understatement?"

Then she smiled. That warm and friendly open smile which had won him over. She'd always tried to act so strong, but when he'd seen her smile at wounded soldiers, offering them compassion, he'd been won over time and time again. Reagan had reminded him of his mother—not in looks, but in strength and fortitude.

His mother Ariana had been compassionate, strong, independent. She'd loved his father, even though his father hadn't seemed able to love her back in the same way.

When his mother had died he'd been so lonely. There had been no love in the palace. His father had stood on formality. As had his elder half brother Alek. Only his mother had given him affection.

Reagan hadn't known he was a prince. She'd been so honest. So warm. He'd craved that warmth. Needed it like air. She'd treated him like everyone else on the unit and with her he'd been himself. There had been no formality. No protocol. It had been nice to be himself for a change, instead of Prince Kainan.

If there hadn't been a war… If he was still the spare…

He didn't want to drag her into the tumultuous situation that was still happening in his country. Still, she'd borne his child and she would be in danger if word got out. If he married her he could protect her. He had to do right by

her, even though that would mean her life wouldn't be her own anymore. Even though he would be condemning her.

Yes. That. He rubbed his temples, felt his throat tightening again.

"I'm sorry there's so much. I swear we're almost done with the orientation."

Can we take a break? he signed.

She cocked an eyebrow. "A break?"

Coffee?

He had to get out of this room. He felt as if he was suffocating again. Like when he'd woken up after the blast and not been able to breathe, with a tube in his throat, burns on his body.

"Okay…"

She seemed unsure. Confused.

He was confused too—about this whole situation.

When he'd felt this way in the past, surgery and practicing medicine—his work—had helped him get through so much. Saving lives made sense to him. It made sense of this mixed-up world.

And he couldn't do that anymore. He couldn't be a proper surgeon because he couldn't speak, and couldn't sign when his hands were busy. He couldn't lead his broken country for the same reason. He was trapped in limbo.

They walked in silence to the coffee cart.

Even though there were Hermosian guards all through this hospital, and he was being monitored by the Canadian government, no one besides those watching him for his own protection knew he was King.

He was free here.

Kainan could breathe—although he hated hiding here until the surgery was done. He wanted to be on the front lines, saving lives.

Even though he didn't have a voice.

He would soon enough.

That was if it was successful. Sometimes Kainan was positive that he wasn't going to survive the surgery.

Reagan ordered him a coffee, just as he liked it. Hot, dark and rich. No sweetener. She was so thoughtful and he was a monster.

You remembered, he signed.

"You drank it every day religiously, Kainan." She wrinkled her nose. "I can't stand black coffee. I don't know how you do that."

Kainan took a sip. It didn't taste as good as the Hermosian coffee he was used to, but it would do.

Hermosian coffee is much better. It is naturally sweet.

Reagan snorted. "I remember what it tasted like. Black coffee is black coffee."

No, it is not. This is nothing compared to what my country grows.

"That we can agree on. Hermosian coffee *is* better," Reagan said as she dumped sugar in hers.

He shuddered and she made a face at him, making him smile.

They wandered over to a table in the hospital atrium. Snow was falling gently. He was still not used to snow, but it had a nice calming effect.

"What do you think of snow?" she asked.

Cold. He took a sip of his coffee.

"Yes. It must be a culture shock for you."

A bit. He nervously began to flick at the plastic spout on his coffee cup. *Our son...*

"Peter," Reagan whispered softly, a bloom of pink on her high round cheeks.

An interesting name.

"I always liked it—and Peter Pan was the boy who never

grew up." Her voice trembled, but only for a moment. "It suits him."

Peter Pan lived forever by not growing up, yes?

"Well, I suppose so. He never aged as long as he stayed in Neverland."

There you go.

Peter. His son was named Peter. Though Kainan hadn't put Peter Pan and his son's name together at first. When she'd said his name was Peter all he'd been able to think of was St. Peter, the patron saint of fisherman.

Isla Hermosa had a thriving fishing industry, so the thought of St. Peter made him happy, but it frightened him all the same. Peter was a prince.

"You're frowning again," Reagan said.

He smiled. *I frown a lot lately.*

"Why?"

I've been through a lot. Then he sighed. *I suppose we both have.*

"Our time in Isla Hermosa feels like a lifetime ago." Pink tinged her cheeks again. "I am glad you're alive. I didn't tell you that."

Kainan's heart melted. *I'm glad to see you again too.*

"So, Michael told me you're awaiting surgery for your voice?"

He clenched his coffee cup. *Yes. I hope it works.*

Kainan didn't tell her the risks he was taking. The chances that he wouldn't live through it. She didn't need to know.

Reagan nodded. "I'm sure it will, although I'm sure scar tissue is an issue in your case?"

Kainan's stomach turned. It was indeed adhesions and scar tissue that were impeding his throat. Choking him from the inside out.

I don't want to discuss it.

"Fair enough," she said.

He felt bad, but he didn't want to think about the surgery. He needed his voice by the New Year, because on January first he was supposed to be on a plane to Isla Hermosa to attend his own coronation.

Without his voice he was trapped. He was blessed that he knew American Sign Language, but without his voice he couldn't properly rule and nor could he practice medicine. And without the surgery he might die.

So he was trapped. There was no choice over his surgery. It had to be done.

A ring tone sounded and Reagan glanced down at the phone in her hand, frowning.

Peter? Kainan signed, his heart sinking.

"No, incoming trauma. I'm needed," she said. "It must be a lot of trauma coming here or I wouldn't have been called in to help."

Go, Kainan signed. *I can find my way around.*

"Not everyone knows ASL."

Kainan pulled out his phone and typed in the word *Go*. His phone repeated it back. She smiled at him.

"I'll be back as soon as I can."

He nodded and watched Reagan disappear, a pang of jealousy coursing through him. How he wished he could be in the fray with her. Like old times.

He tossed the coffee cup in the garbage and wandered through the hospital.

He wanted to be free. And even though he wasn't in a palace, he was alone and shackled here.

You're not alone. You have Reagan.

Only he didn't have Reagan. She wasn't his. Not yet.

His stomach turned with guilt at the life he was going to impose on her.

And he hated himself for it.

CHAPTER THREE

THE INCOMING TRAUMA took longer than Reagan had expected. A multi-vehicle crash with multiple traumatic injuries kept her in surgery for hours, and by the time she got out it was evening. She was exhausted, and wondering what had happened to Kainan.

He wasn't answering his pager at all, and she couldn't help but wonder if he had gone home.

She couldn't really think about it right now. She hadn't heard from Sophie, Peter's nurse, since she'd gone to see Peter earlier. Which was good. Of course it was protocol not to disturb a surgeon when operating. Still, no one had come to find her afterward. So Peter had to be okay.

It had been the longest stretch in a while since she'd got an update and she was worried.

She'd worry about Kainan later. Right now she had to see Peter and make sure that he was all right.

As Reagan approached the pediatric critical care unit she met Sophie coming off her shift.

"Sorry, Sophie. I was in surgery. If you paged me and I didn't answer…"

"It's okay, Reagan. Nothing to mention. Peter is stable, but there *is* something you didn't tell me."

"Oh?"

"You didn't tell me that Peter's father is Dr. Laskaris."

Reagan's eyes widened. "I... What? How did you find that out?"

"He's in there now. At first I wasn't going to let him in to see Peter, per your restrictions, but he said he was his father."

"And you believed him?" Reagan's voice rose an octave.

Sophie blushed. "He offered to take a genetic test. It's still in process. We let him in the unit, but he's not in Peter's pod and he's not allowed to touch him. He's just sitting there, in the room you sleep in, watching him."

Reagan felt terrible for snapping at Sophie.

"I'm sorry, Sophie. You did absolutely the right thing. Dr. Laskaris *is* Peter's father."

"Well, I really grilled him. But you told me Peter's father died on Isla Hermosa and Dr. Laskaris is Hermosian. Also, you brought him in here earlier, even though he doesn't have privileges yet."

Reagan smiled. "I meant to tell you earlier, but I was in complete and utter shock. I thought he was dead."

Sophie grinned. "I'm sure you were. I know I would be too, in your situation."

Reagan laughed nervously. "You can let Dr. Laskaris in to see Peter whenever he wants."

"I'll make a note on his chart tomorrow."

"Thanks, Sophie. Have a great night."

Sophie waved goodbye as she walked away. And for one moment Reagan envied her because she had freedom.

When Reagan had found out she was pregnant she'd known her life would change, but she'd been expecting diapers, daycare and a messy apartment.

Not this.

Never this.

She buzzed in to the pediatric critical care unit after putting on the gown and gloves that were mandatory. The

new shift on the unit had started, and she greeted the people she knew all too well.

Kainan was standing in the little room next to Peter's, watching their son intently through the glass partition. Reagan couldn't read his expression but it didn't matter right now. All that mattered was that Kainan was there.

He was with Peter.

Her father had never been there for her. He'd barely acknowledged her. So to see Kainan with Peter softened her heart.

Maybe he did care about Peter. Maybe she had it all wrong.

"I'm sorry I'm so late," she said, coming up beside him. "I tried paging you, but you didn't answer."

My phone died, he signed. He held it up. *Forgot the charger. It's back at my place.*

"Oh." She cleared her throat. "I'm glad you're here."

He nodded and smiled at her, those dark eyes twinkling. *Me too.*

Her heart skipped a beat. "I told Sophie you're his father. A genetic test isn't needed."

It's okay. Actually, I don't mind. I would like it done all the same.

Heat bloomed in her cheeks. "Of course. You need verification. Facts. You are a doctor."

What are you talking about? He looked confused.

"You'll need scientific proof that he's your son."

He frowned. Looked concerned. *No, not at all.*

"Really?" she asked in disbelief.

Really. He turned and looked back at Peter. *In him I see me.*

Her heart skipped another beat, because she'd had that thought so many times when she'd looked at Peter.

She saw Kainan.

"Then why did you agree to the test? Why do you want it?"

Blood types. I'm curious about whether he's a universal donor, like me. It runs in my family.

"He does have a universal blood type."

Kainan smiled. *Good.*

"The cardiomyopathy is genetic, but it doesn't run on my side."

I don't have it either.

"You're sure?"

The royal family of Isla Hermosa has been recorded for a long time, he signed. Then he tensed.

"Uh…what does the royal family of Isla Hermosa have to do with anything?" she asked, confused.

Nothing. I was thinking of something else.

"Okay." Reagan couldn't help but wonder why he was getting so defensive about this. "Still, it's not on my side."

It's not on mine either, he signed. *Stop implying it's my fault.*

"I'm not."

Fine. Good, Kainan signed sharply.

Something was bothering him. "Sorry."

No, I am sorry. Family is a touchy subject for me. The war was hard for so many.

"Yes," she said sadly. "I remember that."

Peter is all I have left.

That made her pause. It made her nervous, thinking he'd take Peter away.

Kainan had rights, but she couldn't lose Peter.

Tears were threatening to escape, and she didn't want to cry in front of Kainan or in front of Peter—even though Peter wouldn't even know it if she did.

In the pediatric critical care unit she had to be strong. She was a warrior. A fighter for her son. There couldn't

be an inch of give. And she didn't want to appear weak in front of Kainan or anyone.

If she did her weakness might be used against her.

Great. Now I'm being paranoid and sounding like my mother.

She had to get a grip. She was stressed, tired and stressed—in that order.

Kainan stepped closer, and before she could stop him he drew her into his arms. Her body reacted instantly to his touch. She closed her eyes, drinking in his scent, her body trembling because she'd never thought she'd experience this again.

She'd thought he was dead.

He was supposed to be dead.

And it had been so long since someone had held her. Her parents never openly showed affection and neither did she. Being in Kainan's arms brought her carefully constructed walls down a little. It was overwhelming to be held by him. Actually to be comforted. Just like it had been the night Peter had been conceived.

"Come," he said, his voice rasping, and she knew that it was a strain for him to speak. But with her head buried in his neck as she drank in the sensation of being held she couldn't see him when he signed anyway.

Reagan let Kainan lead her out of the pediatric critical care unit.

She was in a daze.

She was exhausted.

Kainan took the gown off her and disposed of it. Then he removed the gown he was wearing.

Reagan shook herself out of the daze she was in. "Peter. I can't leave him."

You can leave him for one night.

"He has no one else."

There's a team of medical professionals in there to take care of him, Reagan. You need sleep and a decent meal.

"I have to stay here," she said firmly.

Reagan, he's stable. If he's not they will page one of us. Come back to my place and I'll get my charger. There you can shower and have a meal. Let's get your things from your locker.

A hot shower and food that wasn't from the cafeteria sounded heavenly, but she was terrified of leaving the hospital.

The nurses and doctors on the pediatric critical care unit had tried to get her to take a night off every once in a while, but she couldn't do it.

"I can't," she whispered.

My place is right next door.

She cocked an eyebrow. "You're staying at the Royal York?"

He nodded. *Yes.*

"That's pricey."

He shrugged. *I have money, and none of that matters right now. Come, let me take care of you. You shall sleep and I will be on call for Peter tonight. Let me take some of the burden off your shoulders.*

"I would like that…" She cleared her throat as emotion threatened to overtake her, but she controlled it.

Those dark eyes softened as he stepped forward and cupped her face briefly, and the simple touch eased her.

No feeling guilty. To take care of Peter you have to take care of yourself. Let's go.

She nodded and he put his hand on the small of her back, as he'd done when they had gone to his tent in Isla Hermosa. It was nice.

After they'd gathered the small suitcase that she always kept at the hospital and put on their winter coats—because

it was December, and the wind chill off the lake was brutal—they walked out of the hospital together and dashed across York Street. It was quiet, as there were no commuters out and about. However, there were a few hockey fans coming and going.

Kainan raised an eyebrow in question at the hockey-goers, with their blue-painted faces and shouting.

"Leafs. It's hockey."

He nodded, but didn't sign anything, just squeezed her hand as they scurried up Front Street to the entrance of the Royal York hotel.

Through the revolving door Reagan stepped—into another world. She had only been in the Royal York once, and knew it was opulent with its art deco interiors from a golden age of Toronto.

"This way," he whispered, and pulled out a gold card, which meant that Kainan had a suite.

He took her to the private elevator that was used by the elite guests at the Royal York.

He swiped his card and the elevator doors opened. They got on and took the elevator to the top floor. Then he led her down a hallway to the very end, and swiped the card to open the door to a luxurious suite.

She dropped her bag and stared at the main room with its plush furnishings, and then wandered in to see a king-size bed in another room, a kitchenette. As she approached the window she could see that there was a view of the waterfront over Union Station.

"Wow…" she whispered. "I've never been in one of these rooms before."

He smiled and jammed his hands in his pockets. *Food first, shower or nap?*

"Shower first, if I can. Then food and maybe a nap. But

I'm not entirely sure that I'm going to stay here, Kainan. I might have to sneak out and head back to the hospital."

He chuckled and then plugged his phone into the charger on the desk. *You go have a shower and I will order you some food.*

"You don't know what I like," she teased.

I think I remember bits and pieces. Go shower, and then after you eat we'll discuss whether you or I should go back.

"Deal."

She found the bathroom and flicked on the light. There was a plush white robe and thick, soft towels. Much better than the staff change room. She pulled out her toiletries bag, digging for soap and shampoo.

It didn't take her long to find everything she needed and soon she was turning on the shower. It was nice to have this moment to herself. And she didn't feel rushed here, like she did in the hospital staff room.

This was one of the first times she'd been out of the hospital in months. Paying her rent and utilities was done with a simple app on her phone or over the internet. She had no pets. No plants. Her life was in the hospital.

As she stepped under the shower and let the water wash away her stress she realized that in the hospital she carried the weight of the world on her shoulders. She carried the weight of her son and the life that he might not get a chance to experience. It was only in the safety of the rushing water washing over her that she let it go for the first time in a long while.

She turned off the shower and grabbed a towel to dry her hair and face.

There was a knock on the door. She wrapped herself in a robe and opened the door. Kainan was standing there.

Are you okay?

"I'm fine."

He pursed his lips together. *You were in there a long time. I was worried you'd fallen asleep in there.*

Warmth flooded in her cheeks. "How long have I been in here?"

An hour. He grinned.

"An hour?" She looked down at her hands, which were wrinkled like prunes from so much water. She must have zoned out.

Come, there's food. You can stay in the robe.

She nodded and followed him out of the en-suite bathroom into the living room area, where there were salads, cheese, fruit and a big bowl of pasta. Her favorite kind too. Fettuccine Alfredo.

He'd remembered.

"Don't think me ungrateful, but how did you order all this?"

Through the computer. The hotel and I have an understanding.

"It smells delicious. I can't remember the last time I had real food instead of cafeteria food."

Then let's eat, instead of standing around here and talking about it.

He motioned for her to sit on the couch and remained standing until she sat.

Always the gentleman.

Even in a war zone. It had always been ladies first. And once, when a particularly crass soldier had got a little handsy with a nurse, Kainan had been there to jump into the fray and put that soldier in his place.

Of course since it hadn't been a Hermosian soldier there had been some international logistics to work out, and eventually both commanding officers had had Kainan and the other soldier duke it out in a boxing ring in the middle of the mobile army hospital.

You're smiling, Kainan signed. *What are you smiling about?*

"I was thinking about that time you boxed that soldier. Totally laid him flat on his back even though he was twice your size."

He made a funny face. *He wasn't twice my size.*

"The man was trained in special ops and he was broad."

Broad is one thing, but "broad" is often confused with muscle and mental agility.

Kainan winked and Reagan chuckled.

What made you think of that? he signed.

"I was just thinking about how you're very much a gentleman."

He raised an eyebrow. *Boxing made you think of me as a gentleman?*

"Isn't boxing the sport of kings?"

No, that's horse racing. There was a twinkle in his eyes. *I believe that boxing is the sport of manly self-defense. I believe many fine gentlemen were pugilists a long time ago.*

"Ah, see—there you go. It *is* a gentlemanly sort of sport."

Not anymore. Women box.

"Right, but still…"

Fine, I concede. So, you were thinking of me boxing and you came to the conclusion I was a gentleman?

"No, I was thinking about how you stood until I sat down, and that led me to remember your boxing."

A smile quirked his finely shaped mouth, making her recall for a brief moment the way he kissed.

Now you are blushing.

Reagan saw him sign it, but she remembered the sound of his voice and the way he would softly exhale on her neck. It had been a long time since she'd desired anyone, because the last person she'd felt that rush for was Kainan. Since Peter had been born she hadn't had any feelings like that. She had been just numb and existing.

She felt guilty for allowing those feelings to creep back in. So she picked up the bowl of pasta. "I'm glad you remembered my favorite."

Kainan sat back. The spell that had been woven over them was broken and that was a good thing. Reagan didn't have time to start anything up, even if Kainan *was* the father of her baby. Her life revolved around her son and making sure that he survived long enough to have experiences like this.

She had to protect Peter from hurt because there was always an expiration date. Kainan would go back to Isla Hermosa. Kainan would probably leave them again. Her heart could take it—Peter's couldn't.

The conversation had taken an interesting turn before they'd started eating, and Kainan was trying to remain a gentleman but it was so hard when it came to Reagan. He'd forgotten how much he liked being with her. She brought out a side in him he'd thought he'd buried long ago.

He'd forgotten about laying that officer out in the boxing ring after he'd laid into him publicly outside of the ring when he'd started bothering that Canadian nurse.

Men like that annoyed him.

You could still be a strong, alpha male and respect women.

If only his brother had learned that.

Or his father.

"Mama, why are you crying?"

His mother had wiped away her tears with the back of her hand and then wrapped him up in her arms, holding him.

"Are you sad, Mama?"

"Never, Kainan. Never when you're here."

Kainan had glanced over her shoulder to his mother's bed and seen a newspaper. There had been a picture of

his father, with his arm around a woman who was not his mother.

His father had been a beloved king, but his affairs had been notorious.

Kainan had vowed he'd never be like that. Even if he became King he would never be like that. Of course he'd never thought that he *would* be King. That was something he'd never wanted.

Never.

All he'd wanted to be was a surgeon.

Being King would be a huge responsibility. His life would not be his own anymore. His life would belong to his kingdom and the world. There would be no more privacy. It would be a life of sacrifice and stress.

Could he really do that to Reagan? To Peter?

There was no choice. He had to do what was right and make Peter legitimate.

He glanced up after they'd finished eating and saw that Reagan had fallen asleep. She was curled up on the couch, her head resting on the overstuffed armrest.

She looked so peaceful.

He hated dragging her into this, but it was the perfect solution. He would marry her and they would be a family. Then they would return to Isla Hermosa, and maybe he would be able to heal what was broken in his country.

There was a knock at the door. He got up and peeked through the peephole to see his head of security, Andreas, in the hallway.

Kainan opened it.

"I'm sorry for intruding, Your Majesty."

Kainan held his fingers to his lips to silence his security guard and motioned behind him.

Andreas peeked over his shoulder and nodded. "I'm sorry…"

"What's wrong?" Kainan asked hoarsely, rubbing his throat.

"Word has gotten out that the missing Hermosian King is hiding somewhere in Toronto."

Blast. "How?"

"The papers here are running it. Though your picture is not in the papers. Just the story. Someone has leaked it."

Kainan's stomach clenched, and all he could see was his father's face instead of his as he thought of that newspaper on his mother's bed, stained with tears.

Dammit.

Kainan wished that he could let out a few more strings of expletives, but that would wake Reagan, so perhaps it was best that he currently didn't have the ability to do that.

Please keep me informed, Andreas, he signed. *Let me know if the press come anywhere near the hotel or the hospital.*

"We've been keeping a low profile, Your Majesty. The only people on this floor are your security detail and you. Much to our chagrin, we're letting you go to the hospital alone and trying not to be too obvious."

Kainan smiled briefly. *I know that it's hard for you, but it's for the best.*

"What's for the best is for you to remain hidden and safe until you can return to Isla Hermosa."

I am safe.

"Your son is unprotected at the hospital," Andreas said.

A cold rush of dread crept down Kainan's spine. *How do you know about him?*

"I *am* head of security, Your Majesty."

We're done talking about this, Andreas. Keep me posted about the leak.

Andreas pursed his lips together and bowed. "Yes, Your Majesty."

Kainan shut the door and scrubbed a hand over his face.

The idea that news about him was getting too close for comfort made him think of his helpless son, clinging to life in a hospital bed. He didn't want the press to find out about Peter. He had to protect him.

Kainan flung open the door and ran after Andreas.

Andreas turned around, confused. "Your Majesty?"

Don't be obvious about it, but protect my son, he signed. *I don't want people coming to the hospital. He needs to protected at all costs.*

Andreas smiled. "Of course, Your Majesty."

Work your magic with administration, but please just keep Peter safe.

"I will, Your Majesty. Right away."

Kainan nodded and turned back to his room. He shut the door gently, so as not to wake Reagan. She was still sound asleep, curled up on the couch.

He approached her and gently scooped her into his arms. She didn't even wake, and he couldn't blame her for being so exhausted. He felt guilty for not being there when Peter was born. For not knowing and being able to help her.

Kainan carried her to bed and set her down, covering her up. She sighed, but didn't wake. So he stood over her, staring at her face and fighting the urge to touch her, to run his fingers over that graceful neck and through her soft, dark silken hair.

To cup her face and kiss her.

Yet, as much as he cared for her, in this moment his duty was clear.

He cared for her and Peter too much, and in caring for them he would have to burden Reagan. Even as vulnerable as she was, there was no choice.

He needed to make Reagan his Queen.

CHAPTER FOUR

COMFORTABLE. THAT WAS her first thought. But she shouldn't be this comfortable.

Reagan woke with a start and couldn't figure out where she was at first. She was definitely not sleeping on the cot in the pediatric critical care unit, because it was too quiet in here and the bed was too soft.

She sat up and then remembered that she was in Kainan's hotel room at the Royal York.

She heard a sigh and looked over to see that Kainan was sleeping next to her, still in his street clothes. He wore a dress shirt, but the tie that he'd been wearing was gone, and the shirt was unbuttoned. He was lying on top of the covers, his ankles crossed and his hands across his chest.

He looked so peaceful. She wondered how long she'd been sleeping, and when she glanced at the clock on the bedside she saw that it was nine in the morning.

Oh, my God. Peter!

She'd slept through the night. Away from Peter and the pediatric critical care unit.

How could she have been so foolish? What if something had happened to him?

She got out of bed quietly, so as not to wake Kainan. She found her things and quickly dressed, brushing her hair,

which had dried naturally and now had a horrible kink in it. That was solved by tying it up in a bun.

She cursed under her breath. Angry at herself for leaving Peter's side. She had been weak when Kainan had convinced her to leave the hospital. She had to be stronger. She couldn't let Kainan sway her so easily.

Who are you kidding?

Even after all this time Kainan was the only one who got through her barriers, and she was angry at herself for letting him through.

Once she was dressed she snuck out of the hotel room, quietly shutting the door behind her. When she turned around, though, she jumped back in surprise to see several men in dark clothes loitering about the hallway.

They'd been talking, but stopped when she shut the door. They watched her with a sense of reverence, almost awe. Whatever it was, it was super-creepy.

"I'm sorry, miss," one man said, stepping forward.

He had a slight accent similar to Kainan's, and she wondered if they were Hermosian refugees as well.

"Did we wake you? These walls are very thin."

"No, it's okay."

"We're sorry if we startled you. Congregating in the hall before we all head to a…a workshop is not proper."

"It's okay," she repeated.

The man nodded and the other men smiled, stepping back as she scurried down the hallway toward the elevator. She pressed the button and the elevator appeared instantly.

If she didn't know better then she would almost swear those men were security guards.

That's ridiculous. Who are they guarding?

She shook that thought away as she pulled on her winter jacket in the elevator. She pushed through the crowds of people in the lobby of the hotel and then went downstairs

to the concourse level and took the Avenue from the hotel to the hospital.

That way she wouldn't have to go out in the cold.

Reagan weaved her way in and out of the morning rush of commuters who were walking the concourse in underground Toronto from Union Station to all the tall office buildings that connected to the PATH system. When the trains came in the concourse level was flooded with people.

It was a great system, but so crowded during certain times of the day. Like now. But Reagan was a pro at fighting her way through crowds.

At the hospital level, she punched in her access code and took the elevator up to where the staff change room was located. She stashed her coat and the bag of clothes and changed into a fresh pair of scrubs and a lab jacket.

First she would check on Peter, and then she would do her rounds.

You're not doing rounds anymore, remember? You're supposed to be working with Kainan and you left him in the hotel.

Reagan groaned inwardly.

Well, she'd just stay with Peter until Kainan came to start his shift at ten. That was when they would head down and work with the medical students who were coming in.

When she got to the pediatric critical care unit the morning shift had started and Sophie was back at the PCCU's desk.

"I'm so sorry, Sophie—" Reagan started.

Sophie looked confused. "For what?"

"I fell asleep…at my apartment."

It was a lie, but she didn't want to divulge the fact that

she'd spent the night with Kainan, even though Sophie knew that Kainan was Peter's father.

"I went there to take care of some business and just crashed."

"Don't worry about it, Reagan. Nothing happened. Peter's stable." Sophie opened up his file on the computer. "I don't see any notes that you were paged."

"I wasn't paged." Reagan bit her lip and sighed. "Actually, I didn't even check to see if I *was* paged. I just woke up and raced over here. I was feeling incredibly guilty for not being here."

Sophie smiled and gave her shoulder a sympathetic squeeze. "You have the right to sleep. We all know you're always here and always reachable. Hovering won't heal him."

She knew that, but she didn't want Peter to be alone. Like she had been when she was seven and had had her tonsils out. She'd been alone. Her parents had never come to visit her.

They'd been working.

She'd got a lot of pity then from the nurses.

Even though Peter was too young even to know she was there, she didn't want him to be alone as she had been.

"I have to be here," Reagan said firmly.

It was her duty to be here for Peter. Her parents might be standoffish, but Reagan had sworn she'd never be like that. She *had* to be there, even if she could use a break, but thoughts still ate away at her. Made her feel like a terrible mother.

"I know. I've been a pediatric nurse for a while now, and I know that you need to be here. Peter knows that you're here, but you need to take care of yourself too. When he gets his new heart and gets out of here you're going to

have to contend with a baby, and then a toddler. He's not going to know that he has to take it easy, and you'll need your strength for that phase. Usually my sickest little ones are the ones who are the most mischievous when they get out of here."

Reagan laughed and tried to picture it, though it was hard to see because of her uncertainty. "I'm looking forward to that."

"It's not easy to see it, but it *will* happen. I have faith that it will."

Sophie picked up her charts and started to do her rounds of the patients she was in charge of. Reagan let out an exhausted sigh and headed over to Peter's incubator.

She lifted the blanket that covered him and a smile crept across her face. There was a brief sense of relief to see him stable.

But she didn't know what to do.

Not that she could do much when he was at this critical point in his life.

He was stable. Sophie wasn't hovering currently. Sophie was doing her rounds and Peter was just lying there. All she wanted to do was hold him, but she didn't want to stress him by picking him up.

So she just stood there, watching him, feeling absolutely useless and helpless at the same time. She'd felt this way before, but usually when he was ill and she wasn't sure he was going to make it, when she didn't have time to ponder these thoughts. To let them really sink in.

Now she did, and Reagan didn't like it very much. But she couldn't think that way or she'd go mad.

There was a tap on her shoulder and it was Kainan.

You left, he signed.

"I'm sorry. I didn't realize that I had…" she lowered her

voice to a whisper, heat blooming in her cheeks "…spent the night."

Why are you whispering? Everyone knows that we've once spent the night together before. The evidence is right in front of us.

There was a mischievous twinkle in his eye and he grinned.

Reagan chuckled. "Sorry."

Don't apologize. You didn't leave a note or anything and I was worried.

"You were worried?" she asked, shocked.

Of course. I went to sleep with you there beside me and I woke up and you were gone.

"Sorry, I should've left a note."

Yes, he signed gently, and then his gaze drifted down to Peter and she could see hesitation in his eyes.

It stung.

She'd thought he cared for Peter. His hesitation now worried her. She didn't want Peter to be rejected by his father the way she'd been rejected by hers. That rejection had caused loathing in her mother, and Reagan knew her mother blamed her for her husband's distance.

"How did you know where I was?"

Andreas told me.

Then he frowned and pursed his lips together, as if he hadn't meant to sign that. As if it were a slip-up.

"Who is Andreas?" Reagan asked, confused.

The man in the next suite. He saw you this morning when you snuck out.

"Oh." For some reason she didn't quite believe Kainan. There was something he wasn't saying.

Once he said you'd snuck out I put two and two together and knew where you'd be.

"Of course." She sighed.

Kainan frowned. *What's wrong?*

"Nothing." She couldn't look at him right now. He wasn't telling her the truth and she was having a hard time trusting him. "What time is it?"

Almost ten. Are you ready to meet the medical students?

"No, but I suppose we must. We put them off yesterday when I was called into surgery." She smiled the fake smile she'd mastered. "Are you ready?"

Of course. He grinned.

There was a confident air about him. One she envied.

"Well, let's go, then."

Reagan waved at Sophie on her way out and Sophie nodded in response. Reagan would be in the hospital. There was no way she was going to leave Peter for another night.

"So this Andreas…" she started.

What about him? Kainan asked.

"He sounded Hermosian to me."

Kainan frowned. *What makes you say that?*

"I spent over a year in Isla Hermosa. He reminded me of someone, but I can't remember…"

Déjà vu, that's all. It's being around me. You think anyone with that type of accent is Hermosian, he signed, cutting her off.

He was annoyed.

"Why are you getting so angry?"

I'm not angry.

"You're being very touchy about it."

I don't know where Andreas is from. He arrived at the hotel with some coworkers around the same time I did and we've met in the hall a few times. Can we just drop it?

"Sure."

And she should. She didn't want to get involved with him. Peter was her priority. The only problem with that was that Kainan was Peter's father.

She couldn't lock Kainan out. For the sake of Peter she had to care, had to be involved and let Kainan in.

Plus you cared for him once.

Yes, she had, but that felt like a lifetime ago. They'd both been very different people back then.

"Good." He said the word out loud and then cleared his throat, interrupting her thoughts.

It was apparent that he was still annoyed about the course their conversation had taken, and for some reason Reagan couldn't help but wonder if he was hiding something about Andreas. And, if he was, why?

It's not your concern.

But Reagan knew when people were lying, and she had the gut feeling that Kainan was lying to her.

The question was why.

Who cares?

And that thought made her force those doubts from her mind. She really didn't have time for this. What Kainan did was his own business. She didn't have time to form a relationship with Kainan outside the bond of their son and their professional relationship. All she had time for was her son.

That was all that mattered.

Kainan opened the door to the lecture hall that was inside the hospital and gestured for her to take the lead.

Right now she had to focus on translating the American Sign Language for the medical students in this room. This was her new assignment. She was here to work with Kainan and that was it. Her feelings with respect to Kainan couldn't be allowed to come into play.

She had to keep reminding herself of that fact.

When Kainan had been able to speak, and before civil war had torn his country to shreds, he'd been at the forefront

of surgery. He'd been on a fast track to win a Nobel Prize in medicine for his surgical advances.

Of course then his father had died and his brother had taken over. He hadn't even lasted a year and then everything had gone to heck.

One of the perks of working here in this hospital in Toronto, while waiting for surgery to correct his voice, was being able to continue with his medical research. He was looking forward to that.

That was, of course, if he could train his medical students in triage in time to work on his research. It had been a long time since he'd taught. And he wasn't sure he had the patience for it.

Of course with Reagan by his side it would be a snap. Not only because she would be able to help him communicate with these eager medical students, but because when they had worked together in the field, in the mobile military hospital, everything had just seemed to flow.

And as he worked with her now, guiding his students through triage in a mock active war zone, he was happy to be with her again.

He'd forgotten how well they worked together. Two surgeons from two different countries, different backgrounds, but they came together seamlessly to create perfection.

Just like Peter.

His heart swelled with pride for a brief moment as he thought of the beautiful boy who was clinging to life in the pediatric critical care unit.

Everything was right when he was with Reagan. It thrilled him, but terrified him just the same.

If his brother were still King, then he would be jumping into the fray with her, begging her to stay with him. But now that *he* was King he didn't have his own life, and he hated the thought of ruining her life too. As much as

he loved his country, he hated being King. He hated the shackles, the restrictions it entailed.

It was tearing him up inside. Just as it had destroyed his mother. And although Reagan was strong, she was vulnerable, and he didn't want to hurt her or overtax her.

"Mother, why are you so sad?" he'd asked once, when his mother had barely looked at him.

She'd put her arm around his shoulders as she'd sighed, looking out at the sea.

"I want to be free, Kainan."

"You are free. You are the Queen."

"I know."

Kainan turned his focus back on the students. This was his task now. He couldn't let memories distract him.

"Good," he said, to a student who was performing a very complicated stitch with makeshift tools.

"Thank you, Dr. Laskaris." The student was beaming.

Kainan nodded and moved on.

As he walked the room, watching Reagan showing a couple of medical students a technique for draping with plastic, he saw Andreas out of the corner of his eye, standing outside the window of the lecture hall where they were with the medical students.

Kainan's stomach dropped to the soles of his feet.

There was a determined look about Andreas. Kainan had known Andreas for some time, and he knew when his head of security was stressed. And Andreas was stressed now.

Kainan darted out of the room. Reagan called after him, but he ignored her as he caught up to Andreas.

"The press know," Andreas said, not mincing his words. "I do not know who leaked it, Your Majesty. The press are outside the hotel and in the avenue below us…"

Are they here in the hospital?

Andreas pursed his lips together and nodded.

Dammit.

Kainan raked his hand through his hair. He was enraged that he'd been discovered, and if he found out who had sold him out he was going to ignore his Hippocratic Oath and do horrible things to that individual.

"Kainan, what's…?" Reagan trailed off as she looked at Andreas closely, and she wasn't just recognizing him from this morning either.

Kainan's heart skipped a beat, because Andreas had been a soldier as well as a bodyguard during the Hermosian civil war. Andreas had been injured and Reagan had been the one to aid him.

And, by the way Reagan looked at Andreas now, she was picturing him with his head shaved, instead of with the long dark hair that Andreas now sported.

"I know you," she whispered.

"Of course—we met this morning," Andreas said, trying to bluff it out.

Reagan shook her head. "No, you were a soldier. I treated you. I remember you with shorter hair and you…you are Hermosian."

Andreas looked worried and sent Kainan a look, which Reagan caught.

"What's going on?" she asked, her voice rising. "And don't get annoyed with me, Kainan. I *know* something is going on. There's something you're not telling me."

Let me explain, Reagan, Kainan signed, and scrubbed his hand over his face.

He saw that Michael McNeil, the Chief of Surgery, was rushing toward them.

"Dr. Laskaris—a word!"

Reagan frowned. "Michael? Are you okay?"

"No," Michael said hurriedly, and then he crossed his

arms, looking directly at Kainan. "I have press surrounding my hospital."

"Press?" Reagan asked.

"Yes, and they're blocking the ambulance bay. I have all my security guards trying to keep them out, but how do you keep people out of a hospital?" Michael looked annoyed. "Dr. Laskaris, they're looking for *you*!"

Kainan's stomach knotted. He was angry, but he felt defeated, because there was no sense in hiding now.

He'd been found. Even though he'd been trying to keep a low profile until after his surgery, when he hoped he'd have a voice again.

Reagan looked confused. "Kainan, what's going on?"

Andreas cleared his throat and Michael stood behind Reagan, his hands on his hips, looking just as confused as she was.

Kainan took a deep breath and mustered all his strength to whisper breathlessly, "I am the lost King of Isla Hermosa."

CHAPTER FIVE

"You're...what?" Reagan asked, not sure that she'd heard Kainan correctly. "You're a king? The Hermosian King? I thought he died?"

Kainan sighed and turned to look away.

"Dr. Laskaris?" Michael asked.

Andreas stepped forward. "He became King when his brother King Aleksander the Seventh died after an explosion in the palace. As you're all aware, King Aleksander's rule was tenuous, at best..."

Kainan spun back round, and there was a fire in his dark eyes that scared her.

I am King. My brother is dead and I am the missing King, he signed.

Reagan frowned. "The name Laskaris isn't associated with the Hermosian crown, and you told me when we first met that your family was from Greece."

Kainan sighed. *My mother was born in Greece. Isla Hermosa was founded by the Spanish and the Greeks. The name Laskaris is tied to the Hermosian crown, but it is kept for the "spares." Like me. I didn't want to change it when I became King. I am still Dr. Laskaris.*

There was a sadness to his expression which softened her a bit. It was apparent that he wasn't happy with his new position in his country.

"You *were* injured in an IED blast?" Reagan asked. "At the front?"

Yes. I was injured trying to save my brother, but that was for nothing. He died after the explosion. I am the last of my line, so the Canadian government thought it prudent to take me away from my country. They brought me here, where I recuperated, and now I wait for surgery. I cannot sit idly by and do nothing. But it is not safe for me to go back yet.

Reagan nodded, but it was hard to take it all in.

Why hadn't he told her that he was a prince when they were working together? She'd thought he was just a surgeon.

But had they ever really talked about personal stuff?

No, they hadn't. Not ever.

It explained why Kainan had that air of command about him. Why other people in the Hermosian Army and the wounded civilians had been in such awe of him. He'd been a prince and she'd been too blind or naive to see it.

Another scary thought sank into her mind. If Kainan was King that meant Peter was a prince.

Peter might not be able to stay with her if it came to a custody fight. Even at his tender age Peter had a duty to the country of his father's birth. He belonged to Isla Hermosa.

Not to her.

As if sensing her apprehension, Kainan signed, *This changes nothing. Peter is your son. I will not take him from you.*

She wanted to believe him, but she was having a hard time processing all this.

"I'm surprised that your brother allowed you to serve as a doctor in a field hospital," she said, because she didn't know what else to say. She didn't know of many surgeon kings.

My late brother didn't care much for me. I was only the

spare. Kainan turned to Andreas. *Please help Dr. McNeil deal with this security situation.*

Andreas bowed deeply. "Yes, Your Majesty."

Michael and Andreas walked away. Kainan turned to her, pain etched across his face.

I am sorry, Reagan. I could tell no one. Not until I'd had the surgery. Canada needs to protect me until my coronation.

"When is that? When is your coronation?"

New Year's Day.

"And your surgery?"

The twenty-sixth of this month. It's risky.

"How risky?"

With the severe amount of scar tissue...

He frowned and her heart sank. She knew.

"It's bad, then?"

Yes.

She nodded, but still the reality of it all was not sinking in. "That day at the palace…"

I tried to save Alek, but Alek wouldn't leave. The fool thought I wanted to be King.

"Why would he think that?" she asked.

My brother was a fool. The IED went off as I was trying to get him out of the palace and he didn't survive his injuries. So here I stand. King of Isla Hermosa. A voiceless king.

"I don't know what…" She trailed off as she thought about Peter upstairs. The sense of dread was threatening to drown her. The thought of the press pushing their way into Peter's room was too horrible to think about. "Do the press know about Peter?"

Kainan shook his head. *No, they do not. They do not know about you or Peter, and I plan to keep it that way to protect you both.*

She nodded, but she wasn't sure that he would be able to. She wasn't sure about anything, and she didn't even really know him anymore.

Reagan had thought that Kainan was just a simple Hermosian surgeon. Nobody famous, just a person who tried to save lives, like her. But instead he'd been living this whole double life when they were on the island.

He was a king. Kainan might have called himself the "spare," but he was still royalty. It was a little too much to take in at the moment.

No wonder there was so much security surrounding Kainan at the Royal York. No wonder the Canadian government had insisted that Kainan come here, Dr. Shaw was one of the best otolaryngologists in the country. It also explained why he was being put up in such an opulent hotel.

Kainan was being protected.

"Dr. Laskaris, Dr. Cote…what should we do now?" asked a medical student.

Reagan and Kainan both spun round to see a few of the medical students in the doorway. A couple of them were staring at Kainan with wide-eyed awe.

These students must have heard about the civil war that had ripped the island nation of Isla Hermosa apart. How the late King Aleksander had been a tyrant and driven the country's resources into the ground. As well as cutting off a lot of trade and manufacturing, King Alek had been an ill-informed, misguided playboy who had cost a lot of lives.

And they probably all knew about the missing King too.

The missing King who was standing in front of her. Who was the father of her baby.

At least the press doesn't know about Peter, and we have to keep it that way.

"Why don't you head back to the university? Class

is dismissed for today," Reagan said, making an executive decision.

The students turned back into the room to gather up their stuff and Reagan started to walk away, because she needed to let all this sink in.

Kainan caught up with her as she headed down a quiet hallway that was rarely used. The beds on that wing were closed, and she needed the peace of the closed ward to regain her composure. But she had a feeling that was not going to happen, because Kainan had followed her and insisted on signing.

I meant what I said. This changes nothing, Reagan. My being King changes nothing about this situation. We're in Canada. We're not in Isla Hermosa.

She wanted to believe him, but she couldn't.

It's Kainan, a little voice said, but that didn't matter anymore. She didn't know him. Not really. The man she'd thought she knew didn't really exist. He was a stranger.

Nothing changes, he reiterated.

"Oh, really?"

"I am still me," he whispered breathlessly.

"I don't know who that is." She stopped to face him. "I never really knew you. We spent all that time together, working side by side, but we were strangers."

Kainan scrubbed a hand over his face. *I couldn't tell you I was spare to the heir. Do you know how many women found out who I was and immediately changed. They just wanted my wealth. They wanted status. With you I could just be me.*

"You *knew* I wasn't like that."

In the end, yes, I did. But you can understand my hesitation. At the beginning I knew nothing about you either.

Reagan thought about this, then nodded. "How many

women are we talking about?" she asked, trying to ease the tension a little.

Kainan smiled. *Okay, not that many. When women found out who I was they pursued me. I wasn't the playboy my brother was.*

"I just wish you had told me."

What would telling the truth have done? Nothing. We were at war. I don't think of myself as a leader. I wasn't trained to step into my father's shoes. All I ever wanted to be was a surgeon, and it was refreshing to be just that when we were working together.

"What does this mean for our son?"

Nothing at the moment. He is illegitimate.

Her eyes widened at his words. *Nothing at the moment.* What did he mean by that?

Despite what he'd said about nothing changing, did he mean to legitimize Peter and take him away? And then she recalled what legitimizing meant to a royal. It meant marriage. And if it meant what she thought it meant, she would need more than a moment. She would need a lifetime.

There was no way she was going to marry Kainan just because they had a son together—just because they'd once had feelings for each other and had had a great night of sex.

That was not something to base a marriage on. Her parents had married for that, and her mother had resented her for pushing her father away. First of all because he'd wanted a son and then because he'd thought Reagan was a burden, cramping his lifestyle.

Reagan didn't want a marriage like that.

She never wanted to get married.

"At the moment?" she asked, trying not stumble over the words.

If we marry...

Reagan began to laugh at the absurdity of it all. "No, I don't think so."

Kainan's dark eyes narrowed. *I didn't ask you.*

"I'm saving you the trouble. There's no way."

Reagan, he's my son too.

"I am very aware of that, *Your Majesty.* But just because he's your son it doesn't mean that I'm going to marry you. Just because you're King it doesn't mean that I want to marry you."

Kainan rolled his eyes. *This is exactly why I didn't tell you. You've changed.*

"I thought that was why you liked me—because I wasn't after your title or your money. I'm still not, by the way. I haven't changed."

You're more cynical.

"I have every right to be!"

Why? he asked.

She couldn't tell him. She didn't want to share with him or anyone her painful past. To do that would be letting him in, leaving her exposed.

Reagan softened. "I'm sorry. I can't marry you. I don't ever want to get married."

Kainan nodded and then took a step closer to her. *Are you saying you never cared for me in that way?*

"I cared for you, Kainan. It just feels like a lifetime ago, and you are not the man I thought you were either."

And you would've turned me down back then?

He reached out and touched her cheek briefly, before signing again.

You would've turned down a proposal of marriage from me then? When I was the man you thought I was?

Yes. I would.

Only she didn't say it out loud. That was for her only.

"We were friends. Did you really want to propose to me back then?" she asked, but her pulse was racing.

His simple touch still affected her and she recalled the moment when he'd finally taken her in his arms and kissed her.

She remembered it with vivid clarity. The sweltering heat, the sound of the waves crashing against the shore and all the chaos that had seemed to still around them in that moment.

"If things had been different…" Kainan whispered, then stroked her cheek again.

His arm slipped around her as he tipped up her chin and captured her lips in a kiss. She closed her eyes and drank it in. This stolen moment that took her right back to that time.

And even though she didn't want to feel this way about him, because she didn't have an inch of her heart to give him, she couldn't help but be swept away.

It was like a dream.

All those months when she'd thought he was dead, and right now he was a reality.

He was here.

Alive and kissing her.

He was affecting her, bringing down her walls.

She couldn't let him in.

She pushed him away. "Kainan, it doesn't change any-thing. I never want to marry. Royalty or not, it doesn't change how I feel about marriage."

Reagan, I can take care of you and Peter.

"How?" she asked. "You can't give him a new heart by making him a prince."

He looked crestfallen. *I can protect you both.*

"From what?"

Those who wish to end the monarchy of Isla Hermosa.

She frowned. "But you said it yourself—he's not legiti-

mate so he's not a threat. If I marry you so you can protect us, I'm actually endangering us further."

Kainan's shoulders slumped. *You'd still be a target if people found out. I am sorry. I just... I want to protect you both. I haven't done much for you, but I can do that. Let me do this. It's the right thing to do.*

She reached out and grabbed his hand. "Being here now is enough, but we need to protect Peter. His last name is Cote, not Laskaris. The only people who know that you're his father are the pediatric critical care unit staff and Michael. They won't say a word."

My security team knows.

Reagan's stomach knotted. "You'll have to keep them away from him. They'll attract attention."

He pursed his lips together, annoyed. *I will not call them off. I don't even think that I can anyway. They're protecting the monarchy of Isla Hermosa.*

"Then the press will find out."

Security will keep them out of the hospital.

Reagan rolled her eyes. "Don't underestimate the press."

Fine. They will keep their distance. But the moment something happens to you or Peter I am bringing about the security detachment in force.

"Deal." She held out her hand to shake his.

Kainan didn't take it. *I'm going to check in with Andreas and make sure that everything is good.*

"Okay. I'm going to check on Peter and then see if they need any help in the emergency department, since we sent the medical students home early."

I want you to have dinner with me tonight.

"How is that keeping your distance, Kainan? Won't the press see me having dinner with you?"

Not if you come to my hotel room. No one will notice you and my guards can provide a distraction.

Reagan crossed her arms. "Why do you want me to have dinner with you?"

Kainan pinched the bridge of his nose. *Why must you question everything?*

"I'm not leaving the hospital tonight, Kainan. I shouldn't have left yesterday. I'm needed here."

To do what? Peter is stable.

"I'm not leaving. So, no, I'm not having dinner with you tonight."

Fine, but I'm not giving up on this.

Kainan walked away and Reagan shook her head. She knew he was stubborn enough that he would persist until she agreed, but she wasn't going to leave the hospital tonight.

She was going to stay right by Peter.

With this threat of the press, and people who would do harm to Kainan, she was going to make sure that no one got to Peter.

Kainan waited outside the pediatric critical care unit. He didn't want to go in on the off-chance that someone from the press had snuck inside. It was killing him not to see Peter, but this was for the best.

Until he could make Reagan his wife and legitimize Peter he had to keep his distance from his son. Only he didn't want to. He didn't want to be like his father, a distant, remote figure.

If the press found out about Peter then all hell would break loose. Yet Kainan had to legitimize him. He had to marry Reagan and provide for them both. It was the right thing to do.

He saw Reagan walking toward the pediatric critical care unit, her head down and rubbing her neck. She looked

tired and he didn't blame her. He needed to do more. Reagan needed help, even if she didn't trust him.

He had heard from Sophie that Reagan had spent every night since Peter was born watching him. Except for last night. She hadn't even had a chance to recover much from the birth. She was always there, beside Peter.

One night of sleep would not make up for all the nights she'd lost. All the time she hadn't taken to heal. All the weight she had on her shoulders.

Kainan wanted to help her because the guilt of not being there for her was eating away at him like so many things did, but this was more real. This was a weight that he would gladly bear, that he *wanted* to bear for her.

"Reagan." He said her name uncertainly, because he wasn't sure his voice would be able to say it in a way for her to hear him.

She stopped and looked up. "Kainan—I thought you had returned to the hotel. Your security detachment isn't here."

Not that you can see. They're always around.

Reagan gave him a halfhearted smile. "What're you still doing here? I told you I didn't want to have dinner."

I know, but you do have to eat sometime.

"I'm not leaving the hospital, Kainan. I told you that."

I know, and that is why I have arranged for dinner in the classroom.

"What?" she asked, raising a finely arched brow.

It's cafeteria food, and I know that you said yesterday that you were tired of cafeteria food, but seeing how you won't leave the hospital, and I don't want to draw attention, I didn't really have a choice.

She crossed her arms, a smile spread across her face. "You *are* persistent."

I may be King now, but I haven't changed that much.

"Is a king supposed to change?" she teased.

I don't know.

They both laughed at that.

Come on, he's stable. He's fine right now. Eat first, and then you can man your post by his bedside, or I can man the post and you can sleep in a proper bed.

"You want to take a shift by Peter's bedside?" she asked, surprised. As if she didn't quite believe him or the help he was offering.

Yes.

"You? Shouldn't you be resting before your surgery?"

That's not for a few days yet. Let me take a shift. I want to do it.

"I don't know…"

She looked over her shoulder at the door of the pediatric critical care unit and he knew the pull she was feeling. He was feeling it too.

It was hard not to when your child was lying there sick.

You are no good to him weakened. You need to eat, Reagan. Come.

Reagan tore her glance away and nodded. "You're right."

Of course I am. I am King, after all.

It was a tease, and Reagan rolled her eyes, but she laughed all the same.

"Lead the way, my liege."

I'm not your liege, Reagan. You are not Hermosian. He held out his arm. *However, I am a gentleman, so if you'll do me the honor and let me escort you?*

Reagan took his arm and they walked away from the pediatric critical care unit to the classroom that was at the far end of the hall, on the other side of the hospital.

They didn't say anything. It was night, and the hospital was quiet. All the regular appointments and coming and goings that happened during the day, making the hospital a busy place, were gone. There were a few staff members

walking past, because the emergency room never stopped running, but for the most part the hospital was deserted.

The lighting was low and it was very calm. The cafeteria was only serving coffee and sandwiches. The gift shop was closed and through the atrium window he could see snow falling softly.

In a couple of days it would be Christmas, then his surgery, and then New Year's, which would be his coronation.

If he survived the surgery and *if* the surgery was successful.

Kainan couldn't remember the last time he'd celebrated Christmas. He'd always made excuses to his father in order to avoid the holiday since his mother had died. So for years, he hadn't celebrated it. He'd worked and he'd enjoyed that.

And then war had broken out.

He'd spent last Christmas with Reagan, in the mobile military hospital. She had sung Christmas carols to the soldiers. Just thinking about that made him smile.

"What're you smiling about?" she asked.

I was thinking about last Christmas with you.

She smiled. "I remember that night."

You brought a lot of hope to those wounded soldiers.

"It was Christmas—it's all about hope. Although I wouldn't really know…"

Did you not celebrate Christmas as a child?

"No. Well, sort of. My parents never really liked to spend time with me. I had a grandmother until I was about seven, who made the holiday special, but after she died my parents were very cold to me. They didn't want me and they made it clear."

He frowned. *I'm sorry, and I can understand that.*

"You understand? I thought your father was a great king?"

Yes—a great king, but a very cold, detached father. I

was the spare, so he didn't spend a lot of time with me. Besides, Christmas was all pomp and circumstance. It was all for show.

"Sounds like we both had it rough," she whispered. "Still, Christmas is a time for hope."

Do you feel hopeful about this Christmas?

The wistful smile disappeared, to be replaced with sigh. "I'm trying, but it's hard. This is Peter's first Christmas and he's spending it here."

Kainan understood. He wished it was different.

At least he's still alive.

She smiled at him, her eyes glistening. "Yes. He is."

Kainan opened the door to the classroom, where he'd set up a small dining area. He'd borrowed plates and cutlery from the cafeteria, with Andreas's help. He only wished there were candles or something, so he could set some mood lighting, but candles weren't allowed in the hospital. He wanted to make it special to her.

He pulled out a seat and beckoned for her to sit. Once she'd sat down he pushed her chair in and then took the seat next to her. The table was too long, and he didn't want her to have to shout across the room. This way, if he wanted to speak to her then he wouldn't have to shout.

He longed to speak to her as he'd used to be able to do. With his voice he could offer to hold her hand, touch her and comfort her.

At least she could understand him, though. Not many people knew how to use American Sign Language. He had learned it in medical school, because he'd wanted to converse with hearing impaired or nonverbal patients in his medical practice. He'd had no idea that it would become a part of his life.

"What's for dinner?" she asked.

Kainan lifted the lids on the salads he'd ordered be-

fore the cafeteria had shut down. *I believe it is called Cobb Salad.*

"It looks good. Actually, the cafeteria makes a great Cobb salad."

Well, this is just the starter. The main course is macaroni and cheese. I can't say that I've had the pleasure of trying macaroni and cheese.

"You're pulling my leg," Reagan said.

No, it's true. It's not really a staple on Isla Hermosa, and I grew up in a palace with a team of cooks. Macaroni and cheese wasn't in their repertoire.

"Then you missed out, my friend," she teased.

He chuckled. *I took a peek at it. I highly doubt that.*

Reagan smiled brightly, her dark eyes twinkling under the fluorescent lighting.

You have beautiful smile, Reagan.

Pink crept up her neck into her cheeks. "You've told me that before."

It's the truth.

"Why are you doing this?" she asked.

Doing what?

"This dinner. Why?"

I'm doing this because I wasn't there for you when Peter was born. I see the burden you carry and I want to help. Don't be on the defensive so much. You can trust me.

She looked away. "It's dangerous for you to help right now."

I know, but at least I can do this. I may not be able to directly help him, but I can help make things easier for you.

Her spine stiffened a bit. "I don't need help. I got myself into this situation and I can handle it."

I believe I was part of this "situation", as you call it. Unless Peter was another immaculate conception, I had a hand in helping you.

Reagan sighed and relaxed. "Okay, thank you for dinner. I appreciate it."

Kainan nodded. *Eat. You need to eat to keep your strength up. You're no good to our son if you get sick or collapse from exhaustion.*

Reagan nodded and they ate in silence, but it wasn't awkward. It felt right, and it was nice just to sit there with her and enjoy the peace and quiet, alone in this section of the hospital.

When they'd finished, Reagan leaned back in her chair. "That was good. What did you think of the macaroni and cheese?"

It was...interesting.

He made a face and she laughed, then she picked up her phone and frowned.

What's wrong? Kainan asked when she looked up again.

"It's Peter. His stats are a bit low." She bit her lip and then got up. "I have to be with him."

Kainan nodded. *Go and keep me posted. Please.*

Her expression softened. "I will. Thank you for dinner. I really appreciate it."

He nodded and she left the room.

Kainan sank back in the office chair he was been sitting in, spinning a bit as he tried not to think about what was happening to his son, or the fact that he was helpless. It was too much to bear.

He had to marry Reagan to protect her, to protect them both—especially if he didn't survive the surgery. Although he was very aware that he would be ruining her life *and* Peter's by staying and subjecting them to royal protocol.

He should just walk away. Only he couldn't. And the fact that he couldn't scared him.

CHAPTER SIX

IT HAD BEEN a couple days since their impromptu dinner that night in the classroom. It was the nicest thing that anyone had ever done for her in a long time. Actually, Reagan couldn't remember the last time someone had done something so nice for her.

Maybe there was still a piece of the man she'd thought she knew in there. Kainan had promised her nothing would change with respect to Peter. He wouldn't try and take him away.

Could she believe him?

She sighed, hating the doubt that still crept in.

He had been trying really hard, but since that dinner he had kept his distance both from her and Peter. It broke her heart to see him keeping Peter at arm's length, especially when Peter wasn't doing particularly well at the moment.

You asked him to stay away, remember?

And she had. He was doing what she'd asked.

It had been to keep Peter safe. Now she wasn't so sure that it had been the right decision.

Peter needed both his parents, and Kainan was alive. It was a miracle, and she shouldn't keep Kainan away from Peter or vice versa, but there was danger attached to Kainan and that made her fear for her son. She feared Peter might be hurt when Kainan returned to Isla Hermosa.

It was across the Atlantic. If Kainan had meant what he'd said about not trying to take her son away from her, Peter wouldn't see Kainan much. As King, Kainan's duties would take over—and what would happen when he married?

A king needed a queen.

You could be that queen.

No, she couldn't. Her life was here.

What life?

Still, she was protecting Peter's heart. She didn't want him to feel abandonment as she had. It was the right decision that he stayed away, so the press wouldn't discover Peter. News of Kainan's presence in Toronto was in all the papers. Not that she'd had a lot of time to read in between her duties at the hospital and being with Peter.

All she'd had time for was the headlines.

The world was waiting for Kainan to say something. Anything. Yet he couldn't. Not until after his surgery.

Reagan knew that Michael was overwhelmed in keeping the press out of the hospital so that they didn't pry into Kainan's life. Or hers.

At least there had been no mention of her. Which meant they didn't know about Peter.

That was good, but who knew how long that would last? It was something she didn't want to think about it.

She watched Kainan now, from a distance. He was sitting in the empty classroom, writing. When they'd served in Isla Hermosa he had told her that he was at the forefront of a new surgical technique that would save lives, but the war had put an end to that.

He was researching again now, while the medical students were on a break for the upcoming Christmas holidays. That meant Kainan didn't really need Reagan unless he was out and about in the hospital. Although she couldn't

help but wonder how he would be able to develop a surgical technique when he couldn't speak.

To develop a surgical technique he had to be able to perform surgery, and without his voice that was something he couldn't do at the moment.

She was impressed by him. He was so strong. That was what had drawn her in last time. She smiled to herself, still watching Kainan. How did he get to her? Especially when no one else did.

It was thrilling, but unnerving. Those walls of hers had protected her for so long, and yet Kainan could get through to her.

"You do remember me, don't you, Dr. Cote?"

Reagan spun around to see a security guard—the one who had spoken to her in the hallway at the Royal York. The one she remembered working on in the field. Kainan's security guard—Andreas.

"I do. It took me some time. I wasn't used to seeing you with hair."

The security guard smiled. "I prefer this length over the required shaved head for military service. His Majesty does not care if I keep my hair long, as long as it doesn't interfere in my duties."

"I'm sorry I didn't recognize you right away, sir," she said sheepishly.

He smiled gently. "It's Andreas—and do not worry. I suspect you have a lot on your mind, especially in regard to your son being so ill."

Reagan nodded. "I appreciate the fact you're keeping an eye on him. He's not Hermosian…"

"He may not have been born there, but he is still half-Hermosian. He is heir to the throne—that's if he is legitimized." There was hope in his eyes as he looked her.

She chuckled nervously. "Right…"

That wasn't going to happen, but Andreas didn't need to know that.

"I thank you for saving my life that night and for singing me those Christmas songs. I have never forgotten that moment."

Reagan smiled. "I was just doing my duty—as were you. There is no need to thank me."

Andreas dipped his head. "Ah, but you sang so sweetly. It gave me such hope. You *still* give me hope."

Warmth flooded her cheeks and she discovered she didn't like the attention he was lavishing on her. "How do you mean?"

Andreas opened his mouth to say something further, and then looked over her shoulder and froze. "My apologies. I must get back to my duties."

Reagan turned to see that Kainan was standing in the doorway. His hands were in his pockets and he was glaring at Andreas. It was an expression that meant business. It caused a shiver to go down her spine.

Andreas skulked away and Kainan's gaze never left his retreating form. He looked like a true king—or at least like the ones she'd seen depicted in movies.

"That was rude," Reagan snapped. King or not, she didn't like it when people treated others badly.

He was treading where he should not, Kainan signed, and mouthed a curse word.

"What're you talking about?"

There are affairs of my kingdom that do not concern you. You do not need to know about them.

"Okay..."

And he does not need to know our personal business.

"I agree," she said, relieved.

Kainan's expression softened. *How are you? I have not seen you these last couple of days.*

"I've been busy. Actually, I'm on my way to see Peter's pediatrician in his office. I came to see if you wanted to come."

Kainan frowned. *What's wrong?*

Reagan sighed. "Peter hasn't been doing so well and the doctor wants to touch base."

His brow furrowed and she could tell that something was bothering him.

Does this doctor know who I am?

"That you're his father and the King of Isla Hermosa? Yes, he knows, and he's signed the confidentiality agreement that Michael has forced upon all those dealing with our special situation."

Kainan let out a sigh, relief on his face. *Then I would like to go and hear for myself.*

"Okay."

Kainan hesitated. *That's if you want me to go?*

"I wouldn't have offered if I didn't."

I have been staying away, like you asked.

Her stomach flip-flopped with guilt. "I know, but perhaps I was wrong."

He cocked an eyebrow.

"Yes, I was wrong. Don't stay away."

She was afraid Kainan that would leave, and that would hurt Peter, but Peter not knowing his father at all and growing up to learn that Reagan had kept Kainan away would be worse.

Peter needed Kainan.

Kainan smiled, those dark eyes twinkling as his gaze held her captive. *Then I won't.*

"Good."

Kainan locked up the classroom and they headed toward the pediatric wing of the hospital, where Dr. Braccio worked.

Reagan sighed. "You know, I sometimes wonder if I would have been better off without my parents."

Why is that? Kainan signed.

"They never wanted me. Their resentment was horrible. I wouldn't wish that on anyone."

You had no love?

"Did you? You said your father wasn't the best."

Yes, but my mother loved me. He smiled wistfully. *So I was lucky.*

"I'm glad you're here, Kainan. Peter needs you. He needs both of us. I didn't have my parents when I really needed them and…it was miserable. You're here, alive, and Peter should have every opportunity to get to know you."

Kainan nodded. *Thank you. I want to get to know him too…before I have to return to Isla Hermosa.*

Her stomach clenched. "You have a country to run."

Let me worry about that. You know I will be there for Peter if he needs me. Of course I could be there all the time if—

She knew where he was going and she didn't want to go there.

"How is the research coming?" she interrupted, changing the subject but feeling the awkward tension that was between them suddenly.

Good. I am glad to be working on it again. It was my one true passion. I never wanted to be a king. I just wanted medicine.

"I know—you've told me."

And what is your grand passion, besides our son?

"I don't know," she said. "I enjoyed my time in the military, and when I left Isla Hermosa I was excited to be working at this hospital in trauma. I guess I never really thought beyond those plans, because I found out I was pregnant and my focus shifted."

Come on, there must've been something?

"I once wanted to teach medicine," she admitted. "I wanted to teach at my alma mater."

Where was that?

"I went to medical school in London, Ontario. It's a small city, about two hours west of here. I just loved London. Toronto is my hometown, but it's too big for me. The prices of the homes are astronomical here, but in London housing is a bit more affordable. I could actually buy a small house and Peter would have a yard to play in. Of course when Peter was born so ill I really had no choice. I had to stay here."

She laughed nervously.

"It's not as wild as your aspirations to win a Nobel prize for medicine or anything."

It's still a good aspiration. He smiled at her. *It's good to dream of something like that, because that sounds wonderful to me. I didn't have the luxury to go and play outside when I was a child.*

"Oh?" she asked.

Well, there were always threats when it came to the Young Princes. More so with Alek than me, but still... If I did get to go outside then I was followed by Security. There were a few times I managed to sneak away.

"And where did you sneak off to?" she asked with a smile.

To the ocean. I was fascinated by tidal pools and I liked to swim. My mother was terrified of the ocean. Her brother was carried away by a rip tide and died when she was a young girl, so when she found out that I was sneaking away from my bodyguards and heading to the ocean to swim I got in a lot of trouble. I was shipped off to boarding school in Switzerland. Just mountains—no ocean.

"I'm sorry you didn't have freedom. I didn't have a huge

amount of freedom growing up in the city. There wasn't many safe places to play—and forget about learning to ride a bike. I grew up on the Danforth."

What's the Danforth? Kainan asked.

"A part of Toronto—a neighborhood. It was busy, so I played in a shoebox-sized yard. My parents didn't really take me anywhere. We didn't travel. I think I was a bit of a burden to them."

He frowned. *Well, if it's any consolation I think I was a bit of a burden to my father too.*

"Not your mother, though?" she asked.

No, never my mother. Even though she died when I was ten. I was at boarding school when she got sick. I was brought back in time to say goodbye to her.

His expression softened and he had a faraway look in his eyes, like the one he'd had the day before he'd been sent up to the front lines, when he had been staring at the smoke rising from the gates of Helicia.

"I'm sorry to hear that. How did she die?"

Cancer. She did not suffer long. All she wanted was her freedom... He sighed.

"Freedom? Was she a prisoner?"

In a way. She wasn't locked up, but a member of the royal family has to follow certain protocols, certain rules, and my mother was a bit of free spirit. He smiled sadly. *She loved my father, though he never really loved her. Not in the same way.*

Reagan could understand that. She'd often wondered if her parents really loved each other because they seemed so cold and so indifferent. She had never been quite sure that they were capable of love. At least Kainan had had love. His mother had loved him, and from the way Kainan described his mother it sounded as if he'd loved her too.

"I understand," she whispered.

You do? he signed, looking confused.

"My parents were very emotionally closed off to me, and to each other. I didn't have the best childhood."

I'm sorry.

"I sometimes wonder if I can be the mother Peter needs." She blushed, annoyed with herself that she'd let that slip.

You're an excellent mother, Reagan.

Her pulse quickened as Kainan reached out and took her hand and they continued their walk to the pediatrician's office, moving in silence the rest of the way.

They stopped in front of Dr. Braccio's office and Reagan took a deep breath. She had a feeling about what Dan Braccio was going to tell her about Peter. She'd read his chart. Peter was dying. And time was running out for him to get a new heart.

Kainan, as if sensing her apprehension, gave her hand a squeeze and nodded with determination toward the door.

You can do this. You have to do this.

Reagan let go of Kainan's hand and knocked on the door. Dan Braccio answered. "Reagan, come on in—and you must be Peter's father."

"Kainan," Kainan said carefully.

"Welcome—it's nice to meet you." Dan shook Kainan's hand, and as Reagan sat down on the edge of the chair Dan shut the door behind them, locking it so that no one would barge in.

Which was not a good sign.

Reagan's heart started to race and Kainan placed a hand on her shoulder to steady her, as if he knew that she was terrified.

"I'm glad you both could come, and I'm not going to mince words with you as you're doctors." Dan took a seat behind his desk. "Peter's cardiomyopathy is progressing rapidly."

"How long?" Reagan asked, her voice trembling slightly.

"A month, maybe, if we're lucky," Dan said sadly. "The pediatric cardiologist, Dr. Bruni, is very concerned."

Tears stung her eyes but she tried to keep it together. A month? That was it? That was all she'd have left with her son?

This couldn't be the end.

A year of life was all he got?

Her world was crumbling under her.

"He has been moved up the priority list on UNOS," Dan said. "He's right at the top now. But you both know that infant hearts are hard to come by. I wanted him to get a bit older."

"He's three months old now—that's surely got to give him a better chance?"

Reagan was grasping at straws, but she wasn't ready to accept defeat yet. Not when it came to Peter. He was her whole world. She didn't have a contingency plan for life without him.

"Yes, I am glad he's not newborn. That does give us a slight advantage. It's easier to find an older heart for an infant as opposed to a newborn heart, but it's still difficult." Dan opened up Peter's file. "We do have a better shot now."

Kainan tapped her shoulder and she saw he was signing. Dan was watching and waiting for her to translate.

"Kainan would like to know the specifics of what will happen. Will he go on a left ventricular assist device?" she asked.

Dan nodded and looked at Kainan when he addressed him. "I would like to hook him up to an LVAD as soon as possible." He slid the consent form toward Reagan. "He's no stranger to surgery, but I hate having to do this to him…"

"I know," Reagan said dully. "But it's his only hope."

Dan nodded. "I'm sorry, Reagan and Kainan. I truly

am. This is not an easy situation. I don't like delivering this kind of news."

Reagan didn't respond. What doctor *did* like delivering this kind of news? None that she could think of. But it was a part of the job and being on this end of the conversation sucked. Big-time.

It was as if someone was trying to cut her heart out with a blunt instrument and hand it to her while it was still beating.

If only she could give her heart to Peter she would. She would give up her life for him. Anything to have him live.

Reagan clicked the pen she didn't even remember picking up and signed her name on the form, dating it before sliding the form back to Dan.

"When will the surgery take place?" Reagan asked stonily. She was numb.

"As soon as possible. He needs to go on the device. I'm having my team and the cardiothoracic team prep him for surgery and ready everything I need. I hope to have his surgery done within the next couple of hours."

Reagan nodded. "Can I be with him?"

"Yes, but you won't be able to handle him. I'm sorry. We have to take every precaution to prevent infection. This will be taxing for him."

"I understand." Reagan stood. "Thank you, Dan."

Kainan went ahead of her and unlocked the door, holding it open for her. There were so many emotions rushing through her she wasn't sure what to do. Instead she bottled everything up tight.

There was no time for her to feel.

Right now she had to be strong for Peter.

Kainan seemed to understand. He said nothing, just walked beside her. This time he did not reach out to touch

her and she was glad, because if he touched her she would
lose it, and she didn't want to fall apart right now.

They gowned, gloved, and put on surgical masks before
entering the pediatric critical care unit.

There were a few nurses and a couple of young pediatric surgical residents hovering around Peter's crib, and
Reagan let out a hiss of pain and turned away. She couldn't
stand to look.

Kainan's arm came around her and she looked up into
his eyes.

"Be strong. You are strong," he whispered, his voice
hoarse.

He winced, and she knew that uttering those words had
been hard for him, painful as well. His words, his voice—
even broken—gave her strength.

"I don't know if I'm *this* strong," she said, her voice
cracking with the emotion that she could barely contain.

Kainan removed his arm and signed, *You've been here
before. Peter needs you. He will pull through. This is his
best chance.*

"I know." She turned back around and stood on the periphery, watching as they readied Peter for surgery. Sophie
glanced up once from her work to nod briefly, and then
turned back to Peter. Kainan stood beside her.

"I have never heard him cry," Reagan whispered urgently. "Well, not since the day he was born."

Kainan's expression was pained, but he said nothing.

"I would love to hear him cry again." Tears were welling up in her eyes. "Just one more time. If I had a Christmas wish it would be that."

*When he gets a new heart you will hear him cry all the
time. It will probably drive you crazy.*

Reagan smiled. "I would like that."

At least after the LVAD surgery you can hold him. In fact, it'll be encouraged. He'll need all your strength.

The surgical team came in and transferred her fragile son to a gurney, along with all his wires and tubes. He looked so small. She took a step forward, aching to reach out and touch him, but restrained herself.

"Touch him," Sophie whispered. "He needs you."

"I was told not to," Reagan said.

"Touch him. It's just a touch," Sophie encouraged.

Reagan nodded, tears rolling down her cheeks as she bent over her sick boy and touched his head through her rubber glove, kissing the soft skin that she'd never got to touch through the surgical mask.

"I'll be waiting," Reagan whispered. "Right here."

Kainan stepped forward, but then he hesitated and turned away, shaking his head. He couldn't do it, and it hurt her that he wouldn't reach out to touch their son, but she saw the pained expression on his face and understood.

She knew that look of pain—she lived it every day.

The surgical team rolled him out of the pediatric critical care unit. Reagan followed them. She would follow the gurney until she could do so no longer. Until it entered the surgical floor, where she would not be able to follow because she was a parent in this moment, not a surgeon.

It was hard to stop at the double doors that closed off the surgical wing from the rest of the hospital, but she stopped and watched as they rolled Peter away.

She hated being in a patient's shoes. She hated being on this side of the door.

Kainan was beside her. "Come," he said.

Reagan shook her head. She wouldn't let him take her away. It was as if staring at those double doors would somehow protect Peter, somehow bring him back to her.

"Reagan," Kainan said more firmly.

"I'm not leaving."

Before she knew what was happening Kainan was scooping her up in his arms and carrying her away, in broad daylight.

"Are you crazy?" she screeched. "Put me down!"

Kainan didn't respond, and he wouldn't look at her as he carried her to a small exam room that was dark and unoccupied. He set her down and then shut the door, locking it, then pulling down the blinds.

"What do you think you're doing?" she yelled at him. "People could've seen—people probably *did* see, you maniac!"

Let it out, he signed.

"Let what out?"

Let it all out. You can't bottle up that emotion forever. Let it out. Stop locking your emotions away.

She just stared at him at first, because she was so stunned at what he was suggesting, and all she could hear was her mother's voice in her head.

"Honestly, Reagan. You're a big girl now. Stop crying. It's embarrassing. You can hold it together," her mother had hissed at her when she'd cried over the fact her dog had died. "Big girls don't cry."

"I don't have anything to let out." Her voice trembled.

Reagan, you don't have to hide with me.

The moment she saw what he'd signed it was like a floodgate opening up. She broke down weeping, covering her face with her hands, and let it all out—every piece of raw emotion that she had been bottling up inside her since Peter had been born.

Kainan took her in his arms and she clung to him. He ran his hand over her head, but it was hard for him to do that with the bun she had in her hair.

Still, it was what she needed.

She needed to be held. Her body trembled as he held her, the pain washing through her. The strength in his arms calmed her.

"There was nothing you could've done," Kainan had said back then, gripping her by the shoulders and shaking her. "You did everything you could."

"I didn't. I didn't save his life. That's what I could've done and I couldn't even do that!"

"His injuries were too severe. He stepped in the path of an IED. There was nothing anyone could've done, but you gave him comfort."

"Comfort?" She'd wiped away her tears.

"You held him and he passed away peacefully, knowing that he was safe and that he was without pain. You did all you could. In fact you did more. Not many surgeons in this military hospital would do the same."

He'd pulled her into his arms then, giving her a hug, holding her close so that she would calm down as she cried in his arms.

"He was so young," she'd whispered against his neck. "He didn't get a chance to live."

"Some never do." He'd tipped up her chin, those dark eyes so reassuring, so understanding, and she'd known that he also felt the pain she'd felt in that moment.

"You did everything you could. You were strong for him. You *are* strong."

Reagan looked up at Kainan now, longing to hear him say those same things.

He did say those words. You just didn't hear them.

She studied his face. There were a few more scars, some creases in his face from worry, and some grey in his dark curls. It suited him. But those dark eyes were the same. They were reflecting back the pain that she was feeling.

Acting on the need to be close to him, she kissed him.

And it was as if she had come home. His arms wrapped around her, pulling her tight against him as they kissed. How long had she dreamed of this moment but been thrown back into reality, remembering that he had died?

Only he hadn't died.

He was here with her. He was here with Peter.

And for one brief moment, as she sank into the kiss that eased her sorrow, her pain and her worry, she forgot about it all. She forgot that he was King, that their son was dying and that she had been alone for so long.

She finally broke off the kiss and laid her head against his chest as he ran his hands over her back. He was still holding her as they stood in silence. The only sound was her own breath and the steady rhythm of his heart under her ear.

They stayed together in that stolen moment of peace, comforting each other as their son fought for his life.

Then Kainan's hand stilled and he moved away, knocking her out of the peaceful reverie.

I'm sorry for carrying you away like that, but it was the only way, he signed.

"I know. I'm sorry I called you a maniac."

He smiled, a dimple forming in his cheek. *I'm used to it. You've called me worse things before.*

She frowned. "When?"

Your Majesty. He made a sarcastic face, as if to drive home the point that she had said it in a spiteful way.

"I'm sorry about that too."

He shrugged. *I deserved it.*

"Still, thank you for being here with me. Thank you for bringing me here."

I thought you would've learned by now not to bottle up your emotions so much. You were about to burst.

She nodded. "I know. Thank you for coming to my rescue again."

He smiled, his expression softening. *You're welcome.*

Warmth crept up her neck into her cheeks. "I'm sorry for kissing you as well."

Never be sorry for that.

His dark eyes glinted with the promise of something more. Something she knew all too well. And as much as she wanted that, she couldn't do it. She couldn't divide herself between Peter's care and Kainan. It would be too much to bear. Peter and work—that was all she could handle.

Work was the only thing that kept her sane. It was structured and, though it was never predictable, she knew what she was doing. She could detach herself emotionally from it.

Starting something up with Kainan was not the answer, because she knew that she would never be able to detach herself emotionally from him.

He was definitely *not* predictable, and she wasn't sure she could handle losing both Peter *and* Kainan.

The thought of losing them both scared her beyond all reason. And she wasn't prepared to invest in that.

CHAPTER SEVEN

THE SURGERY SEEMED to take an eternity.

Kainan had stayed in the hospital until he was certain that Peter had pulled through and been hooked up to the left ventricular assist device. He'd done it with flying colors. Then he'd gone with Reagan to the pediatric critical care unit, where Peter had been moved to an isolation room.

There was only enough room for the nurses and the doctors to navigate and one chair, which was where Reagan had curled up in her street clothes with a hospital gown over her. She'd looked completely uncomfortable, but Kainan hadn't been able to get her to budge.

There had been no place for him. So he'd left.

He had to put some distance between himself and the hospital anyway. He felt so helpless.

Ever since he'd become King and been whisked away to Canada he'd felt this way, but it came into painful Technicolor how truly helpless he was when he gazed into the incubator at his son.

He was just like his father, who had been absent for most of his childhood. Kainan was following in his father's lead and he loathed himself.

You didn't even know Peter existed. That's why you weren't there, he told himself.

Only that didn't make him feel any better. Things had

to change. He refused to be like his father. His father who hadn't taken care of his illegitimate children...his father who had broken his mother's heart and been distant with his legitimate children.

Kainan refused to force Peter into an unhappy childhood like he'd had.

He'd already missed so much. Three months of Peter's life. And if he didn't get a new heart soon Kainan would never know him. Never speak to him.

Reagan said he didn't cry, that she'd barely heard Peter's voice.

Just like me.

Peter had no voice but he was still here, fighting to live.

Reagan was strong. She would be able to handle the burdens of royal life. He felt guilty for having to impose them upon her, but it was the only way to protect them if he died.

Remember how it broke your mother, though. How it hardened Alek and you.

He had almost lost it when he'd seen Reagan bend over Peter before they took him to surgery. She had bent down and whispered to him to be strong and she'd touched him, kissed him through the surgical mask.

It had alost been too much for him to take. It had taken all his strength to keep himself from breaking down.

Reagan had been so strong and he so weak in that moment. The thought of losing his son had too much for him to bear, but Reagan had needed him. He knew she liked to have walls up, not to show any weakness. But when she cracked he would swallow his worry, his sorrow, and step up to bear it for her.

He wanted to take Reagan and Peter's pain for them. To be better than his own father. If Kainan didn't survive his surgery, if Peter wasn't legitimized, then Kainan wouldn't

be able to leave his fortune to them. It was the only thing he could think of doing to protect them.

It had made him think back to that night on Isla Hermosa, when the chaos had died down after the rebel attack on the front lines. When his foolish brother had demanded that the youngest and most untrained of the Hermosian Army should advance.

And that boy who had been no more than eighteen had taken the brunt of the explosion. All they'd been able to do was patch him together, but they had known it wouldn't stop him from dying. That boy had been alone and dying.

The boy had been from the coast. Most likely a fisherman's son, looking to supplement the family income from a dwindling industry by signing up to serve in the Hermosian Army. He'd probably been fresh out of training.

It had been apparent to Kainan that the boy hadn't been fully prepared for what awaited him, and it had broken his heart. It had broken his heart to see the youngest of his country dying in the name of his foolish brother.

In that moment Kainan had blamed himself for the boy's death, because he'd known that when Alek had begun to run amok he should have done more to rein in his brother. He'd tried. He'd tried hard. But then his brother had sought to end his life.

So Kainan had backed off and tried to help the people in another way. Serving as a surgeon on the front lines. But in moments like that, when that boy had lain there dying, afraid and alone, Kainan had questioned his choices.

And then Reagan had appeared, out of the darkness, in the quiet of the hospital where those on duty had been making their rounds on the patients who would live and trying to clean up the mess that the onslaught of injured soldiers from the front had caused.

She'd given the boy more medicine. More of the pain-

killers that had already been given to him. And then she'd sat next to him. Reagan could speak fluent Spanish, which was the mother tongue of Isla Hermosa, and she'd spoken to the boy.

Javier had been his name.

She'd held him. She cradled him in his arms and sung to him, just as she had sung to Andreas, and Kainan had realized that she sang to many of those who were injured.

All he had been able to do was watch in awe as she'd administered the simplest form of healing: love, patience and human contact.

Reagan had held Javier as his tremors had ceased, as his breathing had become more shallow and as he'd breathed his last.

And she'd held him for a long time after. Singing to him…some sweet melody, something he had never heard before. But it hadn't mattered what she was singing. It had been her voice. It had been her kindness, her purity. So like his mother, who had helped the less fortunate, who had given everything to his father and got nothing in return.

It was in that moment that Kainan had melted for her. She might bottle up her emotions, but her compassion for others made her a brilliant, strong woman and he had desired her.

Only her.

He had seen her reaching out and comforting their son in the same way she had comforted Javier and all those other countless injured men and women from Isla Hermosa, Canada and the United States. It hadn't mattered to her what side they'd fought for. She had afforded each and every single one of them the simple gift of human compassion and caring. To her there had been no borders, no colors and no religions. No conflict had been too great to stop her from delivering what they had all needed and that was love.

Reagan had cared for them all. She had judged no one.

And at that moment, seeing her being separated from their child, Kainan had realized that their son might never know what kind of strong woman his mother was and what a failure his father was.

It had broken his heart, and it had been too much for him to take in so he had turned away, missing that moment when they'd taken his son away.

He had turned back to find her trembling in front of the surgical wing, her eyes wide and her body looking as if it was about to bend and break under its burden. She'd been trying to stay strong, but her walls had come crashing down with the weight of it all. Of carrying the burden alone for too long.

That was why he'd picked her up and carried her away from it all. He hadn't cared who saw him in that moment. He'd wanted to afford her the same amount of care and compassion she'd shown to everyone else. To make up for not being there when she'd needed him.

He wasn't sure he could *ever* make that up to her, but he'd try.

She'd helped so many and yet there had been no one helping her. He had seen that. She'd been alone and she'd been standing there so lost. So broken.

And he'd taken her in his arms, as she'd taken Javier in hers, and he'd held her. Comforted her. And then she'd kissed him.

He'd thought about her kisses ever since they'd parted. As he'd been transported on his way to Canada, with an endotracheal tube breathing for him, with no voice to cry out, he'd thought of her.

He'd longed for her.

When she'd kissed him he'd forgotten about being King.

About the conflicts in Isla Hermosa. About his late brother and the damage he'd wrought.

All he'd cared about was the fact that he was in her arms again.

It had taken every ounce of his strength to step back from her when she'd broken the kiss, because he'd burned for her. He still did.

And that was not proper.

It was selfish of him.

Perhaps he was just as selfish as his brother was?

No. You're nothing like him.

Still, he'd needed to put some distance between them, and yet now that it was morning he realized that, no matter how much distance there was between them, he would still feel the same.

His blunder of picking her up and carrying her to that boardroom, where he could hold her, had cost Reagan and Peter something. Their privacy.

Word had got out to the press about his behavior with Reagan. The world knew about her and Peter. Peter was no longer safe.

There were pictures of him carrying Reagan. And although he'd thought they were alone in that boardroom someone had managed to get a picture of them kissing.

He loathed being King in moments like this. Private, precious moments were made into entertainment for the rest of the world. Something cherished became tawdry and debased. It was no longer a beautiful moment between Reagan and him. It belonged to the world.

He headed back to the pediatric critical care unit and watched Reagan sleeping. The guilt of subjecting her to this intrusion on her privacy was eating away at him.

I should've kept my distance from her in Isla Hermosa. I should've kept away.

He shouldn't have been so reckless, so selfish, but he could be *himself* around her. She gave him a sense of freedom that he'd never known. So he had been selfish, and had pursued her. When it came to Reagan he lost all sense.

Within a few hours the press and the rest of the world would know all about Reagan, and know that Kainan and Reagan had worked together in Isla Hermosa. He felt guilty that Reagan's life was going to be exposed. The press would chew her up and spit her out. They would twist everything about her.

He was going to try hard to protect her.

Reagan stirred and then sat up, seeing that he was standing by her.

"What time is it?" she asked groggily.

Seven in the morning, Kainan signed, and handed her the coffee that he'd picked up in the hotel when he had been wandering. It was gourmet coffee, from his own country.

"Thank you." She took a sip. "Hermosian?"

He nodded. *You look like you didn't have a very comfortable sleep.*

"No, the chair was uncomfortable." She glanced back through the window. "But I'm used to cramming myself into hospital chairs and getting only a few hours of sleep while I'm waiting."

Was there anything to worry about last night?

"Nothing. Last time I talked to Sophie she said he was doing well." A wobbly smile spread across Reagan's face. "This will extend his life while we wait."

That's good.

Reagan stood and stretched. "I'm sorry, I'm a bit of a wreck. I can go change quickly, in the staff room, and then we can get to work."

No work today. I talked to Dr. McNeil. Christmas Eve is in two days and the medical students are already home

for the holidays. I can work on my research and you can take some time to be with Peter.

"You spoke with Michael?"

Kainan held up his phone and grinned. *My robot voice did.*

Reagan laughed. "Well, if you need help with your research I can do it. I really don't want to be idle. I need to keep busy."

He didn't want to talk about his research, because it was no longer something he could focus on. Once he returned to Isla Hermosa he would no longer be a surgeon or be able to practice medicine. All his years of research would be left unfinished, and it was hard for him to think about, but it was a sacrifice he had to make.

He changed the subject. *Reagan, you do realize that in a couple of days, if Peter stays on this upward trajectory, he's going to come out of his medicated coma and he'll be able to come home.*

Reagan's eyes widened and she sat down slowly. "What?"

I thought you knew? Kainan signed.

"I *do* know." She shook her head. "It's just that he's never been home. Never. I had the nursery sort of complete…but it's not ready. My home is not ready."

Well, let's go check out your place and get it ready, then.

"You have your research to do."

It can wait. It had waited this long. *My security detail can take us there in the town car and I will help you.*

"You're abusing your power now, Your Majesty," she teased.

How? It's their duty to help the King's son. He grinned.

Reagan sighed. "I suppose so. I don't think I'm ready for this…"

Ready or not, you have to do this. There will be no need

for him to be here while he waits for a heart. They will move him to the pediatric ward, out of this critical care unit, get us used to the portable ventricular assist device, and then we can take him home.

"We?"

Kainan smiled and then knelt down in front of her. *You know that I can protect you, Reagan. Please let me take care of you.*

"Kainan, I'm *not* accepting your proposal of marriage. Besides, you said that keeping us secret was the best form of protection that you could give us. If I…" She trailed off when she saw his expression. "The press know, don't they?"

Kainan nodded sadly. *When I carried you into the boardroom. There was someone from the press watching and they got a picture of us kissing.*

Reagan groaned. She set down her coffee cup on the floor beside the chair and rubbed her eyes. "This is horrible."

I'm sorry.

"It's not your fault."

It sort of is. I am King, after all.

And nothing about his life was his.

She laughed at that. "You're not helping."

Marry me. I can protect you.

"No. I can't. I can't think about that now, and I can't consider entering into that life with Peter still so fragile."

Kainan's stomach knotted. He'd known it was a long shot, but he'd had to keep trying. It was the only way to protect her and Peter, to provide for them. He had to do better than his father ever had.

Will you at least let me assist you with your apartment? he asked. *If you're with me I can protect you from the press.*

"Okay. Do you want to go now, while they still have Peter sedated?"

Kainan nodded. *I will go tell the team to get ready and you gather your things.*

"It's going to be a short visit to my apartment," she warned. "I want to be here when he wakes up. It's important that I'm here."

Of course.

Reagan picked up her coffee cup and left the pediatric critical care unit. Kainan sighed and looked back at his son, who still needed a machine to survive.

He knelt down, and even though he couldn't touch Peter he stared into his son's face. Emotion overcame him. This was his child. His flesh, his blood. He couldn't lose him.

"I will do better by you," he whispered. "I swear."

He bowed his head. He would be better than his father ever had.

Even if he wasn't there to show him.

She was trying not stare at Kainan, who was looking out of the window, his chin resting on his hand. She wanted to tell him that she'd seen him, that she'd heard what he'd said to their son.

Any kind of reservation had melted away when she'd heard him whisper, "I will do better by you. I swear."

Reagan had had to leave the room or break down in front of him.

Kainan might be King, but he was good deep down. He was still that man she cared for.

He looked over and smiled. *Comfortable?*

"Very."

Reagan was thankful that Kainan had access to a town car, and that the car's windows were tinted, but the Hermosian flags that flew on the hood sort of gave them away.

"I thought you wanted to be the hidden King?" she said lightly.

Well, since word got out I thought it was time to use the embassy car that is kept here in Toronto. We can park anywhere. He grinned.

"That's good. There's not much parking near my place."

She didn't like it that they were in an embassy car, but if the world already knew about her then there was no sense in hiding. She could face whatever they threw at her. She was the one who'd got involved with Kainan.

Although it made her feel a bit nervous to be out with him.

How far away is your place?

"I don't know. It's fairly new. I got it when I first came back to Toronto and was preparing for Peter's arrival. I just know the distance in subway stops."

"What's the address?" the driver asked from the front seat. "There's GPS."

"Three-sixteen Richmond Street West. It's not that far, I guess. Like I said, I only know by subway stops and how many blocks I have to walk."

"You're right, Dr. Cote. It's not far. We'll be there and back in no time."

The driver plugged in the route map and Reagan turned back to Kainan.

"Thank you for helping me. I'm sure my place is a disaster. I really didn't have a lot of time to settle in. I was trying to work as long as I could at the hospital, to save up and have a decent maternity leave, and then… Well, you know the rest."

Peter was born and was so ill. Sadly, I do know the rest.

Kainan glanced out the window.

Perhaps he'll be on the regular pediatric floor by Christmas? I hear they do a lot of celebrations for the children in there over Christmas and New Year's.

"Maybe he'll be home in time for New Year," said Reagan. And that thought was scary indeed.

A strange look passed over Kainan's face. *Yes. Perhaps.*

It didn't take the driver long to navigate the streets to her condo complex. He parked in front—legally, not having to resort to the embassy park-wherever-you-want privileges.

Kainan slid out first and then helped Reagan.

"No press here," she said, relieved.

I am glad of that. Especially since they know what you look like. I am sorry they were snapping your picture so much as we came out of the hospital. And you were bombarded with questions.

"I ignored them." She took out her key and opened the main door.

Before she called the elevator she opened up her mail slot and pulled out the copious amount of mail that had been piling since she'd last been there. One of the things on top was a Christmas card from her parents.

A knot formed in her stomach as she thought about them. Thought how they didn't really care much for Peter—or her, for that matter. Still, what was socially acceptable was to send your offspring a Christmas card, and that was exactly what her mother had done. She was following protocol.

You haven't been back here in a while, I take it? Kainan signed, cocking an eyebrow as he glanced at her mail.

"No, I haven't."

What if you go into arrears on something?

"I do everything on my phone. There's an app for that," she teased.

She called the elevator and the doors opened up. She punched in her floor.

Her apartment was at the end of the hall. When she got to the door something seemed wrong. The door was splin-

tered around the lock, and instead of having to put her key in she just turned the knob and it opened.

Kainan moved past her and into her apartment first. Reagan took a step inside and saw her place had been trashed.

The furniture was turned over and all her boxes had been opened up. Her things were everywhere, but her television and stereo were still there. Her computer was as well, but it was plugged in, and when she touched it, it woke up. It was on, and it looked as if her system had been hacked. All her personal files...

She began to tremble. She hated it that this had happened. Her life was strewn across the floor in a shambles...exposed.

Kainan came from the bedroom.

This doesn't seem like a robbery for valuables. It looks like they were looking for information.

"Information about *me*?" she asked, in shock still.

Or your ties to me.

Kainan began to text.

"Who are you texting?"

"My security team" he said hoarsely.

He finished the text.

"I can't believe this has happened." She wanted to sit down, but if the police were going to come she didn't want to disturb any of the evidence. "Is your team calling the police?"

Kainan nodded. *I'm sorry this has happened, but I can protect you.*

Reagan snorted. "You've said that before, and look what's happened."

I'm sorry.

Reagan ignored him and set her mail down on her kitchen table. She made her way to her bedroom. The con-

tents of her nightstand drawer had been dumped out on her bed, and her dresser had been rummaged through.

The few pieces of jewelry she had were still there. Kainan was right. They had been looking for information.

She went over to the walk-in closet and opened it to look at where she had started setting up a small nursery for Peter. Nothing had been touched.

Tears stung her eyes when she saw the crib that was waiting for him and the fine layer of dust on the wood. She was the worst mother ever. She hadn't even made it up. The sheet and quilt, even the hanging mobile, were still in a box.

All she had managed to do was set up the crib and a change table. There weren't even diapers in there yet.

"Big girls don't cry, Reagan. This was your choice!"

Reagan cursed under her breath. Angry at herself. Angry for letting her mother's words back in.

How was she going to bring home a baby on a ventricular assist device and have him live here? This was no place for him. She was not ready for him to be out of the safe confines of the hospital. How was she going to be able to deal with this?

She picked up the small teddy bear that she'd bought for Peter three days before he was born. She held it close and tried not to cry again. She couldn't do this alone.

She didn't have to. Kainan had offered to help her. Kainan was *here*. But she wanted him to help her without having to make promises that she wasn't sure that she wanted to keep. She'd never wanted to get married. Not really.

Why couldn't they just work on raising Peter together?

Because Kainan will go back to Isla Hermosa after his surgery. He is King.

She had to do this on her own. Her parents were right in that she could only rely on herself. Peter was *her* responsibility. She had always been going to do this on her own

anyway. Kainan's presence didn't change that. She had to protect her heart.

Kainan would do right by Peter, of that she was sure, but she wasn't so sure he would do the same for her, and she couldn't risk it.

He was King and he had a duty to his country. She understood that. She respected that.

Reagan set the bear back down. She would have to get used to doing things on her own. She couldn't leave Toronto. She had to stay close while they waited for Peter's new heart.

Kainan would return to Isla Hermosa to lead his country and Reagan would have to parent Peter on her own.

As she'd planned to do all along.

CHAPTER EIGHT

It DIDN'T TAKE long for the police to arrive, and all Reagan could do was stand to the side and watch them go through her things, dusting for fingerprints and looking for evidence. She felt so exposed, so vulnerable, and she hated every minute of it.

"You say it doesn't appear that anything has been taken, Dr. Cote?" the constable in charge asked.

"Everything seems to be here—my computer, my television, and even some money that I had hidden in my sock drawer. Until I clean I won't really know."

The constable nodded.

Kainan signed and the constable glanced at her in question.

"He says he thinks that my personal information was stolen. It appears my computer was hacked into," she said.

"Why does the think that?" the constable asked.

"Because he's the King of Isla Hermosa and…we have a child together."

The constable was shocked. "This may have to be taken up with the RCMP."

"I understand," Reagan said stonily. "I know you'll do what's best."

Only right now she wasn't sure what that was.

The constable nodded. "We'll take your laptop in and

have our forensic team go over it. There could be a digital trace."

"Thank you, Constable."

"No problem, Dr. Cote. Make sure you get your locks changed. As soon as we hear anything we'll give you a call."

The constable turned back to his team and they began to bag the evidence that they wanted to take a closer look at.

Reagan turned away. "What do you think they were after?" she asked Kainan.

They're were looking for information about you, me and our son. I have no doubts. Kainan shook his head. *I'm sorry this happened.*

"At least they didn't touch Peter's nursery. It's just as I left it."

Where is Peter's nursery? he asked.

"It's in the bedroom, in my walk-in closet."

Kainan frowned. *A closet?*

"It's a large closet, with a light. Lots of space. I was even able to fit a chair in there."

A closet seems highly inappropriate.

"Oh, yes? And what would you have me do? I'm alone and this is what I can afford."

His expression softened and she felt bad for snapping at him. It wasn't his fault that she'd thought he was dead.

You can't have a ventricular assist device in a walk-in closet.

"I'm aware of that now, but when I was pregnant I didn't think that my baby would be *on* a ventricular device."

Kainan sighed. "I'm sorry."

"It's okay. It's not your fault. I just feel…" She trailed off. *Violated. Afraid. Insecure.*

Only she didn't say those words out loud. She had been

taught never to say things like that out loud. Never to show weakness.

"I'm tired."

Are you sure that's all? Kainan asked.

Reagan scrubbed a hand over her face. "I really should get back to the hospital. We've been gone for ages. What if Peter wakes up?"

It will take a while before they wake him up. He has been sedated for so long. You won't miss it. Besides, you have to get these locks changed and we have to clean up this apartment.

Reagan nodded. "You're right. I'm just feeling a bit anxious right now."

And you have every right to be.

"We've got everything, Dr. Cote," the head constable said. "We'll keep you updated."

"Thank you, Constable. Have a merry Christmas."

"You too, Dr. Cote."

Reagan opened the door for the retreating police officers and shut it behind them. "I suppose I'd better call a locksmith to come and change the locks."

I'll start cleaning in the bedroom.

"I don't know where to start…" Reagan muttered.

One room at a time.

Kainan wandered away to her bedroom. She had no doubt that he was going to check out the nursery she'd set up and tell her that it was unsuitable. And he wasn't wrong. It was unsuitable.

What am I going to do?

She felt lost at the moment. Everything was overwhelming her.

Step one: call the locksmith, and then you can think about step two.

Reagan looked up a local number on her phone and di-

aled, hoping someone would be able to come out on short notice right before Christmas.

Kainan wandered around the bedroom. It was small, but it was cozy. It was Reagan's room. Or it had been until a stranger had come in and violated her privacy.

Kainan clenched his fists, biting back the rage he was feeling thinking because someone had been in here. Someone who wanted information about him and Reagan.

This is all my fault.

If he hadn't got involved with Reagan this would never have happened.

He picked up a drawer that had been pulled out and tossed on the bed, slid it back into the dresser, remembering...

"Hey, can I get a picture of you?" the stranger had asked.

Kainan had looked up. "What?"

"You're a prince of Isla Hermosa, right?" There had been a blinding flash. "Come here."

"Who *are* you?" his mother had screamed as she'd thrown herself in front of him. "Get off my property!"

"Easy, Your Majesty. The public just wants pictures."

His mother had stood, her fists clenched. "Get off my property!"

The guards had soon been there, dragging the man away. When the photographer had been out of sight his mother had collapsed, trembling as she'd turned to him.

"He didn't hurt you, did he, Kainan?"

"No, Mama..."

He needed to protect Reagan, he thought now. And he couldn't protect her here.

He began to pluck clothing off the floor and fold the items, placing them back in the drawer. His gaze fell on the closed closet door. Kainan's pulse quickened as he thought

about Peter. And, though he knew he shouldn't look in the closet, he did.

He opened the closet door and flicked on the light.

Reagan had been right. It was a large closet, but it was a closet nonetheless, and his throat tightened when he saw the crib, the bedding in a bag on the floor, and the teddy bear that was lying on its side on a change table.

She had made it homey and cozy for their son. She had done the best she could, but it wasn't enough. Not for him.

He closed his eyes and guilt ate away at him for not being there. For not providing for them. She'd been all alone. This was not good enough for Reagan. She deserved more.

How? This will continue to happen. People will always pry into her life.

Even if Kainan didn't survive his surgery Peter was his heir and the press would be curious about him.

His throat tightened and it was hard to breathe. He closed his eyes and tried not to think of the moment when he'd tried to speak and hadn't been able to. When he hadn't been able to breathe.

"Kainan?" Reagan called out, and then she appeared in the doorway of the room.

Kainan set the bear back down, sitting him upright, and stepped out of the closet, closing the door behind him.

"Checking up on my handiwork?" she asked.

He smiled. *Perhaps.*

"The locksmith is here and I've cleaned up the living room the best I can. Once the lock is changed and I've grabbed a few things I want to get back to the hospital."

Of course. And I will have Andreas pack up the baby's things.

"What're you talking about?" she asked.

You can't stay here. It's not safe.

"Kainan, this is my *home*. This will be Peter's home. Where else would we go?"

I will get you a new place. One that is more suitable.

"I don't think so."

I do think so, Kainan signed. *Peter needs a larger room and you need to be moved somewhere safe. My security team will handle it.*

"No, I'm not uprooting my life, Kainan. That's too much to ask."

You won't marry me, and you won't let me protect you. Let me do this. I can't have you come back here and be pestered. Not when Peter needs to rest and heal.

Reagan bit her lip. She was clearly thinking about it, but she didn't answer.

It will be days before he's discharged, Kainan signed. *More than enough time to get you a new place, close to the hospital, and move you. You won't have to do anything. Let me do this, Reagan. Please.*

"Fine," she said. "But it has to be close to the hospital."

I will find something.

He was relieved he could do something for them. That he could take care of them this way.

Kainan texted his team to let them know what he required. The new place would be large enough to house Reagan and Peter, and Kainan would be in a suite next to him, with his security detail.

Though Reagan didn't need to know that bit of information yet.

The press knew that he was at the Royal York and were camped out there permanently, so moving to a new location with a secure entrance would be better. He would be closer to Peter and Reagan and maybe, just maybe, he would be able to convince Reagan to marry him. Then he could keep them safe behind the palace walls.

Really?

That was his father's thinking, and he hated himself for it, but he felt powerless and didn't know what to do.

He was broken.

But he wasn't going to let Reagan or Peter out of his sight.

Kainan dropped Reagan at the hospital, where she wanted to be, and then went with Andreas to see a new place.

The condo was located two blocks south of the hospital and on the lakeshore. It had two suites, side by side, and one of them would comfortably house his security staff and himself. The smaller suite was larger than Reagan's current home, and would be more than adequate for her and Peter.

The only downside was that it wasn't on the subway route, but it was only a block to Union Station and the hospital was right across the street from that.

Reagan could walk or Andreas could drive her. If he was still here. If Kainan's voice surgery was successful then Andreas would return to Isla Hermosa with him.

But you can come back.

He wasn't sure about that. Would Reagan forgive him if he left?

He wasn't sure.

"They're just waiting for your signature, Your Majesty. I have made sure that they have signed confidentiality agreements and I have paid in cash," Andreas said, interrupting his thoughts.

Thank you, Andreas. How soon can we move in?

"Today," Andreas said. "I can have movers go to Dr. Cote's apartment and pack it up, so we can get her into this new home by tomorrow morning."

Do that.

Andreas nodded and opened the door to the condo com-

plex. Kainan went through all the paperwork and signed everything that was needed.

Tonight he would tell Reagan about the plan over dinner. Even if he had to bring it into the hospital again. He wasn't giving her a chance to say no this time. This was for their own protection. This was something he could do for them.

They would be in their new home in time for Christmas, and perhaps this way he could show Reagan he was in. That if he left he would still be there.

How can you be "in" as King?

And then there was his surgery coming up. With the amount of scar tissue in his throat it was risky. He might die, abandoning Reagan.

He shook that thought away as he took the keys from the realtor and followed Andreas to the top floor of the complex.

"The suites are at the end of the hallway," Andreas said as he led Kainan down. "Dr. Cote's is twenty-nine B and you're twenty-nine A."

Kainan nodded and turned the key to Reagan's new place. It was bright and large. There were windows which faced the icy grey waters of Lake Ontario. He could not see the CN Tower from this viewpoint, but that was okay. The view of the islands and the water was all he needed.

It reminded him of Isla Hermosa. Endless water and islands scattered all around the main island. The only difference was that Isla Hermosa was tropical and here there was snow. And the grey, ice-filled water was a bit unforgiving.

Kainan was not a fan of winter.

Still, this was a much better space than her current home. She was surrounded by tall buildings there. It was stifling, as if there was no room to breathe. Here at the top of this complex, with Lake Ontario stretching below him, he felt he could breathe.

"Do you like it, Your Majesty?" Andreas asked.

Kainan nodded. and then handed Andreas the key that Reagan had given him when the locksmith had changed her locks.

Please make sure that Reagan is moved in right away.

"And what of you, Your Majesty?"

Get some furnishings. My room can be packed up later. I want us to have a close-by option—especially since we don't know how long Peter will still be in the hospital.

Andreas nodded. "Very well, Your Majesty."

Thank you for all your assistance, Andreas. I don't think I express it enough.

Andreas was a bit taken aback by that. "Thank you, Your Majesty."

There was a buzz on Kainan's phone and he looked down to see that it was Reagan texting him. There was news about Peter.

I have to go back to the hospital. Kainan slipped his phone in his pocket.

"I will take you back there right now."

Kainan followed Andreas out of the apartment. He was glad things were moving forward with Reagan, because he was running out of time.

Reagan's pulse was racing. They had just moved Peter from the pediatric critical care unit to the regular pediatric ward. He was doing so well on the ventricular assist device that they were going to bring him out of sedation.

She would be able to hold him. She hadn't held him in so long. Her arms were aching to hold him, but she was terrified too.

Deep down she was scared of this whole thing. It was a way to extend his life, but there was a set time-frame. Peter needed a new heart. There was no other choice.

There was a new set of nurses on duty and she waited with bated breath as they moved about the room. Peter was moving, and there were more subtle movements as the sedation wore off.

She'd done a rotation on Pediatrics when she had been an intern, but she had forgotten how resilient kids were. How they bounced back.

She'd texted Kainan to come, because he'd wanted to know when they were going to wake Peter up.

She knew he was out property-hunting, but she seriously doubted that he would find anything on short notice. And, even though he didn't want her going back to her apartment alone, she was going to head back there and get Peter's nursery ready.

Kainan came into the room.

"Glad you could make it," she said, and she *was* relieved that he was here.

How is he doing? Kainan signed.

"Good. He's strong."

Kainan nodded and picked up the chart to read the notes. A brief smile crossed his face as he shut the chart.

This is good!

"I'll be back in a few minutes, Reagan," the pediatric nurse said. "I have to check on my other patients."

"Thanks, Maria," Reagan said.

Maria nodded and left the room.

Reagan took a step forward and stared down at her baby, wrapped up in his crib. There was a cannula running from his chest to the machine that sat on the table next to the crib. The machine that was pumping blood instead of his heart now.

His poor, weak heart.

She reached out to touch him but then took her hand

back because she wasn't wearing gloves. She looked up at Kainan, unsure.

What's wrong? he signed.

"I'm not wearing gloves—just a surgical gown."

Did they tell you that you needed to be gowned and gloved?

"No, they didn't. I just put this on out of habit."

Kainan smiled gently at her. *Go ahead.*

Reagan reached out and touched Peter's smooth, soft skin. Emotion overcame her as she ran her fingers over his tiny hand and then over the dark curls on his head.

"I've waited so long for this," she whispered.

The tears were threatening to spill, but she cleared her throat—because this wasn't the end of scares. This was just a way to keep him alive longer, until a heart became available.

She couldn't let her guard down yet.

Peter stirred under her hand and she gasped. His head moved and he opened his eyes, blinking. And then those dark eyes that were so like Kainan's looked toward her. His brow furrowed as he tried to make sense of what he could seen through a drug-induced fog.

"Peter…" she whispered, she knelt down to look at his little chubby face. "Mommy's here."

Her voice hitched in her throat and it took every ounce of her strength not to cry as she connected with her son in his crib.

Peter's eyes closed, but he smiled. So many stages of his life she'd missed. Babies grew so fast and she was missing it.

There will be more stages that you will get to see, she told herself.

And for the first time in a long time she confidently believed that.

Then Kainan knelt down and stared at his son, his eyes glistening, and he beamed as Peter opened his eyes again and looked at Kainan.

"He has my eyes," Kainan said, and Reagan could see the pride in his face.

"Did he open his eyes?" Maria asked as she returned.

"He did," Reagan said, standing up.

"That's wonderful. It will take a while for him to fully wake out of his sedation, but he's doing very well," Maria said.

"How long do you think it will be before he's discharged?" Reagan asked, nervous about the answer, because here in the hospital he was safe.

"It's hard to say. It depends how well he does and his pain management. But since you're both surgeons Dr. McNeil will probably discharge him as early as Christmas Eve. And that will be an excellent Christmas gift!" Maria continued, checking Peter's lines as Reagan stood there in shock.

"That soon?" Reagan murmured in disbelief. "I have a lot to do to get ready."

Maria grinned. "I'm sure. Why don't you go do that, Dr. Cote? He will likely be asleep for a while longer. Get some diapers and get his nursery ready."

Reagan was about to argue when Michael entered Peter's room. He looked a bit panicked.

"Reagan, I'm so glad I found you," Michael said breathlessly, and then he saw Kainan. "Dr. Laskaris, I'm glad you're here too."

Dread crept down her spine. "What's wrong, Michael?"

"A section of the roof has collapsed at the shopping center. A lot of people are injured and I'm short-staffed due to the snowstorm that just rolled in off the lake. It's dumped three inches of snow since it started two and half hours ago."

"What?"

Reagan opened the blinds in Peter's room and couldn't even see the courtyard of the hospital. Just a wall of white.

"They're bringing them in on foot and our emergency room is packed," Michael said. "I could use you both."

Kainan signed, and she knew what he was thinking.

"Kainan wants to know how he can help even when he can't communicate," Reagan said.

"He can work with you, Reagan. I'm sorry to pull you away from your son, but it's all hands on deck."

Kainan nodded with determination and picked up his jacket.

"We'll be right there, Michael," Reagan said.

Michael left at a sprint.

"Don't worry, Dr. Cote. Peter will be fine," Maria said.

Reagan nodded, but she was unsure about leaving him. Still, she was needed. She was a surgeon and there were lives to be saved.

Kainan held open the door for her and they walked together to the staff change room, where all the on-call doctors who'd been able to get in were getting ready for the onslaught of patients.

There was also a team of doctors who would be working on clearing the operating theaters of nonessential surgeries and keeping the flow to X-Ray and the CT scanner free and clear. As well as finding bed space in an already cramped hospital.

Reagan changed quickly, stuffing her clothing into her locker. Kainan stood beside her, unbuttoning the dress shirt that he'd been wearing.

"No locker," he said quickly as he stuffed his clothes into hers.

"Save your voice, Kainan," she said as she shimmied

out of her dress pants and pulled on her scrubs. "You're going to need it."

He smiled sadly and nodded as he grabbed a pair of men's scrubs from the shelf behind him.

She thought about all those times in the tight quarters of the field hospital and how much carnage they had seen and worked together on.

This was going to be the same.

A section of the roof falling in a packed shopping center at Christmas… The thought made her sick to her stomach.

After they were dressed and ready to go, with disposable surgical gowns and gloves, they headed straight into the chaos of the emergency room.

Michael was in charge as he spoke to his surgeons and assigned stations, putting the residents outside to receive the patients as they came in from the ambulances.

Kainan went straight to work and began to set up other triage areas for the less critical. Reagan translated for him and helped him to divide a hallway that was rarely used into small pods for the less injured.

The waiting room was packed as well, with patients who had wandered in with things like colds, sprains and an assortment of other cases. They would have to be seen to. and Michael mobilized a group of residents to take care of them and prioritize.

Reagan and Kainan worked well together, just as they had always done. She knew what he was thinking before he had to ask her, and vice versa.

"Just like old times, eh?" she teased.

Kainan made a funny face. Before he could respond there was the wail of sirens. Ambulances were working their way through the snow. Orderlies were outside, working on shoveling a clear path as the first ambulance pulled up.

"Reagan and Kainan—you're up!" Michael called over the commotion.

Reagan went outside, the bitter cold biting at her cheeks as the ambulance came to a stop. The doors opened and the paramedics jumped into action.

"Male, age forty-five, multiple injuries to the torso and abdomen. Glasgow coma scale of two on arrival."

Reagan and Kainan helped the paramedic push the gurney through the snow and they took their patient to one of the trauma bays that were being used for priority patients. A man with multiple crush injuries to the torso and abdomen and a GCS of two was a priority.

Kainan signed off on the paramedics' charts while Reagan began to go over the man's ABCs. One pupil was blown. and she was worried that when he fell he'd hit his head hard and there might be a hematoma.

Kainan worked on the other side of her. He snapped his fingers to get her attention and signed, *Free fluid in the lungs. I'm going to do a chest tube.*

Reagan nodded. "Left pupil is blown. I want to get him down for a CT."

"Chest tray," Kainan said gruffly to the intern who was in the room with them, and he rolled his shoulders, wincing from the pain of exerting his voice. But he didn't hesitate as he cut away the man's shirt and examined his chest.

"Any lacerations from the debris that landed on him? I see blood," Reagan said as she started a large-bore IV and hung painkillers and fluids.

Kainan held up two fingers.

Reagan counted at least four wounds to the man's abdomen. There was also dark bruising under his skin. "He needs a CT scan as soon as you get that chest tube in."

She cursed inwardly as she tried to picture how the debris had fallen on the patient and what organs it might have

damaged. Because there was fluid in the man's lungs she had no doubt that he was suffering a hemothorax, but what other damage had the debris caused?

"Here you are, Dr. Laskaris," the intern said, handing the chest tube tray to Kainan.

Kainan nodded and went about listening and finding the best place to insert the chest tube. He quickly wiped the skin and then made his move.

The patient flexed in a decerebrate motion, arching his chest and his head, arms straight out, everything stiff in response to the chest tube being inserted.

As it did its job the patient's vitals steadied. Kainan smiled and secured the tube and they readied the patient to go down for the CT scan. Reagan needed to see what she was dealing with before she went in there and tried to fix the damage that had been done.

Kainan moved beside her silently, anticipating her every move. Just like in Isla Hermosa.

They were as one.

And, though she'd always prided herself on being a lone wolf, she was glad he was here in this moment. That he was here with her now and that she didn't have to explain her every move. He just *knew*.

And that thought scared her.

It scared her to think that she needed him when she had never needed anyone before.

CHAPTER NINE

"CAN YOU MOVE the retractor, please?" Reagan asked, and Kainan adjusted his hold on it.

Their patient had some head trauma, but nothing as serious as what was going on in his abdomen, because there were crush injuries and he was bleeding internally. The CT scan had shown her what damage had been done.

The spleen had been lacerated and was bleeding heavily. A kidney had been pierced, as well as his bowel, and the diaphragm, which was why his lungs had filled with blood. The heart was fine for now, as was the liver. Still, the bleeding needed to be controlled so he didn't die before they had a chance to repair his injuries.

She was hours into surgery. They were still hanging blood, but she was getting ahead of the damage. Even though Kainan could not speak he knew what to do, and she didn't often have to ask for his assistance. It was if he knew what her next step would be before she did.

They worked so well together. She'd forgotten how much she enjoyed working with him. Working with him to save lives.

The King of Isla Hermosa.

She shook her head, trying not to think about that fact. He was a surgeon too. He hadn't been a king when they'd worked together, when he'd taken her in his arms.

He had just been Kainan.

Now he was King, and yet here he was helping save lives. How many world leaders would do the same? It was at this moment that she saw the man he'd been before—the man she'd known and cared for.

She watched him briefly as a resident worked on stitching, studying him over her surgical mask. Those kind eyes were looking down at the work the resident was doing with keen interest, and she couldn't help but smile as she thought of him by her side, working with her as if nothing had changed.

It was nice, even though the situation was not. And her pulse quickened as she thought back to that kiss they'd shared, when Peter was in surgery for the ventricular device. His strong arms had comforted her, as had his kiss, and their connection had grounded her.

Kainan was her rock.

The realization shocked her, and she wasn't sure how she felt about it. She had been taught not to rely on anyone. So when had she begun to rely on Kainan so much?

It made her stomach twist in a knot, because she *had* to be self-sufficient. She couldn't rely on him, no matter how much she wanted to.

He was King of a foreign country and would eventually have to return to it. She couldn't leave Canada—not until Peter had a new heart. She had to be careful not to let *her* heart do all her thinking, which was what was happening when she was around Kainan.

She had to start thinking logically. She had to be careful. Peter's heart wasn't the only one that was fragile—hers was too.

They had been working on this man for hours, but he was going to make it and that was the most important thing. After they'd finished up here they would have to scrub out

and head back down to the emergency room and continue to work, to take the pressure off a bombarded trauma room.

On a tray across the operating room she could see her phone sitting there, silent, as a nurse monitored it.

Peter's fine. And after this is all done you can hold him.

Just that simple thought sustained her. It kept her focused.

She finished the surgery and gave instructions to the scrub nurse and the intern for the patient's postoperative care. Kainan followed her out of the operating room and they scrubbed out.

"Where to?" Kainan asked, and then winced, his throat paining him.

"Have you had your throat looked at by your otolaryngologist lately?"

Kainan sent her an exasperated expression. *Of course.*

"It's just that I know if you use your voice more than you should it can cause problems. I would hate for you to risk your surgery."

It's already a risky surgery and there is a lot of scar tissue.

"Why have they waited so long?"

The surgeon wanted to wait until I was strong.

"And...?" Reagan asked, drying off her hands. "You're stronger now."

Kainan pursed his lips together. *The surgery is coming, but there's no guarantee it will work.*

"I think it will," she said.

Why do you think so?

"A king needs a voice," she said.

I have you.

It was like a punch in her gut. "I won't always be there to be your voice, Kainan."

Why not? You could be my Queen. It's a solution that

would work for us both. We'd give Peter stability and you could assist me in my rule.

"I'm a surgeon, Kainan. Could I still practice medicine as Queen of Isla Hermosa?"

Kainan's shoulders slumped and she had her answer. She felt bad for Kainan, because soon his surgical career would be over. He was a king, and when he returned to Isla Hermosa he wouldn't be able to practice medicine any longer.

"You need to stop proposing to me, Kainan. You know my answer. It's no."

But the more time she spent with him the harder it was to say no. The dream of a happy family she'd always craved was tempting, but nothing worked out the way it was supposed to and she didn't want to risk it.

He didn't say anything, and didn't look her in the eye. It was hard to disappoint him, but she couldn't let her heart make this decision.

If her heart had had its way then she would have said yes the first time he'd asked her. The moment he'd walked back in her life.

You're a fool, her heart told her, but she knew that it would never work. The only person she could rely on was herself.

They headed back down to the emergency room and it was still chaotic. As she surveyed the scene her gaze landed on a tall man with dark hair in one of the beds. Alone and clearly in pain.

"Isn't that Andreas?" she asked.

Kainan spun around, pained as he rushed to his security guard's side with Reagan at his heels. He had been hurt, but it looked like just a flesh wound.

"Andreas," Reagan said sadly. "You were at the shopping center?"

"Dr. Cote…" He grimaced, and then his gaze fell on Kainan. "Your Majesty. I'm sorry."

For what? Kainan signed.

Andreas leaned back against the pillows, his face with the grey tint of pain and blood loss.

Reagan pulled his chart. "Your leg was caught under a cement beam, but it's not broken, and the laceration missed your femoral artery. That's good."

Andreas nodded. "It's just a flesh wound. I was trying to protect a child from the falling debris."

Kainan winced and bowed his head, gripping Andreas's shoulder.

"You have lost a lot of blood," she said, then bit her lip and stopped the resident who was dealing with Andreas. "Has blood been ordered? His platelet count is low."

"Yes, but the blood bank doesn't have any universal blood. There's another blood bank across the city, and they're trying to get through with the type of blood he needs, but the storm and this accident has depleted our reserves," the resident said.

Dammit.

I will donate blood, Kainan signed. *I'm Hermosian and I can donate for him.*

The resident looked confused.

"He can donate," Reagan said. "He's a universal blood type and both of them are Hermosian. Ready a transfusion kit and get this man on plasma while I handle the donation."

"Yes, Dr. Cote." The resident ran away.

"We'll be back, Andreas. Do you need anything for the pain?" Reagan asked.

Andreas shook his head. "No, Dr. Cote. I am fine. The child I helped lives, and that's the main thing, but I cannot accept blood from my King."

Reagan frowned and Kainan's brow furrowed.

You will, Kainan said.

"Your Majesty, I can't take your blood."

It's just blood, Kainan signed furiously. *You will take it and that is a royal decree.*

Andreas sighed and closed his eyes. "Yes, Your Majesty."

Kainan pulled the drapes around Andreas's bed. His face was like thunder. Andreas's injury was obviously bothering him. It bothered Reagan too. She hated to see Andreas hurt again. When he'd been injured during the Hermosian uprising it had been because he'd pulled a younger soldier out of the line of fire.

It seemed bizarre that on the front lines of battle in a foreign country they had more blood than here in a vast city, and all because of a snowstorm which was hampering their ability to get to it. It was silly.

Kainan took a seat in an exam room just outside the emergency department. He pulled off his white lab coat and stuck out his arm.

The resident brought Reagan the kit she would need to get the blood donation from Kainan. Reagan began to ready everything while Kainan stared at the wall, still fuming.

"Are you all right?"

Kainan nodded, but he wouldn't look at her.

"What's wrong? Are you mad at Andreas?"

No, he signed. *I'm angry at myself.*

"Why? You had nothing to do with his injury."

I sent him out to furnish my new apartment.

She raised her eyebrows as she wiped his arm with rubbing alcohol. "*Your* new apartment. I thought you were looking for a place for me and Peter?"

We found that too. They're next to each other.

She raised an eyebrow. "How convenient."

A small smile tugged at his lips. *Peter is my son too, and I want to be close to him for as long as I can.*

Right, because he would have to leave. There was an expiry date on his time in Canada.

"Sorry, of course you do." Then she realized what he was saying. "You got apartments that are available now?"

Kainan nodded. *With the right amount of money.*

"Kainan, how *much* money?" She'd agreed to a new place, but she didn't want him spending great sums of money on her.

There is no mortgage to worry about, Reagan. You can raise Peter there comfortably. And when I'm in Toronto I can be close to him.

Reagan cursed under her breath. "You shouldn't have done that."

He's my son too. I just want him to be comfortable. And I want to take care of you.

"Kainan, I have to be self-sufficient. I *can't* rely on you. When you leave it will just be me and Peter."

Kainan didn't respond. He set his jaw firmly in that stubborn way of his and looked away from her.

"So, when are the movers coming for my stuff—or have you arranged that too?" she asked sarcastically.

He grinned and she groaned.

"I'm probably already moved in, aren't I?"

In the process.

She shook her head and then tied the tourniquet around his arm. "Make a fist—and no more signing."

Kainan rolled his eyes, but that smug grin was still on his face.

She got the blood transfusion started and then removed the tourniquet. Kainan was a pro at this.

"It's not your fault for sending him to that shopping center, Kainan. A roof collapsed. No one is at fault. Things happen."

Kainan didn't say anything. He just closed his eyes and looked at the ceiling. She couldn't blame him. One of the things that bothered her about medicine was blood donation. It was good to do it, but she'd got a bit queasy the couple of times she had donated over the years.

"What you're doing for Andreas is good," she said. "You're a good king to your people. You may think you need a voice, but you don't. Your actions speak louder than your words ever will."

He raised his head and looked at her then, those dark eyes twinkling, and he mouthed the words *thank you* before closing his eyes and staring back up at the ceiling.

Kainan stood and watched as Andreas received his blood transfusion. After he'd donated he'd felt a bit dizzy, and Reagan had got him some orange juice and let him rest before she'd been called away by a resident.

When Kainan had felt better he'd headed back to the emergency room and gone to check on Andreas, who had already been hooked up to an intravenous and receiving Kainan's donation.

The color was returning to his friend's cheeks now.

Kainan still felt incredible guilty that Andreas had been put in harm's way. Twice.

He didn't like putting people's lives at risk. He was a surgeon. He *saved* lives.

You're no longer a surgeon, though.

And that thought sobered him. He was King, and a country full of lives depended on him. His life was no longer his.

Still, there was a part of him that didn't want to be King. Being back in the operating room and working with Reagan had been amazing. He'd forgotten what it was like to save a life. He hadn't practiced surgery since the day Reagan had left Isla Hermosa.

He missed it.

Missed the thrill of it all.

Still, if he died on the operating table with a surgeon trying to save his voice then there would be no monarchy for Isla Hermosa. Peter was too young to be King and he was the last of his line.

Unless you appoint a regent to take Peter's place. An illegitimate king can still rule when he comes of age, as long as he's claimed, in writing, by the current King.

Reagan came in and glanced at Kainan in the seat next to Andreas's bedside. Andreas was still sleeping.

"You okay?" she asked.

Tired, but I will live.

"So will Andreas. Don't worry—your blood helped."

I know. Even if he didn't want it.

"I don't get that."

Because I'm King and...

"And?" she asked.

"It's not right," Andreas repeated, still in delirium.

Kainan chuckled softly as he looked at Andreas. *He's my half brother.*

Reagan's eyes widened. "Your half brother?"

Yes, though not legitimate. Andreas thinks of his adoptive father as his real father, not the late King. His adoptive father claimed him as his own, which is why Andreas could never be in the line of succession. He was luckier than me.

"Luckier? Why?"

He was loved and doted on. He had freedom. I did not. Kainan scrubbed a hand over his face. *I envied him for so many years.*

"Do you still?"

He looked up at her. If he'd had Andreas's life he probably wouldn't be a surgeon, and he wouldn't have met Reagan. For the first time he didn't envy Andreas's different upbringing.

No.

Pink bloomed in her cheeks. She cleared her throat. "How is your voice?"

He spoke aloud. "My throat is tight…sore. I should go see Dr. Shaw. Can you keep an eye on Andreas?"

She nodded, her gaze soft. "Yes."

Andreas opened his eyes. "Your Majesty?"

Kainan stood up and squeezed Andreas's shoulder. *Rest*, he signed.

Kainan left Andreas to sleep. He made his way out of the emergency room and to Dr. Shaw's office. Dr. Shaw had been the surgeon who'd looked at his throat when he'd first arrived in Toronto, and he had the information from the Ottawa surgeon about the surgical procedures that Kainan had endured in the field.

Dr. Shaw was packing up for the evening when Kainan knocked on his door. Dr. Shaw also knew American Sign Language, because of all the hearing-impaired patients he worked with. Which was fortuitous.

"Dr. Laskaris—or should I refer to you as Your Majesty?"

Kainan smiled. *Kainan will suffice.*

"It's some crazy storm out there, eh? I think I'm going to leave my car in the employee garage and take the subway home—although the tracks at Rosehill are covered."

I'm worried about scar tissue. I've been using my voice, Kainan signed.

Dr. Shaw's eyebrows rose. "Have you? How much? I told you not to overdo it."

Kainan ignored that. This was his chance to be strong for his son, for Reagan. He needed his voice.

Could you please check?

"I can." Dr. Shaw set his bag down and took a seat, firing up his computer as Kainan shut the door. "Hopefully you haven't overtaxed yourself too much."

I hope not. I need my voice by the New Year.

Dr. Shaw nodded and examined his throat, frowning. "The surgery may not work. Although during your last scan there were not as many adhesions. I would like to get another scan, but I can still do your surgery on December twenty-sixth."

Kainan nodded. *Of course. When would you like the scan done?*

"Tomorrow morning, if that's okay? I know your boy just had surgery…"

Tomorrow is fine. My son is stable and I need to get this taken care of.

Dr. Shaw nodded. "Dr. McNeil told me that when you asked for the surgery I was to make it happen as if you were a head of state."

I appreciate it, and I'm sorry for inconveniencing you, but I was told you were the best.

"You're not inconveniencing me, Kainan." Dr. Shaw stood and Kainan did as well. "It's my pleasure. Come by my office tomorrow at seven in the morning and we'll get you down to the MRI and get it done. We'll see what we're working with. And stop using your voice!"

I will.

"I'm serious—no more talking. No more exercising it. I will see you tomorrow, Kainan."

Kainan shook Dr. Shaw's hand before heading back to the emergency room. He texted Andreas's second in command to see how the move was going and to let them know what had happened to Andreas.

He had to step up and do what was right.

He was terrified that he wouldn't survive surgery, which meant he would lose Reagan forever, leaving her and Peter alone.

Never know his son.

Never have happiness.

CHAPTER TEN

REAGAN HAD BEEN separated from Kainan since just after he'd donated blood for Andreas. She'd got pulled into another surgery. An injured person had been brought in and could only communicate in Spanish.

She'd planned to take Kainan into surgery with her, but then she had been informed that this man was a Hermosian refugee and, given Andreas's reaction to Kainan donating blood, she'd thought it was best to keep the King out of the operating room.

Her patient was sedated, so Reagan went about repairing the injuries that he had sustained when the roof had collapsed on top of him.

Thankfully, no one had died in the accident.

Not even her first patient, Mr. Lucas, with the multiple crush injuries and the head injury. Reagan had saved his life.

When she came out of surgery the chaos in the emergency room had died down, as had the snow.

It was after midnight, which meant that it was Christmas Eve now. Officially.

She was exhausted, but she had to find Kainan.

When she went down to the emergency room, where the staff were now cycling through the non-emergent cases that

had come in, she saw that Andreas was being moved to a room for overnight observation.

"Dr. Cote," Andreas said, smiling.

"How are you feeling?" she asked.

"Better. I would like to leave, but they want to keep me."

"You just had a major laceration and a blood transfusion. You need to rest here. Have you seen Kainan? I'm afraid I had to go into surgery and I lost track of him."

"Yes, I saw him a few hours ago. He was going to speak to another doctor before he checked on Peter, and then I believe he was headed back to the hotel to pack up his things because his new residence will be ready soon."

"I heard about that," Reagan said, crossing her arms.

Andreas grinned. "He will have the key to your new place, and I know that my team has got everything in your old place moved out. Do you want me to put your old place on the market?"

"I can handle that, Andreas. You need your rest."

"If you want to speak to Kainan you'll need this," Andreas reached in his pocket and pulled out a gold elevator keycard. "It's my extra copy and it will allow you to access his room."

"Thanks. I think I will go see him after I check on Peter."

Andreas nodded and the orderly wheeled him away.

Reagan turned the keycard over in her hand. She really needed to talk to Kainan, especially since they were planning on discharging Peter soon. They had to talk about the arrangements and what would happen when Kainan returned to Isla Hermosa.

How much longer could he stay here? He had duties to do.

Reagan pocketed the card and went to the staff change room. She got out of her scrubs and put them in the laundry hamper, changing back into her street clothes.

She went to check on Peter and found he was still asleep, but he stirred when she touched him gently. Things were looking up. Even though Peter relied on a machine to keep him alive, he was here and responding. He was no longer in a medicated coma.

Even if Kainan left she would have Peter.

Except Peter wouldn't have Kainan.

That made her sad, but the timing was off. Kainan was King and his country needed him, and Peter needed a new heart. He had to stay in Toronto while he waited.

Reagan kissed her son's head and then left the hotel. She needed to have something to eat and a nap, and Kainan was the one who had the key to her new place where supposedly her bed and all her belongings were.

She didn't even know the address!

Reagan slipped down through the abandoned PATH walkway, which was devoid of commuters now, with the underground shops closed for the night. Then she went up the spiral staircase that connected The Royal York to the underground.

She was heading toward the gold elevators when she saw that Kainan was hanging out in a deserted piano lounge. He was playing the grand piano. The music was sad and haunting.

She headed toward him. Such strong hands, but gentle in the way he handled patients…and her. He was an imposing king, but he was so kind and sweet with their son.

It had completely knocked down her barriers to see him with Peter.

All her fears about Kainan being distant and not caring about Peter had evaporated away.

Kainan *cared*.

And she was lost to him. She was weak when it came to him and in this moment she didn't care.

Kainan glanced up as she approached him and smiled halfheartedly, scooting over so she could sit next to him.

"I didn't know you played," she said.

He didn't respond, but finished his piece and then turned to her.

I don't play often, but it helps clear my head. Where were you?

"I got pulled into surgery on another injured patient. He was a Hermosian refugee."

Kainan grimaced. "A Hermosian refugee?"

"Yes," she said carefully.

"Did he live?"

"Yes."

"That's good." Kainan rubbed his eyes. "I feel responsible for him—for all my people. As King, I feel it was my duty to keep my country together. My people shouldn't be here as refugees."

"It wasn't your fault that war broke out in your country. You weren't King then."

"I know, but I'm King *now* and it's my responsibility."

"He's safe here in Canada. As are you."

Kainan nodded, but didn't smile. He was sad, and it was apparent that the burden of his people weighed heavily on him.

That's good.

"I came to ask you where I live now," she said with a small smile.

Yes, I suppose that's important. Kainan reached into his pocket and pulled out a key. He handed it to her. *Your new condo is Golden Centre condos on Queens Quay. Your apartment twenty-nine B.*

"Thanks." Reagan pocketed the key. "They're going to send Peter home later today, and it's Christmas Eve."

Kainan nodded. *I know. It will be good. What should we do?*

"I need to go to my new place and make sure that Peter's room is ready." She was puzzled. "What do you mean, what should *we* do?"

To celebrate?

"I don't know." She laughed. "I never thought that I'd have anything to celebrate. I think I just need to ready Peter's room and make a home for him. I think that's all I can handle now."

Would you like to go there now? We can take a cab. Most of my security detail is over at my new place anyway.

"They left you alone here?"

They don't know that I'm here, actually. They think that I'm still at the hospital.

"I suspect that they wouldn't be too happy to learn that you were here."

Kainan shrugged. *Do you want to go?*

"Yes. I wouldn't mind having a short nap in my own bed for a change."

Kainan nodded. *That can be arranged. Let's go, then, it's late.*

They walked out of the empty piano lounge and headed out onto Front Street. The snow had stopped falling and the streets had been freshly plowed. Even though it was long after midnight there were still taxis waiting outside the prestigious hotel.

Kainan opened the door and Reagan slid in, telling the cabdriver the address. It didn't take the cabdriver long, on the deserted streets of Toronto, to get to the new condo building.

Reagan's mouth hung open when she saw it. She knew exactly how much these suites were. When she'd first moved back to Toronto, just pregnant, this building had

been half-complete. She'd looked at purchasing a suite, but hadn't been able to swing it.

It was the perfect location. Even better than her apartment on Richmond Street West.

Do you like it? Kainan signed.

"It's too much," she whispered.

She paid the cabdriver and they got out of the cab. Kainan opened up the main door with his key and waved to the doorman. Reagan decided she would introduce herself later.

They rode the elevator, almost to the top, and down at the end of the hallway were two apartments. One was his and the other was hers.

She opened the door and saw the contents of her apartment were now in her new place. Her apartment on Richmond Street had been sparsely furnished, but because her old place had been smaller it had looked all right. Now she could see how sparse her belongings really were in this large new condo.

Kainan gestured and she followed him into a smaller room. He flicked on the lights and there was the crib, the chair and everything. All made up. Emotion overwhelmed her, and she covered her mouth to keep herself from crying.

It was too much. All of it. No one had ever shown her this kind of kindness or generosity before—not even her parents. Michael was like a father figure, but he had his own family. The only time she'd felt somewhat complete was when she was in Isla Hermosa with Kainan.

And then she'd thought he'd died.

Now this.

It was too much, and she wondered why she was fighting him. They could be a family.

She shook her head, because how *could* they be a family. How could she fall in love with a man who was King?

Are you okay? Kainan signed.

She nodded, overcome by his generosity. "It's wonderful. Thank you."

Kainan touched her face and then took her hand and placed it on his chest. Those dark eyes that had always been her downfall were tender and she couldn't help it.

She wanted to be with him.

Even if it was just one more time. She wanted to feel safe in his arms, to forget the world around them for just one moment. To forget all the horrors of this life and know that they had this. They shared so much.

She stepped closer and touched his face, running her fingers over the scars on his face and neck. He closed his eyes and under her other hand she could feel his heart beat faster. He wrapped his arms around her, pulling her against him.

Reagan closed her eyes and kissed him, melting into him as she had done so long ago. As she'd done a couple of days ago when he'd taken her to that room to calm down when she'd been so terrified of Peter having the surgery to attach the ventricular assist device.

Even without words he knew what she was thinking. He knew what she needed. Who needed words when all that was needed was action? And in this moment, that was all she wanted.

She wanted to feel his arms around her again. Even if it was only one more time. She wanted him.

She didn't want to think. All she wanted to be was lost— in his arms, in his kisses. All she wanted to do was *feel*. She'd been numb for so long.

Kainan's kiss deepened and he pressed her against the door, their bodies flush together.

The kiss ended and those dark eyes glittered with desire.

"Yes," she whispered.

And that was all he needed.

He picked her up and carried her to the bedroom, where

her bed was made up in the center of the very large room. There were no window coverings, and all she could see was the darkness of the lake outside her window. There were no other buildings, no one to look in and see them, just the darkness of the frigid water and the sound of another squall blowing in off the lake.

Kainan couldn't believe this was happening. It was what he wanted. All he'd ever wanted. There had been no other woman who'd made him feel this way.

He cupped her face as she undid his belt, watching her eyes, those beautiful brown eyes which made him weak in the knees, and those full pink lips he loved to kiss.

"All I want is you, Kainan. Right here. Right now."

And that was all he needed to hear. Like the snow squall that was raging outside the windows, there was a storm in his soul. He needed to possess her again and never let her go. There was no turning back for them.

Even though he wasn't supposed to use his voice, because of the scar tissue forming in his throat, he whispered against her lips. "No protection."

This seduction, making love to her, was a part of him that he'd thought long gone. He'd thought the Kainan he'd been before his brother had died and he'd became King was long gone. He'd been so focused on duty versus desire he had never prepared for this moment when desire would win over. She made him forget his duty.

"It's okay," she said, kneeling in front of him and unbuttoning his shirt. "I'm on the pill. I won't get pregnant."

And what about last time? he signed, teasing her.

"I wasn't on the pill then. That was an entirely different situation."

He chuckled and leaned his head against hers. "You'... sure?"

"Yes. Very sure. I want you, Kainan."

She opened his shirt and ran her hands over his chest. Her simple touch made him burn with need for her. He wanted to possess her again and again. He'd lost all sense of reason.

There was no way he could turn back. She made him *feel*—made him feel as if he could breathe and love. Things that he'd thought he would never feel again.

And although he wasn't sure what was going to happen in his future, he knew one thing to be true—and that was he never wanted to let her go in this moment.

He kissed her again, running his hand down her back, cupping her bottom to pull her tight against him. He didn't want any space between them and he didn't want to let her go.

All these thoughts ran through his mind. The things he wanted to tell her. How he'd thought only of her since they'd parted. How the memory of her had got him through so much.

How there was only her.

"I've missed you," she whispered, and then she let out a little moan of pleasure as he kissed her throat down to her collarbone, feeling her pulse quicken under his lips.

Kainan had nearly lost his mind with his want for her. *This* was what he'd been dreaming about for so long.

If he wasn't careful he would just take her—right here and now, half dressed—and he didn't want that. Not in this moment.

Kainan wanted to take his time with her.

He wanted to do right by her.

He'd been waiting so long for a chance. A chance to be with her again.

"Kainan…" she whispered, running her hands down his back, her touch leaving goose bumps across his skin.

He couldn't wait, and they made quick work of the rest of their clothes. He undid her rich mahogany brown hair

from its confining bun and ran his fingers through the silken softness. Nothing was between them now. It was just the two of them...bared to each other and vulnerable.

I love your hands on my body, he thought as her hands moved over his skin.

"I can tell you like that," she whispered.

And then she continued teasing with her fingertips, running a finger down his neck, over his chest and lower. Her hand splayed against his abdomen before slipping lower and gripping his erection in the palm of her hand.

He groaned.

She chuckled, and then nibbled his neck. Every nerve-ending in his body was alive as she stroked him. His blood was on fire, and he tried to hold back another moan but couldn't keep it in. Reagan's touching him was driving him wild, and he was afraid that if she kept it up he would come. Only he didn't want her to stop.

Her mouth was on him now, and his hands slipped into her hair. His throat tightened but he couldn't stop. The pleasure was making his body wild with need.

He pulled her away and pushed her against the mattress, pinning her there below him. Reagan bit her lower lip and tried to wrap herself around him, but he let go of her wrists to push open her legs.

"Kainan..." she begged.

He grinned, and wouldn't give in to her pleas.

"Kainan, what're you...? Oh, my God," she gasped as he did what she had done to him. Tortured her the way she had him, driving her wild with need.

"Please," she begged.

He didn't respond, just ran his tongue around the most sensitive part of her, making her cry out. He wanted her to come, but he wanted to be inside her too. He was greedy and he wanted all of her.

Reagan arched her hips up and he moved over her, staring down into her eyes, then bent down to kiss her as he entered her slowly.

He groaned. She was so tight, so hot. It took every ounce of his control not to take her fast. It had been so long since he'd been with her. There hadn't been another since her, he'd never had a desire for any other.

It was only her.

Just Reagan.

He sank deeper into her and quickened his pace. He couldn't hold back. He slipped a hand under her bottom, bringing her closer and angling his thrusts as he took all of her. It was hard to hold back, but he wanted Reagan to come first, and it didn't take long before she was crying out his name, tightening around him.

And that was when he sought his own release.

When it was over he rolled away, trying to catch his breath, but it was only a moment before he pulled her close against him. He didn't want her far from him. He needed her.

"Kainan…" she whispered in the darkness, her breath fast and heavy like his.

He ran his hands over her soft body and kissed her gently.

"Sleep," he said hoarsely. "I'm here."

Reagan smiled up at him and sighed.

Soon she was asleep, the even sound of her breathing letting him know she'd drifted off. The wind was howling outside, a high-pitched wail which usually set him on edge and made him shiver, but there was no shivering with her warm body pressed against his.

Tonight he had her.

Tonight she was his Queen. Even if it was only for one night.

CHAPTER ELEVEN

THE ALARM WENT off at six o'clock in the morning. At first Kainan forgot for a moment why he'd set the alarm so early, because all he wanted to do was lie in Reagan's arms all day long. Then he remembered that it was Christmas Eve and Dr. Shaw wanted him at the hospital so he could do another MRI and check the extent of new damage and scar tissue in preparation for the surgery coming up soon.

Try as he might, Kainan hadn't been able to keep silent when he'd made love to Reagan. He'd lost all sense of logic and reason, and now he was paying for it.

His throat was hoarse, sore and very tight. It was hard to breathe, but last night had been worth it.

Kainan disentangled himself from Reagan's arms and slowly got out of bed.

"Where are you going?" she whispered, and flicked on a light which blinded them both. "It's dark still."

I'm not trying to sneak away.

"Where are you off to then?" she asked, sitting up.

To the hospital.

"Is it Peter?" she asked, panicked.

No, it's me. He ran his hand through his hair. *I just need another MRI scan. There's more adhesions in my throat.*

"Oh," she said quietly, worried. "That will complicate the surgery."

Yes, and it also complicates my breathing, not just my voice.

She cocked an eyebrow. "I'm worried about you. Worried about this surgery."

He grinned and touched her face, whispering, "I am not."

It was a lie. He was, but there was no choice.

"What happens if you…? What happens to your country?"

Peter could be King.

Reagan frowned. "Peter is not legitimate."

You can change that.

She rolled her eyes and shook her head. "Are you crazy?"

Reagan, please. We belong together as a family.

She looked unsure, and for some reason he got an inkling that he was getting through to her. Maybe she would agree to be his Queen. Then he could take care of them.

That's if you survive the surgery.

He didn't want to think of that. He didn't want to think of putting Peter in a position of having no childhood. Perhaps he was being selfish, like his father. Still, he wanted both of them. He needed them both.

"I'm worried about this surgery, I really am," she said.

It touched him that she cared so much.

I don't know when or if I can have the surgery, he signed, and then started to pull on his discarded clothes.

"I'll go with you to the MRI."

He shook his head. *No, you need to go to Peter. They could be discharging him today. I will have a security detail available for you and a town car to bring you back here with him. Do you have a car seat?*

"I did…it's probably in the closet in his nursery."

He nodded. *I will be fine. I promise to keep you posted, and tonight we'll celebrate as a family.*

"Just don't do anything rash. You can be a voiceless king, Kainan. There is no shame in it."

I am not ashamed. I just want answers. If it can be resolved, then I would like to speak again—I would like to address my people. It was maddening not being able to work on my own during that trauma. I had to follow you like a shadow. I couldn't go into the operating room as lead surgeon because how can I sign with my hands inside a person? I have to return to my throne strong.

Kainan finished dressing.

Do not worry, Reagan. Everything will be okay. We'll order in food for tonight and celebrate our first Christmas, the three of us together.

She smiled. "You can invite Andreas and the other members of your security team. Andreas is family. He's Peter's uncle, whether he wants to admit it or not. And he cares for you."

I will try to convince him, but Andreas takes decorum very seriously. He didn't even want my blood. Kainan straightened his tie. *When the MRI is done I will come see you—or, if they decide to discharge Peter before I'm done, I will meet you here.*

"Okay…" she said, but he could tell that there was uncertainty in her voice and he wished he could tell her more. Tell her how much he cared, but that he was scared. Scare of ruining it all. Scared of breaking her heart if he died.

The pressure he felt was keen.

As he left Reagan's apartment he ran into Andreas, who was limping to the apartment next door with a cane.

"Your Majesty," Andreas said, wincing as he tried to bow.

Don't. Kainan stopped him. *Rest. Diego, another one of my security guards, is taking me to the hospital for a test.*

"The MRI?" Andreas asked hopefully.

Yes.

Andreas looked worried. "I should be with you, Your Majesty."

It is fine. Reagan is next door. Keep an eye on her, if you must.

"You spent the night with her? Has she agreed to be Queen?"

Not yet. Rest, Andreas. That's an order.

"Thank you, Your Majesty."

Kainan nodded and went downstairs, where Diego was waiting for him. He didn't say much and opened the door to the tinted-windowed town car. Diego knew where Kainan needed to go.

First the MRI, then the embassy. Time was running out. Kainan had to put his affairs in order before he had surgery, and he was angry with himself for letting it go this long. But he'd been too afraid before.

Now, with Peter and Reagan, Kainan was experiencing something he had not felt in a long time, and that was hope. He was always going to make sure everyone was protected if he died on the operating table, but that hope gave him courage. He wasn't going to die during surgery. He was going to fight. He was going to live to know his son and to return to Isla Hermosa and take his place as King.

Reagan was torn.

Last night in Kainan's arms had been so amazing and it had felt right. She had felt as if she belonged with him. And then he'd shattered her by telling her that he was still contemplating going through a risky procedure to restore his voice.

It wasn't so much the surgery itself that was terrible, but Kainan's injury…the scar tissue.

The idea was too much for her to bear, and she was torn

between what she'd been taught her whole life and becoming a family with Kainan.

She found a towel in one of the boxes in her bedroom and had a quick shower in her brand-new walk-in shower.

When she walked out of the bathroom, she glanced out of the window toward the icy waters of Lake Ontario.

Right now it was full of foreboding. A stormy, gloomy body of water that had always freaked her out. But then she thought about the spring thaw and the summer, when she would be able to watch the ferry head from Queen's Quay to the islands, and that brought a smile to her face.

There was Centerville, out on one of those islands, and she thought about taking Peter there one day—taking all the rides with him and walking on the beaches there. She thought about all the things they could do. But now, instead of seeing only her and Peter in the picture, she saw Kainan.

Would it really be so bad to be his wife?

Once Peter had his new heart she could move to Isla Hermosa. Despite the war, she had enjoyed her time there—the ocean, the tropical weather and the lush jungle.

There was really nothing to keep her in Toronto after Peter got his heart. She could practice medicine in Isla Hermosa. Perhaps she could do even more, like teach the future physicians of Isla Hermosa. She'd always wanted to teach.

Maybe she *could* have it all?

Be careful. You can only rely on yourself.

She shook that thought away, because right now she was feeling something she had never felt before and that was love. The picture she had in her mind of her future didn't have to be Toronto or London, Ontario…it could be Isla Hermosa and Europe.

And Kainan.

She couldn't lose him again. She'd thought that she had lost him once and that had nearly destroyed her. This was

her second chance, and she would be a fool not to take it, but she was terrified beyond all reason.

Reagan got dressed as quickly as she could and then dug the car seat out of Peter's closet. Starting tonight, with Peter home for Christmas and Kainan here, she was going to make her life right.

She couldn't be scared anymore.

She wasn't going to ruin this second chance that she had been given.

As she locked her door, the door to Kainan's apartment opened and Andreas hobbled out.

"Andreas! They let you out?" she asked.

Andreas turned and smiled at her. "Yes, Dr. Cote. I am fine now."

"You need to rest," she said. "Where are you going?"

"Out. There is no food."

"You should order in."

Andreas sighed. "I was going to go to the hospital and check on Kainan."

"I thought someone else was with him? You really should rest."

"I should be the one to go to the hospital with him," Andreas said grimly.

"You really need to rest. But tonight come over and have dinner. You are family."

"I beg your pardon?" said Andreas.

"He told me that you're his illegitimate half brother."

Andreas frowned. "I wish he hadn't."

"Kainan cares about you."

Andreas sighed. "And I him."

"So come over and celebrate"

"No, it is not proper. There's nothing to celebrate. The surgery is too risky, and if he dies he will be leaving the country without an heir."

"It's a risky surgery, for sure, but—"

"The odds of his death are high."

Reagan's heart skipped a beat. "What are you talking about?"

"He has extensive scar tissue…"

"Kainan could *die*?" Her world spun out of control.

Andreas nodded. "Although your son could still be King if you marry him."

Reagan's heart sank. So that was why Kainan wanted to marry her. Why he constantly pestered her to marry him. It wasn't because he cared for her—it was all about the crown. It was all about saving his kingdom because he expected to die. He was going to abandon her and Peter after all, and abandon them to a life she didn't want.

If she hadn't had Peter then he probably wouldn't have bothered with her.

You've opened your heart to the wrong man, Reagan. You always do. This heartache is all your fault.

Reagan couldn't even respond to Andreas. She just turned on her heel and carried on her way. She didn't know what to think.

She was hurt that Kainan had used her. Played her for a fool. He didn't really care for her *or* Peter. He saw them as a means to save his country. To save its monarchy.

And it hurt.

Had their night of passion been a part of his game?

She slammed the "down" button at the elevator as hard as she could and it felt good to hit it—but it didn't quell the feelings of betrayal she was experiencing right now. The pain…

The fact he'd lied to her and hadn't even been able to tell her the truth.

Why had she thought she could trust him? She knew

better than to listen to her heart. Her heart was thing that always got her into trouble. She was a fool.

She hailed a cab and climbed in, directing the taxi driver to take her to the hospital. She didn't know what she was going to do when she saw Kainan, but she knew one thing was for certain now. She was never going to marry.

Never.

CHAPTER TWELVE

AFTER KAINAN'S MRI he was scheduled for surgery with Dr. Shaw on December twenty-sixth in the morning. There were risks that the scar tissue was now threatening his ability to breathe, and that was not good. Dr. Shaw had put him on oxygen just now, and he was feeling light-headed because breathing was getting harder.

He had to get it done sooner rather than later.

When the surgery had bee booked he went straight to the embassy to talk to his delegates about his possible death.

Kainan had decided that it was time that the monarchy did not have absolute control over the people. Time for him to take a step back, so that if he died Peter would not be trapped as he had been.

He could be a figurehead, and he could help his people, but Kainan had to give them the tools to help themselves, and soon his delegates would be in the process of dealing with the Canadian officials in order to make that happen.

Which meant the deadline for him to be crowned was a moot point. He had it struck out in one of his last acts of power.

The burden that had been lifted from his shoulders was great.

He felt free.

He was still King, but it was different.

This was now a monarchy on his own terms—a monarchy that would serve its people. They could vote in a prime minister. There would be a democracy.

And Kainan would oversee these things to make sure corrupt people didn't get into power as long as he was their figurehead.

When he got to the hospital he went straight to Peter's room to talk to Reagan, but when he got there the room was empty.

Peter was gone and so was Reagan.

His heart lurched and he began to panic, thinking that something had happened to their son.

A pediatric nurse came into the room. "Dr. Laskaris, they've been discharged. They were discharged about twenty minutes ago, so they're probably at home."

Kainan breathed a sigh of relief and mouthed his thanks to the nurse before rushing out of the hospital. He was texting Diego when he saw Andreas limping in.

Dammit.

"Your Majesty," Andreas said. He looked concerned.

What's wrong? Kainan asked.

"It's Dr. Cote. She knows. She knows about the risks of your surgery."

His stomach sank like a rock. *How does she know? Did the press find out?*

Andreas shook his head. "I told her."

Kainan saw red, felt his blood boiling, and it took every ounce of his strength not to hit Andreas.

You did what?

"Your Majesty, I had to tell her. I am also the one who broke into her apartment."

Why would you do that?

"I wanted to push her into your arms. I wanted to protect my country and your birthright. Your son's birthright."

Kainan mouthed a few choice curse words and scrubbed a hand over his face. *I can't believe you did this, Andreas. You've ruined everything!*

"How? She knows the truth now."

I was going to tell her, but I was also going to tell her that the monarchy no longer exists.

Andreas was confused. "I don't understand…"

I'm forming a democracy, Andreas. I will still be King, but I will just be a figurehead. I will help the people rebuild Isla Hermosa and they will vote in a prime minster and elect officials. The people will run Isla Hermosa. I will not.

Andreas blinked and then bowed his head, ashamed. "Your Majesty, I'm sorry that I doubted your abilities."

Kainan sighed and gripped his half brother's shoulders. *It's all right. I just pray that it's not too late to turn this around with Reagan. I still want her as my Queen, but only when she wants to become my Queen. And Peter can inherit one day, but he doesn't have to. There will be a government.*

"I'm glad to hear that, Your Majesty."

Andreas turned and they walked out of the hospital together.

Have the police come for you yet? Kainan asked.

"No, I know how to get away with murder, Your Majesty," Andreas teased. "I can fake an apartment break-in without being caught."

Kainan smiled. *I will still need a head of security, but I think that you should run for prime minister when we go back to Isla Hermosa. You would be a fine elected leader. You're a war hero, as was your father before you.*

Andreas nodded. "Perhaps—but right now I want to make sure you and your family are taken care of."

Kainan hugged Andreas. *I'm still ticked off at you for sticking your nose in where it doesn't belong.*

"I know, but if I hadn't then everything would've been lost."

Diego pulled up in front of the hospital and Kainan helped Andreas in first and then climbed in himself. He had to make things right with Reagan before it was too late.

When they got to the apartment Diego helped Andreas out and Kainan ran inside. At least he knew that she would be there. Everything of hers was still there, and he had a key so she couldn't lock him out.

When he got to their floor he passed a locksmith and saw Reagan standing in the doorway, her arms crossed and her face like thunder.

He started to sign. *Let me explain—*

"Save it," she said. "Andreas told me everything."

Not everything.

"He told me that you needed me to marry you so you can legitimize Peter and that when you die he'll be King? Is that correct, or is there more to that story?" she asked.

That was true, but now there is more.

She raised an eyebrow. "I'm listening."

That was true up until this afternoon. Now I have changed everything. I don't need to marry you for Peter to be King.

Reagan reeled as if she had been slapped. "How nice for you."

Reagan, I'm creating a democracy. I will just be a figurehead now.

She didn't say anything, but he saw he was getting through to her. She hadn't shut him out yet.

Peter will become King whether we are married or not, he signed. *And he too will only be a figurehead. Isla Hermosa is to become a democracy. And with that the old monarchy was replaced. My officials at the embassy and back home are working with the prime ministers of Can-*

ada and Britain to make this happen. There will be peace now because of this.

"I'm very happy to hear there will be peace," she said softly.

But…?

"You lied to me. You constantly asked me to marry you because you said you wanted to protect me."

I did.

"You *did*?" she asked, her eyes shining with tears. "And that's the trouble. Now that I'm not needed anymore, you're free. You don't need me."

Reagan, I still want to protect you.

"I wish I could believe that, Kainan. I really wish I could. But first you lie to me and then you don't tell me that you're King of a country. You don't contact me and tell me that you're still alive."

I couldn't tell you I was alive. I was in hiding. Besides, I didn't know where in Canada you were.

Reagan ignored him. "You told me your surgery was risky, but not how risky. Why did you feel the need to lie to me?"

To protect you!

She nodded. "I don't believe it. I can't. You've broken my trust, Kainan. You've hurt me too much. You're welcome to be a part of Peter's life, but I will fight you if you try and take him out of Canada and away from me. He's too fragile to live a life like yours."

Reagan, please don't turn me away.

Although he wouldn't blame her for doing so. And he couldn't sign the words he needed to say because he wanted to *say* them. To use his own words to tell her he loved her.

I need you, Reagan. I want you in my life.

Reagan sighed and a tear slipped down her cheek. "I wish I could believe that, Kainan. I wish that I could."

She turned back into her apartment and shut the door. Shutting him out of her life.

He sighed sadly, but he wasn't giving up.

He'd come too far to give up on her now.

Even if she didn't want to marry him, he was going to have Reagan in his life and he would do anything to win her back.

He would not be the man his father had been.

It was heartbreaking to spend Peter's first Christmas alone with him, especially when she'd thought Kainan would be there.

She'd thought for a brief moment that they were becoming a family—and then she'd found out the real reason why he wanted a family.

To protect the crown when he died.

He needed them, but not in the way she'd hoped he would. Did he even really *want* them?

Still, this was the way she'd *thought* she was going to spend Peter's first Christmas, when she'd been pregnant with him and had thought Kainan was dead.

It was scary how dependent she'd become on Kainan without really realizing. She'd got used to having him around.

They had even planned to spend Peter's first Christmas together, but since she'd turned him away on Christmas Eve she hadn't seen him.

It was now Boxing Day, and she was considering going next door and talking to him. Perhaps she'd been too harsh on him. She wanted him involved in Peter's life, but that was it. They could work together for as long as he was at the hospital, and they could work together to raise Peter, but that was where she had to draw the line.

She couldn't risk her heart again.

But you love him. Love is always worth the risk.

Her phone started ringing and she answered it.

"Reagan, it's Michael."

He sounded completely stressed out.

"Michael? Is everything okay?"

"UNOS called. There's a match, and I've sent a recovery team to Ottawa to get it. There's a heart for your son. You need to bring Peter in right away."

Her heart skipped a beat.

So soon.

She'd only just got him home. She had been enjoying her time with him and now she had to take him back and put him in the hands of the surgeons.

"I'll be right there. Thank you, Michael."

Reagan hung up the phone. She could hear Peter stirring through the baby monitor.

She grabbed the baby monitor and left her apartment, heading straight to Kainan's. She knocked on the door. She could feel panic rising.

Diego answered the door. "Dr. Cote?"

"Is Kainan here?"

"No," Diego said. "Andreas took His Majesty over to the hospital early this morning to have his surgery."

"His surgery? Right…that's today too."

The world began to spin out of control. Peter and Kainan were both having surgery on the same day. She could potentially lose them both.

"Is everything okay, Dr. Cote?"

"Can I get a ride to the hospital? It's Peter—they've found him a heart."

"Yes, of course. I will meet you downstairs in ten minutes."

Reagan nodded and went back to her apartment as Diego

closed the door. She went straight to Peter, who smiled when she entered the room.

Her body shook and she smiled back at him. "My little love," she whispered as she carefully picked him up and held him tight.

What if this was the last time she got to hold him? What if he didn't survive?

Right now she wasn't in the mind-set of a surgeon. She was in the mind-set of a mother who was terrified about what she might lose.

And Kainan was going to have surgery too.

She could lose it all in one fell swoop.

She had to make things right.

Reagan kissed Peter's head. "I'm going to make it right for you. I swear."

She would do better for her son than her parents ever had for her.

She packed up Peter's ventricular device and got him into his car seat, covering him with a blanket. She grabbed everything Peter needed and hurried out of the apartment.

Kainan was in pre-op with Andreas. He wanted to see Reagan. He'd gotten word that a heart for Peter had been found.

Screw this.

He got out of the bed where he'd been waiting for Dr. Shaw.

"Your Majesty?" Andreas said in alarm.

Tell Dr. Shaw I will be back in time for my surgery. I have to see Reagan and Peter.

Andreas nodded. "Yes, Your Majesty."

Kainan pulled on his street clothes and left the room. His throat was tight and his pulse was racing. He cleared his throat and rolled his shoulders. It was hard to breathe.

It had been getting harder to breathe since Reagan had locked him out of her life.

She was his air. His freedom. And he needed her.

It was stress that was making him feel this way, and he knew he wouldn't relax until he saw Peter and Reagan.

He made his way to the pediatric floor, where they were prepping Peter. He could hear him crying. He'd never heard him cry before. Reagan hadn't let him see him since he'd been discharged two days ago. Not that he blamed her. He'd ruined everything by not telling her the truth.

Hearing Peter cry was an amazing thing.

It was strong.

Reagan turned around and her expression softened, making his heart skip a beat. He wanted to comfort her, but didn't want her to push him away.

"What're you doing here?" Reagan asked.

I'm his father, Kainan signed.

"I know, but I thought you would be in pre-op yourself."

Who told you?

"Diego. You're going through with it?"

Of course.

"You could die," she said, biting her lip as if she was holding something back. "If you're just to be a figurehead then you don't need to go through with this surgery. There are less riskier surgeries to remove adhesions."

I do.

"Kainan, it's too risky."

He nodded. *So is this.*

They both turned to Peter as the gurney came in and the pediatric cardiologist, Dr. Bruni, entered the room.

"Reagan and Kainan." He nodded at them both. "The heart is on its way from the airport. We're now going to take Peter into surgery and remove the ventricular device and put him on bypass. You both know the procedure. He

will be in the pediatric critical care unit for some time and will be on anti-rejection drugs for the rest of his life."

Reagan nodded and Kainan felt numb.

She stepped forward and kissed Peter goodbye.

Kainan took a step toward his son. The last time he'd gone off to surgery Kainan hadn't even been able to look at him. It had been too painful—as was this.

What if something happened and he didn't ever get to know his son?

What if he died in the operating room himself?

Better me than Peter.

He touched his son's head and then kissed him. He couldn't say that he loved him. He had no voice with which to say it. But he hoped Peter knew that he did.

He couldn't lose Peter. Kainan wanted time with him. Parents were never supposed to outlast their own children, though he'd seen it every day when he was a surgeon.

Life was complicated and messy. And he wanted Peter to experience it all.

He stepped back and they wheeled Peter away.

Reagan broke down in tears, sobbing into her hands, her shoulders shaking. Kainan took her in his arms and she clung to him.

"I'm sorry," she whispered against his neck. "I'm so sorry."

When she looked up he signed, *What for?*

"For pushing you away. I never gave you a chance to explain anything. You were carrying around this tremendous burden and I should've been more sympathetic. I know what it's like to carry around a burden as big as that, and I'm sorry I didn't give you the chance. I was afraid."

Of what?

"Of relying on you and losing you. I've never had anyone before. Never had love…or a family. Not really."

Me neither.

"Only you have ever cared for me."

I understand. I had people to rely on, people to protect me, and I was never alone—but I really was. I was scared of relying on you too, Reagan. I was scared of...

Kainan felt his throat tighten and he touched her face. The room began to spin and he shook his head, trying to focus.

He was finding it hard to breathe.

And he couldn't call for help.

He couldn't tell her what was happening.

"Kainan?" she said, panic in her voice.

I love you. That was the last thought he had before everything went black.

Reagan screamed out as Kainan's knees buckled under him and she helped him to the floor. As she laid him out she couldn't hear any breath sounds. She hit the panic button on the wall to call a code and then she tried to breathe for him, compressing his chest to keep his heart beating.

He'd stopped breathing.

She couldn't lose him for real this time.

She hadn't even had a chance to tell him that she loved him. That she forgave him and that she wanted to try and make it work. That she was tired of carrying her burden alone and that she now knew it was okay not to handle everything on your own.

It was okay to lean on someone else—especially someone you loved.

The code team came for him. They got a tube down his throat and started manually ventilating him.

She had to take a step back.

She couldn't work on him.

They whisked him off to surgery.

"I can't lose him," Reagan said out loud to herself. "I thought I'd lost him once. I can't go through that again."

And she made a vow then and there that if Kainan came out of surgery she was going to make things right—just as she'd promised Peter.

She needed Kainan. She loved him.

As much as she had been taught that she didn't need anyone, she knew she needed Kainan and he needed her. She wasn't going to squander her second chance.

Not this time.

Pain was the first thing that Kainan felt. His throat was raw, as if it had been shredded with a thousand razor blades. His mouth was dry.

It took him a moment to realize what was happening and then he remembered. He had been with Reagan and they had just taken Peter away when he'd collapsed.

He tried to sit up, but it hurt.

"Don't try and sit up," Reagan said gently.

Kainan opened his eyes and smiled at her. He signed to ask her what had happened.

"Scar tissue blocked your airway. Dr. Shaw was able to get at it all, and repair your vocal cords, though it may be a few days before you will be able to speak. If you can't speak don't worry—it will come. You're in the ICU, still."

Peter? he asked, signing.

Reagan grinned, her smile bright. "He made it through. He did beautifully and is in the pediatric critical care unit."

Kainan let out a sigh of relief. *I want to go see him.*

"We will. You're still coming out of the sedation. Dr. Shaw wanted to make sure that you had some extra rest after your surgery yesterday, so he kept you in a medicated coma for a night."

What day is it?

"The twenty-ninth. The New Year is coming and your move to a democracy went through. Your coronation will wait and your people are voting for their first prime minister."

I am sorry about all that.

Reagan touched his face. "I know, and I'm sorry that I didn't give you a proper chance. I was so scared of relying on anyone. I've been used to doing things on my own for so long."

You have no reason to apologize.

"I do. I was devastated when I thought you were dead, Kainan. It crushed me. It felt like I'd lost my best friend, my partner, and then you came back and you were so distant. It killed me. I just didn't want to risk my heart. I wasn't even sure that I was feeling anything, what with Peter."

I am the one who needs to apologize. I left you alone and I didn't try and reach out to you. You carried our son alone, dealt with his devastating diagnosis alone. I should've been there. I felt like I was failing you the way I failed my brother.

"You didn't fail your brother—he failed you *and* your country," she said.

He shook his head. *I should have tried harder to stop him. I could've done more to control him. And then maybe, just maybe, there wouldn't have been a war. Lives could've been spared.*

"Everything happens for a reason, Kainan. You weren't your brother's keeper. You did the best you could."

I'm sorry, Reagan. I'm sorry for deceiving you, for abandoning you. I love you more than anything.

Reagan leaned over and kissed him. "I love you too. And, if the offer still stands, I would like to be your wife."

Kainan grinned. *It will always stand, but are you sure?*

I have to return to Isla Hermosa at some point. Your home is here in Toronto.

"My home is with you and our son. That's all the home I need." They kissed again. "I love you so much, Kainan."

"I love you too," he whispered.

Kainan developed a slight postoperative fever, which was not uncommon after the amount of blood that he'd lost. So he wasn't allowed to see Peter until New Year's Eve.

As he walked to the pediatric critical care unit, with Andreas following closely behind with a wheelchair, he couldn't help but think about how this should have been the night he'd prepared for this coronation. Now, instead of a coronation, a parliament was being formed. It was an exciting time for Isla Hermosa and he couldn't wait to go back.

As soon as Kainan and Peter had healed, they would go back to Isla Hermosa and begin to heal the country—from the ground up.

Kainan had decided that the palace would be repaired, but would no longer be his home. It would instead house the new government that was being formed right now.

He much preferred his original home outside the city gates of Helicia—if it still stood. From there he could see the ocean and the beach. It reminded him of his mother and her longing to be free.

And, though he was still King, he would have more freedom now that Isla Hermosa was a democracy.

He wanted a safe place for Peter to play—not a prison for him to grow up in, like Kainan had had.

Reagan had been by his side. She'd moved between the rooms, taking care of him *and* Peter. Now that they were getting closer to the pediatric critical care unit, where Peter was, Kainan became nervous. Peter was no longer sedated and Kainan had never yet got to look into his eyes. Not really.

They put on gowns and were buzzed in.

Kainan walked toward his son's crib.

Peter was cooing and kicking, despite the incision in his chest.

As soon as Reagan came into view Peter responded happily to her presence and Kainan's heart melted.

He moved closer to the crib and Peter's eyes locked on his. Peter stared at him and Kainan could see eyes so similar to his studying him. Emotion overcame him as he reached out and touched his son. Peter grasped his finger, squeezing it before smiling up at him.

Kainan's heart swelled, and instead of signing he opened his mouth, to hear his voice—not a whisper, but his *voice*—respond to his son.

"I love you."

He was no longer voiceless. He had a voice, his son had a new heart, and the three of them together were one. They were whole and healed.

EPILOGUE

Two years later, New Year's Eve, Isla Hermosa

"IT'S ALMOST TIME, Your Majesties," Andreas said, bowing as he came into the room.

Kainan's pulse was racing as he smoothed his hand over the traditional red military dress jacket that had once been worn by his father. His pulse was racing.

"You can do this."

Kainan smiled down at Reagan, who was dressed in white and wearing his mother's tiara, as well as some other jewels that had been hidden and saved during the war.

He sighed and nodded.

This was to be his first speech in Isla Hermosa since he'd returned, married Reagan and introduced the world to his son Peter, who was taking to his new heart so well. He'd spoken to his people briefly, but hadn't given his first address in the new parliament that had been built in the restored palace.

Which was where he was now standing.

He was dressing in his mother's old room.

He, Reagan and Peter lived in his mother's seaside villa, outside the capital city of Helicia.

For the first year after his return Kainan had kept to himself as he and Peter had healed.

His surgery had been a success, but it had taken some time for him to speak properly again. There were times he was still unsure of his voice.

Reagan took his hand and squeezed it. "Your voice is strong. You can do this."

"Did I tell you...?" He took a pause. "How beautiful you look?"

She blushed. "Don't even *try* to get out of this by complimenting me. I'm not letting you off the hook."

Kainan chuckled and held out his arm. "Are you ready for this moment? Standing by my side as I address parliament?"

"No!" She laughed nervously as she slipped her arm over his. "I'm afraid I'm going to mess something up. I'd rather be at the free clinic in town."

Kainan beamed at her. "You're giving my security team a hard time, you know. Andreas is finding it difficult to calm Diego down when you work at the clinic."

"Why?" she asked. "It's perfectly safe. I'm a *surgeon*, Kainan. You promised me I could continue as a surgeon. I don't want the crown jewels or the palace. I just want to work."

"You just want to work?" he teased. "What about the beach house and our son?"

"Well, of course. And there's also one more thing," Reagan said.

"What's that?"

"You."

She kissed him—just a light feather kiss, but it made his blood fire and he suddenly didn't want to be there any longer.

"Diego is very concerned about you working in the clinic."

"Why?" she asked.

"Diego can't stand the sight of blood."

"He should leave the room, then."

Kainan shook his head. "He's devoted to his Queen. He cannot."

Reagan's arm trembled. "I'm not used to that."

"You're doing fine."

Then Andreas opened the door.

Kainan held Peter's hand. Peter laughed and smiled at his parents. And Kainan's tension melted away.

In his son he saw himself, but he also saw Reagan. Peter had Reagan's spirit—the spirit that reminded him of his mother.

Every day Peter grew stronger, and their life in Isla Hermosa grew more idyllic. The beach house was the perfect hideaway for them to live in peace.

"Your Majesty," Andreas said with a hint of pride. "Prime Minister Monterro is ready for you."

"I am ready," Kainan said, but inside he was nervous.

This was the first time he would be addressing his people since the successful election of Alejandro Monterro as their first prime minster. Judging by the way Isla Hermosa had bloomed in the last couple of years, Alejandro was the perfect choice. And Kainan respected him.

Reagan squeezed his arm.

As Kainan escorted Reagan through the door he reached down with the hand that had been resting on his ceremonial sword and took his son's chubby hand in his.

"You're breaking protocol," Reagan whispered.

"I think that it does not matter anymore," Kainan whispered back.

They smiled at each other.

The three of them walked side by side towards the double doors. One the other side was Isla Hermosa's parlia-

ment and a handful of reporters. Not only were his people watching, the whole world was watching.

Before the double doors opened Kainan turned to Reagan and she let go his hand and took Peter, because he had to walk in alone first.

"I couldn't have done this without you," he said, touching her cheek.

"You were always going to have the surgery—your voice would've been restored."

"I know, but you're the reason I'm alive. You and Peter have given me a reason to live. I love you."

Reagan's eyes glistened with tears. "And I love you."

"Me too," Peter chirped.

Kainan laughed and tousled his son's hair. He turned to Andreas and nodded. "I'm ready now."

Andreas beamed and opened the doors.

Kainan was blinded by bright lights, flashing bulbs.

"His Majesty, King Kainan the First!"

It was shouted over the din of scraping chairs as everyone stood.

Kainan gripped the hilt of his sword tightly, taking a step through the double doors into what had once been his father's throne room, but now held Isla Hermosa's democracy—

It was a step towards his destiny.

A destiny not only as a king, but as a father and husband.

As a man who had once again found his voice. A voice he never would have found if it hadn't been for Reagan.

This was all for her and Peter.

There was no turning back—and, thanks to Reagan, he never wanted to.

With her by his side he could do anything.

* * * * *

*If you enjoyed this story,
check out these other great reads from
Amy Ruttan*

*NAVY DOC ON HER CHRISTMAS LIST
CONVENIENT MARRIAGE, SURPRISE TWINS
HIS PREGNANT ROYAL BRIDE
ALEJANDRO'S SEXY SECRET*

All available now!

MILLS & BOON®

MEDICAL ROMANCE™

THE ULTIMATE IN ROMANTIC MEDICAL DRAMA

A sneak peek at next month's titles...

In stores from 25th January 2018:

- **The Doctor's Wife for Keeps** *and* **Twin Surprise for the Italian Doc** – Alison Roberts

- **Falling for His Best Friend** – Emily Forbes *and* **Reunited with Her Parisian Surgeon** – Annie O'Neil

- **From Bachelor to Daddy** – Meredith Webber *and* **A Surgeon to Heal Her Heart** – Janice Lynn

Just can't wait?
Buy our books online before they hit the shops!
www.millsandboon.co.uk

Also available as eBooks.

MILLS & BOON®

Coming next month

THE DOCTOR'S WIFE FOR KEEPS
Alison Roberts

'So…it's the sensible thing to do, isn't it?'

'Sorry?' Had she been on another planet while Luke was polishing off her dessert and had missed something he'd said?

'To marry someone that you're already great friends with.'

'Oh, no…' Kate put her hands over her eyes. 'This is about that pact again, isn't it?'

'Is it such a crazy idea?'

Kate dropped hands, her eyes widening. *'Yes.'*

'Why?'

'You can't just marry someone because they're a *friend*…'

'Why not? Seems like a pretty good place to start, if you ask me. You always hear people say "I married my best friend".'

Kate could feel furrow lines appearing on her forehead. 'Yes, but…'

'But what?'

'But they have more than that to begin with. You've got to have more than that.'

'Such as?'

Kate could feel colour creeping into her face now. 'Um…attraction?'

Luke leaned towards her. His eyes had a mischievous glint and his mouth had a cheeky curl on one side. 'You don't think I'm attractive?

'It's not just about looks. There's got to be…um… chemistry.'

'Ahh…' Luke sat back in his chair, nodding slowly. 'I get it. You mean the sexual compatibility thing.'

Kate had to close her eyes for a moment so that she could concentrate on breathing. There didn't seem to be enough air in here any more. Her cheeks still felt hot.

Her eyes snapped open. 'Can we go now?'

'Sure.' Luke still seemed perfectly relaxed as he signalled that he was ready for the bill.

'I'll wait outside for you. I could do with a bit of fresh air.'

The air was fresher than she'd expected and Kate pulled on Luke's heavy, wool-lined anorak she had grabbed from the peg on her way out. It was far too big for her but it was warm and…she wrapped her arms around herself and let her chin sink so that her nose was buried in the lining…it smelt like Luke. All macho and masculine and…totally delicious.

She was so lost in the moment that she didn't hear Luke coming up behind her. Wasn't aware of him until she heard the low growl of his voice right beside her ear.

'I think we'd be very compatible.'

Instinctively, she lifted her head to turn towards that compelling growl and Luke's fingers captured her chin. In slow motion, he tilted his head and closed the gap between them. Kate knew he was going to kiss her and now her brain felt just as weak as her knees. She couldn't have stopped this happening if her life depended on it.

Copyright ©2017 Alison Roberts

Continue reading
THE DOCTOR'S WIFE FOR KEEPS
Alison Roberts

Available next month
www.millsandboon.co.uk